The Damascus Way

ACTS *of* FAITH, BOOK 3

The DAMASCUS WAY

DAVIS BUNN
&
JANETTE OKE

BETHANY HOUSE PUBLISHERS
Minneapolis, Minnesota

The Damascus Way
Copyright © 2011
Davis Bunn and Janette Oke

Art Direction by Paul Higdon
Cover design by Jennifer Parker
Cover photography by Mike Habermann
The Damascus gate image on the back cover by Holy Land Art / Alamy

Scripture quotations are from:

The King James Version of the Bible.

The HOLY BIBLE, NEW INTERNATIONAL VERSION.® Copyright © 1973, 1978, 1984 by International Bible Society. Used by permission of Zondervan Publishing House. All rights reserved.

The New King James Version of the Bible. Copyright © 1979, 1980, 1982 by Thomas Nelson, Inc. Used by permission. All rights reserved.

Published by Bethany House Publishers
11400 Hampshire Avenue South
Bloomington, Minnesota 55438

Bethany House Publishers is a division of
Baker Publishing Group, Grand Rapids, Michigan.

Printed in the United States of America

Library of Congress Cataloging-in-Publication Data

Bunn, T. Davis.
The Damascus Way / Davis Bunn and Janette Oke.
p. cm. — (Acts of faith ; bk 3)
ISBN 978-0-7642-0558-3 (hardcover : alk. paper) — ISBN 978-0-7642-0866-9 (pbk.) — ISBN 978-0-7642-0867-6 (large-print pbk.) I. Oke, Janette, 1935- II. Title.
PS3552.U4718D36 2011
813'.54—dc22

2010037076

Joining with the apostle Peter, we dedicate this book to
". . . them that have obtained like precious faith with us
through the righteousness of God and our Saviour Jesus Christ."

Paul wrote, "There is neither Jew nor Greek, . . . there is
neither male nor female: for ye are all one in Christ Jesus."

What a privilege to be part of that world-wide Church,
anticipating the wonderful day of his second appearing.
He says, "Surely I come quickly. Amen.
Even so, come, Lord Jesus."

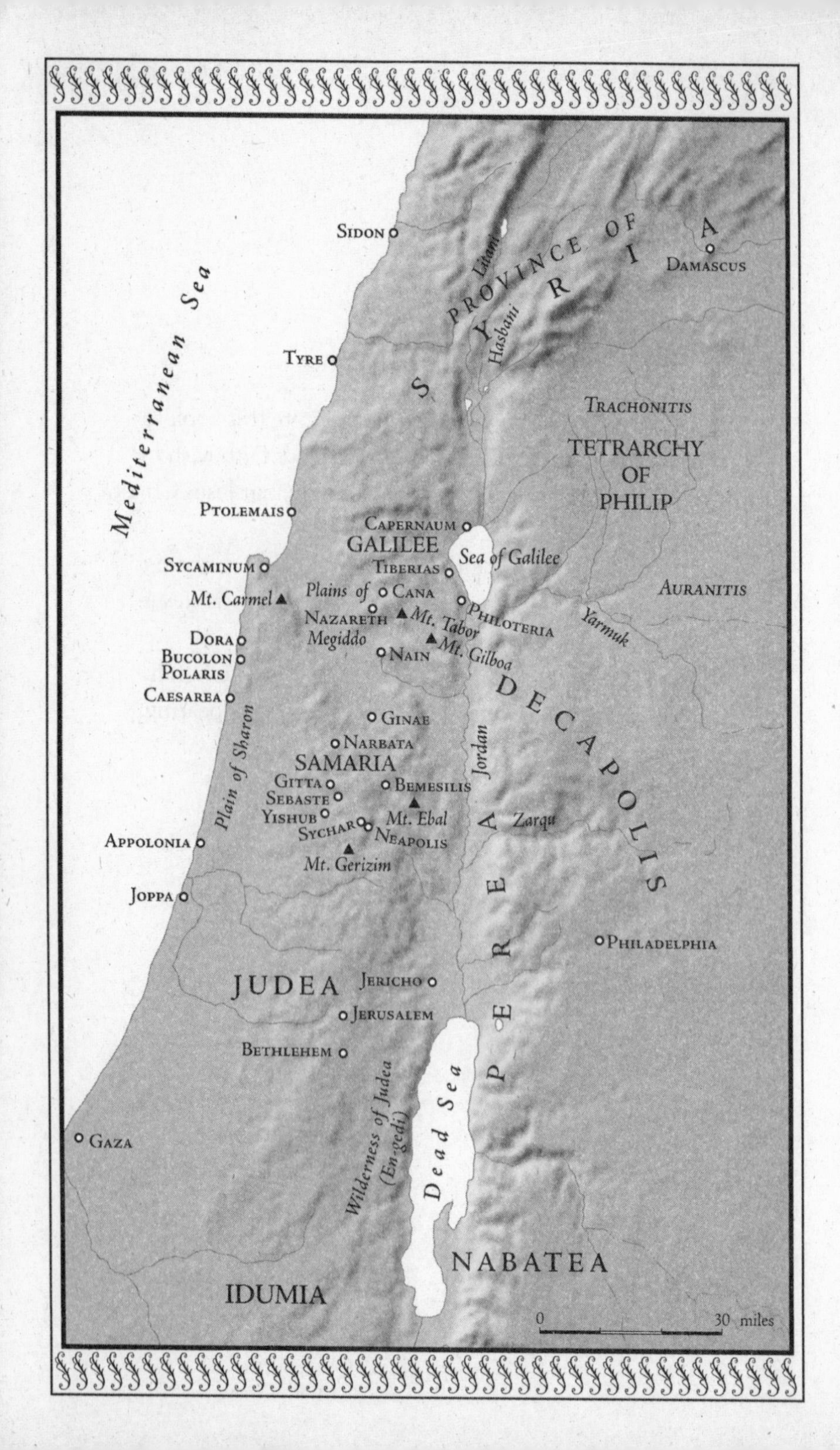

Sidon
Mediterranean Sea
PROVINCE OF
S Y R I A
Litani
Hasbani
Damascus
Tyre
Trachonitis
TETRARCHY OF PHILIP
Ptolemais
Capernaum
GALILEE
Sea of Galilee
Tiberias
Sycaminum
Plains of
Cana
Mt. Carmel
Auranitis
Nazareth
Mt. Tabor
Philoteria
Yarmuk
Megiddo
Mt. Gilboa
Dora
Nain
Bucolon Polaris
Caesarea
DECAPOLIS
Ginae
Plain of Sharon
Narbata
Jordan
SAMARIA
Gitta
Bemesilis
Sebaste
Mt. Ebal
Yishub
Zarqu
Sychar
Neapolis
Appolonia
Mt. Gerizim
Joppa
Philadelphia
JUDEA
Jericho
PEREA
Jerusalem
Bethlehem
Dead Sea
Wilderness of Judea (En-gedi)
Gaza
NABATEA
IDUMIA
0
30 miles

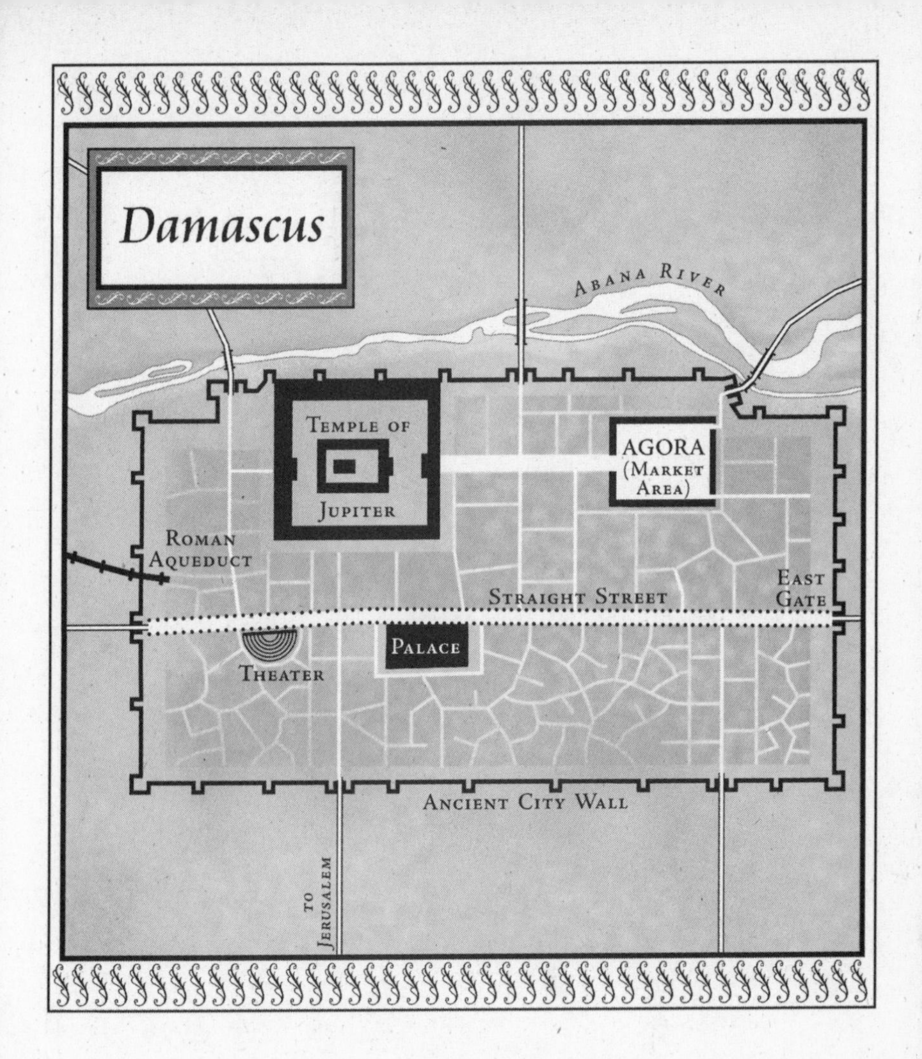
Damascus
Abana River
Temple of
Jupiter
AGORA
(Market
Area)
Roman
Aqueduct
Straight Street
East
Gate
Palace
Theater
Ancient City Wall
to
Jerusalem

CHAPTER ONE

Tiberias
Circa AD 40

THE LATE AFTERNOON sun bore down with such intensity that little shivers of heat rose from the brown earth. Overhead not a cloud floated against the blue of the sky, nor a whisper of breeze stirred the leaves of the olive trees. Julia strode down the well-worn path toward the compound's outer gate, her thoughts intent upon the morrow. Her father had only just returned, yet on the next dawn she would say good-bye. Again.

A sigh of frustration escaped her lips. Why was it always this way? Julia lived in anticipation of her father's homecomings. The pleasure in his eyes at the sight of her lingered long after the farewell, when once more he took to the road.

Julia struggled to accept her life for what it was. Her father, Jamal, was a merchant, and she knew his profession required travel. Yet in her heart she questioned why he could not stay longer. Why must it always be one good-bye after another? *Other girls . . .*

Julia stopped and stared down at the pathway. She was not like other girls, she knew. Though the mystery of *why* remained unclear.

Her life seemed to be a relentless contradiction. None of its parts seemed to fit together. She had puzzled over this many times but had never come to a clear understanding. And her mother never spoke of it, though Julia was certain she felt it too. For some strange reason Julia could not fathom, they were not a part of the Tiberias community. They lived in a spacious, well-presented home, with servants enough to care for their comforts. Yet no guests came to their home. None invited them to theirs.

Her mother spent most hours in her favorite rooms or in the central garden. She touched appreciatively the beautiful gowns Jamal brought, but while he was gone they hung unattended. Helena remained in comfortable homespuns until the moment a servant announced Jamal's caravan was drawing near the city gates. Then the entire household shifted to a state of high energy. Servants scurried about, drawing fresh water, running to the markets, bringing out the incense jars, placing fresh linens in the bath. Julia did her own dashing . . . along the dusty road out from town, straight to the common area where the camels gathered, moaning and complaining over the loads burdening their backs. To the place where her father surveyed the caravan's unloading. Where he greeted her with that special smile and arms spread wide. His hair glinted copper in the sunlight, and his eyes shone hazel through the leathery skin of his face. A while ago he had stopped swinging Julia around in his strong arms. "I suppose you're getting too old for that," he had said, with something in his voice she could not quite understand as he held her close.

And when they would arrive home together, the whole house looked different. Smelled different. Was different. Her mother met them at the door, a warm smile on her lovely face and one of the silk garments gracing her figure. "Welcome, my lord," she would say with a deep bow, and he would draw her close for just a moment as they looked into each other's eyes, seeming to feast on the sight of the other's face.

The evening meal was different too. All sorts of delicacies Julia barely knew existed seemed to show up at the table. Talk and laughter circled what was usually a silent room. After the meal Jamal would open a bundle and present treasures from strange and exotic places. Silks and spices. Perfumes in beautifully carved jars and hair combs of pearl or amber. Jewelry, bracelets and rings and chains of fine gold. Her mother always exclaimed over each gift, eyes showing her pleasure and charming smile echoing her declarations of how lovely it all was.

Her mother seemed to blossom in the presence of Julia's father, like a desert flower in the spring rains. It was at these times Julia realized how beautiful Helena still was. And Jamal also told her so. Over and over. Helena flushed or smiled quietly, smoothing back the long dark curls he loved to see gathered loosely about her face. It was the same the entire time he was home with them. Their whole world changed.

But they did not go out, not as a family. Not to the markets. Not for any of the town's activities. Not to visit a neighbor. Certainly not to the synagogue, for her father was of Greek lineage from Damascus and rather irreligious. Julia knew her mother's roots were Hebrew—Samaritan, actually, though she never discussed it and put Julia off if she tried to ask questions concerning her heritage. The little family remained in the compound together every minute Jamal was at home. Enjoying one another. Laughing. Talking. Even gently teasing. Pretending that *this time* it would not end.

Julia loved those treasured moments. And it made the inevitable parting that much more difficult.

Often Jamal was away for many months at a time. The lovely gifts disappeared from sight. Her mother went back to a simple hair braid, her soft homespun, and her sad, haunted eyes. And Julia? She too went back to simple garments, the plain shawl tossed carelessly over her shoulders. But she could not bear to set aside some of the favorite pieces of jewelry he presented to her, now that she was older. Somehow, just touching them, hearing the jangle of them on her arms, brought him a little closer. Because otherwise her world remained dreary and ordinary, and all the enchantment her father brought with him was gone.

Julia roused herself from her reverie, sighed deeply, and impatiently brushed at a tear. *He is still here in Tiberias*, she told herself with a shake of her head. Was that not enough? She would make the most of their last evening together.

Her step quickened, her sandals making little puffs of dust with each step that swirled about her hem. She shifted the cloth-covered basket to a more comfortable position on her shoulder. Jamal would be looking forward to his afternoon meal, unless supervising the caravan's preparations had distracted him from noticing the passing of the sun. Sometimes she felt her father was so absorbed in his duties he would have gone the entire day without eating. But her mother insisted on sending refreshments out to him. And Julia was delighted for any excuse to see him.

The path took her out through the entrance to their compound and into the busy roadway heading out of town on the edge of Galilee Lake toward the caravanserai. When she arrived, the enclosure was filled with moaning camels, bleating sheep, scurrying caravan drivers, and barefoot herders, all hot and dusty and out of sorts. She wanted to hold her breath against the stench of animals and sweat-glistened bodies. She felt a stir as she passed, but no one spoke. She was not surprised at this, realizing even the newer herdsmen would know the wealthy merchant Jamal showed a sharp tongue and a quick temper where his daughter was concerned. No one dared raise his ire, especially with that camel scourge in his hand. She held her shawl over her nose and hurried forward.

She knew exactly where she would find him. She had been there many times over her growing-up years. His camels held the choicest spot in the entire enclosure, the one closest to the well and the watering trough. Even from a distance she could hear the strange braying of camels vying for position as servants attempted to pour fresh water from the goatskin buckets into the trough.

Again she shifted the basket, her eyes scanning the busy, noisy scene before her in search of the familiar form. And there he was, his back to her, bent over as his hand ran the length of a camel's front leg. She moved quickly up beside him and lowered the basket from her shoulder.

"Is she able to travel?" At her soft question Jamal straightened, and yes, the light in his eyes reflected his great pleasure. Her heart did a joyous skip.

"Julia, my dear." He reached out a hand toward the basket she held. "Come, daughter. Let's find some shade."

He led her through a gate and up a slight rise to a tent and swept aside the flap to let her enter. Rich dark carpets covered the ground beneath her feet as she stepped inside. Cushions tumbled haphazardly in deep piles against one wall, and she reached for some and tossed them together to make comfortable seating for them both. She loved it there. It was her favorite place in the entire world. Just the two of them . . .

If only . . . but she refused to let her thoughts pursue that direction. "Will she be able to travel?" she asked again.

"She is fine. She took a nasty kick at the watering trough, but the swelling has gone and she is not limping."

Julia knew she should be pleased. This camel served as the caravan's lead animal. She set the tone for other animals and held them all to a steady pace. Julia tried for the smile she was sure was expected. Yet in her heart she couldn't help but think—even hope—that if the camel was injured, perhaps this next journey would be delayed.

"Now, let's see what you have brought." Jamal had placed the basket on a cushion and was lifting the cloth. He nodded appreciatively at his favorite honey cakes. "You spoil me, my dear."

"It is really Mother who spoils you. I merely carry the basket."

He nodded. "What a fortunate man I am. Two lovely women to take care of me." He waited as she poured a mug of the cool tea. "So, what orders do you have for me? What would you like me to bring back when I return?"

There it was again. A reminder that he soon would be leaving. With first dawn he would once again take to the trade route with the caravan, the drivers, the loads of merchandise in which he traded. She would say her brave farewell, accept his warm embrace with a smile, and then spend the rest of the day lamenting quietly in her room. It was always the same. The joyous welcomes, the heartrending good-byes.

Suddenly a new idea surfaced and she leaned forward. "Father, may I . . . well, why should I not travel with you?"

He stopped in the middle of drinking his tea. "Join me on the road?"

"Yes. I could—"

But already he was shaking his head. "The trade route is no place for a young maiden. Particularly one as lovely as you are, my Julia."

"But—"

"No, no, no." The words came in quick succession. "No place for a young girl. It is not safe. Not proper." He shook his head emphatically.

She knew it was useless to argue further. He gulped a second cup. "I had not realized how I thirsted. Will you share a honey cake with me?"

She shook her head and stood to her feet. "No, thank you, Father. I think I will go and say good-bye to Sheeka."

He smiled around a generous bite of the cake. "They like you, those camels. They always seem to settle down when you speak to them. It is much better to have them in good humor when beginning a journey. They work harder. Less restlessness and stubbornness. You go ahead. I'll join you as soon as I have finished here."

Julia pushed aside the tent flap and walked toward the grumbling, spitting camels. She had noticed it herself. For whatever reason, the camels did indeed seem to become more docile when she talked to them and stroked the long hairy necks.

Camels were considered smelly, moody, and disgusting, she knew, but Julia liked the beasts. Why, she did not know or even try to understand. Perhaps it was the simple fact that when they arrived, so did her father. He had even allowed her to name each one. It had given her pleasure to think of him calling them by the name she had chosen when they took to the winding trails and roads toward those distant cities such as Damascus and Jericho.

She reached her hand out to Sheeka's neck. It would not do to approach one of the other camels first. Their leader would be sure to express displeasure in angry grunts and moans.

"How are you? Is your leg feeling better?" she said softly. "You have a long trip to make. Are you sure . . . ?" She crouched down to assess the injury for herself, running her hand gently over the tender area. Sheeka's rumblings softened. "I think Papa is right. You are—"

"You, there." It was a loud voice from behind her. "The camels are thirsty and the trough is empty. More water."

Julia glanced over her shoulder at a dust-covered caravan guard, sword glinting at his leather belt. Obviously just arrived from the trail, he was roughly clothed and red-faced from the desert sun. He scowled at her from under a dark, shaggy mane. He was young, she could tell, too young to talk with such imagined authority. And almost too young for the short dark beard that covered his chin. Julia allowed her eyes to skim across his face, then to each side, trying to determine to whom he was speaking.

"The camels," he said again, motioning to the herd crowding up behind him. He paused and looked directly at her. There was now a question in his tone as he added, "They thirst. It's been a long trek."

She straightened slowly. So his gruff orders were directed at her. She could feel the ire rising inside her. He had mistaken her for a servant. Or worse, a slave. Could he not see she had sandals on her feet? That her arms held expensive bracelets? Her earrings were of gold?

She could feel her eyes burning with the fury she felt. Who was this young upstart that he should be ordering her about as if she were a peasant? What right had he to command the daughter of Jamal, the wealthiest and most prominent merchant along the trade route, to do anything? Much less water his animals!

She took a step back, shoulders stiff, chin raised, cheeks burning in anger.

But he did not so much as flicker an eyelash. "Do you not hear? The camels need water."

She gave him a defiant stare. "Then I suggest you water them before your master has you flogged."

She had taken several quick steps before he seemed to have recovered enough to call after her, "He is *not* my master."

She could not resist whirling back to jab a finger in the direction of Jamal's tent. "And I am not his slave—nor his servant. I am his *daughter*."

She paused only long enough to see his eyes staring his shock. His lips parted, and she feared he might be trying to voice an apology, so she twisted away again, her unyielding back no doubt clearly proclaiming her intense irritation. She took some pleasure in imagining his alarm as she stalked away.

Julia brushed at her dusty cotton gown, shook out her thick brown curls streaked with gold—*like my father's*, she thought with satisfaction—and fastened the unruly locks in a tight roll at the base of her neck. Judging herself fit to enter the room where the evening meal would be served, she sighed and opened the door from her private quarters, nearly stepping into Zoe. The older woman stood before her, a tray balanced on one hand and the other poised to knock. She looked as startled as Julia felt.

Julia recovered and widened the opening to allow the servant woman to enter.

"Is Mother not well?"

"A pain in her temples again." The brief words carried an undercurrent of concern that their beloved servant tried unsuccessfully to hide.

This had been happening far too frequently of late, Helena's begging off joining Julia for the evening meal because of not feeling well. "Set the tray on the table by the window, please."

Zoe did as bidden and with a brief nod toward Julia turned to go.

"Wait. Please," Julia added, flushing slightly at the tone of her voice. She sounded arrogant to her own ears. "Please," she said again, "I . . . I really don't like eating alone. Do you mind staying?"

With one brief nod the roles of mistress and servant seemed to evaporate between them. Zoe granted her a look of shared companionship. Almost as a grandmother acknowledging her grandchild. "You are worried too," the woman said softly.

Julia swallowed away the lump in her throat, crossed to the

window, and pushed the heavy curtain aside. Perhaps the day had cooled enough to allow fresh air inside. The light was moving toward dusk as evening shadows stretched across the courtyard and the limestone floor of the room. One lone star held a solitary place in the night sky, blinking faintly as though beckoning others to join it. "Did you bring two cups?"

Zoe had eased herself onto a stool. "No—just the one."

"Never mind. I have another with my water jar. I'll fetch it."

Julia poured two servings of tea before taking her place in the chair at the small table's opposite side. She pushed the tray toward Zoe, hoping the frail-looking elderly woman would eat. What would she and her mother ever do if something happened to Zoe? Julia looked steadfastly at the woman she had known all her life and asked the question that was uppermost in her mind. "Is Mother truly ill?"

Her eyes held Zoe's as she spoke, challenging her to tell the truth.

The old woman shook her head as she spoke. "She worries."

It was the answer that Julia had expected. "But I cannot get her to tell me what it is that concerns her," she said. "Does she share her heart with you, Zoe?"

The elderly woman hesitated. "Helena—your mother—does not speak of it, but I . . . well . . ."

"You have known Mother far longer than I. She sees you as the only friend she has. We both love her. We need to talk about anything that might help her." Julia reached across the table to Zoe's hand.

The pleading words clearly had an impact on the woman. She refused to meet Julia's gaze as she said, "It started long ago. Back in Samaria, where your mother was born, she was a cheery, carefree girl. Then when . . . when things . . . happened to the family and they were left with nothing but debt, Helena was forced to be the answer to the need."

"The 'answer'? What do you mean? How?"

"Your father said he would take the small market stall and . . . well . . . Helena in exchange for the sum owed. He even, generously it was said, offered some denarii as well. And then Helena was brought here. I came with her."

Julia felt her body stiffen. "My father?"

Zoe only nodded, her eyes fixed on the hands tightly knotted in her lap.

"He married her?"

There was no response from Zoe.

"You mean . . . ?" Julia couldn't finish. She could feel her heart pounding in her chest.

When Zoe spoke again it was in a gentle tone. "Julia, that is the way of things. You can't change it. Your grandfather had died. Helena's mother, your grandmother, accepted the only course that might save her family. Otherwise they all would have been sold into slavery. Or left in the streets to beg. Helena was a beautiful young girl. Your father noticed her. He offered a way out of—"

"But he loves her," Julia protested.

Zoe's eyes lifted. "Yes. Yes, he loves her, your father does."

"But he—he *purchased* her?" Julia still could not grasp it. "She was simply payment for a *debt*?"

"In . . . in a manner of speaking."

"She's not his wife—she's his *slave*." The terrible word came out far too harshly. Oh, the shame of it! Julia could feel hot tears scalding her eyes. No wonder the town women crossed to the other side of the street to avoid her. No wonder guests never arrived at their door. "So that is why we are treated as lepers—"

"No. No, I am quite sure the neighbors, the townspeople, do not know."

"So my father hides her away to shield her from wagging tongues?"

Zoe shrugged and picked at a snag in her shawl. "It is a common enough thing for men in Jamal's position. I do not think he gives it thought at all."

The very words made further anger churn through Julia. Had he really no idea of what this meant? "She is a common . . ." But Julia couldn't say it.

Even so, Zoe's head lifted and she said quickly, "Are you to judge? What do you know of how it began? Or what it is now? Do you not see them when they are together?"

Julia's words were equally impatient. Angry. "Where does he go all the time, Zoe? Is he always just traveling the roads with his merchandise as he claims?"

Again Zoe sighed, but Julia could tell she would not lie. "I understand he has a home—a family."

"Where?"

"Damascus."

"So he cheats us both. His Damascus family and us. Do they know about us?"

Zoe slowly lifted her shoulders. "I have no idea. It is really none of our concern, Julia. We should ask no questions. Nor should we—"

"Does Mother know? Of that other family? Does she know?"

Zoe nodded.

"No wonder she is ill. She worries. She has no rights, no husband—"

"I do not think she worries much about herself."

Suddenly Julia understood. Her mother was a Samaritan, considered an outcast from Judaism—neither a member of the Jewish community nor of the Gentiles. Even her Hellenized name labeled her as other than a true Hebrew. And now it turned out she was a kept woman—could not even claim to be the wife of a wealthy Greek merchant. She clung to a most tenuous position against another woman, another household, another family. . . .

So what rights does that give her only child? Julia placed her untouched food back on the tray. "And I am a girl. Mother has no son to care for her should she be turned out." Julia stared directly at Zoe. "Why did she not have more children?"

"She did want them. Cried for them. But her womb had closed. She said Jehovah deemed her unfit. . . ."

Julia pushed away the now-cold tea and rose from her chair. She crossed the few steps back to the window. More stars had found their places in the darkening sky. To her left a sliver of moon did its best to offer what little light it could. From the courtyard, squabbling voices of outside servants hung on the stillness. *Likely the guards disputing over the hours of watch*, she thought numbly as her fingers traced a path across the windowsill.

She turned back to Zoe, her only anchor in a tilting world. "You've always known this?"

Zoe nodded. "Yes, I have been with your mother from the beginning—back in Samaria." Sadness darkened her eyes, and the hand she lifted to push back her shawl trembled.

"You have spoiled me," Julia scolded softly. "You leave me feeling like an overly pampered child."

Zoe straightened, her eyes flashing a silent protest. "You have enjoyed the finer things of life. You have father and mother and love—"

"And I have not taken responsibility for anything. But I will. I must find a way to help Mother. Surely there is something that can be done."

"I think there is one way," Zoe said slowly, staring into her cup, then lifting her gaze to Julia's. "Remember my trip back to Sychar a few weeks ago? I had permission to travel with your father's caravan to see my family. Well, I saw more than my family. I talked with a neighbor, another Samaritan, someone I would not have claimed as a friend those long years ago when your mother and I lived there. But she has changed—she is a different person now. She told me all about it. She met a man some years ago—a prophet of Israel—at the city well. This rabbi spoke to her, and she became his follower, along with others. It seemed too much to believe when I first heard her story, but she urged me to find a group of his followers when I returned to Tiberias and let them tell me more. I did. They are in a village nearby. These people of the Way, as they are called, are everywhere. More and more of them."

Zoe's voice took on an emotion Julia had not heard from the servant before. "He is not just a prophet. He is our promised Messiah. He did not come just for the Jews. He came for all people. Even us Samaritans. To bring salvation. And freedom."

Julia was more curious than convinced, but she asked, "Where is this prophet?"

Zoe frowned. "Well . . . he . . . they crucified him."

"What are you saying? He is dead?"

"Now, this is the part I found hard to believe at first, but it is true," Zoe said, hurrying on. "He came out from his tomb. People saw him. A few at first, then more. He talked with them. Ate with them. He gave them messages and promises about the future. They know that what he said—"

"I don't understand." Julia shook her head at the preposterous story.

Zoe stood now, her eyes filled with an unusual light. She reached a worn hand to place on Julia's shoulder. "Come with me. We are meeting again tonight. Let one of the leaders explain what I cannot. Come. Please come."

It was pure nonsense. A dead man coming to life! But . . . where else was there any promise of help? What harm could it do to listen to their account of this man, whoever he was?

Julia finally nodded assent, watching as the old servant's eyes took on a further gleam.

CHAPTER TWO

Tiberias
Six Months Later

"ALBAN!" THE VOICE of Jamal, Syrian trader and owner of both the caravan and the trading grounds outside Tiberias, carried far. Especially when he was in a temper. "A word with you!"

Alban quickly left Jacob's side and started toward the open tent. Clouds of dust shimmered above the campsite while camels snorted and stomped and bellowed—some impatient to begin the journey, others complaining over the enormous loads being fastened upon their backs. Most were simply being camels.

Jamal's tent was a decidedly elaborate affair with its wooden corner posts ornately carved and painted in whorls and other exotic designs. As the dawn wind had not yet stirred, all four sides of the tent were raised. The floor, layer upon layer of woven carpets, held a throne-like chair with gilded arms. Jamal was seated upon it, a brass table to his left holding quill and ink along with parchment and tea. The traveling abode was situated upon a small hillock just outside the camp's perimeter, providing Jamal a bird's-eye view of the entire caravan.

Alban knew the man's practiced eye would have missed nothing. As he approached the tent, the head servant started forward with the traditional bowl and towel. Alban would be invited to wash hands and face and feet. But Jamal impatiently waved the man aside. "We will not keep our chief guard a moment longer than required."

Alban remained, as expected, at the edge of the tent. His dusty sandals did not touch the carpet's border. "Sire?"

"It is considered a bad omen to begin a journey with a quarrel among the men."

"Among followers of the Way," Alban said quietly, "there is no such thing as omens."

Jamal brushed that aside with a wave. "I do not follow any man or deity. And it is good for us all that I do not. I lead, Alban—I lead! And I hired you, a former Roman centurion, to guard my caravan. Not to create discord among my guards."

"I hear and obey, sire."

"My caravan departs with the sun. I want my chief guard's attention focused upon the protection of my goods, not on his young assistant. Perhaps I should replace him—Jacob is his name?"

"He is my right hand," Alban assured him quickly. "And one of your finest guards."

"I've heard nothing but good reports about him," Jamal allowed. "So why is it you insist upon staining the dawn with your arguments?"

Alban knew that beneath the trader's usual joviality lay a streak of dangerous wrath. He sensed the man's force lurking within his now easier manner. "Jacob is at times a difficult and stubborn young man."

"While you at his age were no doubt an angel with wings of gold and a smile that melted the hearts of your elders?" Jamal sipped from a golden goblet. As soon as he placed it back on the table, the hovering servant refilled it. Steam poured out the long spout, and the air was suddenly perfumed with mint. "Tell me—I forget. Jacob is your nephew?"

"My charge. I rescued him from slavers when he was but a lad. A few years ago I was appointed his legal guardian. His sister's as well."

"You and he are bound by ties strong as blood," Jamal noted, his former ire seemingly evaporated like the steam from his cup. "Which no doubt explains why I heard you two squabbling like father and son."

Alban sighed. His wife, Leah, had admonished him over the same point. And more than once. "I apologize if we have disturbed your morning, sire."

"Not just mine! The caravan master is already anxious enough, what with the threat of bandits and Zealots hovering about the Samaritan plains, ready to snatch my hard-gotten goods!"

Jamal had returned from his last journey suffering from some illness. At the urging of the best physician in Tiberias, he had reluctantly agreed to stop his traveling, at least for a time. But the decision had not been easy, and Alban knew the merchant chafed at the thought of his caravans departing Tiberias without him.

"I shall guard your caravan and your merchandise," he now told the man, "with my life."

"Your loyalty is not in question, Guard Captain." Though he had returned to his easy manner, Jamal's eyes were iron hard. "Now I command you to go out and make peace with your Jacob."

Alban bowed as expected. "Sire."

He returned to where Jacob was helping load the donkeys that carried the caravan's own supplies. Jacob looked over his shoulder at Alban's approach and yanked so hard on the strap the donkey bellowed.

Alban held both arms wide. "I ask that there be peace between us."

Jacob kept busy lashing covers over the provisions they would need for the next four days. "Only because Jamal ordered it."

"The command was his. The peace is my own."

Alban could see that Jacob remained stubborn, but he kept his irritation in check. Finally Jacob gave a short nod, though refusing to meet Alban's eye, and swiftly turned back to his work.

Alban watched his charge for a moment longer. Jacob's growing strength and manhood were evident. At times Alban could still see the youth peering out from the dark eyes. But the trader's ire granted Alban a fresh perspective. He realized Jacob's shoulders were now broader than his own. The lad's legs and arms were finely muscled. At almost twenty, Jacob was half a head taller than Alban himself. He was still so wiry that Alban outweighed him, but Jacob was all lean strength and filled with the vigor of youth.

As he walked toward where his horse was tethered, Alban reflected on how Jacob restrained his movements nowadays when they trained together. Clearly Jacob was reluctant to best his master and mentor. Alban sensed the eagerness in his charge, the joy he took in his growing abilities with sword and staff and spear and bow. At the same time, Alban felt as though Jacob considered it all simply part of a thrilling adventure. But Alban knew the truth. These days, the roads of Judea and Samaria and beyond carried a growing risk. This was one of the reasons Alban felt such urgency in drawing the young man away from this vocation. Yet Jacob threatened to toss aside the new opportunity Alban had presented. Alban's arguments only threatened to tear their relationship apart.

At the caravan master's plaintive cry, Alban swung onto his horse and signaled the other guards with a shrill whistle. He and

Jacob both saluted Jamal as they passed the merchant's tent. Then Alban faced the new day and the open road.

In his heart he knew there would be no peace with Jacob this day.

From the outskirts of Tiberias their caravan descended toward the plains to the southwest. November had scarcely begun, yet the wind carried a chill more suited to February, heavy with coming rain. The camels snorted and balked, and the drovers' shouts were plucked away by a rising wind. Bandits used wind and rain to mask their attacks. Alban signaled with his whip hand, ordering the nine armed men to begin circling the caravan. Jacob's team traveled in one direction, while his own moved in the opposite course. It permitted them to cross paths repeatedly and enclose the caravan in a tight loop. Alban's strategy was one Roman troops had developed.

By late afternoon the caravan remained safe and the wind had subsided, but Alban and his men were exhausted. They camped beneath the shadow of a Roman garrison marking the entry to the Plains of Megiddo. Alban ordered his men to unsaddle their mounts and give them an extra feed. He began patrolling alone on foot, though he too wanted nothing more than rest and food. His bones ached. He missed Leah and their beautiful son, safe at their home on the outskirts of Capernaum. Alban sighed and wondered if he was getting too old for such duties.

Jacob approached him, carrying a skin of cold tea and a soldier's repast of dried meat and onions wrapped in flatbread. While the young man fell into step beside him, Alban ate and drank. When he was done, Alban wiped a hand across his lips and repeated his words from that morning. "I would have peace between us, Jacob."

He clearly had been expecting this, for he instantly said, "Then you will speak no more about this idea of yours."

"It is a good plan, Jacob."

"Not for me, it is not. I want nothing to do with it."

Alban kept his voice calm, though it required great self-control. "I wonder if this might be God's will for you, my friend."

Alban could tell Jacob had started to round on him but stopped and continued simply walking alongside. "I talk with God. Every day," Jacob finally said. "He hasn't said a thing about this to *me*."

Alban was about to rejoin that perhaps it was because Jacob continued as always in his headstrong way, refusing to *ask*. Jacob wanted to *tell* God. But as Alban opened his mouth, he glanced over. Jacob's features were taut with barely repressed anger. His shoulders were hunched in the manner of a warrior ready to strike. He looked ten years beyond his age.

Alban took a deep breath and let it out slowly. The lad whom he had loved and cared for as a son was becoming his own man, for better or worse. Alban said simply, "According to the tradition of your people, you became a man when you reached the age of thirteen."

Jacob snorted. "And now you're going to tell me I should obey my elders, yes?"

"No, Jacob. I admit I would like to say that, but I won't." Alban pointed to the Roman road they had just traveled, running straight and true until it disappeared between the first of the low-lying hills. "Beyond those first hills lies the valley of Tiberias, overlooked by Herod's castle. Then the Sea of Galilee, then the Parthian hordes."

"I know all that. You've taught me such lessons for years beyond count."

"Hear me out. Is that so much to ask?" Alban took Jacob's shoulders and turned him to face southwest. "There lies Samaria, filled with bandits and Zealots. All of them stalking caravans just like ours, waiting for a chance to strike. Beyond are the Arabian desert princes, whose generals would like nothing better than to capture a rich caravan, then claim it was lost in the empty wastelands. To the north is Lebanon, where once-proud Phoenicians have turned to piracy and plunder."

Alban saw him squint into the distance, as though searching for what he could not see. And was satisfied that at least Jacob listened carefully now. "What I am trying to tell you is this: If you stay with our work, sooner or later you will be forced to kill another man. Can you live with this stain upon your soul?"

"You do." Jacob did not look at him.

"I know no other life, Jacob. I have trained with sword and bow and spear since childhood. I fight to defend, to wound. But no longer will I kill." He paused and looked at Jacob until he turned his head. "But, Jacob, I cannot train you in such a manner and hope you will remain alive."

Jacob studied him now with an intensity that left Alban hard-pressed to meet the younger man's gaze. "I have done the same as you up to now."

"Perhaps you could indeed continue this as well. But there is great risk in this approach. Especially for one who has not yet gone through the fire of combat and emerged bloodied but not unto death."

Jacob nodded slowly. "I understand."

Alban felt hope surge. He repeated the words that had started their recent argument. "In the past nine months, three of my caravans were attacked by bandits. We saved all three from pillage. As a reward, Jamal has offered this trading center in Samaria to me."

"I hear you," said Jacob, impatience coloring his voice. "But you do not wish to run it yourself. Why do you think I—"

"Jamal made it clear I was to find someone else to actually manage the stall. He wishes me with the caravans."

It was a move worthy of Jamal, the shrewdest caravan merchant Alban had ever known. Jamal explained he had taken over a market stall some years ago from a widow. Her departed husband, a friend of Jamal, had left her not just alone but owing a great deal of money. Along with other items, he said, Jamal had accepted the stall in payment, clearing the woman's household of all debts, and also leaving her with enough silver to support her for years.

Jamal sent a series of underlings to run the enterprise for him. He was convinced, though, that these servants all were robbing him. Alban thought Jamal was probably right. The shop stood at the juncture of the four busiest roads in all Judea. Yet it had not made a profit in years. So the trader offered the whole thing as a gift to Alban, his loyal guard captain, one who deserved this kind of reward for a job well done. Though, in truth, they both knew it cost Jamal nothing except the chance to relieve himself of future headaches.

Alban paused, realizing he had been speaking his thoughts aloud. Jacob remained silent, walking alongside and directing most of his attention to the plains stretching out beyond the camp's perimeter. Now and then, however, he glanced at Alban. Showing a hunter's patience. Alban said, "Forgive me. I must be more weary than I realized."

"You do not look well."

"My chest burns," Alban admitted.

"Go and rest. I can handle the first watch."

"I know you can." Alban coughed and hunched over his chest, feeling like the action drained his body of breath and energy. Jacob's hand slipped underneath his arm, and the young man supported him easily. Alban straightened slowly, once again reminded that the concerned companion was a lad no longer.

Jacob said, "Sleep the night through. I will take responsibility for setting the watches."

Alban started to turn away, then stopped and asked once more, "You are certain you do not want to take hold of this opportunity in Samaria?"

"I can think of almost nothing," Jacob replied, "that I want less."

"Then what is it, please tell, that you *do* want?"

Jacob turned his face toward the setting sun. "That I wish I knew."

CHAPTER THREE

Jerusalem

ABIGAIL HURRIED DOWN the side passage, one hand clutching her wrap tightly against her chin, the other gripping the front of her robe. She had debated about bringing the produce basket in case she needed to deflect any questions about what she was doing out alone. But the wind was treating the street like a funnel, howling and tearing through the space. The sky overhead was dark like the hour after sunset, though it was scarcely midafternoon. A few other people scuttled past her, their heads bowed against the gale, and Abigail passed unchallenged.

She skirted around the city's southeastern plaza, the one which held the Freedmen's Synagogue. Though five years had past, Abigail still avoided the synagogue where her beloved Stephen had been plucked away by a mob and brought before the Sanhedrin. By now there was an additional reason for holding to side lanes, as the square had become a gathering point for those who hunted down followers of the Way.

As she approached the Essene Gate, Abigail spotted four

women bearing jars of oil along with baskets covered with damp cloths to keep out the dust. She assumed they also were headed for the caravan sites beyond the city boundaries, and fell into step just behind them. Two Roman guards huddled against the interior wall, sheltering against the wind. The women were given no more than a glance.

In the plains beyond the city gates, the unfettered wind nearly stopped their forward progress. Abigail tried to be heard over the bluster, asking the nearest woman where she might find Jamal's caravan. Then she heard someone shout, and a shape emerged from a nook in the outer wall. "Hello, sister!" he called as he ran over to her.

"Jacob!" It remained an astonishment to have to reach up in order to embrace her brother. Though she had seen him only four months previously, still he seemed to have grown another handsbreadth. Within her embrace, Jacob's shoulders felt as solid as the wall's stones. "When did you arrive?"

"Three evenings back."

"But why—?" Abigail refrained from further questions as he drew her toward a nearby tent. It was one of those foreign affairs, with double walls and more square than the familiar Judean shelters. The exterior canopy was pinned at an angle, like a sail, while the interior wall was formed of thick carpet matching that underfoot. The dual cloth walls were so effective that once the door flap fell into place, the tent's oil lamps burned with scarcely a flicker. With the wind's howl now muffled, Abigail no longer needed to raise her voice. "I am so glad to see you, my brother, but why did you not come to see me instead of sending a message?"

"We are being watched."

Abigail stared at this brooding stranger who resembled her brother. She had seen vestiges of the man emerging the last few times he had journeyed to Jerusalem. But some further change had come about since then. Something had jolted Jacob's world so the lad she knew and loved was being overtaken by a man.

She asked, "You are certain?"

"They skulk about the caravan site. They carry clubs. When challenged by the guards, they challenge back. Like a Roman soldier might, or a Temple guard. Only these men are Judeans, and wear no robes of office."

"I know of whom you speak." Abigail dropped her voice and felt a shiver through her body. "They use the Freedmen's Synagogue as their meeting place."

"Where Stephen used to preach?" Jacob shook his head. "You *must* leave this city, my sister."

"We've had this discussion," Abigail said with a sigh. "Many times. My place is here, Jacob."

She expected Jacob to argue with her. As had occurred the last time he had visited the city. And the time before that. In truth, the growing threat to believers had been subtle enough for her to ignore it most days. But she knew Jacob also could sense the mounting pressure, the growing risk. Abigail prepared herself for the ongoing dispute. She was not leaving the city where she had met and loved and wed and lost her man. And bore his child.

Instead, Jacob merely said, "Forgive me, Abigail. I have not even asked if you might care for something to eat or drink."

The reserve evident in Jacob's voice and stance left her unsure how to respond. She finally said, "Tea would be nice, if you have any."

"Of course." He slipped through the curtains that divided the tent in half. Abigail thought she glimpsed another figure in the shadows, but was not certain. Jacob swiftly returned and handed her an earthen mug. "Some dates, perhaps?"

"Thank you, brother, but I am not hungry."

"You are staying fed, then."

"Oh yes. We are more than well taken care of."

"I was worried. My man went first to the compound in the Old City and found it abandoned. It was only by chance I found a shopkeeper who is a follower and knew where you had gone." He cocked his head. "Why do you smile?"

" 'Your man,' " Abigail repeated with a chuckle. "How you have grown."

Jacob smiled briefly, and for an instant the little boy emerged once more. Then he turned somber again. "There is something you need to . . . to see."

His eyes seemed to darken further.

"What is it, Jacob? Is it Alban?"

Jacob drew back the dividing tapestry. "Come."

Jacob was aware his manner was unsettling to Abigail. He wished he could do something to bridge this distance between them. But the fact was that he felt beset by more than he could manage. When Abigail spotted the figure lying upon the pallet, she drew back. Jacob said, "Don't fear, sister. It is indeed our Alban."

Her face creased in alarm, and her hand went to her mouth.

Jacob shifted the oil lamp close over the man. Alban's features were slick with fever-sweat. His cheeks were hollow, his half-closed eyes glittered in the lamplight. A slight smile curved his lips around the coarse murmur, "Hello, dear one."

Abigail knelt beside the bed. "What has happened, Alban?"

"I assure you, it looks far worse than—" The words were interrupted with a cough that shook his entire frame.

Jacob caught him in what had become a practiced manner, holding him and fitting the mug of cold tea to his lips. "The tea is sweetened with honey," he told Abigail quietly. "It eases his throat."

Alban drank, nodded, and allowed Jacob to lay him back on the pillow. "I grow so very tired of honey," he murmured.

"How long have you been like this?" Her voice sounded as horrified as her expression.

Jacob answered for his guardian. "He was not feeling well when we left Tiberias. Every day on the road, it worsened. And since we arrived here. Twelve days in all."

She asked Alban, "Are you eating?"

Jacob again replied for him. "Not nearly enough."

"Jacob is doing his best to fatten me up, never fear."

"We are to leave tomorrow," Jacob told Abigail. "The caravan master has held off, hoping for his guard captain to recover. But we carry fresh supplies for Caesarea. We can tarry here no longer."

"You must not travel," Abigail said quickly, looking again at Alban's pain-wracked face.

The man seemed ready to argue, but Jacob settled a hand upon his shoulder. The silent admonition was enough. Alban asked Abigail, "Will I not be too much of a strain upon you and the followers?"

"How can you even ask such a thing?"

"These are not the best of times, and—"

"I cannot understand why you waited this long to ask for our help."

Jacob explained, "He wanted to continue with the caravan."

Abigail swept her hand the length of Alban's sleeping pallet. "That is utterly out of the question."

"And," Jacob went on, "we were both fearful of the watchers."

He saw the concern tighten her features and felt the same response in his gut. To name the threat was to give it strength, reality.

Still, Abigail merely asked, "Where are they now?"

"Gone," Jacob replied. "Since the wind heightened this afternoon."

"Then we must make haste." Abigail addressed her words to Jacob as she looked at the supine form. "Are there those who can help carry him?"

"Too dangerous." Jacob had spent many dark hours thinking this through. "We need to move him without anyone knowing who has left."

"But you just said the watchers were gone."

"Even so, we do not know if they have allies in the camp." Jacob disliked troubling his sister more than she already was. But she needed to understand the risks. "The watchers did not patrol the entire caravan site. They were intent on finding a specific—"

"They . . . they were after you, Jacob?" Her head came around swiftly with the words.

"I think they were not certain whom they sought. If they wanted Alban or myself, they needed only to come asking by name."

Alban said weakly, "Which is a reason you should not become involved, Abigail. I should not have suggested—"

"I am *already* involved, Alban." Her hands punctuated her statement as she added, "I have been *involved* since the day you rescued my brother."

Alban's only response was the feverish gleam in his eyes, the hoarse sound of each drawn breath.

Jacob told them, "I have a plan."

When Jacob emerged from the tent, the sky was the color of pewter, a sullen grey lanced with fragments of afternoon light. Jacob crossed to the nearest corral, where six donkeys huddled together, facing away from the storm's wind. Jacob shouldered his way among them and pulled upon the ropes of the two youngest beasts. One donkey brayed a single protest, then fell into step.

Jacob drew blankets and saddles from the packs. The donkey to his right swiveled about so as to watch him. The beast's eyes, surrounded by white circles, had a mildly astonished look. Its sides shivered in the chill, but it did not resist.

As Jacob took two cloths from his belt and lashed them across the donkeys' eyes, a voice said, "You are leaving, then."

Jacob turned to face Latif, a Judean drover from the outskirts of Damascus. He was a quiet, steady hand upon the road, and gentle with his camels. He was also a follower of the Way. Jacob had learned this in a manner that was customary in these dark days. One quiet word murmured to a sunlit dawn had passed from Latif to Jacob, something that might have been ignored except for the fact that Jacob knew what to listen for. In the ensuing days, they had taken cautious measure of one another and were becoming friends. Jacob replied, "Alban is no better. I need to take him to safety."

Even robed as he was against the chill, Latif was a small man, though his slight frame held astonishing strength. "Safety is not a word I would choose for our people, especially not in Jerusalem."

"Just the same, he will be better off here than with us on the road to Caesarea."

Latif reached across and rubbed the donkey's nose. The beast whickered softly at the man's familiar scent. "Do not hurry back. Stay with them the night. It is dangerous traveling the streets after dark, and I will stand guard in your place."

Jacob nodded. "It would be good to spend some hours with our friends."

"Tell Alban I shall continue to pray for his recovery." Latif stroked between the donkey's ears. "Can I speak to you in absolute confidence?"

"Of course."

"These are uncertain times. I am in need of . . . of a friend."

Jacob noted the man's tight glances, cast in every direction. The hand that stroked the beast's muzzle trembled.

Latif went on, his voice just above a whisper, "I serve our community in a most secret way."

"I don't understand."

"I am a courier. We risk our lives to keep the followers in contact with each other. The further our clan spreads from Jerusalem, the more vital our work becomes."

Jacob shifted closer, though no one was nearby. In fact, the entire caravan site appeared empty. The tents that filled the encampment were bowed on their windward side like earthbound sails. The ropes hummed a constant whine. The camels knelt and calmly chewed their cud. Even the wells, which normally were centers of bustling activity, were vacant.

Jacob said, "Why are you telling me this?"

"I fear the Temple's henchmen are after me. Why else have they been lurking about, watching us like vultures?"

"There could be any number of reasons."

Despite the chill, Latif's features were beaded with sweat. Jacob could smell the man's fear. "They know a courier is here, and they hope to flush me out. I sense it in my gut."

Jacob doubted the man was correct. But it was clear enough that nothing he said would lessen the man's anxiety. "What would you have me do?"

Latif's eyes scouted the empty site once more, then he slipped his hand inside his robe. It emerged holding a slender leather satchel. "Take this. I was to hand it to another who leaves for Tiberias, but I am being watched and cannot make the contact. They must not find it. Hide it well."

"But what am I to do with this?" Jacob wanted to step back, but he forced himself to stay and listen to his friend.

"If I am wrong, and we leave here safely, you can give it back to me. And you can forget we ever spoke. But I am not wrong." He thrust the satchel into Jacob's hands. "If I am taken, return to Tiberias as soon as possible."

Latif quickly explained the procedure Jacob was to follow exactly. The man stopped now and then, asking Jacob to repeat the instructions. Upon his arrival back in the Tiberias encampment, Jacob would be approached by someone within the camel pen. Jacob was to wear a red headband and carry a basket of herbs to treat the animals. He was to speak a phrase which Latif urged him to repeat several times until he was sure Jacob would remember it correctly. After the phrase was spoken, his contact would respond by drawing the sign of the fish in the sand. Jacob would then also draw the sign of the fish. Only then was Jacob to pass over the satchel.

Latif ended with one more caution. "It must be just as I have said. And be careful. There are eyes everywhere. Now, do you have it clearly in mind?"

"I think so, yes, but . . ."

"In this there are no uncertainties, Jacob."

"Of course." Jacob tried to swallow.

"And if I am taken, I place three of my camels in your charge. Jamal has given me a special assignment to . . ."

"You have a double mission?"

"Two. Separate. They are not in any way related."

"You are obviously a man to be trusted."

"And I in turn trust you. With them both." Latif might have shaken his head, or perhaps it was merely a nervous tremor. "Keep safe the packet, Jacob. Guard my camels," Latif implored, his dark eyes saying far more than his words. "Now go. And if I am taken, pray for me."

Jacob wanted to protest further, but the man turned and hurried away. Jacob slipped the satchel inside his robes, fitting it tight against his abdomen, and refastened his belt. He tried to tell himself that Latif's fears were merely overwrought imaginings. All of the caravan's associates bore the strain of the road and the storm. But as Jacob turned toward the tent, he felt the satchel riding against his skin. The man's fears seemed to emanate from the leather, working deep into Jacob's own gut. He looked forward to the morrow, when he could hand this back to Latif and forget the exchange had ever taken place.

With their eyes protected from the swirling dust, the donkeys made no protest as Alban was helped into the saddle. The man was so weak that both Abigail and Jacob were required to give him a hand up. It was the first time Jacob could ever recall his guardian needing help to do anything. The realization left him reluctant to leave Alban's side. "Are you sure you will be able to ride?"

"It's a good plan," Alban said, coughing weakly. "And you were right to insist I remain here in Jerusalem."

Abigail darted a glance at Jacob. Such an admission was troubling indeed. "Be ready to assist him," Jacob murmured as he made a cradle of his hands for Abigail to step into the saddle of a second donkey, then moved it alongside Alban.

"I will be fine," Alban said.

Both Alban and Abigail were dressed in cloaks of the Damascus style, free-flowing robes of a golden color with hoods that shadowed their faces. The woman's robe differed from the man's only by the tassels that rimmed her hood, and which now were whipping wildly in the wind. Jacob, attired in a Syrian servant's robe, grey with a striped cloth belt, gripped the reins and pulled the two donkeys forward.

With a slight reduction in the gale, the Roman guards had returned to their posts outside the gates. A metal basket, as large as a kettle, burned several logs and flung cinders in a steady stream into the evening sky. Jacob had hidden the leather satchel beneath the carpets in his tent. Even so, he felt as if it were still burning the skin of his abdomen as they approached the gate. The guards huddled against the wall, eyeing them sullenly, but made no challenge.

They passed well to the east of the plaza fronting the Freedmen's Synagogue, though the maneuver was probably unnecessary. The streets of Jerusalem were largely empty. Most of the stall owners already had shuttered their shops and left for the comforts of home and fire and food. Overhead the wind buffeted the rooftops, like the rumble upon a giant's drum. The donkeys' clopping hoofs held to a steady cadence as Jacob hurried forward. The only sounds between them were Abigail's quiet directions and Alban's occasional cough.

Soon enough, Jacob required no further instructions, for he knew where they were going. He stopped before the familiar gate and rapped loudly with his staff. The face that appeared in the recessed portal peered at Jacob and his two shrouded passengers in the near darkness. The bearded man barked out, "We are closed. Come back tomorrow."

"It is I, Master Carpenter."

"I know you not."

"Jacob. Your former apprentice. Let us in. Please."

"Jacob . . ." He squinted doubtfully through the gloom. "I still do not—"

"You once accused me of only being good at holding up the side wall."

"Can it be?" The scrape of the bar being lifted, and the carpenter flung open the door. "Merciful heavens, it *is* you."

"As I said." Jacob led the two donkeys inside, and the carpenter quickly closed and barred the gate. "Help me with Alban."

"Alban is here as well? And Abigail, I see! Dressed as foreigners from beyond Judea's boundaries." He helped ease Alban to the earth. "What has happened to you, my good man?"

"It is nothing," Alban said, wheezing hard from the journey. "A cough—"

"And a fever strong enough to eat him from the inside out," Jacob said as he tethered the two animals. "Our caravan must leave tomorrow. But Alban needs rest and time to heal."

Abigail greeted the large man and asked, "Is there place for one more? I can move—"

"No, no, not necessary. For a friend in need? Of course we have room!" The carpenter fitted himself to Alban's other side. "Come and settle your bones by the fire, brother."

"I do not wish to make trouble," Alban said.

"We can pay," Jacob put in.

"No more such talk. We do not speak of payments here." The carpenter glanced over Alban's bowed head. "You look like your own elder brother, Jacob. How long has it been since—?"

"Five years."

"And long ones besides. But from the looks of you, you have made good use of the time."

Alban wheezed out, "Jacob has become my good right arm."

Abigail followed close behind the trio. "So he will take good care of your caravan, Alban, and you can rest easy and recover before getting back to your Leah."

Alban coughed again and would have doubled over save for the grip the two men had on his arms. When the spasm ended, he said, "Yes, I have been gone from Leah too long . . . and from our son, Gabriel." Even speaking their names seemed to soften the lines of pain and weariness in his face.

"We comfort and care for one another." The carpenter was a simple man, with hands as large as the mallets he used. He led Alban through the familiar doorway into what Jacob knew as the main workroom. "You are joined with us in the family of our Lord. Of course we will help, and you will soon be ready to travel home to your wife and child."

The workroom had been swept clean and the tools stowed. The high-ceilinged chamber was filled with torchlight and tables and perhaps thirty people. At the other end, large doors opened into what Jacob recalled was the storage area for wood and finished products. Here in this place, all was warmth and friendship. Nods and smiles greeted the newcomers.

Jacob allowed himself to be seated at a table with some men, and Abigail settled herself on the other side with the women. Alban was given one of the few chairs set near the great oven and the warmth of its fire.

The master carpenter, Josiah, stepped to the front of the room and spread his arms wide, as if embracing the whole gathering. "In the name of our risen Lord," he sang out.

Jacob bowed his head with the others for an opening prayer, the men rocking back and forth their agreement and fervently echoing amen at its close. A psalm was sung. Another prayer. A second song. Then bowls of fragrant stew were passed along the rows by several young women.

Jacob held his bowl below his chin and enjoyed the meal with the others, responding when spoken to but comfortable with mostly listening.

When the women were gathering the dishes, Abigail moved nearer to Jacob. "We have so little time together, my brother."

Jacob nodded somberly. It was true. His visits were always a brief stop when he came with the caravans. At the same time, he wished Abigail could be convinced to leave this city. It truly was not a place for her and her little daughter. He would feel much more at ease were she to move near Leah up north. But he did not speak his thoughts. Abigail had already heard them many times. Instead he asked, "Where is the little one?"

"Asleep upstairs." Abigail's face glowed with her smile. "You are not the only one who has grown."

"You are living here now?"

"For six months. Ever since the . . . the men came to our quarters at the upper room where our Lord shared his final meal." Abigail shuddered at the memory. "I was away at the time, continuing Stephen's work with the orphans and widows. Three of our dear friends still are missing. The Temple guards will tell us nothing."

Jacob shook his head, but he did not want to hear more bad news. Not tonight. "Is my little niece as lovely as I recall?"

A woman on Abigail's other side said, "Dorcas holds her mother's beauty. She captures our hearts with her smiles."

It took Jacob a moment to realize who had spoken, the woman had aged so. "Martha! Forgive me, I did not recognize you."

At least her voice had not changed, and she was as blunt and direct as ever. "You have grown into a man as comely as your sister is lovely. I shouldn't be surprised if—"

"Martha," Abigail whispered. "We are preparing to pray."

Martha shrugged and lifted her hands, palms up. "Well, it is good to see you, Jacob. We have need of men of valor," she added. "Now more than ever."

Jacob answered her nod with one of his own. The satchel hidden under the carpets came to mind. He took a deep breath and turned back toward Josiah standing before them at a small table graced with a homespun cloth.

The evening prayer service began with a sharing of the bread and the wine. An everyday occurrence for most there, but for Jacob, this prayerful remembrance of their Lord's last supper with his disciples held a singular intensity. It had been a long while since he'd had this opportunity. He watched as the elders of their group stood before the table and Josiah again prayed, lifting the bread and the cup in turn as he blessed them, then broke the bread into small pieces for distribution.

Jacob thought about the incongruity of the most revered in the group, who normally were the ones being honored and served, to now be carrying the plates of bread and the goblet of wine to each participant. He was reminded of the story he'd heard of Jesus kneeling to wash his disciples' dirty feet. *A servant* . . . kept whispering through his mind as the words of the sacrament were recited. "On the night when he was betrayed, Jesus took the cup. . . ."

Beyond the closed doors and shuttered windows, the wind moaned its way through the darkened inner courtyard. Faces held an otherworldly calm. Most paid the noise no mind. They prayed for those who had particular needs. The first prayer was for "our beloved friend and fellow believer Alban, whose body requires a healing touch." The next was for friends who had left five months earlier for Samaria, from whom there was still no word. Then they all joined aloud in fervent petition for a family that had been hauled away that very afternoon by the Temple's henchmen, led by Saul of Tarsus. The name itself, intoned in grave sorrow by the master carpenter, seemed to cause even the candles to shiver.

From where he was sitting, Jacob could see the workshop's entrance, and beyond was the compound's main gate. Outside those locked and barred doors lurked the same night, the same risks. In here, however, all was peace. He felt that God was very close to him that night, a comfort so strong Jacob could almost hear a voice speak into the deep quiet of his heart.

He glanced again at Alban by the oven's outer wall. The warmth caused his guardian's features to glow, or perhaps it was the same Spirit that Jacob felt burning within his own chest. He knew Alban was sincere in his concerns for Jacob's safety. But Jacob also was certain this was not the life for him. His eyes moved back to the master carpenter, singing in his deep voice, "The Lord watches over all who love him. . . ."

Jacob suddenly realized that for the first time he could look at his former employer without a veil of resentment—over being forced toward a profession he loathed, over working for a man who could not be satisfied. Jacob had never been meant to become a carpenter. Nor was he destined to be a merchant, managing a stall. God might not have spoken to him in words that he could discern. But he knew this just the same.

Jacob slipped off the bench and knelt in the space between the tables, the stones cold on his knees. He bowed his head and prayed with an intensity that was matched only by his heart's calm. *Grant me wisdom, O Lord. Solomon asked this first. I am not as wise as he. I have asked for everything else. Freedom, liberty, strength, riches. But I humble myself this night and accept that without you, and without your direction, all these other things are nothing. I am nothing. Show me clearly what you would have me do. Give me the strength to accept your will. And do it to the utmost of my ability.*

Banging upon the outer gate halted the song as if cut off with a knife. As Jacob sat back on his seat, Josiah moved out of the room and into the courtyard. He demanded, "Who disturbs us at this time of night?"

"A friend!"

Though Jacob could not place the voice, something about it brought his head around.

Josiah grabbed a stave leaning against the portal and gripped it across his chest. "It is late. Return tomorrow—"

"I cannot! The mask of night was necessary in order for me—"

"I know that voice!" Alban was rising unsteadily to his feet. He called as loudly as he was able, "Linux?"

"It is indeed." A pause, then, "Can that be you, Alban?"

"None other." Alban waved toward the master carpenter, whose hand rested upon the latched bar. "He is a brother and a friend. You may open the door."

CHAPTER FOUR

Tiberias

JULIA KICKED RESTLESSLY at covers that seemed to pin her to her bed. She rose to her feet and moved in the darkness across to the window. Her sleep was finished for the night.

She pushed at the latch that held the shutter in place. A chill predawn breeze greeted her. She breathed in deeply of the wintry aromas. Overhead a few clouds scuttled across the sky, hiding all but one curve of the moon. On a distant hill a fire flickered. Camel drivers? Shepherds? Rome's soldiers? Perhaps a group of Zealots. No, likely not. They were far too secretive concerning their whereabouts.

Her thoughts floated back over the previous six months. When she had first accompanied Zoe to the meeting of the group known as the Way, she had gone with the faint hope that somehow they might be the answer to her mother's dilemma. After all, even their name held out some promise of that, didn't it? Zoe had seemed so positive that the people there would offer her both wisdom and comfort. But those first discussions had not been about her mother.

It was all about a Jewish rabbi who had lived, and died . . . and lived again. Julia had been tempted to dismiss it all as sheer foolishness, as she had when Zoe first told her about it. Reason said that it could not possibly be true.

Even so, she had found herself looking forward to the next meeting. It was obvious that this little band truly believed all these things they talked about at their meetings. It had seemed beyond Julia's understanding. Yet they looked like honest, reliable people. Some of them were certainly unlearned, but there were also scholars among them, even one trained Pharisee. These too accepted what was declared as fact. Julia left each meeting struggling with her questions.

Gradually she had found herself wanting with all her heart for this story to be the truth. She felt the rabbi's words, repeated by his followers so carefully and convincingly, calling to her. If only she could throw her cautions aside and accept what they were saying, she had mourned inwardly. Would it change her circumstances? Her heart? For days her thoughts were constantly upon what she had witnessed and heard. Many times she felt prayers of hope welling up within her. *O God, are you really there? Did you send your very son here? Is he our Messiah? Through his death, can you wash me from my sin and self-seeking? Replace my heaviness with joy? My isolation with a sense of belonging . . . somewhere? To someone?*

Last evening, when she had been able to bear her swirling thoughts no longer, she had gone in search of Zoe. "Is it true?" she demanded of this servant who seemed more like family. "Is it really true he was—is—the Messiah that was promised?"

"Oh, yes." Zoe's tone had sounded almost a hymn of praise rather than spoken words. "Oh, yes," she'd repeated, her hand going to her bosom. "He is."

This time Julia had not hesitated. "Then I too want to believe.

I need him. I accept the truth. I can no longer make sense of my world without him."

They had knelt together and Zoe had helped her through a prayer, Julia's voice trembling with emotion. Much to her amazement, a quiet but unmistakable calm had poured into her mind. Her soul. She felt like the disturbing questions had been soothed away, and she was left with a deep sense of peace. She had not felt this way since bounding into her mother's lap as a carefree child.

In the rush of these new impressions, Julia had known this was the answer. Not just for her but for her mother, the dear troubled woman who bore such heavy, painful burdens.

Now she had awakened to a new day, her thoughts still on the wonder of her newfound faith. But filling her heart was the desire that her mother also experience this deep sense of peace.

Yet how would she get her mother to see and accept this wonderful gift? Would she be willing to meet with the group of believers? Julia knew she would be concerned about whether they would accept a Samaritan woman who was nothing more than the unwed chattel of a godless Gentile. The Jewish leaders considered that enough to bar such a woman from all religious functions. Would these Christ-followers also shun her as unclean, unworthy?

Julia suddenly remembered the story Zoe had told about the *other* Samaritan woman, the one Jesus had talked with at the Sychar well some years ago. He had accepted her, changed her life, and given her living water. *That's just what Mother needs, "living water" to wash away the darkness in her soul. . . .*

Tomorrow night was to be another meeting of the Way. Julia's deepest desire was that her mother would be introduced to the man who had that water. But how was she to convince her to go and listen?

There was a shuffling at her door, and Julia knew Zoe had arrived with her first meal of the day. The smiles the two women exchanged spoke far more than words could express. *We are truly like family,* Julia thought as she led Zoe with the tray over to the small table.

The two began removing the plates of fruit and flatbread. "It is a new day," breathed Julia. "A day of hope."

Zoe nodded and handed Julia her mug of tea. "You feel it too."

"Oh, yes. Have you seen Mother yet?"

"She has stirred. But she has not dressed nor eaten."

"I cannot wait to tell her. But . . . do you think she will understand?"

Zoe smiled but shook her head. "Likely not. It is very difficult to understand—to accept—when it is all new. One needs the light of the Spirit to shine the way."

"So you mean I must wait?" Julia felt shock and alarm. "But I will surely erupt with the desire to share this with her."

For the first time in many years Julia heard Zoe chuckle, the laughter crackling strangely, as though she had forgotten how to express mirth. "We can pray now, and if you feel it is right, you can visit your mother as soon as you have finished here."

They bowed together in fervent prayer, certainly a new experience for Julia. Sharing a prayer time with a servant, even though she had known Zoe all her life, was most unusual. Yet it did not feel at all awkward or out of place. There was an even stronger bond now drawing them together.

Julia turned her attention to the meal before her. "Will you continue to pray with me each day?" she asked around a bite of bread and cheese.

"Of course. And I will continue to pray for your mother as I have been doing since I became a believer."

Julia stared at Zoe over her mug. "Did you also pray for me?"

Zoe nodded. "Many times each day."

"And God answered your prayer."

"He did."

"Do you think he will answer our prayers for Mother?"

"It is not presumptuous of me to believe he would love to do so."

Julia pushed the food back and rose to her feet. She still needed to dress, and time was passing. "We need to pray often, Zoe. That Mother will listen and understand. That the Spirit will illuminate her heart. That she will be willing to go with us to the gathering tomorrow."

Suddenly Julia remembered her own struggles. She had been told the Good News many times—yet it had taken her many months to accept it. Now that she believed, she wondered why it had required so long to understand. Yet everything was very new. There were countless questions begging for answers. Though she had a sense of peace, she also was very aware that the same peace was not shared by her mother. And there also was her father . . . how could she make them see? It left her unsettled. Anxious.

"What if Mother won't—how do we make her understand?"

"Foolish child," soothed Zoe, and she reached out to brush Julia's tangled hair. It had been a long time since Zoe had addressed or touched Julia in the familiar way she had often done when she was a child, but Julia was comforted by both now. "My foolish child," Zoe repeated. "We have prayed, and our Lord has heard us. We must trust him to do the work."

She patted Julia's shoulder and turned to gather up the tray, then gave Julia one more smile. "Dress, child. Dress and go see your mother, and I will spend the time praying."

Julia tapped on the door a short while later but heard no response. As silently as she could, she pushed it open a crack.

From where she stood she could see her mother's bed, its covers in total disarray, as though Helena had battled them for an entire sleepless night. But Helena's head was no longer resting on the rumpled pillow.

Julia found her mother sitting in the secluded alcove in the courtyard outside her bedroom suite. Protected from the wind by high stone walls, its flooring designed with patterns of multicolored tiles, the spot offered solitude and a degree of warmth even on a cool morning. The bench tucked up against the southern side held soft cushions, placed by servants early each morning and taken in each night. At the center of the small enclosure an ornate Grecian marble fountain that Jamal had brought back from one of his many journeys danced with colored prisms, creating its own shimmer of rainbows in this world of stone. Helena loved the spot and had claimed it as her own.

She was idly picking at some straws that nesting birds had dropped on the bench. Her hair was loose and framed a pale, expressionless face. One foot was tucked up under her much as a child would sit, while the other swung its sandal back and forth as though in time to some silent inner song.

"Mother?" Julia began hesitantly as she approached.

Helena's head came up and a smile brought life to her face. She moved ever so slightly, indicating that Julia was welcome to join her.

"Zoe says you once more have not been well."

Helena lifted a hand with a small wave, indicating things were up and down with her.

"Mother, I am very concerned about you. You seem to be far from healthy lately. Do you need a physician? I'm sure—"

"Oh my, no." The words were emphatic, and Helena straightened up from her reverie. She shook her head for emphasis. Then her gaze turned back to the straw in her fingers.

"When I am here, things seem right, unbroken," she said softly, slowly, as though speaking to herself. She lifted her eyes to look at Julia. "The way a god would intend them to be. Can you understand what I am trying to say?"

Julia nodded. "There is a sense of peace here."

Helena smiled in response. "That's exactly what I wished to express."

Julia felt she now had her mother's full attention and must seize the moment. "Mother, I was talking with Zoe, and during her trip to Sychar a while ago she met an old acquaintance—a woman she had known previously. She told Zoe the most remarkable story, some very good news."

"News? What possible good news from Sychar?"

"There is not just *a* god—but *the* God. This woman—she met him personally. He was visiting at the well and—"

"The well in *Sychar*?" Her mother frowned. "What kind of god visits *that* town—and a well? Has he need of human refreshing?"

"He . . . he was not there to meet his need but to meet her needs."

This seemed to puzzle her mother even further. "A god, interested in a human? A *woman*?"

"His name was Jesus. He was sent by the God of heaven. The creator God. The one true God who whispers to you about peace."

Her mother was shaking her head. "You believe that? That we . . . that I was created? Made? I'm not simply *here*?" She waved her hand through the air as though to dismiss such a preposterous thought.

"I do."

"If that were so, would not there need to be some reason for . . . for me to be here?"

"Yes, Mother. Yes, there is."

"But I . . . Nothing in my life has allowed me to believe that anything is for a purpose. That it has any other meaning than to exist—and die." Helena's eyes shimmered with unshed tears. She reached out a trembling hand and stroked Julia's cheek. "There is nothing, nothing, that has given me any purpose—any feeling of worth—except for you."

Julia fought back her own tears. "Mother, I thank you for the life you have given me. But there is much more. Truly, there is. I want so much for you to experience this for yourself. Will you come with Zoe and me? A group of Jesus' followers meet near Tiberias. Some of them knew him personally when he was here. They—"

"He was here? In Tiberias? Why was this not known?" She wiped away the tears and turned her large, expressive eyes to Julia.

Julia quickly decided not to attempt any further explanation at the moment. "Perhaps not right here in Tiberias, but . . . but they will tell you all about him. At the meeting I mentioned. Will you come, Mother? Please?"

Helena lifted herself from the bench and moved over to the singing fountain. Her back was to Julia, but her very stance expressed her struggle. Julia saw her reach out a hand and let the splashing water run through her outstretched fingers. At length she turned back, her brow furrowed again. "I can do nothing without your father's permission. He is not one for religions. I doubt . . ."

Julia felt a familiar urge to let her emotions, her questions, burst out with all that had echoed through her mind for weeks now. Why had she been permitted to live with this false conception all her life? Why had she not known the real reason her father was seldom with them? That his other household held the true right to his favor? Did she and Helena truly matter to Jamal at all? Though they already had discussed this and Helena had dismissed it, these thoughts still rankled Julia.

She stirred as she remembered the discussion of the followers about the Messiah's teachings on forgiveness. On loving one's enemies. Her father was certainly not that, but his actions, this deception, had put him on the other side of a great divide. . . .

Helena must have sensed the turmoil in her daughter's heart, for she returned to the bench and gathered Julia in her arms. "Jamal does love us. That is much more than many can say. He is a good man. He has provided for us. He comes when he can. We do have to share him—yes, that is true. But don't you see? That is far better than not having him at all."

"You are not angry? Bitter?" Even as she voiced the question Julia was aware of something at work in herself, something on a deeper level. A soft yearning to forgive him. To feel like his cherished little girl again.

"I have no reason to be bitter. Without your father I might very well be slaving in a grain field gathering gleanings after the harvesters. I could be tramping grapes in a wine press or herding goats on rugged hills. Or begging. Or worse." She shook her head. "Your father has cared for me. And for you. Can I call my lot hard when all I need do is be pleasing to him when he comes? That is no burden. He is kind to me, Julia. Gentle. He seeks my happiness. It is much more than many women have. And because of him I have you."

Julia slid both her arms around her mother, burying her face on Helena's shoulder.

"You think it is my own circumstances that disturb me? The time I spend with him?" Helena asked quietly.

"Is it not?"

"No, my dear. I think little about it at all. Life is not difficult when he is here. When he is with us at our home I know my purpose in life. Life has some meaning. But when he is gone . . ." She was silent for some time before she went on, her voice close to Julia's ear. "When I was a girl in the village, I was raised in a home of market people. There was much to be done and too few hands to do it. We worked hard. Very hard. But I knew my role. I understood my family's expectations. I had a *place*. I knew my way among the market stalls. I knew how to cook. How to clean. I think I would have made a very good servant girl."

That idea brought a smile to Julia's face, and she lifted her head. Her mother? A servant? Helena smiled back, but she was shaking her head.

"Then I came here," Helena continued, "where I cannot be a servant. I have a household of servants. I am to sit—and let them fuss over me. I long to work the ovens, slide in the bread I have kneaded and shaped, and watch the loaves turn golden. My loaves. Smell the aroma of my own fresh-baked bread. Feel the satisfaction of doing something. Making something. But no, I am expected to be a woman of leisure. Yet I am not accepted outside these walls as one. They know I am not of the proper class. So it turns out I have no purpose. I lounge . . . and feel unproductive. Bored. The days drag by with no meaning." She hesitated and her arms around Julia's shoulders tightened. "Except for you—and now . . ."

"Now?"

It was pure sorrow she saw in her mother's eyes.

"I knew it would happen. It was bound to happen, but I . . . I kept telling myself, 'Not yet. Not for a while more . . .' "

"What is it?" Julia could manage only a whisper.

Helena leaned back to look into her daughter's face, then reached out and caressed her cheek. "Your . . . your father is working on marriage arrangements."

"But that is good news, isn't it? I mean, don't you want to be married to—?"

"Not arrangements for me, my dearest. For you. He is hoping for a profitable agreement with some man in some place of which I have never even heard."

CHAPTER FIVE

Jerusalem

BEFORE THE REST of the household went to sleep, the master carpenter's wife and elder daughter prepared three pallets around the workshop oven. The long brick flange, where the wood was treated before drying, held a plate of bread, a bowl of dates, and tea. Abigail briefly brought her sleeping daughter downstairs, and Jacob touched her cheek and murmured he had never seen such a beautiful child. Alban watched them and noted how much he could see of Stephen in little Dorcas. Jacob feared the words might devastate Abigail, but she merely caressed the child's face and softly agreed. "He is there in her every step, every look, every smile."

Linux stood in the shadows observing the reunion with an inscrutable expression on his face. Jacob wasn't sure how he felt about the man—someone who had been good to him when he needed it, but also someone who had denied him assistance into the Roman Legion . . . though Jacob supposed he should thank the officer for that sometime.

Abigail made them all agree not to speak further of Linux's

surprise arrival until she returned the young child to her bed. When Abigail appeared again, it was with Martha at her side. The woman said in her direct, no-nonsense way, "I hope you will allow me to join in." All three men nodded their immediate agreement.

But then Abigail said, "Perhaps we should let Alban rest."

"I sleep too much already," Alban rasped out. "My heart is full, my soul content. I am surrounded by friends." He gestured weakly to them all.

"It can do you little good to continue talking," Jacob protested.

"I shall lie here and listen." And he prepared to do just that, settling back upon his pallet, his gaze swiveling from one face to the other. To Jacob's eye, the man looked at peace for the first time since they had departed Tiberias.

Linux had never appeared stronger. What was more, the man seemed to be utterly at ease, despite what he had already told them of the events surrounding his return to Jerusalem. He pulled a bench over close to Alban's pallet and seated himself, locking his hands around a mug of tea that must have long since gone cold. He studied Jacob with an officer's scrutiny, no doubt observing the evident strengths, seeking weaknesses. Jacob knew the process well. Alban used it in gauging the merit of any man who wished to join their band of guards.

Linux said, "You are a man now, Jacob."

"Yes," Alban said, the hoarseness unable to mask his obvious pride. "He is my strong right arm."

Jacob wanted to point out the irony that Alban was now seeking to place him in a merchant's stall in Samaria. But he held his peace.

Linux turned to his old friend and said, "If you insist upon speaking, I shall say no more this night."

Alban smiled and waved his hand, indicating he would obey.

Linux turned toward Abigail, seated near her brother and Martha on a bench near the oven. "Your little one rests well?"

Abigail's lips curved in a smile. "She sleeps through thunder, lightning, shouts, and song."

Martha added, "She scarcely ever cried, even as an infant. Unless there was good reason. Such as when her mother was late to feed her. Which she sometimes was, with all her other duties."

"You are staying busy, then."

"Stephen began a service for our Lord that is even more vital today," Abigail replied, glancing away from Linux's intent gaze. "Many who have remained here in Jerusalem are in desperate need."

Martha stood and walked over to the kitchen, moving more stiffly than Jacob recalled. There were new lines etched into her features. But her smile came easily enough, and her eyes remained bright with genuine affection. She returned to pour Alban a fresh mug of tea, then asked, "Anyone else?"

Linux held out his mug. When Martha had settled back down on the bench, the soldier turned to Abigail and said, "Might I presume on friendship to observe that you carry the weight of your loss with God's peace."

"Stephen's absence is a wound to my heart every day," Abigail said. "And yet it also grows less painful with time. I feel God's presence even in my loss."

"It is evident," Linux said with a nod.

Jacob scanned the faces around the circle. They all knew Linux had sought Abigail's hand in marriage, and had done so with a Roman warrior's zeal. He had gone so far as to bribe Jacob, offering the youthful adventurer his dream of becoming a legionnaire if Jacob would appeal on his behalf. When Abigail had become betrothed to Stephen, Linux had threatened to tear their friendships asunder. Yet God had worked his will even in this desolate moment, drawing Linux, a Roman, into the believers' fold.

Jacob noted how the others studied the soldier. Martha finally said, "My Roman friend, how you have changed."

"It is our Lord's doing," Linux said.

"God can work only within a willing heart," Martha asserted.

Jacob saw Alban shift on his pallet to cast him a look, but he turned his face away.

Linux's gaze remained fastened on the mug in his hands. "Twenty-nine months ago, I was ordered home."

"We received your letter," Abigail said.

"We have prayed for you ever since," Martha added.

"There is no question in my mind but that I have been held up before God by your prayers," Linux replied. "I traveled to Italy because my sister-in-law wrote to say that my brother was desperately ill and perhaps dying. I will not lie. I went home thinking that this might now be my chance. Finally I would gain all that had been refused to me. The titles, the wealth, the power. All mine. It became the waking dream that transported me across the seas. With each day upon the ship, the desires grew stronger still."

Jacob stared about him, first at the faces of these four glowing in the light cast through the open oven door. A single torch flickered upon the opposite wall. It was a large room, built to handle a dozen apprentices and tradesmen, the ceiling as high as many roofs. A trio of pulleys dangled from the center beam fashioned from the trunk of a massive Lebanese cypress. The master carpenter, Josiah, could build the walls for a new home within this room, then dismantle the frame and cart it piecemeal to the site. The place smelled of fresh timber and the scraps fed to the oven. The far wall held a wealth of tools and measuring instruments. For Jacob, though, the room's familiarity had been a prison from which he feared he would never escape. And becoming a stall holder in Samaria would be exactly the same in all but the name.

Linux was saying, "When I arrived in Italy, I found a misery that had always been there, but until then I had remained blind to it. My desires for wealth and status and power had fashioned a veil before my eyes. This time, I walked the halls of my brother's palace, the rich tapestries hanging from the walls, the gold plates upon his table, looked through the high, arched windows at the serfs, the land . . ."

No one spoke. The only sounds were the wind barred from entering their haven and the crackling fire. Jacob again searched each face in turn. Beloved Martha, the stalwart servant of their Lord, whose sister Mary and brother Lazarus were busy tending to the poor in their home village beyond the Mount of Olives. Abigail, his dear sister, who bore the stain of widowhood with a calm dignity that added to her grace and beauty. Alban, the former centurion who had rescued Jacob from slavers and now made room for him at his hearth and in his heart, and provided employment that nearly lived up to his boyhood dreams. And Linux, the Roman officer who had been transformed by their Lord. . . .

"My brother assumed I had come only for his money," the Roman continued. "He was savage in his attacks, even while prostrate upon his deathbed. I prayed one entire night over this, asking God for guidance. And the next morning it came to me. I went to my brother and told him I wanted nothing. I would accept nothing. All I would ask of him was for him to acknowledge the Lord Jesus as Messiah."

Someone breathed a soft sigh, perhaps it was Jacob himself. All eyes were fastened now upon the man who leaned over his hands and spoke to a distant place. "My brother scorned me. But it meant nothing. No, that is not right. Of course it meant a great deal."

"You had served our Lord," Martha completed for him. "You had done your best. You heard God's call and responded."

Linux nodded slowly, his gaze distant. "I told him of my new faith in Jesus, and I also told the rest of his family. His second wife, stepmother to the twin daughters whose mother died some time ago, prayed with me as well as the two girls. Those girls had become very precious to me even though I had only been with them once before."

"You planted the seed in your brother," Martha said to Linux. "Pray for his soul, and let the Lord do his good work."

"But who will see to his family now?" Linux's concern furrowed his brow. "Who will guide them as I myself have been directed by all of you?"

Finally Martha said, "I shall pray for them, and for the Lord to reveal an answer to this as well."

Linux seemed to find great peace in those words. His features eased, and he leaned back against the wall. "The same sense of protection stayed with me through my return journey. I spoke of Jesus with my shipmates. Two prayed with me, and most of them at least listened."

Alban smiled and wiped at a streak tracing the weathered skin above his beard.

Linux said, "Yesterday, when I arrived back in Jerusalem, I presented myself before the tribune at the Antonia Fortress."

Alban breathed the name Metellus.

"The same."

"He is no friend to us, the followers of Jesus."

"Nor to me. You remember how he considered me allied to the former consul, Pilate's replacement. Metellus sneered that the consul was on his way home now. That I was defenseless. He stripped me of my leadership of the Capernaum garrison. In truth, I had assumed this was lost when I left for Italy, even though I sought his permission prior to my departure. But Metellus found great pleasure in formally ordering me back to Caesarea. I am to report to the garrison commandant and most likely will be sent away. Damascus, Gaul, perhaps even the Germanic frontier. Metellus declared that such banishment was the reward I deserved."

Yet the dark implications did not seem to touch Linux. He spoke in a tone that was more than merely calm, as if speaking of the weather. "I did not reply. To be honest, I am not certain I could have. The feeling of being sheltered by our beloved Lord had never been stronger than that moment. Stronger even than when I was at my brother's bedside. As though nothing in this world could touch me."

Alban coughed, then said, "You truly are one of us, Linux."

Martha reached over and took Linux's hand. "Our brother."

Jacob studied the two of them—the Judean woman, servant to the risen Lord, and the Roman officer, her nation's sworn enemy. Abigail moved from her seat and knelt upon the stones. She said, "Let us pray for Linux."

"For all of us," Martha agreed. "No, Alban, stay as you are."

Jacob shifted over to kneel beside his sister. He felt her work-roughened hand in his own. He heard the others pray, and he prayed aloud in turn. Yet in his own heart he felt the same words resound that he had prayed silently at dinner. Over and over. *Grant me your wisdom, O Lord.*

Jacob returned to the caravan site long before the sun rose. He joined in the preparations for departure in the silver light of an unborn day. The clouds had scuttled away with the night, taking with them the wind, and the air was now cold and dry. The animals had complained mightily when they had been roused two hours earlier. But the loading had warmed them, along with a double portion of oats in their bellies. Now the camels stomped their broad, padded feet, impatient to take to the road.

The moon was a sliver in the western sky, growing pale as the sun lit the eastern horizon. The nearest hills, a wintry purple, were as beautiful a sight as Jacob had ever seen. Many of the drovers groaned their way through the departure routine, coming awake more slowly than the beasts. But for Jacob a morning had never seemed more exciting, beckoning him toward whatever their travels might bring. He rode Alban's horse, a grey stallion with a mane white as sea foam. The horse caught some of Jacob's anticipation and snorted impatiently for them to be done with the preparations and depart.

Jacob made a quick circuit of the caravan. The caravan master's three servants were rolling up the large tents and loading them onto carts to be stored by Jamal's agent in Jerusalem for the next visit.

From his place by the departure gates, the caravan master whistled twice, his signal for the caravan to move out. The camels recognized the sound and were already shuffling into line before the drovers tapped their legs with their quirts. The caravan master, a Syrian named Yussuf, was a lean whippet of a man who had spent ten years as a legionnaire before losing an eye in battle. Alban knew and trusted him. Yussuf had appointed himself master of the guards in Alban's absence. Yussuf directed Jacob to guard their rear, a position most guards disliked. It meant eating the caravan's dust through the long trek. But the ground would be fairly solid from the long rains and the night's chill. Jacob reckoned his only hardship that day would come from solitude. Unless, of course, the caravan was attacked. In that case, the rear guard played a crucial role. Jacob saluted the caravan master and wheeled his horse around. He had no problem with a bit of dust.

Latif, the drover, called softly as Jacob passed. Jacob reined in his horse and started toward the drover, who hissed, "Stand well away."

Jacob slipped from the saddle and pretended to inspect a hoof. "What is it?"

"Look to the north of the gates" came the quiet reply.

The Jerusalem encampment was divided by low stone walls into a series of corrals, each large enough to hold a caravan's animals and tents. The segments held their own wells and drinking troughs. The entire caravanserai was rimmed by a second fence, this one of wooden posts and thorn brush serving as a line of demarcation beyond which the animals and drovers were not permitted to camp. Along the camp's perimeter were market stalls catering to the caravan trade—blacksmiths, leather workers, feed merchants, and inns. The encampment had just one entrance.

When Jacob lifted his head and peered over the horse's neck, Yussuf and the first string of animals were moving slowly past this point. Jamal's caravan was a large one, numbering over seventy camels and half again as many donkeys, but it seemed even longer than usual. Latif's much smaller string of camels remained kneeling within the corral, waiting their turn to move out.

Jacob noticed that the man's string contained only six camels. Which meant three of Latif's animals were missing. Which was impossible. News of an injured or ill camel traveled like the wind through a caravanserai. "Where are your other beasts?"

"With Yussuf. Never mind that now." Latif motioned with his chin. "See who stands by the gate."

A customs officer stood by the main entrance, surveying the departing animals as was usual. Such officials were universally loathed. The officer was protected by two Roman soldiers, who leaned upon their spears and watched the caravan with bored indifference.

"I don't understand," Jacob said, keeping his face turned away from Latif. "They often check for one reason or another. Any excuse . . . Or contraband? But you aren't . . . ?"

"It's not the tax official," Latif muttered, tightening one of the camel's loads. "Note the Pharisees."

Jacob then spotted the two black-robed men standing well back from the entrance, half-hidden by the awning of a market stall. "Who are they?"

"I . . . I am not certain. But I fear the taller one is Saul of Tarsus."

Jacob felt his blood run cold. "You believe he's looking for you?"

Latif climbed into the lead camel's saddle, then clicked his tongue and waved the leather quirt. His camel groaned and belched and clambered to its feet. The remaining animals did the same and began slowly plodding toward the departure gate. Latif said as he moved past Jacob, "As I told you, Jamal has given me a special charge. One that nobody else in the caravan is to know about. If I am taken, I place my camels in your care. They are now with Yussuf. He knows nothing—and is wise enough not to ask." With one last dark look he went on. "But I do not think that is why Saul is here. The satchel? It is safe?"

Jacob nodded and swung himself into the saddle, his legs trembling enough that his horse sensed the fear and danced sideways. Jacob reined him in, patted the stallion's neck, and muttered without hardly moving his lips, "How can you be certain they are here for you?"

"I'm not. But why else . . ." Latif might have shaken his head, or perhaps it was merely a nervous shudder. "Never mind. We will know soon enough. I have spoken with Yussuf. He knows you are to guard my camels and report back to Jamal."

Jacob started to protest further, but Latif waved the quirt and growled, "To be seen with me endangers you and everything else.

If I am taken, pray for me. And, Jacob, the satchel is vital. Deliver it as instructed."

Jacob pretended to survey the rearmost camels as Latif plodded ahead. When he reckoned it was safe enough, Jacob turned around, keeping the last string of beasts between himself and the officers by the gate. The two Pharisees remained little more than ghosts, their black robes merging with the awning's shadows.

Then he saw one of them move one step forward, and Jacob's breath caught in his throat.

He recognized the Pharisee instantly as Ezra, the powerful Jerusalem merchant who had sought Abigail's hand in marriage. Since the death of his sister, Sapphira, Ezra had become a menace to all followers of the Way.

Ezra turned to say something to the other man. Though Jacob did not recognize him, he did not need to. He had heard enough descriptions of Saul of Tarsus. Tall, lean and hard, both in form and expression. His eyes were fierce and dark, a religious version of a bird of prey. They stood together, this pair, Ezra and Saul, their gazes burning with a dangerous light.

Jacob dropped from his saddle and unknotted the long desert kerchief from his neck. He wrapped it about his head and retied it so that it draped about his face in the fashion of a desert tribesman. This practice was adopted by drovers and guards alike, when the sun burned or the wind blew with brutal force. But this day was cool, and the breeze fresh. Even so, Jacob was not the only man who fashioned a protective burnoose.

Heart pounding, Jacob matched his pace to a heavily laden camel and observed the two priests between the camel's neck and the pile of trade goods. They had identical beards, pointed like spears, only Ezra's contained a weaving of silver. Their faces were taut with a shared fury.

Jacob saw Ezra lean again toward the younger Pharisee and

mutter something. Saul pointed at the approaching drover, Latif. Ezra jerked a nod.

Saul turned and called to someone behind him. Jacob's heart fluttered more rapidly still as five Temple guards stepped from the market stall's recesses.

Together the guards and Saul approached Latif. Saul's words were lost amidst the bellowing camels, but the result was clear enough. The Temple guards dragged Latif from the beast's back. The man was forced onto his knees in the dust beside the road as his camels were pulled to one side.

Word of the confrontation must have reached the front of the line, because Yussuf's horse suddenly pounded its way back along the line of beasts and reentered the main gates. Jamal's caravan master was already shouting his protests before he slipped from the horse's back. "What is the meaning of this?"

"I am here on Temple business." Saul's voice carried the deathly chill of a poised dagger. "You are warned to stand well away."

"But this man, Latif, is Syrian!"

"He is a *Judean* from Syria! And thus he falls under Temple law." Saul's eyes tightened. "As do you."

The string of Jamal's camels plodded past the point where Latif knelt in the dust. Jacob kept his head lowered so his face remained hidden by the folds of his burnoose. Over the thunder of his heart, Jacob heard Yussuf demand, "By whose authority?"

Saul drew a scroll from his robe. "I am here under the direction of the Sanhedrin. They have ordered this man's arrest."

Yussuf, the former legionnaire, had battled his way through bandit attacks and desert storms. But Jacob saw that the sight of that scroll, bearing the Temple seal and the gold standard of authority, left the man subdued. "Latif is a trusted friend," he said, voice quaking.

"And you should show greater wisdom in selecting your friends, else you share this man's fate."

Jacob heard more than a warning directed at the caravan master. He sensed an implacable will in this Saul of Tarsus—everything the rumors had suggested, and more. Here was a man so certain of his authority that he would sentence any man who opposed him to death. Willingly, swiftly, and without a moment's qualm. Jacob was glad for the camel that hid him from view.

Legs trembling, Jacob led his horse forward beneath the gates' crossbeam. He heard Yussuf say, his voice now stronger, "Well, and what of the drover's camels? Are they to be arrested as well?"

This time the second Pharisee spoke. The same voice of the man who had sought his sister's hand, yet different. It sounded colder now, more stern, carrying the same implacable force as Saul. "We have news that this man is both a follower of the banned sect and a carrier of contraband."

On this point, Yussuf must have felt he was on firmer ground. "Search his articles, then. But the camels belong to Jamal, my master and his."

Ezra hesitated. "This would be Jamal, the merchant of Tiberias and Damascus?"

"The very same."

"Then the animals are not ours to take." Ezra's voice had lost some of its strident force.

"And what of these goods? Am I to leave them here in the dust for you to scramble through and take what you will?"

Saul shouted with indignant rage, "We are not common thieves!"

Yussuf remained silent.

Ezra said, "The goods must be inspected. We will do so immediately. If there is nothing amiss, you may take them with you."

Jacob slowed his forward progress as much as he dared till the last camel was his only shield. He heard Yussuf ask, "And what of Latif?"

"I have already told you," Saul growled. "You should take greater care in your choice of friends."

"I hear and obey. Only I beg you to make your inspection with haste. This delay will—"

But an impatient motion of the man's hand silenced further objections.

Jacob risked a glance back. His heart wrenched at the sight of Latif kneeling in the dirt, his eyes clenched shut, hands clasped to his chest, lips moving, no doubt uttering a fervent prayer. Jacob yearned to turn about, spur his horse, draw his sword, and . . . *What then?* What could one lone man do against two legionnaires and a cluster of armed Temple guards? Jacob turned his face back to the open road, walking alongside the horse's head for best concealment.

Yussuf called behind him, "Jacob! Ride forward and pass the word along. Follow the coast road. I will meet you when this inspection is finished."

Jacob swung onto his saddle and lifted his arm. His mouth tried to form the words *I hear and obey*, but his throat was too tight to utter a sound. He kicked his horse's side and galloped ahead.

He had never considered himself a coward until that moment.

CHAPTER SIX

Jerusalem

LINUX SLEPT LATE and woke feeling groggy, hoping he would soon be able to cast aside his long voyage's lingering weariness. He looked around the workshop and rolled off his pallet, staggering outside to wash his face as a common soldier would, simply dunking his head in the water barrel behind the building. Josiah and his apprentices chuckled at the sight of the dripping Roman soldier, who had slept beneath a tattered blanket next to their curing oven, so deeply that not even the crank of bellows and the whack of mallets had awakened him. When Linux lifted his dripping head from the barrel, he immediately returned it for a second dunking. This time when he came up for air, he blew a great spout of water at the nearest craftsmen. They scrambled back, laughing louder now.

Josiah tossed him the cloth he had just used to dry his own hands. Linux wiped his face with it, nodded his thanks, and accepted a dipper held by the youngest apprentice. He drank his fill, declined any more, and returned to the workroom. He sat down on the floor beside Alban's pallet. "Where is our young Jacob?"

"He left before dawn. I would imagine his caravan is already on the road to Caesarea." Alban showed no emotion with this piece of news. Linux judged his thoughts to be elsewhere.

"Is something troubling you, my friend?" When Alban did not reply, Linux said, "Jacob will do an excellent job."

"Of that I have no doubt." Alban hesitated, then said, "He and I . . . well, we have a disagreement."

"And what is it that furrows your brow?"

Alban related the information about Jamal's gift of the market stall in Samaria. Linux heard him out, then said doubtfully, "I have difficulty imagining Jacob as a merchant."

"He would be safe. He would have stability, and the stall would supply him with an excellent income."

"Jacob has reached how many years now? Twenty? He doesn't hanker after a safe little place in the middle of the Samaritan plains. He wants a life of adventure."

"These are most perilous times to go adventuring."

"You have trained him well. He will no doubt . . ." But Linux could see Alban was ready with further reasons, so he swiftly changed the subject. "You are looking better this morning."

"How could I not?" Even Alban's voice sounded stronger. "I am surrounded by friends. Sheltered by faith. Prayed over, cared for, and loved."

"You speak of a heaven on earth," Linux said, grinning.

"Yes," and Alban's tone turned gentle, "and my two most beloved await me at home—truly at least a piece of heaven on earth." He stared at the carved wooden cross nailed to the opposite wall, then shook his head. "If only that were so for all the followers."

Somehow Linux had missed the cross the previous night, the first such carving he had seen. "The situation is dire?"

"Not as bad as it may soon become." Alban motioned toward the cross. "Josiah awoke suddenly last night, feeling an intense dread for his family and his apprentices. As he prayed, he saw a vision of that cross. He carved it while the rest of his house slept. I watched him nail it into place this morning."

"I wondered why I had not noticed it before now." Linux nodded, not so much at Alban's words, but at his own response. A simple acceptance of the fact that Josiah had approached the Lord on his knees, and the Lord had spoken through an image. It might not have been the answer the carpenter had sought. But the peace Linux felt while staring at that simple cross caused his chest to burn.

To Judeans the cross was perhaps the most hated symbol of Roman rule. The deadly silhouette had scarred too many hilltops, signifying the most ignoble of deaths, a lingering torment that carried shame for all who witnessed it.

And yet here it was, portraying a hope that transcended their worries and fears. Merely looking at this bit of carved wood lifted Linux beyond himself, carried upon a promise as strong as it was eternal.

Linux watched Abigail and Martha, along with little Dorcas, join the group for the midday meal. Josiah's family, along with several clans related to the apprentices and craftsmen, all gathered for prayer, then ate in silence, as was apparently the custom in this household. Except for Dorcas. Abigail's daughter, a bright and cheerful four-year-old, ate from her mother's plate, then played in the shadows beneath the table. She chatted to a little rag doll and sang snippets of hymns, causing Linux to smile and yearn once more for the nieces he had left behind in Italy. By now the clouds had dispersed, and the wind was not so severe. Tables set up in the rear courtyard were flanked by a long row of date palms. The entire area smelled of sawdust, glue, woodsmoke, and honest sweat. Linux would have found himself content, save for the somber expressions surrounding him.

When the meal was finished, Martha brought Alban's pallet outside and arranged it by the side wall. Alban, certain he was just fine seated at the table, waved her off, but Martha firmly told him, "You will lay yourself right here where the sun can warm your bones."

"But I am—"

"Do as she says, my man," Linux warned good-naturedly.

Alban made a show of further grumbling as he found a comfortable position on the pallet. Josiah approached, his forearms streaked with sawdust. He wiped his hands on the cloth hanging from his belt. "Another of our brethren vanished in the night." His low voice and his expression told them more than his words.

His wife moved up beside him and handed her husband a ladle of fresh water. "It is the way of Saul's men. They come in the dark hours and take who they please, waving orders from the Temple at any who protest."

Josiah shook his head. "I do not know what I would do if they took one of my boys."

"We are leaving the city," the woman said, her voice now low also. "Tomorrow at dawn."

"This has been my family's home for seven generations," Josiah said. "The house and the work. My father was a carpenter and his before him. Jerusalem is in my blood."

"You are not running away," his wife assured him, no doubt repeating an argument from a previous conversation. "You are saving your family."

"I have work to complete, and pieces I've promised—"

"You will be taking your tools with you, and you can send back the items when they are ready."

"It is not the same. I need to be here to find more work."

"If they take you or your sons, what good will more work do us?" Her words held no anger, and little force. Clearly their discussion followed a well-trod path. She said to Alban and Linux, "We have found an olive farm near Sebaste. There is an old barn where my husband can do his carpentry. There is wood enough. And peace. We leave at dawn." Her nod was as firm as her tone.

Josiah responded with a seemingly reluctant nod of his own, then turned to the others silently watching. "You may stay here as long as you wish."

Alban said from his pallet, "You all should leave Jerusalem as soon as possible."

Martha's response was to glance at Abigail.

Abigail said quietly, "I cannot leave Jerusalem."

The master carpenter's wife sighed but did not speak. Overhead, the wind rattled the palms. It sounded to Linux as though the weather itself argued with Abigail's declaration.

Abigail said, "I must continue Stephen's work. I serve the widows and the orphans. They have no one, no place—"

"There are fewer of them left in Jerusalem with every passing day," the carpenter's wife said. But she spoke to her hands, maintaining the same emotionless tone she had used with her husband.

Abigail said, "I feel God is present. He guides and he comforts me. He will keep us." She lifted her little girl into her arms and held her close until Dorcas squirmed away.

Alban asked her, "Can you not do this work in another place?"

Abigail adjusted her shawl more closely about her. "Being in Jerusalem is important. Somehow I feel Stephen, his blessing, here."

Alban shifted on his pallet. All eyes but Abigail's turned toward him, and Linux expected further objections. Instead Alban told them that Jamal the trader had deeded him a coveted market stand at the juncture of the trade routes in the Megiddo Plains of Samaria.

A house in a nearby village came with this bequest. Alban reported Jacob's refusal to take over the stall, insisting on continuing his increasingly dangerous assignments as a caravan guard.

This information was met with silence. Finally Abigail said, "I also must stay for Martha's sake. She has pains in her joints. Travel will only—"

"Do not use me as your excuse," Martha broke in. "I am ready to go today."

"But you refused to join Mary and Lazarus at your home," Abigail said.

"How ever could I leave you here alone, my dear one? You've heard what is happening. The situation worsens with each passing day. The clouds are looming. The storm approaches."

"Think of the little one," the carpenter's wife said. "What happens to Dorcas if you are taken by Saul and his men?"

"I have thought of little else," Abigail said just above a whisper, and she used the corner of her shawl to clear her eyes. "But if I leave Jerusalem, I shall lose my last remaining connection to Stephen. . . ." Her voice broke.

Alban said, "Stephen awaits you at the end of life's road. Of that I am absolutely certain."

Linux hesitated, then said, "I am not sure how much I should say right now, but in my last conversation with Stephen, he asked me to protect you as best I could. I feel it is my duty to him and to God to tell you that what the others say is very true. I have only been back in this country a few days. And already I know the situation to be far graver than I had heard. The Sanhedrin considers the followers a threat worse than the Zealots. The new consul has granted the Temple Council every authority in the matter. The tribune will not raise a finger to protect you. It all adds up to one certainty. If you stay in this city, you most likely will be arrested . . . and worse."

Abigail remained silent. Martha asked, "What of Alban's illness? We cannot leave him here on his own."

"I could arrange for a cart," Linux said. "No, old friend, do not argue. Not this time. I will travel with you and see you settled. We will send news back to Leah in Capernaum that you are on your way to health and will be home with her shortly."

Dorcas must have noticed her mother's distress. She clambered to her feet, the doll gripped in one hand and the other plucking at her mother's shawl. "Mama. Mama?"

Abigail again lifted the child into her lap, stroked the small face, and sighed. She gave one short nod.

The carpenter's wife moved nearer her husband and said, "We all leave at dawn."

CHAPTER SEVEN

The Joppa Road

JACOB WAS FULLY aware of the two separate routes leading from Jerusalem to Caesarea. They began as one through the hills west of Jerusalem. But once the road descended to the plains, the main Roman road headed north and west, running in an almost straight line to its destination on the coast above the Mediterranean. This road was paved in stones and so was easier on the camels' foot pads, but it led through a desolate region. Bands of Zealots were increasingly active in this often empty stretch. The safer coastal route dated from the times of King David, or so the legends went. But in places it was little more than a rocky trail.

Yussuf still had not rejoined the group when they reached the main turn. Jacob doubted any of the caravan's other members had heard Yussuf's final orders to him, and feared there would be disagreement or resistance to his temporary authority from the drovers, or perhaps from guards who knew him not. Yussuf was a strong and experienced caravan master, appointed by Jamal himself. Jacob was just another guard, especially now that Alban was laid up in

Jerusalem. Jacob was certain at least some would question his right to direct them.

As the road took its final curve and descended to the valley floor, Jacob spurred his horse forward from his end position. He half expected to be challenged, either by a drover or one of the guards. Instead, several of the men he passed waved their quirts in a desert salute.

Jacob arrived at the lead position when the road's split was less than a furlong ahead. He reined in beside the guard at the head of the caravan, a man whose name was lost to him at that moment. "You know the road ahead?" he asked.

"I have never traveled further west than this point."

"You are from Syria?"

"Nabataea."

This was news. Nabataea was a small kingdom south of Syria. Some years it was part of the Roman empire, other times it switched allegiance to the Parthians. Nabataea was known as a haven for bandits. And further, the Zealots were said to have paid bribes to Nabataea in order to set up permanent encampments beyond the reach of Roman soldiers.

Jacob's surprise must have shown, for the guard said, "Yussuf trusts me. As does Jamal."

"And so do I." Jacob nodded. "My name is Jacob."

The guard raised a hand. "Hamman. You are Alban's son?"

"He is my guardian." Jacob hesitated, then said, "My family were traders. Their caravan was attacked. I was only a child at the time. I alone was saved from their fate by Roman soldiers led by Alban, the centurion."

The guard nodded slowly, then said, "And the bandits were most likely either Nabataeans or Parthians allied to my country. You have reason to be surprised, finding me here."

Jacob did not reply to the comment. Instead he said, "One of us must ride at the back. Our rear is unguarded."

"You know the coastal road?"

"I have traveled it several times. Jamal has put you on point duty, though," Jacob added slowly.

"Those who know you say you are as trustworthy as Alban." Hamman wheeled his horse about. "I will guard our rear."

Jacob saluted the man in the Arab fashion, the thumb and forefinger traveling from forehead to lips to heart. The guard responded in the same manner, then rode away.

When the first animals arrived at the turn, Jacob did as Yussuf would have, rising from the stirrups to stand in the saddle. He shrilled a whistle loud enough to be heard far down the line, then swept the arm holding his leather quirt down in a single motion, pointing to the road ahead.

His new vantage point now leading the caravan seemed to magnify the landscape. Everything Jacob saw was now etched with crystal clarity. The plains were laid out like a sea of rock and sand. To his left, south of the road, dark clouds moved in solemn precision, laying down solid columns of rain. Behind him the hills rose in timeless splendor, grey and shaded where the clouds gathered, ocher and gold where the sunlight touched. The caravan stretched out behind for a full Roman mile. Jacob turned his face back to the west and the empty road. He took a long breath and tried to tell himself it was the same cool dry air he had breathed all morning. But he had never ridden at the head of a caravan before. This was Alban's position, and Yussuf's, and Jamal's. Each breath was spiced with adventure. And just a touch of trepidation.

Yussuf had still not rejoined the caravan when it arrived at the first night's stopping. A village had sprouted where the road turned south and the smaller northern trail broke off. The caravanserai, rimmed by thorn brush, was located east of the village. A ramshackle fence marked the area set aside for travelers.

As the long procession of camels, horses, carts, and drovers approached, Jacob felt eyes upon him from up and down the caravan's length. He was the most junior of the guards in age and experience and knew fewer than half of the drovers by name. But when no one else stepped forward, Jacob rode ahead to where the village elders awaited them.

Such caravans were the mainstay of the village economy. Jacob bargained hard, but feared the price he was offered for fodder and water and one night in the camp was too high. So he shrugged, raised his quirt, and pointed the caravan north. It was a device he had seen Yussuf use when he felt he was being overcharged. But this was different. Yussuf was nowhere to be found, and the drovers had every reason to refuse Jacob's order. They had been traveling since before first light, and the animals were as weary as the men. Still, Jacob felt responsible for the caravan master's goods and denarii. He whistled Yussuf's signal for moving on . . . and held his breath.

As one, the drovers began turning their animals toward the ragged northern trail. No grumbling protests against Jacob's decision or leadership were heard.

Instantly the elders shouted for them to halt, offering a price less than half their previously stated fee.

Jacob whistled a second time, pointing the lead animals toward the camp entrance. He slipped from his horse and stood by the gate as the first string of beasts entered the camp.

Only when the final camels had passed him, and Hamman had saluted him before riding through the gates, did Jacob draw an easy breath.

Jacob had no idea how he should act in Yussuf's absence, nor how to take on the responsibilities that had thus been laid at his feet. So he tried to do as he thought Alban might.

First he approached Hamman, the most senior of the new guards. In front of the others, Jacob again saluted him and formally thanked the man for his assistance. He then asked if Hamman might aid him by setting guard shifts. Jacob explained, loudly enough for his words to carry to the nearest drovers, that he had been given responsibility for Latif's camels and needed to off-load the beasts and see to their evening feed.

The result was both successful and unnerving. The men responded as if he were already the new guard captain. And yet Jacob was missing Alban more than ever. This was the first time he had been upon the road without his mentor and guardian. Though the tendrils of their disagreement lingered, it was mixed also with a keening sorrow over the absent Latif. And Jacob couldn't help but wonder if Alban had been there, would he have thought of some way to save their fellow believer. Perhaps if Jacob were a better man, braver . . .

Jacob retrieved Latif's three camels, the ones hidden from inspection, from the lead drover. The man, one of Yussuf's uncles, knew not to ask why Yussuf had assigned him these additional animals to oversee. Jacob led them to a space near the entrance, from where he might remain on guard while seeing to the animals' needs. As Jacob tethered the trio, the smallest animal, a female with a wicked disposition, tried to nip his shoulder. Jacob responded to this as other drovers did with beasts who misbehaved, slapping the camel's neck with his leather quirt and shouting loud enough to startle every neighboring beast.

The drover off-loading closest to Jacob chuckled and said, "She's nasty, that one. Latif says she thinks she is too pretty for such labors."

The female camel was indeed a beauty. Her coat turned the color of bronze in the setting sun. She watched him with huge dark eyes framed by long lashes and an expression that Jacob could only describe as reproachful. He touched the camel's neck and felt her shift nervously. He talked softly to her, touching the back of her knees with his quirt. The camel dropped to the earth without further protest.

The drover observed, "You have a way with the beasts. Latif was right to ask for your help."

Jacob resisted the unbidden reply that he had not helped Latif at all. One by one he drew the camels down, so their bellies rested upon the earth. He then untied the harnesses and pulled their loads into one huge pile. The other drover watched Jacob direct the camels so that they formed a triangle around the trade goods, expressions showing their approval.

Jacob worked his way around the beasts, pulling the wooden bits from their mouths, then carefully inspecting each hoof for damage. Camels could tolerate intense heat and go days without water. But their softly padded hooves were extremely sensitive. When Jacob reached the final beast, he once again felt overwhelmed by Latif's arrest. Several times during the day's travel he had felt enormous waves of guilt and worry. He gripped the animal's mane, leaned his head against the long neck, and prayed, asking for Latif's safety. He prayed that he would have the man's forgiveness, and God's. *What could I have done? I could have done something* . . . chased each other through his distraught mind. The female camel seemed to sense Jacob's anguish and groaned long and low.

When Jacob lifted his head and opened his eyes, Hamman was standing beside him. "The guards are stationed and the watches set. And the village elders have returned with sheep for you to inspect."

Jacob straightened slowly. He could see the guard's curiosity, and said, "My heart is heavy over Latif. I should have helped him."

The guard shrugged. "Latif was taken by Temple priests, guards, and Roman soldiers. You would be crazy to have interfered."

"There must have been something—"

"There is. You care for his animals and Jamal's wares. You offer prayers for his safety. Everything else is far beyond your duty."

The guard's blunt practicality gave Jacob a bit of distance from his regret. "Let us see what these elders have to offer for our supper."

The lambs were all as the elders had promised, young and well fed. Jacob did as he had seen Yussuf do on countless other occasions, inspecting each animal carefully. But the elders appeared to remain intimidated by his threat of leaving, and even offered a sack of milled corn and a basket of fresh herbs and spices, including coriander and mint and cumin. Jacob responded as though the earlier disagreement had never happened, bowing deeply and thanking them for their hospitality.

Jacob saw to the meal that had been prepared, ensuring that every drover and guard received an equal portion, speaking briefly with each man in turn. Just as he had seen Alban do on countless other nights. By the time he returned to Latif's animals, night was upon them. Three campfires glowed and tossed embers toward the star-filled sky.

Jacob decided it was time to inspect Latif's wares.

The large slumbering beasts masked his efforts from view. The camels each carried four amphorae, clay vessels as tall as Jacob's waist used for transport by animal and ship. Four full amphorae could weigh as much as three men.

The neck of each vessel was sealed with a wooden stopper and lashed into place with hemp. Jacob chose one, quietly unknotted the rope, and used his knife to pluck out the stopper. His senses were instantly awash with the fragrance of cinnamon. He unstopped another, and the night air was spiced by clove.

But this was indeed a mystery. Trade in such spices was not

restricted. So long as the taxes were paid, Latif could have carried this load from one end of the empire to the other.

On a sudden impulse, Jacob plunged his hand into the vessel containing cinnamon. His searching fingers discovered a packet hidden deep inside the spice.

Jacob searched each vessel in turn and found a total of sixteen packets. Eventually he resealed each container and wrapped one of the camels' saddle blankets around the hidden prizes. He sat there a long while, enough for the knife-edged moon to begin its descent. And he knew Latif's secret, whatever it was, could well mean the end of his own life.

Yussuf's arrival came first as a faint sound on the night wind, the shuffling footfalls and quiet snorts of weary beasts. Jacob was ready, crouched in a defile beside the road south of the village caravanserai. He remained silent and hidden until he could identify Yussuf's silhouette riding against the stars. When Jacob was certain the man traveled alone, he whistled once, softly.

A casual listener might have mistaken it for the call of a night bird. But Yussuf immediately clicked the camels to a halt and slipped from the horse's back. He moaned in imitation of a camel as his feet touched the road, then walked over and patted the lead camel's neck. "Don't tell me you've picked up a thorn," he said, bending to look at its foot.

"It is I, Jacob." His voice was barely above a whisper.

"I know you are weary," the man now said more clearly to the camel, and it groaned softly in response. Yussuf crouched by the camel's left foreleg. "Let me check you out, then we shall go and both have as much rest as the shortened night permits."

Jacob said hoarsely, "I have found the secret wares that Jamal placed in Latif's care."

The camel snorted and groaned and permitted Yussuf to lift the foreleg. Yussuf made a cursory inspection of the hoof, now muttering, "Do I want to know what it is?"

Jacob hesitated. He had been pondering the very same question since he had made his discovery.

Yussuf said, "Never mind. If Jamal has kept it from me this long, it is for a good reason. Only tell me this. Has my caravan been carrying contraband?"

On this point, Jacob was certain. "Neither you nor Jamal have broken laws, Roman or Judean."

Yussuf took the knife from his belt and scraped at the animal's hoof. "Saul and that Judean merchant with the viper's face spread all Jamal's wares on the earth and sorted and searched." His tone, though kept to a low pitch, held his fury. "They were much enraged when they could not find whatever it was they sought. They kept me far too long, forcing me to travel the hills by night. Thankfully, as it turns out from what you have just told me, Latif's camels were already far north with you. My little caravan disturbed the sleep of no bandits. Were it not for that pitiful sight of Latif in chains, I might be smiling."

Jacob crouched behind a creosote bush, and its pungent aroma filled his senses, strong as the guilt that still battered his heart. "If only I could have done something . . . rescued Latif."

"You showed good sense in hiding yourself." Yussuf's voice had hardened. "Else you would be chained alongside Latif, and I would be out yet another trusted ally."

Jacob's fists pressed against the hard-packed earth. "You were a stronger man than I was. You stood up to them even when they threatened you with death. While I did nothing to defend my fellow brother in our faith."

Yussuf snorted. "Of such things as faith or prophets, I know little. But this I do know. You are free to breathe this night air and walk the lands because you hid yourself this day. But Latif? Though they found nothing they still insisted on holding him. What they were looking for—or what they hoped to find—I do not know. Nor do I wish to. The less one knows in this day . . ." He did not finish the thought but shrugged it away with the dip of a shoulder.

Jacob decided there was nothing to be gained by further discussion on the matter. "I must carry Latif's secret back to Jamal."

Yussuf dropped the hoof, patted the animal's side, and straightened slowly. "You will travel to Tiberias alone?"

"I have thought long on this. If that Judean merchant, the one called Ezra, thinks he knows something, who else might be hunting Jamal's secrets? I will do best as one poor traveler." Jacob pointed behind him, then realized Yussuf could see nothing. "I have taken two of your donkeys. Hamman saw me. I said only that I had to report to Jamal, and that I would await your return upon the road."

"Hamman is a good man—for a Nabataean. He will say nothing. You are armed?"

"I have my sword and knife and staff."

There was the soft clink of metal as Jacob saw Yussuf bend toward the ground. "A pouch of coins awaits you here." Yussuf clicked softly and tugged upon the lead camel's reins. "I fear I will have to walk this final stretch, else my old bones will not let me sleep. Take care, young man. I do trust you know what you are doing."

Jacob watched the camels tramp on westward. He remained as he was until he was certain the road was empty. Then he crawled forward and retrieved the purse before returning to where he had tethered the donkeys.

The hills ahead of him were deepest shadows, the night filled with strange sounds. Jacob kept off the main route, traveling parallel to the Roman road. As the ground started rising into the Judean foothills in the north, the first faint wash of dawn grew ahead of him. The donkeys were stalwart and young, scaling the rocky slope with ease. Jacob continued on until the heat of a new day warmed his face. He led the animals further away from the road, back where a wind-carved gorge formed a natural corral. He tethered each and slipped the loads from their backs. Jacob uncorked a waterskin and filled a shallow depression in a rock with water for them. He drank from the same skin while the donkeys shouldered one another and lapped at the bowl. He filled their feed bags from the load of supplies, checked their tethers another time, and finally unrolled his blanket upon the hard earth.

As he drifted away, he listened yet again to Yussuf's words floating through his mind. He then prayed another time that Latif would be protected, wherever he was. Jacob had heard the horrendous stories of followers being arrested by Saul of Tarsus and the Temple guards. Some were beaten and released, others never heard from again. He asked the Lord if it had been right for him to walk away. Though he didn't hear an answer to this cry from his heart, he felt some comfort in being able to ask.

Latif was the first to be arrested and chained before his very eyes. He fell asleep forming one more prayer for his imprisoned friend. Whatever Jacob did or didn't do, Latif was in God's hands.

CHAPTER EIGHT

Jerusalem

ABIGAIL MOVED SILENTLY about, preparing for bed. In the corner of their small room, Dorcas slept as only the young can—totally tranquil and at peace with her world. Her soft breathing was a gentle stirring in the stillness.

Carefully Abigail lifted back a corner of the blanket and eased her weary body onto the pallet beside Dorcas. Abigail and the other believers had talked far too late. And the day's final hours had been exceedingly busy. There was so much to be done since their decision to depart. Members of the group were determined to leave Jerusalem at first light.

Jerusalem. Leave Jerusalem.

The whole thing seemed unreal. Not what she wanted to do. And yet . . .

As tired as she felt, Abigail knew that sleep was not going to come easily. Her troubled thoughts and churning stomach would certainly keep her awake. She turned away from her sleeping child and finally gave in to the scalding tears she had held back through sheer force of will.

I cannot leave whirled through her mind. No one, not even Martha or Alban, could force her to go. Let them leave, if that was their desire. The carpenter had kindly offered his shop for accommodation to whomever wished to stay behind. Somehow she would manage. There was still work to be done. A few of the believers, for whatever reasons, remained in Jerusalem. Who would be left to help them?

But what will happen to Dorcas?

Abigail lifted herself from the bed, taking a moment to look at her beautiful daughter and tuck the blanket around the chubby shoulders. She drew a long breath and quietly crept to the room's one small window, pushed back the shutter, and peered out into the night.

The sky was mostly overcast, but between those layers of clouds the moon was visible. One lone star shone above the hills to her left. It looked as lonely and deserted as she felt.

Jerusalem stretched before her, devoid of lights or activity. Even the paved streets lay dark and empty. No merchants moved about, displaying their wares. No ringing hooves of Roman mounts. No shouts of children or bustling of women off to market.

Jerusalem. Such an angry city. Such a turbulent, violent city. So much stored-up hate and bitterness and strife. So much emptiness.

For a moment she felt resentment rise in her throat. What had brought them to this state of affairs? Why had so many good people left? Why was she being required to flee?

She closed her eyes to see once again the face of her beloved Stephen. The man who had loved this city. Who had worked for the poor, the downtrodden, the needy. *For what?* What had it all accomplished—save to bring fear and destruction and death? These followers of the Way—who were now more than family to her—were being broken up into smaller groups, then being further scattered to destinations unknown. She felt like she could hardly remember those wonderful days after their Lord's resurrection, the flaming tongues of fire, the wind . . . Where was all of that now—when they particularly needed that strength of purpose, that power?

I hate you, Jerusalem, she inexplicably wanted to cry out against the city stretched out before her in the darkness, but even in her anger and grief she knew it to be a lie.

Jerusalem. The beloved. She knew in her heart she would always love Jerusalem. It was her city. Stephen's city. He had given his life for his Savior—and for Jerusalem. For her people. Abigail realized at that moment that if the same situation, the same choice, were hers, she would willingly do likewise. She laid her cheek against the coolness of the stone and mortar wall and wept once more.

Her tears this time were a mixture of joy and sadness, of bittersweet memories that she would never give up, and her weeping did not last for long. In the morning, perhaps even before the cock crowed, she would leave this city. Perhaps forever.

In spite of her earlier declarations, she now accepted that she would leave with the others. There was no way she could stay. Her reason lay just behind her, sleeping soundly on the straw pallet, curly head resting on the camel-hair cushion, quiet breathing the only song in the night.

Abigail moved slowly back toward the bed and knelt beside her daughter. She reached out and gently enclosed her daughter's tiny hand. And she prayed with more fervency than she had ever prayed before. For wisdom. For guidance. For safety. Because the little one lying before her was the most precious part of her world. And her highest responsibility. Dorcas had been given to her for a reason. It was now her duty as mother to care for her, to keep her safe, to the best of her ability. And as much as she wished to deny it, Abigail knew there was no longer any safe haven to be found in her dearly loved Jerusalem.

The journey from Jerusalem to Samaria began in the wee hours of the morning, most of the travelers on foot. Linux arranged for the animals to be shared, allowing the women frequent rides, particularly Martha. Dorcas had never been further from Jerusalem than the villages beyond the Mount of Olives. Everything she saw was a cause for wonder and exclamations. Sunlight upon cliffs, caverns shaped by eons of wind, hawks soaring in the updrafts. The child met every turn with more excitement. She clung to Linux until her mother scolded her. Then, as soon as Abigail was otherwise occupied, she sidled up close again. First she whispered her question, softly pointing out something new and asking its name. Then she repeated the word over and over, her voice growing stronger. Soon she was once again chattering as swift as the blackbirds. When Abigail attempted again to quiet her, Linux smiled with a small wave of his hand and shook his head. The little girl had captured his heart, along with everyone else's.

Abigail did not appear to have slept. The eyes above her shawl were shadowed and troubled. Linux noticed that so long as Jerusalem's walls remained in view, she cast more glances behind than upon the road ahead. Twice Martha kept her from stumbling. Every so often another one of the women would move up alongside Abigail, urging her softly to rest upon a donkey, or offering a sip of water, or simply touching her shoulder, letting her know she did not walk—or grieve—alone.

Linux did not permit himself many glances her way. His affection for Abigail remained as strong as ever, and yet so altered that it did not bear consideration. He accepted she would never be his, that her heart belonged to another. But his own heart's yearning was not silenced by the mind's awareness.

"Look, Uncle Linux!"

Abigail chided softly, "You must not address him such, child. It is not fitting."

"I would count it as a rare honor if you would permit the child to speak with me in this way," Linux said softly.

Abigail turned away and said no more.

Dorcas watched her mother for a moment, then turned back to ask, "What is this coming our way, uncle?"

"Drovers making their way to market. And behind them come two camels. Surely you have seen camels before."

"Yes. But not that," with another pointed finger.

"Those are cages. For chickens, I imagine. Or perhaps geese." Linux lifted the little one onto a donkey already laden with supplies and pulled it forward toward the front of their little band. "Would you like to move up and see how Uncle Alban is faring?"

Dorcas gripped the gentle beast's mane with both hands, eyes wide. Linux led the animal forward, glad for an opportunity to further limber up his legs.

Word of their departure had spread with the night. Their group had grown to include sixteen families. When he had awakened at first light, Linux discovered the courtyard filling with clusters of families and goods, silently awaiting the signal to rise and depart. Even more followers had joined the procession as it passed beyond the city gates. Linux did not object to their presence, only their slow pace. He wanted them all well cleared of the Jerusalem hills before the next nightfall. But their progress would be set by the slowest among them.

He approached the front of their group to find Alban deep in discussion. Philip the evangelist had appeared with the dawn as they were departing, asking if he might accompany them. As

Linux neared the two, he heard the man saying, "The Judeans and Samaritans have loathed each other for centuries. But surely you know this."

"I fear your words only reveal my ignorance," Alban said. He noticed Linux and asked, "What news from the rear?"

"All is well, save that we travel very slowly."

"There is little we can do about that," Alban said, shaking his head. "We cannot permit any to fall behind, so we must allow them to dictate our speed."

"And risk being trapped in the hills tonight?" Linux kept his voice low.

Alban did not answer immediately. Instead he turned and looked back from atop Linux's horse, which granted him a height at which he could survey the entire group. The cart that had been obtained for Alban now carried eight elderly folk, all of whom were far more infirm than the former centurion. In fact, Alban looked much improved, as though somehow being again upon the road actually increased the speed of his recovery.

Linux knew what Alban saw in that backward glance into the dust. The travelers carried all their worldly goods, and included as many as four generations, from infants to grandparents. None had been willing to leave any of their loved ones behind. Their group stretched back over a considerable distance.

Alban settled back in his saddle with a sigh and said simply, "God will provide."

Linux started to make his case once more but noticed how Philip nodded silent agreement. He kept his peace.

Some oncoming drovers prodded their sheep and the two camels into a shallow defile, almost a miniature cave, to let the larger group pass. Alban offered them a traveler's salute, then called, "What news of the road ahead?"

"Wind and more wind," cried the eldest drover. "And a cold that seeps into one's very bones."

Alban coughed his response, then asked hoarsely, "And the trail?"

"An abomination!" The elder eyed him curiously. "You are Roman?"

"I am. And a Gaul. And a God-fearer—a follower of the Way."

The drover revealed brown-stained teeth with his grin. "To whom do you give allegiance among such a host as that?"

"To God, and our Savior, the risen Messiah, Jesus Christ."

"Him I have heard of. Folks in our village declare him to be the one we have long awaited."

"Your fellow villagers are correct in what they say," Philip put in. "From where do you come, good man?"

"Tephon, straight ahead north as the crow flies. And you?"

"From Galilee, but I have lived with my brethren in Jerusalem since our Lord returned to his heavenly home."

The road-roughened man lifted his chin. "I am Samaritan, and proud of it. I worship the one true Lord, but find no need to hand my coins to the Temple vultures."

When Philip did not respond, Alban offered, "The Temple priests are no allies of ours."

The elderly drover seemed satisfied enough with that. "Where are you headed?"

"Away from Jerusalem," Alban replied. "And toward safety."

"We hope," Philip added. "And pray."

Linux added a silent amen with another glance to the rear.

The elder pointed a trembling staff at the road north. "We have traveled all day, and have seen no trouble. But rumors fly on this bitter wind—"

"Look! Little chickens!" Dorcas's high sweet voice set them

all to chuckling as they looked toward the drovers' cage to which she pointed.

The drover cackled with delight. "Those are not chickens, lass. These are thrush and starling and desert songbirds!"

As though in confirmation, a gold-breasted bird flittered about one of the smaller cages, piercing the air with its music. Dorcas clapped her hands in delight.

The drover signaled to one of his men, who swiftly unlashed the cage and hurried over to her with it. Dorcas watched wide-eyed as he grinned and offered her the hand-woven reed enclosure. She looked a question at Linux, who nodded. "Yes, take it, child."

"A gift," the elder drover said. "For the tiny lass with gemstones for eyes."

"What do you say?" Alban prompted the child.

"Thank you. I like the little chicken songbird!"

The elder laughed again. "And he will like you if you take good care of him."

Linux handed the donkey's reins to Alban and walked over to the drover. The elder squinted his question. Was Linux going to insult his gift with offer of payment? Instead, Linux said, "We are in need of sheep for tonight's meal."

"Those I have. Healthy and young and tender as any you'll find in Samaria."

"Be so good as to select three for me."

The man made a process of choosing, then named a price. Linux paid without bargaining. The elder eyed him again, this time with a glint of respect. Linux had overpaid for the sheep, and thus both pride and need were met. The old man observed, "You shall not make the plains and the campsites, not at the pace you are setting."

"There are old among us. And infirm."

"We use a watering hole that is often dry. But last week's rains have refilled the spot." The unsteady hand pointed ahead once more. "A bit more than halfway through the hills, a canyon opens before you, one running east to west, straight as a dagger's cut. The road takes a sharp left and heads west, hugging the wall. Just after you turn, a narrow breach opens. Keep an eye out, for it is easy to miss. It leads into a culvert that should be the right size—" The man stretched his neck up to view the rest of the group. "You should be safe there."

"Your arrival to cross our path is an answer to prayer," Linux said fervently. "A holy messenger."

The drover cackled once more. "And you are as strange a Roman as ever I have had occasion to meet."

"I am a man remade by Jesus, the risen Christ."

The elder studied him. "If this Jesus of yours can turn two Romans into guardians of poor Judeans, then he is powerful indeed."

"I stand as testimony to the truth of your words," Linux said. "And I shall pray to him tonight for the salvation of your soul, you and all your clan."

They found the culvert none too soon. Daylight had dimmed so Linux feared they would miss the opening between the rocks. They could not light torches along the trail, both because of bandits and because of the wind. The gloom had descended until the clouds rested upon the higher peaks. The road they'd followed was good enough, fashioned as it was by Roman hands. But the way was narrow, and the drops steep, and many of those in the band of believers were not seasoned travelers. Now and then he heard a wail of fear, one high enough to rise above the wind's howl.

Linux had returned the child to Abigail's charge and taken up his station at the rear. He and the master carpenter's eldest son did their best to encourage the stragglers to greater speed. Alban and the evangelist remained at the head of the procession. Alban's cough had returned and sounded worse each time Linux made his way to the front. But he was certain his experienced friend would find them a safe haven. If one indeed existed.

Then, in the murkiness of approaching night, a rustle of hope passed back through the group. There was a passage through the rock walls just ahead. Linux noticed one elderly man sag upon his mount's back and start to slide off. Linux caught him, holding him on the donkey as they moved slowly forward. Rounding the trail's next turning, Linux felt a tremor pass through the old man's frame. A glimpse of the cavern ahead of them and toward the left seemed like the maw of a great beast.

Final progress was very slow as the long string of people and animals began to cluster up against the turn into their haven. At the end Linux stood beside the old man and the donkey for what felt like hours. The elder obviously shared his impatience, complaining querulously, "What is keeping them?"

The only answer that came to mind was "Water."

"What's that you say?"

"Water!" Linux leaned in closer. "There is said to be a shallow catchment. If there's water, they will be filling their skins before letting the animals drink from the basin."

The man faced straight into the wind, glints of wetness streaking down his cheeks. "If I had known it would be like this, I would have ordered them to leave me behind."

"And have your clan settle in a new home without their revered grandfather? Impossible."

The old man looked over at Linux from his perch. "You are a strange one."

"And you, my good man, are the second one to call me such this day."

"You were an officer?"

"I still am. At least, until they catch up with me and strip me of my rank." *Or worse.* But he did not voice the thought.

"They will do that?"

Linux shrugged, but the old man would not have been able to see the motion. "That is in God's hands."

"A strange one indeed. If my daughter had told me this morning that tonight I would be held in my saddle by a Roman officer, I would have feared she was suffering from a dread fever and soon to be joining my dear departed wife!" His chuckle sounded incredulous.

Linux was spared the need to respond by the line again starting forward. They were the last to turn into the narrow culvert. Instantly the wind ceased to pummel them. Overhead it howled its frustration, occasionally showering them with grit, but Linux did not mind. He quickly looked around the large grotto, relieved that it could hold them all and provide a place for rest and nourishment. His own fatigue nearly overwhelmed him.

The elder quavered, "Help me down, will you? I need to ease my bones."

Linux did so, then guided the man as he shuffled toward his family. Already Linux could smell lamb roasting over a fire, hear the laughter of children. He thought he heard Dorcas but could not be sure.

The high-sided bowl-shaped area was perhaps fifty paces across. The early arrivals had joined together family tents, and half the enclosure was now sheltered. A single partition was being erected to form a private sleeping area for the women and children. The ground was covered by a sand as fine as milled flour. A woman rushed over, thanked Linux profusely, hugged the weary old man, and led him away to a place by a fire. Alban beckoned Linux over to another. "There is water for washing, if you don't mind sharing the pond with our donkeys."

When Linux returned, Alban offered him a strip of roasted meat hung from a charred stick. "Our plates and utensils are still packed away—"

"I will miss neither, hungry as I am." As he ate, Linux watched his friend settle onto his pallet. "How are you doing after our long trek, my friend?"

"I feel like my own grandfather. But I shall rest easy tonight, thanks to your locating this haven."

"Not I—it was the drover who directed us."

Philip was sitting with his back against the rock face. "The drover told you because you gained his trust. You, a Roman. I would call that a miracle."

"As would I." Alban laced his arms behind his head. "Philip, back on the road, you started to tell us about Samaria and its people."

Philip turned to Linux and asked, "Do you know anything of the rift between Judeans and Samaritans?"

"All soldiers ever talk about are risk and food and such. Samaria is simply known as a mixture of fertile plains and deserted wastelands. We knew there were disputes between its people and the Temple priests, but it was of no matter. For us . . ." Linux paused as a little figure danced over and halted by his side. "Shouldn't you be with your mother?"

Dorcas shook her head. "Mama is tired."

"Come sit here beside me, then. Do you want some lamb?"

She shook her head and patted her stomach. "I'm very full."

"How did your little bird fare in the storm?"

"Mama gave him water and covered him up. He's sleepy. I looked." She mimed tucking her head beneath one wing. She sat down and leaned against Linux, and he put his arm around her.

Alban smiled at them both, then said to Philip, "Tell us about this land we are entering."

"Judeans have loathed the Samaritans for centuries. The Pharisees go so far as to call them religious deviates, below even the Romans." Philip grimaced an apology at Linux, then continued, "When a religious Judean travels to Galilee, he heads east from Jerusalem and crosses the Jordan before turning north, just so he won't set foot in Samaria."

Philip spoke like an educated man, and his name suggested he came from a Hellenized clan. Because of his passion and dedication, he was known as the evangelist. Linux knew nothing more about him. Philip was a quiet man by nature, a realist who listened long and thought longer before offering an opinion. When he did speak, though, the others paid attention with great care.

Philip went on, "Samaria's boundaries run from the Jordan River to the coast, from Jericho in the south to the Lebanon hills in the north. Originally this formed the territories given to the tribes of Ephraim and Manasseh. During the reign of Hoshea the Second, the Assyrians conquered Palestine's Northern Kingdom. The victors captured a large number of Israelites as slaves. Those who remained intermarried with the new Assyrian colonists. When the Greeks conquered our land four hundred years later, they made the city of Samaria their capital. By the time Herod the Great was given rule over this land, these northerners had established their own temple on top of Mount Gerizim and disavowed all connection to Jerusalem."

Linux felt the little form snuggling closer to his side. Dorcas burrowed beneath his arm to lay her head against his chest, the act of a very trusting child. Before long Linux heard her steady breathing and knew she was asleep.

"It is hard for all of us to ignore such a history," Philip was saying. "And yet the last words the Lord Jesus spoke to us before rising into the sky and departing from us were these: 'But you shall receive power when the Holy Spirit has come upon you, and you shall be witnesses to me in Jerusalem, and in all Judea, *and Samaria*, and to the ends of the earth.' "

Alban said softly, "But it is not merely our coming to Samaria that concerns the apostles, is it?"

Philip's gaze turned to the man on his pallet by the fire. "No," he replied. "It is not."

"If they are to invite Samaritans to join us," Alban said, his voice weak but clear, "why not others? Why not Romans?" He and Linux exchanged a meaningful look.

Philip nodded slowly and continued the thought. "And do we recognize the Samaritans who become followers of our Lord as true Judeans? Or should they be considered merely God-fearers, as Gentiles are who convert? So many questions without clear answers."

Linux recalled something Stephen had told him. "Jesus himself went to Samaria, did he not?"

Philip studied him across the fire. "Several times."

"I can understand," Alban said, "why the idea of believers among the Samaritans might trouble the apostles."

"We have received word that it has already begun," Philip said. "While still with us in person, our Lord preached in a village called Sychar, and followers who have already settled there have told other Samaritans the good news of Jesus. Many are joining us. This is what I told them in Jerusalem. It is no longer a question of 'Do we allow this?' It has happened. I am traveling to Samaria in order to be a witness as our Lord instructed."

CHAPTER NINE

Tiberias

IN SPITE OF Julia's entreaties, Helena resisted joining the small group known as the Way for their evening meetings. Julia was so concerned about her mother that she could not stop urging and pleading. Helena's opposition only grew more firm, and Julia was sure it was because her mother did not wish to displease Jamal. This only served to further broaden the rift that Julia felt growing between her and her father. She tried her best to mask her discomfort in his presence, but she feared sooner or later it was bound to come to the fore. How long could she hide her feelings about what she believed was his injustice toward her mother?

But even with her increasing discontent and uncertainties, ultimately it was her mother's resistance to faith that caused Julia's sleepless nights and daily pleas to God.

As Julia and Zoe walked to a gathering under the cover of darkness, Julia confided, "I do not know what to do. If only she would hear for herself the followers tell of the Messiah, I am sure she would understand. But she refuses to even consider going with us," she finished sorrowfully.

Zoe was quiet for a time. "Perhaps . . . perhaps there is another way."

Julia strained in the shadows to see the woman's face. "If you know of another way, please speak of it."

"You will not think I question your wisdom?"

"What wisdom? I am telling you that I am desperate for a way forward. I have tried everything I know to convince her, and Mother remains unmoved."

Zoe half turned in the silvery light of the rising moon. "Remember what Elias said last meeting? We pray. We live a faithful life before others, that they may see the difference the Messiah has made in our lives. You are anxious. Overwrought, my dear Julia. That is not reflecting the peace that our Savior has given."

Julia stopped midstride. "I forgot those words, Zoe. But now you have reminded me . . ."

The old woman glanced over, then away without further word.

There was enough truth in her eyes to cause Julia to wince. "Have I plagued her with my constant pleading?"

"Perhaps" was Zoe's soft answer.

"But if we are to draw her into the group—"

"Julia, dearest. It is the Spirit who draws people. We can only be the light." The woman turned back to the path.

Yes. Of course. She had heard that too. Why had she not understood what it meant for her? *Live a life of rightness. Seek to follow the blessed Lord, and pray for enlightenment for others.* Elias had said all those things at their last gathering, and still Julia was trying to force her mother into the faith.

Julia hurried her steps to catch up to Zoe. "You are right," Julia admitted, reaching for the woman's arm. "I have been doing it all wrong. I must pray and let the Spirit speak to Mother's heart. She already knows my desires. Prompting her over and over accomplishes nothing."

"I think it has already accomplished something, Julia. Your mother is quite aware of your new faith and also of the fact that the Messiah has come. Now it is up to her to decide if she wishes to be freed from her chains."

"You . . . you don't mean end her relationship with my father?"

Zoe patted Julia's hand that held firmly to her arm. "No, child. Begin her relationship with her Creator."

Julia lifted her head at the sound of approaching feet. She was in the secluded courtyard, a piece of fine cotton and some embroidery silk in hand. She had discovered this to be a wonderful opportunity for prayer.

Her mother now stood before her, the basket designated for Jamal on her arm. Her smile was replaced with a slight frown. "It is near noon, daughter. Your father will be looking for his midday refreshment. I thought you would be coming to the kitchens to see what I had prepared."

Julia stirred. Truth was she had not even thought about her father. Which was strange. In the past she had been anxious to hurry down the paths that led to the encampment. To see her father's welcoming smile and his pleasure at the food she brought. But recently she had come to shrink from the trip. At first it was simply the fact that her father had not married her mother. He certainly could have. Many men, she had learned, claimed more than one wife. It was not an ideal situation from a woman's standpoint, but it gave some measure of security. Some legal protection should something happen. Julia still agonized over her mother's difficult situation.

And her own. Recently it seemed that every time she joined Jamal in his tent, he had some further information concerning her upcoming marriage arrangement. And even though she was well aware of what loomed on the horizon, Julia did not want to talk about it. She did not wish to even think about it.

And it wasn't only her own welfare that was at stake. Helena was still not a believer. Julia had been praying constantly for her mother to reach out for the truth. It was so hard for her to continue to hold her tongue. To refrain from begging. But Julia, with Zoe's steadfast backing, held to her resolve not to raise the issue again—simply to pray.

Julia stirred now. "I was not watching the sun," she admitted as she laid aside her piece of handwork. "I will be only a moment more. You may set the basket by the door."

"Ask your father when he will be home for his evening meal. It seems he has been getting later and later."

"He said he is hard-pressed to have everything in order before he leaves again."

"He is leaving?"

Julia nodded. "Yes, he said so last night when he finally came home." She noted that already Helena's face had clouded.

"With a caravan? I thought they had not yet returned." Helena had rarely troubled herself with the comings and goings of Jamal's caravans, and then only when she was told he would soon be arriving after being gone for a time.

"The main trade caravan is heading for Tyre, I understand, and likely will not return for some time," Julia said as she picked up the warm wrap to keep at bay the day's chill.

"So where will your father be—"

"He has not said." Julia did not wish to say *Perhaps Damascus*, in case the resentment was evident in her voice. *To his real family . . .*

But she would never say that aloud. She knew that would only serve to further hurt her mother.

Julia reached for the basket. She was late and her father would be unhappy—unless, of course, in his flurry of arrangements he had not noted the passing of time.

"I thought he keeps you informed of his—"

"Not always," Julia said quickly. She leaned over to kiss Helena's cheek.

She hurried out the door, leaving her mother with the unanswered question still lingering in her expression.

As she walked quickly along the familiar path, her thoughts churned once again. She had been praying, not only that her mother would come to faith but also for her father. She wasn't quite sure what she wanted God to do about him. Perhaps an apology to her mother. A confession that he had not been honest with them through the years. A change of heart and a marriage that would put her mother on an equal footing with other women in the city. Even as she railed inwardly about the situation, Julia knew there were no easy answers. What could her father do? How could he undo what he had already done? Would it make things look even worse if her parents were legally married after all this time?

When she arrived breathless at the tent's curtained doorway and swept it aside, she was not greeted by a pacing father, anxious for his noon repast. His head was still bent over a parchment—no doubt a list of goods to be packed up for transport. He hardly raised his head at her approach.

"Your food, Father," she said as she placed the basket on a corner of the table and began to lay out the items.

"Yes, fine" was his distracted reply. He did not even turn to her with his usual smile. "I will be just a moment here."

She noted his frown. "Is something the matter, Father?"

"This sale of linens that went to Syria. The price was not

nearly as expected. I wonder if my man there is tending to business as he should. Surely he could have realized a better profit had he been astute in his bargaining. He needs to be replaced. I have had some doubts about his business sense, and this latest makes me sure of it."

He pushed the parchment aside and rubbed at his neck. "A man can only be in one place at a time," he said, his voice sounding tired. "Only able to care for one thing at a time."

Yes, thought Julia. *You of all people should know that.*

"Tea?" she asked, holding her voice steady.

He smiled then and reached out for the cup she was holding out to him. "Now, if you had been a boy," he went on with a grin, "you could have been my right-hand man. I am sure no merchant would take advantage of you with your sharp eyes and wit."

"But I was not a boy," she said with more chill than she intended.

"No—and I would not have traded you for one." He said the words with warmth, restoring some of Julia's fragile peace.

"Sit for a minute and share my tea," he invited. "I have some news for you."

Obediently Julia sat, but she did not bother to pour herself a cup.

He pulled out a sheet that had been laid to one side of the table top and reached for a glass that would magnify the script. "It seems the agreement for your marriage is proceeding favorably. The family is quite anxious to close the deal to obtain the daughter of Jamal."

He did not look at her, which meant he could not see her cringe. When he lifted his head to face her, Julia was surprised to see a look akin to pain in his eyes. "But I shall miss you."

His voice sounded quite ragged with emotion. Julia had never seen him in this state before. He quickly cleared his throat and resumed his former self-assurance. "But life is life. One must make the best of it. You will be happy to know that I have carefully investigated the family. I have discovered no hidden flaws that need concern us. Still . . ."

But he did not finish the thought. Julia wasn't sure whether to be sorry or relieved. All she knew was that this was not what she wanted.

CHAPTER TEN

The Samaritan Plains

WHEN JACOB AWOKE, he discovered he had slept soundly in spite of a rock beneath one rib. He groaned as he rolled over. One of the donkeys brayed a low response, as though agreeing with his discomfort. The sun was approaching its zenith and pounded down from almost directly overhead. Though the snatches of wind which managed to enter the small box canyon carried a distinct chill, the heat from the trapped sunlight was fierce. In an attempt to remain in the shade, Jacob had rolled in his sleep, and then rolled again. He rubbed at the soreness around his rib as he staggered upright.

He stood for a while, then poured water into a rock defile shaped like a shallow bowl. While the donkeys drank he checked their tethers, then refilled their oat bags. Once they were back on the road, they would not stop again until well after dark. As the two beasts munched contentedly, Jacob made himself a drover's meal of crumbly goat's cheese, flatbread, and dried apricots. While he ate, he studied the pile of secret goods he had pulled from the donkeys' packs. When he finished, he announced to the patient animals, "It's time to see if I am right about Jamal and his secret hoard."

Before he had left camp, Jacob had appropriated four burlap feed sacks from the drovers' supplies. Two now held food for himself and the donkeys. The satchel of messages Latif had given him rested at the top of one. The animals also carried four waterskins.

The other two sacks held sixteen packets, wrapped carefully and sealed with a coating of red wax. The same pungent mixture of clove and cinnamon and something else greeted him as he opened a sack. The packets were each slightly larger than his two fists. He selected one at random and used his knife to slice it open.

Instantly his nostrils were filled with an unmistakable scent. Jacob had often heard the fragrance described as a faint taste of heaven. He could well understand why. He shut his eyes and buried his face in the packet. He was filled with a light headiness, as though just breathing the aroma helped to free up all his senses and heal his soul.

Jacob knew that perhaps the most valuable item in the world was frankincense. It formed the core component of virtually every perfume and was used as incense in Greek, Roman, and Judean religious rites. Frankincense was a key ingredient in embalming and burials. And, perhaps most important, for those who could afford it, frankincense was considered to have powerful healing qualities. It was used for the treatment of breathing difficulties, joint ailments, and chest inflammations.

The Hebrew word for frankincense was *levonah*, also the unofficial name of the ancient Phoenician kingdom to the north of Judea. Phoenician traders had held a virtual monopoly on its trade for over a thousand years.

Frankincense came from a tree which only grew in one region of the Arabian desert. Jacob was aware of this because frankincense generated many of the tales shared around caravan fires. Drovers who had made the dreadful journey to Yemen and back were held in awe by their fellow travelers. The one thing worse than the deserts of Arabia was the bandit kings. Only an item as treasured as frankincense made such a journey worthwhile.

Each morsel in the packet had a slightly malleable texture and was about the size of Jacob's thumbnail. The packet he had opened was filled with the spice the color of an old man's hair. Silver frankincense was by far the most valuable of all. Jacob surveyed the two burlap sacks. If even half of these packets held silver frankincense, he was carrying enough wealth to purchase an oceangoing trading vessel and all the men who served it.

No wonder Latif had been so worried about his camels.

Jacob used a hemp cord to reseal the packet as best he could. The red wax coating had alerted him to the contents, for this was the traditional way of masking the intense aroma. Jacob spilled a bit of precious water into the dust by his feet and molded it into clay, which he then used to coat the cut in the packet. He used more of the mud to vigorously scrub his hands. But this was not enough to rid him of the pungent aroma. He would simply need to ensure that no one came close enough to smell him until the fragrance wore off.

He reloaded the two sacks onto the donkey that did not carry his provisions and set off. Jacob remained well off the main road, holding the position commonly used by poor Judeans. He led the two animals along a well-beaten path parallel to the road. His dusty condition left him indistinguishable from the three other donkey drovers he passed. Jacob watched as one elderly man rode while a grandson trotted alongside, picking up sticks for firewood as they traveled. Jacob moved slightly further from the road, slid from his mount, and began doing the same. By the time the climb became steep, the one donkey was so loaded down with firewood and brush that the twin sacks were completely hidden. Because the branches were desert dry, they added little to the donkey's burden.

Jacob made good time. The wind and the altitude kept the sun from becoming too hot. Around midafternoon he found the trail he had sought, a little-used track that branched north and east, away from Jerusalem and toward the Samaritan plains. This was the riskiest portion of his journey, and Jacob wanted to have it behind him before the sun set. The trail rose and fell over mostly empty valleys, and he led the animals on foot.

Jacob passed several shepherds watching their goats and sheep. He offered a quiet greeting and did not stop. Once, when he traversed a particularly steep cliff side, he thought he heard a distant shout, as though a watchman had spotted him and was alerting bandits below. The Jerusalem hills were supposedly patrolled by Roman soldiers, keeping the Zealots well away. But even for Jacob, who had spent nearly four years guarding caravans, the trail's jagged shifts in direction, along with the countless valleys with their endless possibilities for bandit hideouts, left him fearful he might never get out alive.

Jacob traversed yet another ridgeline, turned another bend, and stopped in astonishment as the Valley of Samaria opened up before him. And none too soon, for the sun was just now touching the western hills. Even the donkeys brayed with relief.

By the time he reached the valley floor, Jacob's legs burned with fatigue. He tethered the animals in a shallow defile alongside ruins from some unnamed village—probably abandoned because of the danger from marauding outlaws. He could see no trough or natural depression to hold water, so he held the skin under one arm and poured it gradually into his cupped hand. The donkeys drank in turn, the hair of their muzzles tickling his palm. He then filled their oat bags and ate his own cold supper, watching the last light of day fade around him. The village's ancient stones and remaining timbers rose into the night sky like old bones.

He slept that night with two fragrant sacks for his pillow.

Jacob woke to the sound of voices. At first he thought he had dreamed the faint sounds. Then in the darkness he again heard low murmurs from further into the ruins.

Soundlessly he shifted his coverlet and rose to a crouch. The nearest donkey huffed softly, perhaps in its sleep. Jacob stilled it with a hand to its muzzle, all without taking his eyes from the glow off to his left. A fire was burning low, shielded from the road by a trio of ruined walls.

He had no way of knowing whether they were other weary travelers—or brigands. Either way, Jacob might well have been saved from attack by arriving so bone weary. For otherwise he would certainly have made his own fire.

Thankfully the others were camped at the ruined village's far end. As he lifted his head above the wall nearest to the strangers, Jacob felt a rising wind ruffle his hair and smelled rain. For once he found himself grateful for the coming storm.

Clouds blanketed the sky, ensuring no chance of measuring the distance to dawn. Even so, he reckoned he had at least an hour left of darkness. Jacob untethered the first animal, then quietly lashed the sacks of frankincense and water and feedstuff and his sword to the donkey's back. There was no hope of gathering his firewood in silence. Besides which, his safety now depended upon speed, not subterfuge. Holding the animal's reins in his teeth, Jacob crawled across the sandy expanse and located the second donkey by the sound of its slumbering breath. He woke the beast, stroking his side and whispering to keep him quiet.

Gathering up both sets of reins in his left hand, he led the animals out of the village, heading westward, away from the voices. It was the opposite direction from his destination, but that was not Jacob's concern. He waited until a hillock rose between him and the abandoned village before striking south, searching for the road. By the time he reached it, the faint light of a grey day was streaking the horizon ahead of him.

Jacob climbed onto the second donkey's back, fastened the other's reins to his belt, and clicked softly. He did not draw an easy breath until his overnight encampment was far behind him.

Jacob's view broadened markedly with the dawn. These Samaritan plains formed a wide fertile lowland stretching from the Judean hills to the south to the highlands further north. Mount Carmel, Gilboa, and Tabor shaped a ridgeline that joined with the hills of Galilee, separating the Samaritan plain from Megiddo. These two regions were the heartland of Samaria.

Jacob was fully aware the roads through Samaria were used by Romans, Phoenician traders, Syrian caravans—and only Judeans who considered themselves Hellenized, more "modern" in culture and religious practice than the strictly observant Judeans who would no more set foot in Samaria than they would enter a Roman garrison. To do so would render them ritually unclean.

Despite this restriction, the roads were well traveled. The Samaritan and Megiddo regions remained relatively safe even in these uncertain times. Because of the flat, even terrain, most of the Roman roads and almost all of the major aqueducts passed through here. Which meant the garrisons were suitably manned and alert.

Even so, Jacob maintained the same pattern as before, guiding his donkeys along a well-beaten trail some fifty paces north of the road. By this point, his attire resembled that of just another impoverished villager. He had crawled in the dirt and slept rough and traveled hard, rendering his cloak both filthy and torn. Judea was filled with such poverty, especially in Samaria. Neither the Roman guards nor the customs agent at the crossroads garrison gave him a second glance. He was obviously too poor to pester for a bribe.

Jacob halted for his first meal beneath a garrison's shadow, where the crossroads marked the joining of five major routes. The road straight north was the oldest, known among caravan drovers and guards by its ancient name, the Patriarchal Road, having once joined the twelve tribes. After Solomon's death and the division of the kingdom, it became the only route that linked the northern kingdom of Israel with Judea. Since the Romans' arrival, it had become disused and almost forgotten since the main Roman road ran westward toward Caesarea.

Jacob glanced over at a cluster of perhaps three dozen market stalls that had sprung up around the roads' juncture. He knew the stall Alban wished for him to take over was just like these, only situated further north along the main Roman road. From where he sat he could hear the merchants hawking their wares, a singsong cadence they shouted at each passing traveler. He shuddered at the thought of spending his days in such a manner.

But as he swung his leg over the blanket covering the donkey's back, Jacob suddenly knew if this was truly God's will for him, he would do it. He might argue. He might rant and shout his frustration to the sky. But he would do it. The thought of going against the Lord left him quaking. He recalled the certainty with which Alban had spoken to him. *Why would God speak to his guardian and not to him?* Jacob asked again.

The road stretched out before him, a line of white dust beneath a sullen sky. There were few travelers heading in this direction.

A distant flock of sheep dotted the fields to his left, and a lone cluster of nine camels was visible in the far distance. The solitude heightened his ability to hear beyond the wind, beyond his own thoughts, and accept the truth.

God may have spoken to Alban because Jacob had been unwilling to listen.

Thankfully, the rain never arrived. Jacob saw several dark clouds blot out portions of the valley behind him. The wind freshened, then grew stronger still. By midafternoon he needed his head scarf to protect his face and eyes from the blowing grit.

Toward evening his little procession entered the foothills marking the boundary of the Galilee hills. This region had once been as safe as any, with its Roman fortress looming atop the highest mount. But times had changed, and few of the garrison soldiers ventured out after dark. Between bandits and the Zealots, the armed soldiers still were watching their backs.

The donkeys were tired after being forced to trot all day against the wind. Even so, Jacob pressed them harder still, along with careful glances over his shoulders. Just as Herod's palace came into view, he spotted watchers on a northern hilltop above Tiberias. Unlike the group that had shared his Samaritan ruins the previous night, there was no question who these people were.

"*Hyah!*" Jacob pulled the quirt from his belt and struck the donkey's flank. The animal brayed his protest, for his sides were lathered from a hard day. But there was no choice, not if they were to arrive at all. "Faster! Run, beast! For our very lives, ride hard!"

He knew he was requiring the impossible, for donkeys do not gallop. Their shuffling gait lifts their hooves only a few inches from the earth. Even so, a donkey's strength was revealed at such times, for they could travel longer and harder than any horse, which was why they were preferred on caravans. Horses were ridden only by guards, who needed to shift position with lightning speed. For everything else, the donkeys served far better.

Just as the two animals did now. Though continuing to protest, their miniature hooves danced over the trail as Jacob urged them on with shouts and his quirt. The Tiberian hills formed steep-sided valleys, with sharp drops into shadowy canyons. The Romans preferred to build their roads in an absolute straight line, but here even the world's finest engineers were forced to steer their way around tight curves.

The hilltop palace of Herod Antipas was a mere shadow now, the light failing fast. Jacob heard what might have been a nighthawk calling from the hills behind him. He feared it was in fact the sound of a two-legged predator, and he whipped the donkey harder still. "*Hyah!*"

Rocks scattered down from the hill to his right. Jacob was fairly certain horse-mounted riders were scrambling over the rough highlands, attempting to get ahead of him. Jacob leaned down over the donkey's neck, gripping the reins with one hand and the beast's ragged mane with his other. He moved in close to the donkey's ear and panted, "Do you smell the danger? Can you feel the closeness of their swords? For both our sakes, I beg you, grow wings and *fly*."

He knew this route so well he could have found it in his sleep. Beyond the cutoff to Herod's hilltop domain, the road broadened and began descending down to the Sea of Galilee. The first lights of Tiberias flickered in the gloom. Jacob crouched over the donkey's neck, imploring for ever greater speed. The second donkey had stopped braying now, saving all its breath for the task of keeping up. Jacob risked a glance behind and saw one of the sacks had almost worked loose and was flopping hard upon the beast's side. He had no idea whether it was the frankincense or merely supplies, and there was no way to halt and check. The sound of other hooves was much clearer now.

"Fly, my hairy friend. *Fly!*"

They rounded the next bend, and a third. And the hills abruptly opened. Before him, the lights of Tiberias spread out like a blanket of welcome. To his left, the first walls of the caravanserai opened up.

Jacob heard a shout of pure frustration behind him. Even so, he did not let up until he passed the guards at the caravan site's main entrance. They had heard the cry and the hooves as well, for they stood facing outward, arrows notched and bows upraised.

Jacob did not realize how sore he was from the jouncing race for his life until he slid from the donkey's back and his legs refused to hold him. He held himself aloft by maintaining his grip upon the beast's mane. He flung his other arm around the animal's neck and heaved for breath in time to the donkey's own gasps.

The second beast snuffled its way closer until its muzzle rested on Jacob's ribs. He released the mane so he could embrace both animals. "Well done, the both of you. Well *done*."

CHAPTER ELEVEN

The Samaritan Plains

ABIGAIL WOKE TO the most beautiful sound in the entire world, that of her daughter's laughter.

She adjusted her shawl over her head and emerged from the women's enclosure to discover that most of the camp was awake and readying for departure. Dorcas was playing with a doll the master carpenter had carved for her, as well as trying to mimic the song of her caged bird. Martha watched her, all the while helping another woman fasten a bundle of household goods to a donkey. "If I had my eyes shut, I doubt I could tell which one was singing."

Abigail murmured, "Why was I not awakened with the others?"

"Because you needed the rest more than anyone." Martha's smile seemed unusually warm. "I know how you've tossed and turned through the last nights."

"I must have been more weary than I realized."

The woman alongside Martha said, "You're out of Jerusalem

and beyond the reach of the Temple guards. A mighty burden has been lifted from your shoulders. No wonder you slept."

But Abigail did not feel relieved to have left the city. With each step northward, she felt the last remaining connection she held to her beloved Stephen being stretched to the breaking point.

Martha must have understood Abigail's frown, for she said softly, "Look at your daughter. Is she not as lovely as the sunrise? What joy she brings to your life."

Martha looked again at Dorcas and added, "There is so much of Stephen in her, do you not think?"

The words had been addressed to Abigail, but it was the other woman who said, "Do you know, I had not thought of that until now. But he is clearly planted in the child—his smile, his great heart."

"His eyes," Martha said. Then she turned her head toward Abigail and added in a lower tone, "You will always have him with you." She patted the donkey's side and straightened, hand on her back. "Come, dear Abigail. Let me find you something to eat."

Their entire group seemed to travel with lighter hearts that day. Abigail heard the others speak often of God's hand in finding them such a haven for the night. Not even the ever-present wind and the clouds' gloom could dispel their cheer. As they emerged from the hills and the road straightened and entered the Samaritan plains, they broke into songs of praise. Dorcas sat upon a donkey just ahead of where Abigail walked, one hand intertwined in the mane and the other waving to the clouds overhead as she also sang along.

Martha moved up alongside Abigail. " 'Though the entire world may stand against us, still will I praise my Lord,' " she quoted quietly.

Abigail nodded, and wondered why her heart remained wistful.

When the song had ended, Dorcas turned and reached out her hands. "Mama! Mama! I want down!"

"You're a big girl now. You can ask properly."

"Take me down."

" 'Please,' " Abigail admonished. " 'Please, will you help me down.' "

Dorcas repeated the request, then wiggled free from Abigail's arms even before her feet touched the earth. Abigail said, "Stay close now."

A cluster of children scampered past, squealing their eagerness for the freedom of the broad and straight road ahead. They ran alongside the travelers, filling the gloomy day with their cries.

Dorcas joined them without a backward glance to her mother, her short legs working hard to keep up. Then she broke away from the others and up to where Linux walked alongside the horse carrying Alban. She skipped up and down, her small hands lifted high. Abigail watched as Linux laughed, then reached to heft her onto the horse in front of Alban. Alban stroked the little girl's curls, then said something that made her giggle.

Martha hummed a soft note, observing, "The entire group joins in her happiness, Abigail. It is a gift to all of us."

By midmorning they had arrived at Neapolis, the destination for three of the families. The fields surrounding the town looked fresh, fed by the recent rains. Farmers were busy harvesting the last of the autumn crops, both fruit and late-growth olives, while others scythed fields of golden hay. Yet it seemed to Abigail that the workers all stopped and watched their passage.

Linux must have noticed it too, because when she heard Dorcas call for him to carry her, he instead lifted her off the horse and brought her straight back to Abigail. "Keep her close."

"Is everything—"

"We shall see soon enough," he said. "Tell the other families to gather up their children." He turned away quickly. "Watch for my signal and stay alert."

The fields swept like golden carpets right up to the doorsteps of the town's first houses. Yet even here the sense of unease continued, for people gathered in doorways to stare at the procession. Abigail saw a man turn and speak into the house's shadows. A few seconds later, a lad came racing out, leaping the side fence and scattering a flock of sheep to race toward the center of town.

An old man leaned against the post supporting the next home's roof. In a querulous voice he called, "Where do you come from?"

"Jerusalem," Philip responded.

"You be them that follow the crucified prophet?"

"Jesus of Nazareth, the risen Lord," Philip confirmed.

Alban called out, his voice still weak though loud enough to be heard, "We come in peace."

Abigail watched anxiously as Linux moved back toward one of the families that was hoping to remain in Neapolis. He spoke quietly with them, then raised his voice and said, "We travel with cousins of Ben Isaac."

Alban added, "We have some elderly with us. And infirm. Is there a place where we may water our animals and perhaps find shelter?"

The old man pointed them down the road. "The public well is up ahead, by the market square."

Linux thanked the man, and he stood alongside the road as the families continued on by. He did not speak. Abigail knew that by then all the travelers were aware of his grave disquiet. As she passed him, she saw the knuckles of his hands, chalk white where they gripped his stave. His features were taut, his eyes constantly searching ahead and behind.

Dorcas said, "What is it, Mama?"

"Shah, child. We must take care and stay quiet now."

"I don't like it."

Abigail bent over and lifted the girl into her arms. "You are safe here with me, my Dorcas. We will pray to be brave. Can you do that?" Dorcas nodded and held tightly to her mother's neck and was quiet. She was an armful, especially after the morning's walk, but Abigail did not set her down.

As they entered the main square, Martha whispered, "Let me take the child."

"No, it is all—"

Abigail's words were cut off by a woman's voice. "Is it you?" she cried, her high-pitched voice piercing the quiet of the group.

The travelers halted as one. The animals tossed their heads nervously, their masters' tension making them skittish. One donkey brayed, but otherwise there were no further sounds.

The woman had now emerged from a side lane, and she rushed forward with arms outstretched. "Have you come at last?" she cried out again. She moved from one traveler to the next. "Are my prayers finally answered? I have long prayed for someone to come and teach us."

From the front of the line, Philip said, "Do I know— Am I recognizing you?" He moved toward her.

The woman turned and ran forward, exclaiming, "Praise our God! He has heard me." She dropped to the dust at Philip's feet. "Oh, master!"

"I am not he and deserve no such title." Philip gently took her arm and lifted the woman to her feet. "You were in Sychar, were you not?"

"Yes, good sir. At Jacob's well."

"I remember now. Our Lord spoke with you."

"I gave him water from that well. In Sychar, where I lived then." Her voice was lower, but her words still carried in the stillness. People were now emerging from every lane and shadow and doorway. Moving forward, gathering around Philip, the woman, and the travelers, until they filled the entire square. The woman was saying, "And the Rabbi, Jesus, gave me the water of life. And it changed me—it changed everything!"

Philip was smiling. "And you have told this news to your friends and neighbors."

"Oh yes, over and over—all that I could, which was not very much. Almost nothing." She wiped her face with one hand. "But you have come here. And you now can tell them all that I cannot."

Alban said softly from atop the horse, "Perhaps we should first see to the needs of our group. Then we will talk with you all."

"You all know Helzebah, this kind woman of Sychar. You know her story. How she came to draw water from Jacob's well in that village, and Jesus himself was seated there while his disciples left to buy food."

Philip was standing on the rock wall surrounding the public wells and troughs forming the center of a large square, bordered by market stalls and other buildings. Abigail thought one of them appeared to be a synagogue. Their animals had been fed and watered, and were now quartered in stables off to the left. The three families had been reunited with their kin, and gradually their welcome had been taken up by many other clans of the town. They had brought food and tea and even offered a large dwelling where the elderly, the young ones, and the infirm could settle for some much-needed rest. Abigail could see Dorcas among several other small faces peeking over the roof's edge, watching them from beneath a shelter of woven reeds. The child was vigorously waving with both hands to her mother, and Abigail responded with a little wave of her own, then turned back to listen.

Philip was saying, "Our Lord Jesus promised this kind woman

the chance to drink his life-giving water. Friends, I am here to make that same offer to you today."

Abigail looked around the square, packed with people in every direction, a sea of upturned faces. Many of the other roofs surrounding the square were also filled with listeners. The wind had calmed, and Philip's voice rang out clearly over the masses. "Whoever drinks the water of life, that which is offered by Jesus the Messiah, will find a wellspring rising up inside. The Messiah came to bring this gift to all who will accept it. He invites all of us to receive the gift of eternal life."

A male voice from far back in the crowd called out, "But you are Judean, and we are Samaritans. We are sworn enemies!"

"What you say is true enough," Philip conceded. "And yet the Messiah's coming has changed all that. Remember the prophet Isaiah's words? 'They shall beat their swords into plowshares,' Isaiah said, and, 'The wolf also shall dwell with the lamb, and the leopard shall lie down with the kid.' "

Another voice called, "How can that be?"

Philip pointed to the east, at a lone peak rising above the rooftops. Abigail could see the solitary mountain was high enough for its summit to be rimmed by frost and ice. "Your ancestors worshiped God atop Mount Gerizim, while we Judeans rebuilt the Temple of Jerusalem. And yet Jesus himself told this woman, your neighbor," he said, gesturing toward the woman standing at the wall by his feet, "that a time was coming when God would be worshiped in *neither* place."

"What the man says is true!" she called.

Philip held out both arms to the crowd. "The time has come for you to know Jesus yourself, and to learn to worship God in your hearts."

A powerful sensation came upon Abigail. An impression so strong she felt utterly isolated from the people crowding about her.

Alone in the middle of this great throng. She did not hear further words. She did not need to. Instead, the silent message came clearly and directly to her heart.

How mistaken she had been! She had resisted leaving Jerusalem for all the wrong reasons. She had claimed it was to remain and serve the poor. And yet so many of those who needed her care had left—the vast majority. Day by day, week by week, she had seen the number of believers dwindle, the poor and the widows leaving for safer places. She had seen this, and chosen to remain closed to what this might mean.

The real reason she had insisted on remaining was because she had not trusted God.

She had feared that leaving Jerusalem meant leaving Stephen. And in one way it did mean that. But it also was true that Stephen had already left that city for the heavenly Jerusalem over five years past. Her ties to his beloved memory did not require a *place*. She had Stephen's daughter with her. And the gift of the Holy Spirit.

Further, she had kept herself from serving God in areas where there was even greater need. Just as Philip was doing now.

Philip was saying, "Our Lord spoke of the harvest to come. That harvest, my brothers and sisters, is here, and it is you! The time has come to cast off the chains of your past and see the truth revealed. The eternal gift is yours to claim. Come now, and accept the Messiah as your own Savior from sin, from eternal death!"

As many in the crowd surged forward, Abigail dropped to her knees. She could sense the people shifting and moving about her. But her sense of seclusion in her own small space remained. She bowed her head and prayed with such intensity she felt as though her words were not even her own, coming from some place deep within, a place she was not aware of before. *Forgive me for not being willing to hear your call until now, dear Lord. But I am here and I am ready. Direct me to where I should next go. Reveal to me how I should next serve you. Grant me the wisdom and the strength to trust you in all things. Wherever you lead. Whatever task you set. Help me, Lord.*

CHAPTER TWELVE

Tiberias

JULIA FELT THE shock of what she was hearing send a shiver traveling down the full length of her body. *What is the stranger saying?* Was he truly proposing that she be the Tiberias link in the chain of underground believer communications? *Does he even realize who I am?*

She stepped back a pace, resistance and arguments already forming in her throat.

But it was Zoe who voiced disapproval, her usually downcast eyes wide with concern and rebuttal. "This is nonsense. Julia is a mere child—"

"A woman," the man shot back, almost hissing the words in his effort to be quietly forceful. "A young woman. Which is precisely why she has been selected. She would never be suspected."

"No. No, it is too dangerous." Zoe pushed Julia behind her with one sweep of her arm. Julia could only stare. Never in her life had she seen the usually compliant Zoe stand up to anyone, let alone a man. "I will not have it."

The man took a deep breath, no doubt forcing himself to assume a calmer stance. "I understand your concern. There is indeed danger. In the last weeks three of our couriers have been taken. All men of good standing in our community of believers. Each one was arrested for carrying messages from one group of followers to another. Messages that could have spared injury. Saved lives. But today we have received news of yet another planned raid. If we do not send the warning . . ." He let the words drop, but the thought of what might happen hung heavily in the air between them.

For a tense few moments there was silence. Julia could see Zoe struggling against her own reasoning.

When she did not speak, the man continued, his voice trembling with intensity. "We cannot let the communication lines break down. Many lives have been saved because of those warnings. We realize we must choose the messengers with greater care. Men are automatically viewed as suspect and are watched day and night. We do not know who and where the spies are. We expect they work at the bidding of the Pharisee Saul. He appears to have eyes in every city. Every port. Every market."

Zoe was shaking her head. "But not my Julia," she pleaded.

"She is the merchant's daughter. She has opportunity to move in and out among the caravans. Her presence would not be questioned. And it is well known that her father is not one of us. He has made his position clear on more than one occasion."

Zoe lowered her head, clearly very troubled by what she heard. She pulled at her shawl, drawing it protectively about her face as though to hide from life and its harsh demands.

"She will be given a contact person," the stranger pressed. "Carefully chosen as well. He will also be above suspicion. Not a prominent member of our group. Yet one most trustworthy. We are taking every precaution. We have selected him carefully. Now we can only trust the Father. . . ."

Ah, so he is laying it all in God's hands, Julia thought. The man was right, of course. What else could they do but trust? Every day was a risk. Spies were everywhere. Charges of misconduct, religious and otherwise, were daily laid against one or another of their community.

Zoe's shoulders drooped in resignation. "Nathan, are you sure there is no one else?"

So Zoe knew the man who stood before them. No wonder she had not been frightened when the man had suddenly appeared as they returned from the market. Julia lifted her eyes. The last rays of the evening sun reflected off the distant walls of the hilltop palace of Herod Antipas, making its outline glow like golden embers. The king was not there and had not been for some time. Where he had gone, few knew, and even fewer cared, but his elaborate residence was a constant reminder of the dangerous man who had founded their town.

Nathan continued, "No one is better placed. Else I would not have approached you."

Zoe sighed again, fear still held in her eyes. Julia thought she saw the glint of a tear as the faithful servant turned toward her. Zoe did not ask the question, but Julia knew it hung between them.

"Could I . . . may I have some time to think, to pray about this?" Julia's voice quivered in spite of her effort to control it.

The man named Nathan nodded. He stepped back a pace. Then moved forward again. His voice was little more than a whisper. "Tomorrow. We can wait no longer."

Julia swallowed hard. She had only a few hours to make this decision. A decision that could cost her life, endanger her parents. . . . She felt Zoe's work-worn hand reach for her own, and she clung to the offered support.

"The market. The fig stand of Demetrius," the low voice said.

"Be there at full sun." And without another word Nathan drifted away into the shadows.

The two women stood, clinging to one another. Zoe said, "Your mother will never hear of such a thing. She—"

"My mother must never know," Julia said quickly. "It would only bring danger." She pulled firmly on the sleeve of Zoe's cloak. "Promise me you will tell no one."

Abruptly Julia realized she had already made her decision. And from Zoe's startled reaction Julia knew that the woman was aware of the same thing. She felt Zoe slump forward as though the strength were slowly draining from her. Like a wineskin that had been ruptured. But she saw the servant nod her reluctant agreement to secrecy even as she raised her shawl to blot her eyes.

A sudden knowledge hit Julia, leaving her weak with its truth. She was alone. There would be no one to guard and protect her as she went into this venture. Not even the trusted Zoe would be at her side, sheltering her with loving hands when she was troubled, wiping away the tears when she was hurt. Giving gentle advice or encouragement when it was needed. No. She would be alone. Totally alone.

Even now, Zoe found a way to give her strength. With a shaking hand she reached out to lay it lightly on Julia's cheek. "You are brave, my little one. May God be with you."

The following morning, Julia slowly approached the fig stand of Demetrius. Idly she handled the fruit, casting surreptitious glances into the street and stalls about her. Demetrius himself seemed to be totally ignoring her. He was serving another customer, and as the woman hoisted her basket and turned to go, Demetrius cast one quick glance Julia's way and gave an ever-so-brief nod.

When he did approach her it was as a merchant. "May I help you select some produce? The olives are rich in ripeness, the figs are fresh. Which would you like?"

Julia felt panic fill her being. She had not thought to bring market coins. How could she purchase anything?

She lowered her head and whispered, "I . . . I neglected to bring money."

His voice was also soft. "Next time. For now search in your robe and pretend to withdraw coins. Place them in my hand."

Julia did as she was bidden, her cheeks hot with the necessary subterfuge. The merchant made as if to count the money carefully, then placed some figs in Julia's basket.

"My wife is inside," he said, his voice normal, and he nodded toward the back. "She would like to send greetings to your mother."

Julia hesitated. His wife had never sent greetings to her mother. Nor did any of the other stall keepers. In fact, she doubted that any of the stall owners even knew her mother. But at his insistent nod she picked up her basket and moved to the curtain that divided the market court from the private quarters.

It was not the merchant's wife who greeted her but Nathan. Julia felt her eyes widen. Was this some trick? Was Nathan really who he claimed to be, or was she already caught in the net governed by priestly rule? She hesitated, her eyes quickly seeking some way to escape.

"Come in," said the man in a quiet voice. "You must realize that we could not engage you without first testing to see if you can obey orders. You have done well. But you have things to learn. Do not appear to be without purpose. You have been to the markets before?"

"Many times. With Zoe, our servant woman. Or one of the others from the kitchen. But—"

"I understand. You are not the one sent to make the purchases."

Julia nodded. "The servants . . ."

"Of course. Where do you go on your own?"

She had to think about that. There were few places that she actually went by herself. "Only to see my father."

He pondered in silence. At length he spoke again. "We will need Zoe to come to market with you, as usual. You will appear to be helping in the choosing of merchandise. Do you carry a basket?"

"Often. Yes."

"That is good." He gave a nod. "Now, when you shop, do you carry the coins or does your servant?"

"I . . . we change about, I suppose. We don't really think much about it. Sometimes she brings the coins from the kitchen and keeps them. Sometimes she hands them to me."

"So the people in the market stalls surrounding us are used to seeing either one of you pay?"

"I . . . I imagine so, yes."

"Now, remember, you must be cautious at all times. Trust no one but the people we direct you to. Come here to Demetrius for all your instructions. He will inform you of where you are to meet and when. But you must never shop at only his stall. Go around the market and make the usual purchases. Do not let your eyes appear to wander about as though looking for someone. You are simply shopping for the needs of a household. Dutifully helping your aged servant. Do you understand what I am saying?"

Julia swallowed and nodded.

"That is good."

She doubted there was anything good about the arrangement. Could she remember all of the instructions given? Could she follow them? She felt overwhelmed with it all.

"You are to take whatever Demetrius gives you to the caravanserai. Your contact person will meet you where the animals are kept."

"By my father's *camels*?"

"Yes."

"But my father is not a follower. And he is very protective of his camels. He does not let anyone near them except for his own drivers and his guards."

"We know this."

"Are you telling me this man works for my father?"

He nodded.

"But that is . . . What if my father discovers him? He would perhaps . . . Is not that a grave danger?"

"It is exactly as we have planned. That is the last place the spies will look for one carrying a message for the Way. Your father is wealthy, powerful, and totally demanding. And he has no connection whatever with any religious group or sect. He has made that most clear. To quote him, 'I will abide no such nonsense.' "

"So . . . so you are . . . are *using* my father?" Julia stumbled over the words.

"Only as a shield against evil. Only to save lives of people who have done no wrong." The man handed her a very small cloth-wrapped packet. "This is the only time I will be the one to give you the packet. In the future it will be Demetrius. Do you understand?"

Julia returned a silent nod as she attempted to swallow away her doubt and fear.

"Do you remember the instructions? Today you may hide this packet in your robe before you leave. In the future you will remove it from your basket only when it is safe to do so. Visit your father as usual, then the camels. The contact person will meet you there. Your contact will be wearing a red band across his forehead and carrying a basket of medicine for the animals. He will say, 'The rains have come to Jerusalem.' Repeat those words to yourself."

Obediently Julia did so, her voice low.

"Then you will respond by drawing the sign of the fish. Like this." He outlined the simple body of a fish on the ground with one sandal.

Julia nodded that she understood.

"Now as you go from here, linger at the entrance for a moment and say a few words as though speaking with the merchant's wife."

To Julia's utter surprise the man pulled a woman's shawl over his head and shoulders and followed her to the opening. He displayed only his covered head, the shawl wrapped closely around his face. Julia fought for proper words. "I will certainly tell her," she finally managed, hoping her voice did not sound as fearful as she felt. "She will be most appreciative."

She nodded to the shawl-covered figure, then turned to acknowledge Demetrius as she walked through the stall. To her surprise the man cautiously slipped some coins into her hand and whispered, "Go for further shopping. At the other stalls."

Julia crossed to a stall selling spices, finally choosing some ginger. Would she ever understand the workings of this new game she was to play? A game with risks too great to contemplate.

CHAPTER THIRTEEN

Tiberias

AT FIRST LIGHT, Jacob dusted himself off as best he could and presented himself outside the entrance to Jamal's home. He pounded on the gate. When there was no response, he unsheathed his sword from the scabbard and hammered with the pommel.

The servant who finally answered was known to Jacob, at least on sight. A senior servant who had been retired because of infirmity, he remained unwilling to relinquish his authority. So he made do by quarreling with everyone. He and Jacob had hissed at one another previously, but thus far the claws themselves had remained sheathed.

"What is the meaning . . . ?" His scowl at the sight of a motley donkey drover was terrible indeed. "How *dare* you disturb the peace of this house!"

Jacob normally would have overlooked the man's bluster and simply asked to see the master. But this was no normal situation. He shouldered past the servant. "Out of my way."

"You can't possibly intend to bring those beasts inside!"

But that was precisely what Jacob intended. He had slept in fitful snatches, guarding the donkeys and the sacks all night long. They would not be left anywhere out of sight. "Awaken the master. Now!"

"Guards! *Guards*!"

The donkeys, made nervous by the man's cries and by the unfamiliar courtyard, brayed and resisted along with the elderly servant. But Jacob pulled hard upon the reins and led the two across the entry chamber and into the central courtyard. Once the animals smelled the fountain's water, they came willingly enough. Jacob untied the sacks and set them on the courtyard flagstones. He let the animals drink their fill, stroking their flanks with one hand, while the other held the sword.

The household guards hovered in the distance, watching Jacob's flickering blade in the morning sunlight. Sounds came from the chambers surrounding the courtyard as its members awoke to the unusual commotion. Jacob paid no mind. He was so weary he felt that if Jamal did not appear soon, he might actually fall sleep on his feet.

"There had better be a good reason for this!"

Jacob turned at the sound of the familiar voice. "There is, master."

The large-framed merchant sauntered closer. "Do I know you?"

"I am Jacob, sire."

"Alban's charge? My guard?" Jamal stepped closer still. "Can it truly be you under all that filth?"

Jacob merely nodded.

"Where is my caravan?" He looked at the two dust-covered donkeys, then back at their equally dusty drover.

"They should be leaving Caesarea either today or tomorrow, headed for Tyre."

"And why are you here?"

Jacob lowered his voice. "Latif was taken."

The merchant's face went as pale as old bones. "What do you mean, 'taken'?"

"They were waiting for him. The morning we left Jerusalem, they pounced." Jacob leaned closer and spoke softly, so the curious ears hovering about the perimeter could hear nothing. "They seized his camels, spread out all his goods beneath the eye of the Roman tax agent, and searched everything."

The man's towering strength seemed to melt away in the space of one breath. Jacob gripped his arm and helped him sit down at the side of the fountain. "They knew . . ." the man moaned.

Jacob whispered, "Perhaps. Perhaps not. It could have been a ruse. It is not uncommon for honest folk to be falsely accused. Especially in Jerusalem. The Temple priests were there as well, watching it all like hawks."

Jamal's face had not regained its color. He raised his voice and his arm. "All of you, clear away. I must be alone."

They began to scurry away at his roar. It was followed by another. "Syrus!" The querulous old man emerged from the shadows. "Yes, sire?"

Jamal asked Jacob, "Have you eaten?"

"Nothing but the road's dust."

"Tell the cook to make a plate of something hot. And fresh tea. For us both."

Jacob felt his stomach tremble with sudden hunger. "And pomegranate juice. I have dreamed of the taste."

"You heard the man." When the servant did not move fast enough, Jamal barked, "Go!"

When they were alone, Jacob said, "All is not lost, sire."

"What's that?"

"Before he was taken, Latif charged me with his secret."

Jamal's head rose gradually. "But you said—"

"Latif separated three of his camels. They only searched the six that Latif kept close to himself." Jacob went over to retrieve the sacks, which he placed at Jamal's feet. "It's all here, sire. Every last bit."

Jamal bent down far enough to breathe in the heady aroma of spices and frankincense. He lifted one sack into his arms like a child. "You know what you carry?"

"I opened one of the wax-sealed packs."

Jamal's eyes glazed over. His hands trembled slightly as he resettled the sack upon the flagstones. "The year's entire profits are contained within these bags."

Jacob said nothing, for the servant chose that moment to return bearing a tray.

"Serve my honored guest," Jamal instructed, his bark sounding loud to Jacob's ears.

Jacob could see the old servant would rather have dropped the tray on the ground. But he did as he was told, arranging the plate of food and drink on the edge of the fountain and motioning for Jacob to partake. The man's tone was filled with apprehension as he offered his master a second mug. "Are you— Do you need anything further, sire?"

"We are all most well cared for, all my household—and you—thanks to the bravery of this young man. Now leave us, and make sure we are not disturbed." Jamal gestured the servant away and nodded to the platter. "Eat your fill, Jacob."

As Jacob ate, he related his experiences. Watching Latif kneeling in the dust, Yussuf not yet rejoining the caravan when they made their first stop for the night, Jacob having to take charge of the caravan, Hamman's surprising allegiance, the decision required at the split in the road, the seaside village's response to their arrival, inspecting the containers of cinnamon and cloves. As Jacob talked, he found himself reliving the adventure of it all. Jamal too had become so caught up in the tale he began eating from the same plate. Every now and then he plied more fruit or tea on Jacob, but otherwise the man did not speak. Not until Jacob described his mad dash down the Tiberias road, with the unseen horsemen hot on his back.

"This is true, all you have told me?" He leaned back to search Jacob's face.

Jacob nodded, wiping his fingers and his chin with the end of his head scarf. "Every word."

Jamal stroked his greying beard. "Did they ever tell you *why* they searched?"

"As soon as Yussuf told this Ezra that the camels were yours, they backed down. They did say they were inspecting the goods for contraband."

"Contraband, is it?" Jamal tugged his beard.

"But why pick Latif's camels?" Jacob wondered.

"Do you think they knew what Latif carried?"

"Or thought they did," Jacob nodded. "But as I said, perhaps it was just a ruse."

"Who talked, I wonder."

"Not Latif. It was more than his life was worth."

"So they are aware," mused Jamal further, looking upward to the sky. "At least they know of the possibility. We will need to devise . . ." But he shook his head and said instead, "Send riders out to Jerusalem. Have them carry gold. See if they will release Latif in exchange for payment."

"I hear and obey," Jacob replied, repeating words he had often heard Alban use. "Only, sire, I do not have gold."

"You will, my man. You will. Your reward will come. And more besides. For now . . . Syrus!"

The old man appeared with the speed of one who had trained himself to lurk on the other side of pillars. "Sire?"

"This man is to be an honored guest at my inn. You will show him to the finest of our chambers and clothe him as you would a prince. See that he has everything that he needs."

"A bath," Jacob murmured. "And the best care for the beasts that have saved my life . . . and your wealth."

Jamal's laugh boomed through the courtyard. "They are not donkeys but princes as well! Syrus, see that these three princes want for nothing!"

Jacob descended from Jamal's inn, located near the Tiberias waterfront. Tiberias was actually two cities. Observant Judeans refused to set foot in the portion of town originally established by Herod, which had been erected upon ancient burial grounds. The inn, along with the main market and the harbor area, were clearly separated from the more Hellenized portion intended to serve the king's palace. Jacob headed toward the familiar caravan encampment. As he walked, he did his best to revel in his new-found independence.

Jamal had insisted that Jacob enjoy the hospitality of his inn as an honored guest. Before, Jacob would never have dared enter such fine accommodations. What was more, the Syrian merchant had insisted upon giving Jacob a purse of gold, and promised more besides. Then, even more of a surprise, Jamal had made a gift of his own ceremonial dagger. Everyone in Tiberias knew the knife. It was the length of Jacob's forearm and possessed a hilt of solid gold. Two emeralds adorned the scabbard, which was silver gilt and curved like the blade it held. Jamal had shown Jacob how to wear it in the traditional style, giving him a belt of woven silk, light as a feather and strong as iron, and threaded the scabbard's ring through the belt so that it dangled loosely, yet could not fall away. Jacob had stammered his thanks, but Jamal had shrugged the words away.

Jacob knew he should be pleased with his sudden elevation in status. But a long-past conversation with Alban remained etched in his memory. Occasionally his guardian would speak about his life as a centurion. Not often. Usually such moments came over campfires, late at night, when all the caravan slept except the guards. The stars overhead and the moon created a silver sea, and even the wind seemed to sleep. Such moments were made for secrets, of which Alban had more than his share.

Alban had once told Jacob of his first meeting with Linux, about how he had envied the Roman officer for the ease with which he had moved through the corridors of Roman power. At that time, Alban's burning ambition was to rise further and higher than any lowly Gaul had ever achieved. General, perhaps. Senator. Or even Consul . . .

But during the time he had served Pontius Pilate, Alban had learned a vital lesson: The closer one came to the center of power, the greater the risks. A consul could destroy a man on a whim. The result was that most people sought safety through various deceits. They molded themselves around the prevailing forces, until their spines and their spirits both were permanently warped. They no longer recognized themselves, or remembered why they had sought power in the first place. And they lived in constant fear. No alliance was lasting, no friend true.

Jacob pondered these things as he walked the road leading down to the Tiberias harbor on Galilee, then followed the shore until the road cut away, leaving the town behind and leading on to the open area where the caravans gathered. Deep in troubling thought, he recalled how Alban's face had seemed to age with the telling. He heard Alban's final words echo with each footstep: *A man of power is a prize bargainer. Whatever he offers you, he will take more in return. Your challenge is to know yourself. Give only what you can, while remaining steadfast to your own truths.*

Julia had traveled the path to the caravanserai so often she could not tally the trips, but never had her mind been in the state it was today. Two things lay heavy upon her heart. She still had not worked through her emotions about her father. The man who had kept silent about the true circumstances of her mother, of her. She found it difficult to resume her little ruse of the loving daughter. Respectful? Yes, she could manage that. Obedient? Yes. She would not have thought to question him . . . although the idea of an arranged marriage further weighed down her spirit. There were so many uncertainties, unknowns. Would there be any place for love—the kind of love her parents portrayed, even with the bitter truth her mother had quietly carried all these years?

Besides that heavy burden, today she carried another. The packet resided in a secret pocket of her shawl, carefully sewn by Zoe. Whose hand would be reaching out to accept the covert message? Would she know him when the time came?

Again she rehearsed the sentence. *The rains have come to Jerusalem*, the words she must listen for.

He was to be wearing a red band on his forehead and carrying a basket of healing potions for the animals. Surely that should be enough for her to positively identify the next courier.

In her state of anxiety she didn't know whether to hasten her steps or to drag her feet. But as she neared the compound and heard the noise of the complaining camels, her pace quickened. She had not heard plans of a caravan's departure. It must be a very small entourage or her father would have mentioned it. She must get the message passed on in time.

But first she must go to her father's tent and deliver these provisions. She was to act normal. Perform the same routine she always did. Draw no attention to herself or to what would occur.

Thankfully her father was in the tent, not out surveying his next caravan. A chill breeze was blowing, and Julia was glad to step inside to the relative comfort of the tent's sturdy walls.

Her father's head came up at the sound of the flap being lifted. "Ah—you have brought my tea. Is there any chance that it might still hold some warmth?"

"Zoe wrapped it carefully in many towels," she answered, lowering her basket. "Let us see."

The tea was not hot, but certainly had warmth. She poured a cup and passed it to her father. After his first sip he smiled again. "Perhaps it will thaw my stiff body. I cannot manage the cold like I used to. It comes with getting older, I am told."

Julia forced a smile. Her mind could not turn from the duty still ahead. "Will you have a cake?"

In answer he reached out a hand. "I have little time to visit today. I must go through these final documents I am sending off with a servant."

"I understand." In truth Julia was thankful that she did not need to tarry long. Her nervousness demanded that she get her task accomplished as quickly as possible. "I hear one of the camels has just calved. I will choose a name and come back later to pick up the basket."

He smiled, but his eyes had already turned back to the parchment he held. "You are my blessing."

The very words made Julia's heart skip a beat, but her father did not notice her discomfort. Would he think she was his blessing if he knew what she was about to do?

She pushed at the tent flap and stepped out into the raw air. She drew a few ragged breaths to quiet her nerves, then crossed to where the camels groaned and quarreled. In the corner a cow stood crosswise, protectively guarding her newborn. Julia recognized her as Zadu, one of the older females. The animal had given them many fine offspring over her years. Julia crossed to her, rubbing a trembling hand up and down the shaggy neck.

"Are you as anxious as I am?" she whispered to the grumbling beast. "Look at your beautiful baby. No wonder you worry about him. Or is it her? I cannot tell as it sleeps. You are a good mother, and your babe will be fine. Stop your worrying. Just . . ."

She was about to say more when she became aware of another's presence moving up to the other side of the animal. A hand carrying a basket appeared on the other side of Zadu, matching what Julia had been told. Then over the camel's neck she saw some unruly dark hair spilling over a red band tied across the forehead.

A low, masculine voice said, "The rain came to Jerusalem."

For one sickening moment she forgot what she was to do next. And then it came to her—she was to draw the sign of the fish. Julia reached out and with the walking stick she held in a shaking hand drew a fish in the sand.

The dark hair disappeared as its owner knelt on the camel's other side. Julia saw a hand withdraw a jar of ointment from the basket and begin to remove the cork at its neck. Then one finger reached down and drew a fish in the dust.

"Look as if you are studying the newborn's limbs," she heard him caution quietly.

Julia went to her knees in the sand. It was only then that their eyes met beneath the camel standing above them. She couldn't stop her gasp of disbelief.

He was the first to respond. "Is this some jest?" he hissed. "Someone's poor idea of a hoax?"

Julia did not know if the flash from the dark eyes was from

surprise—or anger. She felt her cheeks burn. "If it is," she replied in kind, "it is not of my doing."

She rose quickly to her feet, anger and humiliation filling every part of her being.

How could this be? How could they have sent her to meet this—this rude young ruffian who had spoken to her so callously back when he assumed that she, Jamal's daughter, was a mere servant or slave. "Water the camels," he had ordered as though he had some right to tell her what to do. She shook out her robe and turned on her heel.

But he had circled the camel, and his quick hand now stopped her. "Wait."

The one word only served to anger her further. "If you do not release me, I will scream and my father's guards will—"

"I am Jacob, one of your father's guards."

"Then you know who I am. Why are you treating me like . . . ?" But she was so angry she could not complete the thought.

He released his hold, but he seemed prepared to grasp her again if she tried to leave.

"Please give me a moment to recover," he said, taking a long breath. "I was not expecting the daughter of Jamal. I had no idea that he had any association with . . . with believers."

"My father chooses his own path," she spat out. "I have chosen another."

"Of course," he murmured, lowering his voice, no doubt a caution to her also.

She did control her tone but the words still held a sting. "And I did not expect them to ask me to take a message to a caravan guard," she hissed. "Someone trained to maim and kill, with no regard for life, seems an unlikely candidate for passing messages of peace and hope." The last words were flung at him like barbs from a thorn bush, and even in her emotional turmoil she recognized the incongruity.

His own eyes flashed. "Other guards take the path of strife. It does not mean that I do."

Julia took a deep breath, forcing her clenched fists to open at her sides. All she wanted to do was to escape.

He went on, sounding courteous but firm. "I believe you came to deliver and receive a message."

She nodded and tried hard to rein in her whirling thoughts.

"It is important that we not allow our . . . our differences to endanger the lives of others," he continued quietly, running a skilled hand along the newborn's flank.

Of course he was right. She reached up to pull her shawl more closely around her against the wind's icy fingers.

He spoke again, his voice low and controlled. "Shall we begin again?"

She merely nodded.

"The rain came to Jerusalem."

"You said it incorrectly. It is to be stated, 'The rains have come to Jerusalem.' "

They looked at one another, and he gave a crooked grin, then shrugged. "I think I have practiced too many times. But I have often thought of the meaning of those words since first hearing them. They contain a truth concerning our Messiah."

Julia had failed to catch any underlying significance in the phrase, but suddenly it came very clear. *Yes, of course.* The rains brought hope and life for the thirsty land just as the Messiah had brought hope and life for the people. She again met the gaze of the young man, this time with what could have been respect.

Jacob withdrew the leather satchel. Before accepting it Julia drew the packet from her hidden pocket and said, "This is for you. Your instructions for delivery are included under the outer flap."

Jacob nodded and slipped the packet inside his cloak. Julia took the satchel and tucked it away.

When he turned to leave, Julia realized how tall he was. How solidly built. No wonder her father had hired him for one of his guards.

He turned back to say, "It is an honor—and a burden—to have been selected for this work." He looked at her evenly. She wondered if she saw a twinkle of humor in his eyes. "And to have this opportunity for a better meeting than our first one."

"My name is Julia," she said, just loud enough for him to hear as he moved away.

The following day Julia observed Jacob from the concealment of a large desert cedar tree, her favorite place in the market square. She had often played in its shade as a child, when the servants would let her tag along as they did their shopping. They had been charmed by her spritely spirit, one that not even her mother's uncertain status could diminish. Julia had known even at that early age that things were not quite as they should be in the household. Her mother had carried a secret shadow with her, close as a winter cloak. She bore this sorrow with a queen's dignity, though, putting on no airs, and thus endearing herself to all the household staff.

Only now could Julia truly understand her mother's remarkable strength of character. There were numerous households about the city with two wives, or a wife and consort, and they mostly were filled with strife. The first wife would lord it over the lesser woman, who would act in a haughty manner, commanding a respect her position did not justify. It was an impossible situation, for being the household's "other woman" meant she was neither servant nor mistress, but occupied some nebulous position in between. Helena could easily have demanded a stronger role, especially as Jamal's true wife was six days' hard journey to the north. But Helena expected nothing, asked for nothing. She carried herself with tragic poise, and would have played the servant herself had others within the household allowed it. The more Julia understood, the more she admired her mother.

And now her father was arranging Julia's marriage, and every morning she awoke with the knowledge that she was another day closer to that dreaded departure. She would be leaving the only home she had ever known. Here was safety. Here were friends, old and new. Here was her community of believers. Here was her beloved mother.

Her father could not fathom why Julia was not more excited at the prospect of marrying into a powerful Baghdad family. And Julia understood her father's frustration. After all, he was elevating her position significantly. No longer would she be merely the daughter of a consort, little more than a slave. Instead she would have the position her mother had yearned for, yet knew she could never claim.

But Julia did not want to wed a stranger, particularly one who did not share her faith. And what would become of her mother? What would the groom's family think of a mere consort's daughter? How would she be treated? And what recourse would she have, utterly isolated, trapped in some distant city?

Julia wiped a hand across her face, trying to rid her mind of such thoughts much as she would a cloud of flies. There were more pressing issues than her own status should the truth ever be discovered.

Julia watched Jacob casually walk down to the stones that rimmed the small fishing port. Nets dried upon makeshift racks to either side of three overturned vessels. Jacob leaned against one of the boats that had not gone out that day, and turned to survey the shore. His gaze drifted across her and continued on. Julia watched as he picked up a rock and sent it skimming out over the water. The lake was the color of washed slate this day, and the clouds brooded low and heavy.

When Jacob turned and started toward the synagogue wall, Julia concluded the day's weather suited her mood perfectly.

Jacob saw Julia leave the tree's shade and walk toward him. He had seen her when he started down the cobblestones to the upturned boats. Concern lurked in the back of his mind about the possibility of sharing Latif's fate with these message exchanges, but he also found himself caught by the lure of Julia's flashing dark eyes and graceful motion. She also possessed her father's aura of barely repressed energy. But in her it emerged as a magnetic fire. Even on such a gloomy day, she seemed to catch the light so it followed her across the square.

Unlike most who called Tiberias home, Julia wore the traditional garb seen in a conservative Judean household. This was especially remarkable for the daughter of a Syrian trader, one who took great pride in letting it be known he bowed the knee to no god. It was no surprise that Jacob had mistaken her for a servant girl the first time they met. Julia's only adornments this day were the bracelets her father had given her. Both her shawl and outer robe were of fine quality wool, yet so frequently washed as to appear more cloud grey than the original sky blue.

But what struck Jacob was the fact that though she was not angry this time, even looked at peace, her eyes held a deep sorrow.

When she hesitated by the synagogue's outer gate, the first words he spoke surprised him. "I was not responsible for Latif's capture."

She looked a question at him, then offered a brief dip of her head. Jacob noted the elderly servant who followed at a discreet distance. He nodded his acknowledgment of her, receiving only an obvious inspection in response.

Besides its position on a major north-south trade route, the fact that Tiberias was primarily a Greek city was no doubt another reason Jamal had chosen it for his second home. Though the ancient burial grounds lay beyond the central town's boundaries, many observant Judeans considered the entire region unclean. As a result, the synagogue was a somewhat derelict affair, and also quite small for a city of this size and commercial power. Herod likely had no interest in its condition, feeling himself above the religious masses that cared about such things.

Julia stood next to the synagogue's perimeter wall, facing in toward the main building. "I stopped by my father's tent last night before leaving the encampment," she said without looking at him. "He has received confirmation from his trading partner in Jerusalem that the drover Latif is still being held by the Temple priests."

Jacob wondered if she realized that Latif was also the messenger. "I would give anything to have him standing here, safe and away from danger."

"Tiberias is not safe either."

"Anywhere is safer for us than Jerusalem." Jacob risked a quick look around. No one was even glancing at them since they stood an appropriate distance apart, the trusted servant nearby. "I did not know you were a follower."

"You know nothing about me."

He nodded agreement, both at the truth of her words and the underlying message. That he was a simple caravan guard, and she the daughter of a powerful trader. "I would like . . ." He started over. "I want to apologize."

Julia turned her head toward him. Only now Jacob could not

bring himself to meet her eyes. "The way I spoke with you at the caravan site . . ." He shook his head. "It was very wrong of me. I expected that . . . Well, even so I should not have addressed anyone—man or woman—in such a manner. This is not what our Lord taught. It is all rather new to me. And then the courier assignment, and I had no idea what or who to expect. I understand now their wisdom in choosing a . . . a woman."

She drew circular patterns aimlessly in the dust with her sandal. "My father often says that to admit a mistake is a sign of great character."

"Your father is a very wise man."

Julia took her time responding. "My father is indeed wise, but he is not a believer." She took a breath and squared her shoulders, again facing toward the wall of the synagogue. "I have another message for you. They say it is very important." She hesitated for only a moment. "But first they want to meet you. They were expecting the satchel to be delivered by another. They fear the chain has been disrupted."

"Who do you mean?"

"I cannot say. I have been instructed that we are not to know anyone beyond our own messenger. It is too dangerous. We cannot leave an easy path that our enemies might follow."

"I am new. Quite by accident, really. Before Latif was taken, he suspected he was being watched and asked for my help."

"Latif was a courier?" She seemed surprised.

"I wondered if you knew."

"I know almost nothing. Yesterday was my first . . . my first encounter also."

He smiled. "It did not go too well, did it?"

She smiled too, feeling a bit rueful. "I am aware Latif was one of my father's drovers. Nothing more. I had no idea he was a follower or served in this way. Does my father . . . ?"

Jacob weighed the question carefully. "Perhaps not. No, I would think not. We must be careful to give nothing away. Does he know that you are one of us?"

"Oh no. He must not. He would never allow . . . Never."

Jacob nodded. So there was much more to this young woman than her flashing eyes, her fiery temperament. He wondered what other secrets she carried.

But she was already moving away toward her servant woman. But she turned back again, her cheeks flushed. "I forgot to tell you," she whispered. "You are to go at once to the cypress tree by the old village well. They are awaiting you there."

He nodded, watching as she walked away. The distance increasing between them, though, was not nearly as wide as that between the fact that she was Jamal's daughter and he was Jamal's lowly caravan guard.

CHAPTER FOURTEEN

The Samaritan Plains

AFTER THEIR VISIT to Neapolis, Abigail and the other refugees from Jerusalem traveled a relatively short distance, less than seven Roman miles, from Neapolis to Sebaste. They were accompanied by several whom Philip had baptized, while the woman named Helzebah and three of her extended family rode ahead to alert the village. The group of believers was welcomed into the town by nearly all its citizens, some waving palm leaves. As they approached the central square, the first drops of rain began to fall along with distant rumbles of thunder.

They all hurried into the inn, where the entire main floor was one large room. Helzebah, the woman who some years previous had met Jesus by Sychar's well, already had organized the townsfolk to shift tables aside, and she now instructed on the care of the animals, begging everyone within calling distance for food and blankets and fodder. The children were fed and led upstairs, where pallets were laid out upon the rough-plank floor. The fire's heat and the warm food and the press of many bodies soon dispelled the storm's damp chill.

Philip rose and spoke once again. He answered their questions in his thoughtful, careful manner. He spoke of the times Jesus had discussed his death, showing he had willingly given his life so all might receive the gift of eternal life. He invited those gathered to pray, to accept the risen Lord as their Messiah and Savior.

Abigail watched the woman from Sychar, how she drank in Philip's words with almost breathless eagerness. Abigail realized that such ardor had drifted away from her own life. She knew that here and now the woman held as great a lesson for her personally as anything she might hear from the Lord's own disciple.

And then a villager stood from among the women listeners gathered in the back, a small, limp form in her arms, and made her way through the crowd to the front, where Philip stood. She knelt before him and held out her baby, murmuring something Abigail could not hear. Philip motioned for Alban to join him, and they each placed a hand on the child and began to pray. The believers immediately understood what was happening and joined in the prayer, their voices rising in a cadence both familiar and beautiful.

"The fever is gone!" the woman suddenly called out over the sounds of prayer. "I have my baby back! Oh, thank you, thank you," and then Abigail heard Philip telling her to give thanks to God. The group stood as one, arms raised along with their voices, now praising God for this miracle. Others pressed forward to ask for their own miracles of healing or deliverance.

Once more Abigail joined her prayer with the others, only this time the petition rose from deep inside her heart. Asking for the fire of the Holy Spirit to be kindled anew. And for her to reach toward God with that hunger, that yearning, that desire to know and serve and love in His name. All around her shouts of wonder and joy rang out as others received the touch they had requested in their bodies and souls.

It was very late that night when the villagers finally dispersed to their own homes and the Jerusalem travelers settled down for the night. Abigail climbed the steps, candle in hand, to find Dorcas. She lay down beside her little daughter and stretched her arm across the sleeping form, weary but full of thankfulness for what she had seen and heard. And what she had experienced herself. "Thank you, Jesus . . ." was all she could remember whispering.

The next morning they traveled north to Bemesilis, and the day after to Yishub and Gitta. At each community, another Jerusalem family found relatives and friends to welcome them and help them establish a new place for themselves. Many from each succeeding village traveled along with them, asking questions about this Jesus along the way.

By the time they reached Narbata, people from the previous villages had swelled their ranks. Their group was now larger than when they had left Jerusalem. They ate another communal meal, Philip spoke, and more were baptized.

Abigail was with Martha on a bench surrounded by local women sitting on reed mats. They were asking questions about Jesus' teachings, about how the Master had fulfilled the prophecies of old. Abigail usually waited for Martha to respond, but she would draw Abigail into the discussion in ways that gave her confidence.

Dorcas was the first to notice Linux standing beneath a massive creosote tree. Abigail watched her daughter run across the square and hold her arms up to him. Linux lifted her up while all the women turned to stare at him. He stepped toward them and said, "I beg your forgiveness for my interruption, sisters."

One close to Abigail's bench murmured, "That I would ever live to see the day when a Roman officer would call me *sister*."

Linux said, "Abigail, when you are finished, may I have a word?"

She realized the women would not continue to listen so long as Linux hovered nearby. She excused herself, rose from the bench, and drew him away.

"I did not mean to disrupt your lesson," Linux said, placing Dorcas back on the ground.

"Martha can teach them far better than I."

"I doubt that most sincerely. She gives them the facts. You sweeten the lesson with your heart and your joy."

Abigail was about to contradict him when Dorcas said, "Mama is happy."

"Indeed?"

Dorcas nodded, her curls bouncing with the movement of her head.

"I cannot see how anyone could be near you for very long, Dorcas, and not be happy," Linux said.

Dorcas smiled. "You are happy too, Uncle Linux?"

He did not answer but led the two of them to the stone wall marking the village boundary. He settled Dorcas down on its edge, and said to them both, "I must depart tomorrow—"

"*No!*" Dorcas called out, with a child's ability to leap from one emotion to the next. Her face showed very real distress.

"I must go." Linux addressed his words to the little girl, but Abigail knew he spoke to her. "Caesarea is a bit over a day's journey to the north and west. Tonight you all will rest here, then your band is turning eastward and heading to Ginae. The day after, you will arrive at Nain, your own destination."

"But . . ." Dorcas was gripping his tunic with both small fists. "No, uncle, you must come with us."

"You have the gift of making friends wherever you go," he said gently. And once again, Abigail was certain he was speaking to her as much as to the child. "I have talked with the elders. The remaining travelers are well escorted and protected. And Alban—"

"No, please," Dorcas continued her protest. "Come *with* us."

"I would like nothing better," Linux replied, laying his hand on her head. "But I am ordered to report to the commandant at Caesarea."

Dorcas looked like she was going to cry. "After that?"

Linux tipped up the little face with a finger. "Dear child. I will come back."

"When?"

"The very instant I am allowed to rejoin you, I shall." For the first time, he glanced at Abigail. "That is, if your mother will permit me to visit."

Dorcas looked at her mother.

"Linux must do his duty, as must we all," Abigail said simply but firmly. "But we will miss his company, won't we?"

Dorcas clung to his arm, looking from one to the other with her eyes full of questions and sorrow.

Abigail studied the two of them as from a great distance. The gentle soldier, even his countenance remade by his growing faith. The change in Linux might be more subtle than the healing of Abigail's injured leg, back in Jerusalem during those early days after the Messiah's return to his Father. Even so, the transformation was no less miraculous. Gone was the sardonic humor masking a bitter rage over fate and his brother's brutal hand. Gone too the need to force Abigail to be his own. In its place resided a kind spirit, a caring nature, and a hunger to grow in faith.

Dorcas now fell to weeping at the prospect of losing her new friend.

Abigail gathered the child into her arms, and Dorcas buried her face on her mother's shoulder.

"I must be on my way." Linux reached out to stroke her curls. "I will leave before the sun is up tomorrow."

Abigail said into Dorcas's ear, "Be a brave girl, and let us bid our friend farewell with a smile."

Dorcas simply shook her head.

"It is so much better if he carries your happiness with him when he leaves."

The little girl's head moved back and forth more vigorously. "I am not happy, Mama. I miss him already."

Abigail was about to say that she did also. But she caught herself and merely said, "I know."

CHAPTER FIFTEEN

Tiberias

WHEN JACOB RETURNED to Jamal's estate to meet with his master, he sensed some change in the atmosphere. For some moments he worried that perhaps Jamal had learned of his meeting with Julia. He sat in the courtyard watching people scurry about, listening to shouts and curses rise from within the house, and felt the pressure mount. *Beware the hospitality of princes.* The words echoed about his mind, and Jacob felt sweat trickle down his spine.

The austere servant with the hawk's beak and hooded eyes finally sought him out. He eyed Jacob with the same dark humor a hunter might give his next prey. "The master will see you now."

Jacob followed the servant down a long passage to gilded double doors leading to the private family chambers. The servant gave a mocking bow, motioning Jacob toward a side alcove. Jacob found his throat so dry he could not swallow.

The alcove was in fact a corridor, lined in stone and sloping downward. Jacob's way was lit by oil lamps flickering in recessed niches. He passed through a second door, this one bound by iron and studded with nails, and descended a curving set of stone stairs. He entered a room almost as large as the interior courtyard, with a roof shaped like barrels cut lengthwise and supported by massive stone columns. Torches burned from iron staves.

Jamal's voice rumbled with gloomy ferocity. "Over here."

The merchant prince was seated behind a massive table, large enough to seat twenty. Packets of frankincense were piled at one end, the red wax glistening in the torchlight. Jamal was busy writing upon a leaf of parchment. Without looking up, he motioned to a copper pot simmering upon a brazier behind him. "Refill my cup, and pour yourself some while you're at it."

The terse order was far from the talkative and jovial man Jacob had encountered on his last visit. Jacob was reluctant to pour the tea for fear he would not be able to mask his tremors. But his throat cried out for liquid, and he did as he was told.

The quill stopped its scratching and pointed at the chair opposite Jamal. "Sit."

Jacob did so, nearly spilling the hot tea. The merchant's head remained lowered over his parchment. Jacob took time to study his surroundings. Here was displayed the merchant's wealth—casks of fine spices, bound chests that Jacob assumed were filled with gold and silver coin, piles of tapestry, elegant robes embossed with gemstones. Rank upon rank of clay amphorae stood in their traditional iron stands, like so many soldiers on parade. The air was aromatic with a myriad of scents, all pleasant. And a kingdom's bounty in frankincense lay heaped on one edge of the merchant's table.

Jamal tossed the quill aside, folded the parchment, and pulled toward him one of the oil lamps to melt a bar of red wax. When enough had dripped down to cover the parchment's fold, he drew out a seal on a gold chain from around his neck and applied it to the wax.

Jamal slipped the chain and seal back beneath his robes and declared, "I have a problem."

Jacob did not know what was expected of him, so he simply said, "Sire."

"Two problems, actually. My caravan from Damascus is late. A week overdue. And no word to explain why." Jamal shoved his chair back so hard it smacked against the stone wall. He rose, linked his hands behind his back, and began pacing. "If we've lost that shipment of frankincense, and if indeed my Damascus caravan has been taken, my business could be facing ruin."

Jacob found his muscles beginning to relax. Whatever it was that troubled the merchant, it was not the encounter with Julia. "Perhaps they have merely been delayed."

Jamal arrived at the chamber's corner and wheeled about. His sandals slapped softly upon the flagstones as he moved back across the room. "Perhaps."

"The weather has been terrible. Perhaps they decided to wait in Damascus for the storms to settle."

"Send a guard to find out."

Jacob started to protest that he had no such authority, then realized if Jamal made such an order, Jacob would have no trouble in passing it on. He suggested, "Three guards traveling together would have a better chance of going out and returning safely, sire."

"Make it three then." Jamal continued to pace. "In such uncertain times, a merchant's destiny is never secure. Do you know, I cannot remember the last time I slept easy through a night."

"I am sorry to hear that, sire."

"Months, certainly. Perhaps even years."

Jacob waited a moment, then prompted, "You said there were two problems."

"Yes, yes. Indeed so. I have just received word that a shipment of frankincense has arrived in Joppa." The pace of sandals against the stones increased. "My trader in Joppa is worried. He fears that others know of what he holds for me."

Jacob then understood why he was there. "You wish to send me, sire."

Jamal halted in midstride. He still had not looked directly at the young man.

Jacob went on, "I am ready to serve, if that is your desire."

The merchant's gaze rose slowly, almost reluctantly. "I had meant to ask if you would favor me by taking Latif's place. But . . . I have no caravan with which you can travel safely."

"Did Latif find safety in Yussuf's company?" Jacob shook his head. "We must assume all your caravans are being watched."

"I suppose I could send you out with a company of guards."

"Sire, there could only be one reason for a group of your guards to travel without a caravan. Especially if rumors have already attached you to the frankincense trade. The Roman tax collectors and thieves would descend on us like vultures on a fresh kill."

"Did you not hear what I just said?" Jamal's fist crashed upon the table. "I must retrieve that treasure while it is still mine to claim!"

This time, the merchant's fury did not touch Jacob. He slowly stood to face his master. "What we need, sire, is a means to mask my travels. Perhaps as a servant attached to a wealthy household, if you know of someone who travels west . . ." Jacob stopped because the merchant now stood as if chiseled in stone. "What is it, sire?"

But Jamal's attention was already fastened upon something far beyond the stone walls. "Wait here."

Julia was surprised when her father appeared in the inner courtyard that held her mother's secluded nook. Days like this, he became so involved in his work he often forgot to eat. Yet there he stood, offering them what to Julia looked like a forced smile.

"Ah, here you are. I have been searching all over." He lowered himself onto the seat next to Helena. "I have some news for you, my dear."

Helena's eyes, which showed both interest and apprehension, turned to look at him.

"It has occurred to me it is time to allow you a reprieve from this little town. I have arranged a trip to Joppa. You will leave today." He turned to include Julia. "Both of you. That young man, Jacob, will be going with you to see to your needs on the route."

Julia could see that Helena's eyes were shadowed with uncertainty. "But why, my lord?"

Jamal's gaze flitted around the garden, seeming to touch everywhere yet see nothing. "Do I need a reason to treat my two most favored with a trip to a place where there is refinement, culture? I have kept you secluded here for far too long."

Julia was beginning to feel her stomach muscles tighten. She tried to moisten her dry lips. She finally managed, "Will you travel with us?"

Jamal appeared to be only more preoccupied. "That won't be possible. I have far too much that needs my attention here." Clearly he saw consternation on both their faces, for he hastily added, "Perhaps later I might be able to join you there. It would bring me such pleasure to show my two ladies the delights of a coastal city. The Mediterranean Sea is such a magnificent sight."

Julia's thoughts were running ahead. *The sea?* She doubted her father had any interest at all in the sea. It was clear to her the true reason for the trip lay elsewhere. What was her father scheming?

Helena still had not spoken. She looked too stunned to even move. Julia decided she must speak for them both. "I thought all your caravans were away just now."

"Yes, yes, they are. But I was fortunate that a trusted friend is leaving today. I thought it a good opportunity to attach you to his caravan. It is a small group—but well guarded. And you will have Jacob as your personal servant and protector." He brightened as though a new thought had just entered his mind. "It will be a great opportunity to begin selecting wedding garments, my dear. You will find the finest of silks in Joppa."

Julia felt like her heart was being squeezed by a powerful hand. She frantically sought for words to protest that she had no interest in anything to do with the marriage.

But Helena chose that moment to speak. "This is all very sudden, my lord."

"Yes, yes, but my friend leaves today. He is unable to delay. There is still enough time for you to make preparations." He rubbed his hands together in a show of enthusiasm. "And, Julia, my dear, since you will soon be traveling far beyond our borders to a much more settled, sophisticated part of the world, you do need some experience about what lies beyond Tiberias."

Helena asked quietly, "Can you not tell us the true reason?"

Jamal went utterly rigid. Only his eyes continued their rapid shifting. "I . . . I . . ."

"You do not trust us, my lord?"

His mouth worked several times. He finally was able to say, "More than I can ever tell you."

The two women simply looked at him.

His head drifted downward. His frame, even his hands went limp. "I face a very grave problem."

Helena moved so she might reach over and touch his hands. "With your business?"

"Very grave," he repeated.

Helena nodded, as though hearing far more than what the man

actually spoke. She said, "You are concerned that to tell us might endanger us as well. Is that it, my lord?"

Jamal looked at Helena, his eyes haunted. "I would not lose you for anything. But I need. . . ." He shook his head.

"You need someone you can trust, to serve you without question." Helena nodded once. "I live to do your bidding, my lord."

The love and the sorrow both were so strong in Helena's voice that Julia could hardly keep from weeping.

Jamal rose to his feet and stared at the two of them. When he spoke, his voice was coarsened by the emotions surging between Helena and him. "Get the maids to help you. You will be somewhat limited in what you can bring. Only one maid will be permitted to accompany you. That is the caravan's rule. And Jacob, of course. He will be your personal servant on this journey." Julia wondered why he was emphasizing that part of the plan, but she was full of questions about the whole arrangement. *And so sudden . . .*

"We will be ready to travel," Helena was saying. "As you have told us."

Jamal laid a hand lightly upon Helena's shoulder. Julia read relief in his eyes, and she again wondered why.

"I knew you would understand and agree to help, Helena. I am in your debt."

The rest of the morning was spent in frenzied activity. It did not help that the maids, led by Zoe, felt as confused by the whole event as Julia herself. This most unusual trip, announced only at the last moment, left them whispering their questions and surmises. Helena was of no assistance, having taken to her bed with one of her headaches. Julia worked alone, giving directives and helping to cram as much as they could into small bundles and bags. Who knew how long they would be gone.

Zoe worked in silence, but now and then Julia spotted her worried frown. She knew the servants sometimes heard news far ahead of others. She asked cautiously, "Will you tell me what it is?"

At length the woman turned to face Julia. "I have news. In truth, it should make us rejoice."

"Is it connected to this journey?"

"Not that I can see, which is why I hesitate to tell you. You already have so much—"

"Tell me. Please."

"It seems there has been a . . . a blessing for Jamal's Damascus family. . . ." Zoe looked away, then back to Julia. "His . . . his wife—in Damascus—has become a believer."

Julia stared at her dearest friend. *A believer?* Yes. Yes, that would be good news. It was always wonderful when someone else joined the followers. *But not yet my own mother* . . . she mourned silently. And now . . . now it seemed Jamal's wife had taken the step.

Did her father know about this? Was this related to their sudden departure . . . or another possibility . . . had his first wife learned of his other family and now was demanding their dismissal? There was no legal reason he should do so, but who knew what pressures could be brought to bear . . . ?

Julia turned to Zoe. "How did you learn of this?"

"One of the servants who has family in Damascus heard it from another who had traveled here. News within the fellowship of followers spreads quickly. Especially when it is joyous news. This woman knew I worked in the household of Jamal. She passed on the information when we met in the market yesterday morning."

Julia thanked Zoe for sharing the information and did her best to hide her disquiet. *Oh, Mother, how I wish this news were about you. . . .* Would she ever be able to care for her soul-weary mother?

CHAPTER SIXTEEN

Tiberias

JACOB WAS FAR more cheerful than he probably should have been. But the sense of unfolding adventure affected him in a rather startling manner. He tried to focus upon the dangers at hand, which were many. Probably more than he could count. He reminded himself that he was headed into the complete unknown. He was personally accountable to Jamal for the safety of his wife, his daughter, and an elderly servant. They traveled with a caravan of strangers. There was no one he knew he could trust, and they faced a long journey. But he also carried another burden. In the rush of preparations he also added one more duty. He slipped away to inform his secret contact that both he and Julia would be away for a number of days, and should important messages come through, other couriers would be required to relay them.

He returned breathless, hoping Jamal had not noticed his brief absence. Nothing seemed amiss as he joined the servants and guards as they hastened to make ready. In spite of all that, he caught himself whistling under his breath as he worked.

Jamal stood by the side of the Roman-style conveyance that already held Helena and Julia. "You will take great care for their safety?" he asked.

Jacob was well aware of both mother's and daughter's presence, only adding fervor to his response. "I shall guard them with my life, sire." He could feel the eyes of the two women upon him.

Jamal tugged at his mantle, kicked one of the carriage wheels, worked his lower lip with his teeth, and said, "This is not my caravan. These are not my guards, you understand." He now looked directly into Jacob's face.

"This caravan is run by an experienced master," Jacob said, attempting reassurance. "Your wares have traveled under his supervision before."

"Not with my wife and daughter."

Jacob glanced inside the draped cart and noted that Jamal's words caused a deep sorrow to spread across Helena's face. A similar wound was in Julia's expression, and she lifted the edge of her shawl and turned away. But Jacob was certain some deep regret was shared by the two women. Over what, he had no idea.

Jamal did not seem aware of their distress. He simply said, "Very well. Keep them safe and as comfortable as the roads permit."

Jacob's short bow was followed by a sincere promise. "I hear and obey, sire."

Jamal stepped closer to the conveyance, and his gaze moved between both women. "Take great care, my dear ones, and make this as short a visit as is possible. Neither our home nor my heart are complete with you gone."

Jacob stared at Jamal, then looked quickly away before his master would notice. Jacob could not comprehend the unspoken message, though he was sure there was one.

Once again sorrow welled up in Helena's gaze. Her parting

words, spoken with unusual directness, were, "I shall miss you, Jamal."

Jacob noticed that Julia did not speak nor look at her father. The cart moved into place, nearly at the front of the caravan to avoid the dust, as Jacob directed the horses pulling it. With one glance back he saw Jamal, standing feet spread and hand shading his eyes, leaning forward slightly as though wishing he too were leaving with the departing caravan.

What does it all mean? But Jacob doubted he would ever know.

Jacob now wore the traditional garb of a Damascus household servant, a simple cotton robe covered by a colorful mantle. His belt was woven with loops of silk, strong as iron mesh, to which he could attach knife and purse and letter pouch. The knife Jamal previously had given him was left in Tiberias. In its place he carried a simple blade of Damascus steel—now hidden in the bed pallet fastened among the bundles on one of the donkeys. Also among the packs was a sword and a second knife, long as his thigh, plus a small shield. Jacob had not thought he would take all of these with him, but Jamal had insisted. Such weapons would not be out of place for a servant entrusted with the lives of a wealthy merchant's wife and daughter.

Jamal had, of course, wanted to also send along a bevy of guards. But the caravan master had refused. The only guards permitted were his own—on this point the man had been hard as stone. The caravan carried goods from a dozen merchants, all of whom might wish the same privilege. But the master permitted only guards under his personal control. Jamal could hardly argue, since his own caravans carried the same rule.

Tethered to the back of the cart by a lead rope plodded the

same animal that had brought Jacob safely into Tiberias. Beside him, protesting slightly about leaving the herd, was a younger animal, as the second donkey from the passage across Samaria had gone lame. This animal, too, carried provisions for the trip.

Jacob's seat was on the outside of the curtains as was befitting a servant, and Zoe rode in the rear seat, as suited her station. The carriage was of a design mostly strange to Judea but common to the Romans. It was in fact a cart topped by a covering held aloft by four posts. The walls were heavy tapestries that could be rolled up or down, depending on the weather. The tapestries' exterior was simple and earthen colored. But as Jacob had helped the two women inside, he had seen the tapestries facing inward revealed bright displays of birds and gardens. On days like this, with a wintry edge to the wind, the interior was no doubt quite comfortable.

From time to time, hands parted the front drapes and a face appeared. Jacob was repeatedly drawn to the sight of Julia. She had removed her shawl, which made her appear rather bold, particularly for a Judean woman. It seemed to Jacob that the dark eyes held questions for which there were no answers. When the face disappeared again, he found himself still held by the memory of those eyes, like finely polished onyx. Jacob repeatedly told himself there was no future in such yearnings. But mental warnings held hardly more force than the call of a thrush from the thorn bush.

Once the Tiberian hills were behind them, the caravan came to a halt in the early afternoon. An abandoned Roman fortress brooded upon a hill to the north of the road. When the well had gone dry, the garrison had moved further north to the Samaritan plains. A few ragged market stalls still maintained a presence for travelers. Jacob withdrew coins from the bag Jamal had given him for the care of the women and went to purchase something for their refreshment. He was glad to find freshly picked pomegranates.

While the caravan's beasts rested and ate, the women remained just outside the carriage, walking around it to stretch cramped legs. Jacob hovered within calling distance, assuming the pose he had often seen house servants take—hands clasping opposing wrists, arms banded just below his ribs, eyes staring blankly. A pair of guards found sport in lingering where he could see them and snickering their disdain. Jacob ignored them. His masquerade was solid. Plus, there were worse duties than inconspicuously observing Julia.

The carriage was pulled by two matched steeds. By the time they again halted at sunset, the strain of pulling the heavy wagon had left the horses lathered and weary. Zoe prepared an evening meal at a small campfire while Jacob took his time grooming the horses. He gave them a small drink and a pair of oat handfuls, and then went back to grooming. He was so absorbed in his task that he did not notice Julia's approach until she spoke.

"Why do you not feed them a proper meal?"

"Mistress Julia—" He scrambled up awkwardly.

Julia pointed to where the horses nosed about their empty feed bags. "They have labored hard all day. Why do you leave them hungry?"

"If you give horses a full meal while they remain overheated, their innards will inflate and the animal will be in pain all night long." He went back to stroking the animal's side with the combing brush. "I'll let them cool awhile longer, then water and feed them once more."

Though he forced his concentration on the animals, he could feel Julia's gaze upon him. Finally she said, "My mother has retired, and Zoe and I are about to begin our evening prayers. We are wondering if you would like to join us."

Jacob turned to her, the comb dangling at his side. He swallowed, then said, "I would be honored, mistress."

He followed her back to the carriage. Two small stools had been set out by the rear portal near the fire. Jacob remained standing on its opposite side while Julia sat down beside Zoe. He had seen such scenes any number of times among believing Judeans, where servants were invited to join the family in times of prayer and worship. Jacob watched as the two draped traditional Judean shawls over their heads. He bowed his head as Zoe began reciting a Psalm from memory. " 'The Lord is my shepherd' " came the familiar words. Jacob found that he was able to ignore Julia's presence as he listened. Heads bent toward each other, one woman murmured her prayer, then the other. Finally he added his own petitions, for their safety upon the trip, for a quiet night, for Alban's recovery. And for Latif, wherever he was this night.

When they had completed the time of worship, Jacob remained as he was, waiting to be dismissed. Instead Julia said, "This Alban you speak of, he is the one who serves as my father's chief guard?"

"Yes, mistress."

"Did you indicate previously that he is your guardian?"

"That is correct, mistress." He hesitated, conscious again how wide the gap was between himself and this young woman. But he knew he must be truthful. "Alban was once the centurion leading the Capernaum garrison. I was his servant."

Both women registered surprise. "My father employs a Roman officer as a guard?"

"He could not have chosen better," Jacob replied. "Alban is from Gaul and trained in all the skills of a warrior. He served Pontius Pilate in the consul's final days, just after the death of our Lord. When he came to faith in Jesus, he was pressured to resign his commission."

He realized neither woman was satisfied with his half-told tale, so he went on. "When I was a child, my family's caravan was attacked by bandits on the Damascus Road. Alban rescued me. My sister escaped, though I did not know of it at the time. We were reunited only a few years back. In Jerusalem at a compound where the believers first gathered."

He knew with certainty how they viewed him now. An orphan who had been raised in service to a Roman. Granted a shred of independence, now in service to Jamal.

But Zoe's tone carried no disdain. "So much tragedy," she said softly. "Your family, they were Syrian?"

"No, they were Judean."

"Ah." Zoe nodded and sighed again.

Julia and Zoe rose and climbed the steps Jacob had set for them into the carriage. As Jacob handed up the two stools, Julia said, "My father is fortunate to have Alban—and you—to trust."

In the torchlight, her face held equal measures of sorrow and strength. He inclined his head. "Thank you, mistress."

CHAPTER SEVENTEEN

Caesarea

As Linux approached the hills ringing Caesarea, he spied a new well that had been dug in the shadow of the guard tower. A simple enough affair, it was a broad pit ringed in stone and sprouting three rough troughs for animals. Several tawdry stalls, little more than rags supported by sticks, provided traveling foot soldiers and drovers a crude meal for a few coins. The city was only two hours away, and such a public well might seem unnecessary. But to Linux it was a symbol of how lawless Judea was becoming. Caravans departing the Roman capital of the country could stop here and water their animals a final time, in case there was no safe haven beyond this point.

As the hills rose to either side and the road snaked through its final turns, Linux felt the old sentiments well up within him. When the city came into view, he rode straighter, his bearing that of a Roman officer entering a Roman city. Guards patrolling the arena's perimeter came to attention and saluted as he passed. Though Linux wore no uniform, they were alert to the scent of power and privilege.

But now, for the first time since entering military service, Linux felt uncomfortable with it all.

The highest hills flanked the beach. Caesarea anchored the end of the Plain of Sharon, which ran along the shore northward from Joppa and Apollonia. The hilltops of Caesarea all were crowned, some with clusters of palaces, others with temples. Jupiter shared the highest point with Saturn, of course. Those two sets of priests squabbled and bickered in every corner of the empire. Linux passed the consul's palace and the hippodrome, then halted by the newly completed garrison. The structure had been begun by Pontius Pilate, but work had continued only in fits and starts, requiring many years to finish. The barracks made up two sides of the compound, with stables lining the northern flank, baths and officers' quarters the south. Linux gave his mount to a stable hand and reported to the officer on duty. Assigned temporary quarters, he dumped his meager belongings and headed for the baths.

Entering the bath's main hall, the calderium, was a return to everything Linux had once known. A group of officers threw dice upon the stones, roaring laughter and crude comments as they gambled. In an alcove by the entrance, an oil lamp burned beneath a statue. Many passing soldiers dropped a coin into an adjoining bowl, another gamble for good fortune. Linux refused a slave's offer of assistance, but sent him for a clean uniform. After shaving himself, he bathed away the worst of the road, dressed, and then moved to the table in the last alcove, where a cold supper was laid out for the bathers.

As he selected fruit and bread for his plate, a man approached the table's other side. "You are Linux Aurelius, are you not?"

"I am." Linux studied him a moment. "Do we know each other?"

"I served under the Legate Bruno Aetius. You were pointed out to me once."

"I thought Aetius took all his officers with him to Damascus."

The Roman hesitated, then dipped a knife into a cup of wine. "Some of us requested the opportunity to remain. A few. Not many."

As the officer was speaking, he traced a curving line upon the tablecloth, the wine forming a crude symbol. As soon as he was done, the officer spilled a bit more wine on the image, then slid a platter over the stain. And waited.

Linux had seen such drawings with increasing frequency. The sign had started appearing after the Temple priests had begun their persecutions. A modest symbol, easily mistaken for something else. The curving line was drawn to a point, then reversed to dip down before crossing over near the start, forming the outline of a fish.

For believers, the meaning was as powerful as it was clear. The sign of the fish signified the last Sabbath meal between the Messiah and his disciples. It was a symbol of peace. Of safety. Of a fellow believer.

Linux said softly, "You are an answer to prayer."

The officer nodded and murmured, "The stable yards. Tomorrow at this hour."

Linux blinked, and the man was gone.

Late the next afternoon, Linux wandered over as instructed to the stables where six men stood admiring a new stallion. Though young, the horse was clearly bred for battle, with a fiery eye and an impatient stamp as an officer swung himself into the saddle. "I am Grattus," he said to Linux. "The unwashed lad holding the reins of your mount there is the scourge of my existence, Octavius."

The mounted young man bore himself with an aristocrat's languor, but his gaze was fierce, and his grip on Linux's hand hard as stone. "My commanding officer would be in dire straits without me, and he knows it."

"Linux Aurelius at your service."

"We're off to check the road north, and perhaps dine with an old friend."

The young deputy added, "Who does not expect our arrival."

"He is a Roman centurion. He should expect bandits at any moment."

Grattus did not bother to introduce the others, customary for an officer leading a patrol of common soldiers. Linux swung up onto his obviously well-fed and rested horse, and they left the garrison and followed the road along the shore, past the port and the main markets, then up to the first line of hills, where they halted.

Grattus pointed out several landmarks while his young officer surveyed the road behind and the foot soldiers trotted at their rear. Ahead of them lay the fishing villages of Dora, Bucolon, and finally Sycaminum at the point where Mount Carmel met the sea. The Mediterranean waters sparkled with a coppery hue beneath the descending sun. A fishing vessel plied its way south, its sail a burnished shield in the western glow. For once, there were neither clouds nor any hint of storm.

Grattus asked, "What say you, Octavius?"

"All is clear, sire."

"Very well." He touched the horse's flanks with his heels and led them down the hillside trail. The road wove its way back and forth before arriving at a small cove. The rocky shoreline was arrayed with half a dozen Roman villas. Grattus glanced around, then motioned for one of the foot soldiers to pound upon the outer portal of the nearest dwelling. As they waited, Grattus said quietly, "We are registered with the guard captain as traveling to this destination. Your name was included."

A servant opened the gate, clearly expecting them, and bowed them inside. More servants emerged to care for their mounts. Inside the main door of the villa the three were greeted in the formal Roman fashion, with bowls to clean their hands and fresh towels. The foot soldiers arranged themselves in the courtyard to wait. Eventually they were led into a central court, where their host rose to greet them.

Grattus introduced the older gentleman as Cornelius, senior centurion within the Italian Guard, the preeminent brigade in Judea. The vast majority of soldiers stationed in Judea and Syria were conscripts drawn from Rome's outermost regions. In contrast, the Italian Guard was staffed by Rome's elite. There were rarely more than two hundred of these guardsmen in all of Judea. Their senior centurion would rank only a trifle below that of the Jerusalem commandant. Linux had once been assigned to their ranks, before becoming an officer on Pilate's personal staff.

As Linux responded to the formal greetings, acknowledging in turn the centurion's wife and sons, he gradually realized why Grattus had been so careful during their journey and arrival.

The house servants and the centurion's personal troops now also entered the center court, along with the foot soldiers who had accompanied Grattus. And several Judeans, whom Cornelius identified as neighbors and friends. The Judeans were all dressed in the Hellenized manner, with flowing robes and oiled hair.

But it was not their mere presence that required secrecy. When all were gathered and silence descended over the throng, Grattus said, "I greet you in the name of the Most High God, his Son Jesus Christ, and the Holy Spirit."

And all the gathering, men and women, officers and common foot soldiers, master and servants, Romans and Judeans, responded in one voice, "Amen."

"He is risen," Cornelius declared.

"He is risen indeed!" rang back from the crowd.

CHAPTER EIGHTEEN

The Megiddo Plains

THE MUCH-REDUCED GROUP turned northwest, Abigail noted. As the elders had assured Linux before he left, the small entourage was escorted by a host of villagers, mostly men, but a few women who refused to end the lessons just yet. Dorcas's mouth turned down at the corners when she remembered Linux's departure. As they prepared to set off upon the road, the little girl asked once more when Abigail thought Linux would be coming back. And her mother repeated that she did not know, but it "likely would be soon."

Dorcas rode upon the donkey, cuddling in the soft blanket, woven in a pattern of alternating squares, that she used when sleeping. Even at midday Abigail was glad for her winter cloak. The winds had subsided, though the weather remained unseasonably cold. When the sun and the trek finally warmed them, Dorcas turned and stared at the empty road behind them, then wondered aloud how Linux would find them again.

Despite the late season, this central region of Samaria remained lush and green. Abigail noted that the road was sheltered by groves of olive trees. Grapevines climbed the slopes rising to the north, and fields of winter wheat flickered silver and gold in the gentle breeze. As they approached the village of Ginae just after midday, the air was filled with the rich fragrance of autumn fruit.

That afternoon and on into the evening, Philip spoke yet again to a large group. Abigail recognized faces among the women, for whole families had traveled along for the opportunity to meet with them once again. Most of their questions were no longer about whether Jesus was the Messiah, but how to deepen their faith, how to live, how to know their Lord better. The band of believers that traveled with Philip shared a sense of meaning that carried into their nighttime prayers, a common passion to be used by God to further his will.

All but three of the families that had left from Jerusalem had now departed to start new lives with friends or relations in the villages they had visited. The remaining found shelter for the night with one family, who moved into their front room, giving the other one to the women travelers and sheltering the men up on their roof. After evening prayers, Abigail settled Dorcas onto her pallet, then joined Alban and Martha outside the front door. Like many Samaritan dwellings, the house was fronted by a long covered portico, which in better weather served as an additional open-sided room. The cooking fire burned in a clay stove in one corner, granting them a bit of warmth against the night chill.

They talked in the easy manner of friends who knew much about one another. There were long periods of silence, for all were tired from the journey and the evening's teaching and prayers for healing. But none wished to say good-bye to the day and succumb to sleep. They spoke of the crowds and their spiritual hunger. They spoke of Linux and what awaited him in Caesarea. Alban suggested they pray for their friend. As they bowed their heads once again and spoke the words, Abigail felt her eyes burning with tears she could not explain away.

Alban was clearly improved, which Martha must have found amusing. "You find healing through travel, I see. Which is odd, since you became ill on just such a journey."

"The two nights of rest in Jerusalem went a long way toward improvement," Alban said with a smile. "And the pace we have set is far gentler than the distance a caravan covers. Not to mention how I am hovered over by friends and carry no great responsibilities."

"Other than to get well," Martha put in firmly.

Abigail asked, "When will you return to Galilee? I'm sure Leah must miss you terribly."

"And your little one," Martha agreed.

"First I will see you settled," Alban said. "Leah knows she is married to a caravan guard captain. She dislikes our times apart, as do I, but she has learned to accept them as a necessary part of our life now."

Abigail hid her relief that he would remain for the present as best she could. She turned to Martha and asked, "And when will you return to your family?"

"When our God tells me to."

"But they—"

"They are fine, I am sure. They are sheltered among friends. They are doing God's will also." Martha reached over and took Abigail's hand. "As am I, dear one. I shall not leave you alone."

A comfortable silence held them for a time. Then Alban said, "I have been thinking over what Philip told me that first day upon the road. How Samaritans are considered by the religious Judeans to be the lowest of the low. In the eyes of many Pharisees, they hold a position below even that of the Gentiles and Roman soldiers."

"And yet we are here," Martha said. "Just as our Lord was while he was on earth."

"And they come," Abigail said.

"*How* they come," Alban said. "Their yearning for salvation is a joy. To me and to our Lord."

They left Ginae at midmorning under scuttling clouds. Once more it seemed as though the entire village saw them off. Philip spoke to the audience a final time. He laid hands on and prayed over many, then baptized a few more. When they departed, the woman originally from Sychar continued along with them. Helzebah had family in Nain, the village where the Megiddo traders lived. She had taken it upon herself to travel with them, ensuring they were greeted properly in their new home.

Alban knew the hills of Galilee were divided into two distinct segments. The southern range split the Samaritan Plain from the Megiddo Plains, or Armageddon, as it was sometimes known. The northeastern hills wove around Tiberias and stretched up to meet the Golan highlands. Between the two, some twenty Roman miles west of the Jordan River, stretched a broad flat region. All the main arteries connecting the northern and southern realms, except for the one Roman road that skirted the western shore of Galilee, met at this point.

Alban rode straight in the saddle this day, his coloring nearly back to normal. His voice was much stronger as he explained the terrain ahead to Abigail. "There before you is perhaps the most important juncture in all the eastern empire." He slid down from his mount to point out one road after the other, naming the destinations. "The port of Joppa lies three days to the southwest, and beyond that the road continues on to Egypt. The southern road there leads to Jerusalem. Along the eastern route lies Tiberias, and beyond that Damascus and the province of Syria. That road leading north and west goes to Tyre, Sidon, and on to Tarsus."

They stood upon a gentle rise, perhaps two hundred feet above the Megiddo Plains. Ahead of her, Abigail could see three caravans traveling the various roads. A faint cry carried upon the wind. "What is that I hear?" she asked.

Alban smiled. "Traders offering their wares. Your new neighbors."

They sounded like gulls crying in the distance. The clouds hung low and turned the plains the color of wet slate. All the verdant growth had been left behind them to the south. Up ahead, the roads dissected what looked like a vast wasteland. Far in the distance rose a lone hill, upon which a Roman fortress held its place like a stone buzzard. The desert plain seemed to go on forever. And over it all, the wind moaned.

Helzebah walked over to them with Martha. The two women had discovered they shared a common characteristic of straight talking and direct opinions. Helzebah pointed to a village perched upon the slopes to her left. "There is your new home. Nain."

The village was the one welcoming spot in the entire vista. The lime-washed homes gleamed like pearls in the gloomy afternoon. The road that climbed up from the plains was steep in places, and at several points seemed barely connected to the ridge. "Is it safe?" Abigail wondered.

"What, the road?" Helzebah huffed a laugh. "Safe enough, when you've walked it a hundred times or so."

Abigail felt a shiver run through her body, and she put her arm around little Dorcas on the donkey beside her.

Helzebah went on, "Nain is perhaps the safest village in all Judea. There is only the one road in and out. Brigands steer a wide berth around this region, you must believe me."

Martha said, her satisfaction evident, "Here is a haven in which we can be secure."

Abigail wanted to agree. But the wind seemed to catch her words and pluck them away, unformed. She held on to her daughter tightly, more for herself than for the little girl.

Nain's only road left them all breathless. The ascent had begun at a modest angle, but steadily grew steeper. At one point several of the donkeys balked when the road emerged from a tight bend and exposed a swooping drop. Alban slid from the animal he had been riding and tied strips of cloth around all the beasts' eyes, speaking softly to them as he did so. "These animals were born and bred in the flatland. They will soon grow accustomed to the climb. After a few weeks they will carry you up at night without a worry."

Abigail was about to say she would never make this journey after dark when Dorcas exclaimed, "Look, Mama. Ants?"

"No, my dear. Camels."

"Little camels?"

Alban shared a smile with Martha. "Big camels," he said. "They look little because we are so high up."

Dorcas clapped her hands and bounced on the donkey's back. "The roads are little too."

Martha asked, "You like all this, don't you, dear one?"

She waved her small hand in as large a circle as she could stretch. "I can see *everything*!"

Martha again smiled across the animal's neck to Abigail. "We can see very far indeed."

"It *smells* nice too," Dorcas said, screwing up her face and grinning.

Philip came to stand alongside the little girl. "Those are the perfumes of northern Samaria. Desert sage and eucalyptus and cedar and sorrel. They all grow wild on these slopes."

Abigail watched her daughter enchanting their little group, and thought upon the difference between them. She had been taken captive by thoughts as grey as the clouds, bleak as the dry hills far in the distance. Yet again she had lost sight of the day's inherent beauty, the *potential* it held.

She stroked her daughter's hair and whispered, "Thank you."

"Why, Mama?"

"You are the sun in my life, little one."

The village was far larger than its first impression. And much more appealing than Abigail would have expected for a hillside town far away from others of any size. Clearly the passing caravans shared some of their wealth with Nain's inhabitants, for many of the homes they passed were freshly limed, their roofs newly thatched, the doors and corner posts fashioned from intricately carved olive wood. The town occupied a plateau perhaps a mile wide and half again as long. Fields of bleating sheep extended out in three directions, back to where vineyards and groves of fruit trees found purchase on the steep slopes.

The surrounding hills formed natural boundaries and blocked much of the wind. The plateau sloped down slightly from where they stood, like a natural amphitheater. Behind them, the view stretched to distant horizons and beyond.

Helzebah hailed an acquaintance who directed them to her family's home. A local drink, pomegranate juice mixed with lemon and mint and water from a natural spring, was served to the group. Soon yet another throng of people began to gather, drawn by the swiftly spreading news that disciples of Jesus had arrived.

The visitors were led to the main square. Abigail studied the village with open curiosity, wondering what her new circumstances would be like. She found alien-looking touches everywhere as they passed, reminders that she was indeed to live and raise her child in Samaria, a distant cousin to her familiar Judean homeland.

"Look! Eyes?" Dorcas pointed to a nearby dwelling.

Helzebah offered, "Those are signs against the evil eye. People in this place believe it wards off bad fortune."

Philip murmured, "I have heard of such things."

Helzebah hesitated a long moment, then said, "There's a wizard who lives in this town. Very famous, he is. Simon is known through all Samaria. I doubt he'll hold out much of a welcome."

But Philip did not respond, for as they entered the main square, a woman hurried up to him. "Please, will you help me?" she cried.

"If I can, indeed I—"

"It's my husband. He's been suffering from such pains for many years now. The wizard has not been able to offer any assistance."

"Where is your husband?"

"Laid out there beneath the eaves, my good sir." She moved alongside Philip, her hands anxiously kneading each other. "We have little to offer you, good sir, but we'll pay you what we can."

"I do not seek your money," Philip assured her. "And I am not your 'good sir,' for we know that none are truly good save the Lord most high."

"Yes, sir," she said with a nod, though the woman seemed scarcely to fathom his words. She must have gathered courage enough to clutch at Philip's sleeve. "There he is, sir."

The man lay upon a portable pallet of woven leather straps, covered by a blanket stained with sweat. His features were stretched taut over his skull, his breath tight and shallow against the pain.

Abigail watched Philip glance across the square, for at that moment a commanding figure appeared from the side lane. The man's long hair was waxed and plaited so it hung across his left shoulder, a silver bell dangling at its end. He wore a fine robe covered in symbols, and more were inked into the skin of his hands and neck. His chin lifted at Philip's open inspection.

Philip turned back to the man upon the pallet. He climbed up the steps onto the portico and knelt by the man's head. "I have nothing to give you, save what has been granted me by the Lord our God. Do you understand my words?"

The man's breathing seemed to become more labored still, but he managed, "Aye."

"Tell me what you want, then."

The man's gaze was fastened upon Philip with a desperate intensity. "I wish to be free of this pain that binds me. . . ." He finished in a gasp.

"Well said, my brother." Philip bowed his head.

Abigail felt a touch on her arm. Martha said quietly, "Come."

Together they stepped forward to stand near Philip. Alban joined them, and they bowed their heads together and began their murmured prayers.

Abigail felt a familiar rush of spiritual winds, the gathering of forces that filled her entire being, until she was almost overwhelmed by the power of God's love. She opened her eyes when Philip spoke.

"In the name of our Lord Jesus, the risen One, I command you, be healed!"

The man's eyes were wide, and his breathing had gone as still as the crowd that surrounded them. "It is *gone*." He whispered the words, then repeated them in a louder voice.

Philip said, "Rise up!" and reached out his hand. The man took it and stood in astonished stages as his wife sobbed her relief beside him. The crowd moved back, giving the man room to step down from the porch. He walked back and forth, staring at his own limbs, then lifted his arms to the heavens and shouted, "I am healed! Glory be to God!"

It seemed as though the entire village followed Philip out of the square. Ahead of the main group danced the man whom Philip had healed, skipping like a child, laughing at a day free of pain. Even the wizard Simon came along, though remaining slightly apart, isolated by more than his fancy robes with their complex designs.

The crowd crossed a pasture filled with sheep and came upon a stand of ancient fruit trees, the trunks gnarled and twisted by countless seasons. In their midst lay a spring, the water bubbling clear as glass from the rocky slopes beyond, feeding a stream which in turn supplied the village with fresh water.

Philip stepped into the water and gave the declaration that for Abigail remained both vivid and fresh. How the water was a sign of having received the risen Messiah and, through this, a transformation of one's whole self. How inward sin was washed away by the blood of the crucified Lamb of God, just as water cleanses the outer person. How acceptance of this truth symbolized an eternal life with God. One by one Philip invited the villagers forward, challenging each with the same softly spoken words: "You may be baptized if you believe with all your heart and receive the Messiah." And each responded, "I believe that Jesus Christ is the Son of God."

Not all the villagers came forward, but Simon entered the water and repeated the words. As Philip lowered him into the waters, the designs on his robe formed a watery cloud that drifted away in the stream. All eyes save Philip's had turned from the immersion, and they watched the dark stain flowing toward the village.

"Rise up," Philip said, lifting Simon out of the water. "Now go, your sins are forgiven. Live to love and serve your Lord."

The villagers went off to prepare a feast for their guests. Helzebah and her relative accompanied Abigail and Dorcas to their new home, the one presented to Alban by his grateful employer, Jamal. Philip and Martha and Alban went along as well.

The small dwelling clearly had not been occupied for quite some time. But it was just as Jamal's deed described. There was a front porch in the Samaritan style, almost as wide as the home's main room. The plank flooring was raised, so the interior would remain dry even in the harshest rains. The door's leather hinges had been eaten away by rats, and inside every surface was covered with a liberal coating of soot and grime. But the rooftop was sound, and the home was well lit by windows facing both east and south. Two smaller rooms occupied the upper level.

Philip climbed the steps to the upstairs chambers and returned wearing a dry robe. By then Martha had laid a fire and made tea. She gave the weary teacher one of the two unbroken mugs they had found, and carried the other to Alban, sitting on a bench on the porch. The men's soft voices formed a backdrop to the women's activities.

Helzebah's cousin had slipped away, only to return with several women carrying one household implement or another. Abigail was moved by their generosity, but did not feel she should accept items they surely needed. But Martha murmured, "They wish to make you welcome in your new home. Besides, they want to reward Philip for his services. I had already explained that he wouldn't take payment. So they are giving the gifts to you, their new neighbor."

Abigail nodded slowly, her eyes filling with tears.

A dozen more hands were now helping. Three men carried a container of lime. They swept the walls of each room, then whitewashed them. Another two had set to work restoring the leather hinges for the door. Dorcas skipped in and out, carrying a cleaning rag in one hand and her doll in the other. Her excited chatter could be heard above it all.

By the time the sun began its descent, the house looked like new, and each room held at least one piece of furniture. The fireplace was sound, its rock-lined opening drawing well, and it all truly began to feel like a home.

The communal meal that evening was eaten in the main square, for no single house was large enough to hold them all. The clouds had moved on, and the mountains, sheltering the village from the night's chill wind, carved tall shadows between the stars. Philip taught them once more, and then led the group in prayer. Abigail listened silently, a sense of peace slowly stealing over her while Dorcas fell asleep in her lap.

Helzebah's cousin accompanied them home, lighting their way with a torch. The excitement and work of the day left them weary. Abigail did her best to thank them all for their kindness as Dorcas slept in her arms. Alban and Philip settled themselves on pallets in the main room near the fireplace. Abigail carried Dorcas upstairs into one of the chambers, and Martha took the other.

In spite of being as tired as she could ever recall, Abigail found herself filled with restless energy. She positioned the room's only bit of furniture, a three-legged stool, by the window and sank onto it.

In the starlight she could make out an overgrown garden rimmed by a stone wall reduced to little more than rubble. Next were four other houses, all the same flat-roofed construction as her own. My *own* . . . She mulled the words over silently. *Thank you, Lord, for this gift*, she whispered. She looked over her shoulder at the precious little bundle in the corner. *I'm so grateful we have a home and neighbors who care. . . .*

But a sigh emerged from someplace deep inside. Abigail struggled to sort through the tangle of feelings that nearly overwhelmed her. Her thankfulness was conflicted by all the unfamiliar that surrounded her. And the unknown future stretched before her like a road with no destination.

She leaned forward, her arms crossed on the window's ledge. Beyond the village, the scene just dropped away. Fires flickered along the valley floor, with a rich silver sea of stars overhead. Here must be the haven from all the dangers she had so feared in Jerusalem. . . .

If only I can find joy once again. If only I can find my place here to give, to serve. . . .

She sat, chin resting on her hand, and stared out through the darkness until her mind began to quiet. She finally slipped under the blanket beside Dorcas. Strange noises and quiet whispers seemed to float about her. The child murmured in her sleep and fitted herself in close. Her daughter's warmth and fragrance gradually gentled Abigail into slumber.

She had no idea how long she slept before the dream. In it, Abigail heard a long-ago sound, her beloved husband whispering her name.

In the dream she opened her eyes to find Stephen lying on Dorcas's other side, the child not separating them so much as binding them together. The small body's presence was a testimony to their love's union.

Abigail wanted to speak, but she could not. And in a way, she was glad of it. For the communion they were sharing was somehow strengthened by the silence.

A faint glow surrounded Stephen, the light just strong enough for her to see him clearly. He was just as she remembered, yet utterly changed. The weariness and stress that had marked their final days together had been wiped away. He looked at her with a love so intense, so complete, she felt as though she were flowing away into nothingness, leaving herself totally exposed, totally open to receiving his love in return.

She awoke to the sounds of her own sobs. Dorcas whimpered in her sleep, no doubt drawn to wakefulness by her mother's crying. Abigail tucked the blanket around the child and rose silently from the pallet. Dreaming of Stephen was something that had happened quite regularly back in the months when Dorcas was still an infant and Abigail had felt her soul torn apart by her loss. She had been relieved—and yet also felt bereft—when the dreams had gradually diminished, then stopped.

She settled her shawl about her head and shoulders and slipped from the room. She sensed eyes watching her, but when she looked into the adjoining rooftop room, Martha appeared to be asleep.

Abigail had thought she was over the worst of her mourning, she told herself as she crept silently down the outside staircase. This nighttime experience had caught her utterly by surprise, leaving her feeling not only sad but defenseless. As if Stephen's death had just happened.

She circled around toward the front door and felt her heart give a silent wail, then a nearly wordless cry of anguish. *What am I to do . . . ?*

Tears veiled her sight as she took one step up to the front portico. She stopped and turned as she felt more than saw a glow.

Abigail cleared her eyes. And there was Philip.

The disciple was kneeling in the dust of the road at the juncture where the village lane opened into the area fronting the cliff face. The night was filled with an unearthly luminescence. The glow was strong enough to turn the surrounding houses a gleaming silver. But the light itself was nothing compared to the sensations filling Abigail's heart. The silence was as powerful as the light, a force that commanded her attention. There was no room for anything, save a tiny glimpse of eternity, one that washed away the fears, the uncertainties, even the sorrow left by her dream.

Abigail dropped to her knees in the dirt. She could see nothing other than Philip now lying prostrate . . . and the light. Whatever the message—whoever the messenger out there in the road—the gifts of power, of love, of hope filled her heart and whispered silent assurances to her mind.

Long after the light faded, Abigail remained as she was. The stones bit into her knees, her back ached from her position. But even these were mere assurances that she had witnessed a miracle . . . and lived. The discomforts reconnected her to this earth. They reminded her that she was there for a purpose. She welcomed the soreness and prayed.

She heard footsteps, and lifted her head as Philip crossed the road toward her. Slowly Abigail eased herself to her feet.

Philip's face carried a trace of the illumination she had seen in the square. He spoke with a breathless wonder. "I am called to the south. To the road between Jerusalem and Gaza. I must leave immediately."

Abigail looked to the east. A slight flush announced the arrival of a new day. She nodded her understanding.

She followed him into the house to start the fire, then climbed the stairs to waken Martha.

There would be no more sleep this day.

CHAPTER NINETEEN

The Megiddo Plains

AFTER A QUICK breakfast, they walked down the winding road with Philip—Abigail and Martha along with Dorcas and Alban. They led one donkey for the disciple's journey, another in case Alban tired on the way back up, and Dorcas rode a third. For once, the early dawn's breaking light was clear and the air windless. When shortly they reached the valley floor, the day and the walk had warmed them enough that they laid their winter cloaks upon one animal's back.

They were obviously feeling subdued by the night's events. Only Dorcas remained untouched, singing softly to herself, patting the donkey's mane in time to her melody, pointing out all items of interest as they passed. Abigail had said nothing about her dream since she had no idea what it meant, or even if it was anything more than reaction to physical and mental exhaustion. Philip's encounter with the Unseen was another thing entirely. Abigail had described to the others what she had seen of it, though she still felt she had witnessed something not truly of this earth at all.

When the village road eventually leveled off, with the southerly juncture now in view, Alban said, "There is so much I wish to say. To ask. But . . ."

"And I also," Martha agreed when Alban did not finish.

Abigail was vastly relieved to hear them voice sentiments identical to her own. "I feel as though I have so many thoughts and impressions trapped inside me."

Philip stopped and turned to face them, his features still carrying a trace of that ethereal light.

Alban said to him, "I have been enriched by your teachings, Philip. I feel that our days together have been a gift. And yet . . ."

Philip remained silent, watchful.

Alban started again, "And yet I feel as though I know you no better than when we first met. Forgive me, I mean no offense."

Philip nodded, as though he expected the puzzling statements. He took his customary time in responding, finally saying, "Those of us called to spread the Lord's message are all very different from each other. We have contrasting gifts and strengths. Who can argue that I share any noticeable trait with Peter, save our love for God? And yet the commission given us by Christ before he returned to his Father is identical for both of us."

Abigail was reluctant to speak. But Philip's silence suggested he was waiting for one of them to respond. She began slowly, somewhat hesitantly, " 'Go into all the world and preach the gospel.' "

Martha nodded slowly. "So the challenge is to do that without getting in the way of the message."

Alban added, "He must increase. I must decrease."

Philip's smile only made the illumination stronger. "That is it precisely. How can I live so that when someone sees me, they are pointed to Jesus? When I speak, is it the Messiah's truths they hear? How can I live that no power is seen to be mine, no authority, no crown, no glory. It all belongs to him. I am the willing, loving servant, providing hands, feet, voice, eyes, and ears for the Holy Spirit to use."

"It is the challenge we all should accept," Alban said slowly. "Once again I am blessed by your words."

They joined hands and prayed, the four adults and little Dorcas as well. For Philip's safety and for the unknown purposes that were sending him south. They prayed for one another. They prayed for the days ahead, and for the growing community of believers here in Nain, as well as the hearts brought to faith during their journey. The prayer was timeless, the joining together as one so strong Abigail felt the same sense of power she had experienced after her dream. And when they finished praying, she also felt a calm strong enough to see Philip off with a glad heart, then turn to the others and say, "Let us go see where I am to work and serve."

The group reached the market of Megiddo fresh and ready for the day. The market stood at the intersection of five major Roman roads. The places of business here were more like actual buildings than mere market stalls, the rear of each being fashioned from blocks of stone. Some families lived above their shops, though Abigail could see why most preferred to maintain their true homes above in Nain. The hillside village was protected from the wind and enjoyed broad vistas. The Megiddo Plains were both dusty and vast, extending to the northwest and southeast, circled on its other two sides by the hills of Galilee.

"Your enemy here is the wind," Alban explained. "And the wind blows almost all the time."

"And the heat," a voice called from the storefront they were passing. "Enjoy the cool of winter while you can. Because for five months each year, this earth you stand upon is an anvil, the sun a hammer."

The man emerging from the stall appeared to be little more than leathery skin over bones. He was as tall as Alban but could not have carried half his weight. The traditional Samaritan robes might as well have been hung upon the branches of some dead tree. Yet his smile was friendly, his eyes bright. "You are here to stake a claim for Jamal's stall?"

"I am," Alban said. "My name is Alban, and Jamal has deeded the stall to me, along with a house up in Nain. I am entrusting it to our friend Abigail here," he explained, motioning toward her.

"Yesterday I watched your comrade standing over my friend and praying for his healing," the man said. "I saw him stand and dance and shout. The night before you arrived, my wife and I had gone to him to pay our last respects. We grew up together, he and I." He offered Alban a work-roughened hand. "I am Yelban. I serve as village elder in Nain, and the same here at the market. I believe you have passed these ways before."

"Many times. I serve as Jamal's guard captain."

"I thought I recognized your face. The family who tends the first corral of sheep, they pointed you out. They claim you are a fair man and honest in all your words and deeds. They say Jamal is fortunate to have you."

"I am honored they would speak thus."

"It is far more than any would say for the scoundrels who last tended the stall."

"Jamal suspected them of stealing from him."

"They did indeed, and not just from your merchant prince. They robbed everyone. If they patted your back, you should search for your purse." Yelban waved them toward his left. "Come. I will show you what remains of your business."

The shop held a prized placement, at one of the elbows where all the roads joined. The structure showed the world two faces. From the front it was a traditional storefront, with a long awning and sunlit shelves where wares could be displayed. In the rear, it was a two-storied stone fortress. The back chamber was one great room without windows. The former occupants had taken the roof ladder when they left, along with all the goods and anything else they could cart away.

When Abigail, Martha, and Alban, with Dorcas climbing right in front of him, clambered up the ladder borrowed from a neighbor stall owner, they saw that the roof was enclosed by more stone, forming a wall at chest height. Dorcas ran over to the wall, begging to be held up to see over the edge.

Yelban pointed out a caravan approaching from the north. "The market knows when a caravan is on its way. They always know."

Alban smiled. "I have heard that the wind tells them."

"More often, we hear from our associates in other caravans." The village elder had a merchant's grin, merry and demanding at the same time. "You can use the roof here for sleeping on some nights. The lower chamber is your strong room. Keep enough supplies in there for five days, for if the winds strike, you will be going nowhere. You know the word *khamsin*?"

"Windstorm," Alban said. "The scourge of all caravans. That and bandits."

"The hills act as a giant funnel, driving the heart of every storm right through this plain. Or so it will feel when those winds strike."

Alban said, "Jamal tells me the stall is set up to sell Samaritan weavings."

"Carpets, tapestries, cloth, robes, tents," Yelban confirmed. "Almost every village woman here weaves. Others work at fashioning shorn wool into thread, or they dye cloth into colors. Samaritan cloth is known throughout the empire."

Martha looked around at the empty shelves, then raised open hands to her shoulders. "But there is nothing here to sell."

"If the villagers trust you, they will provide their wares and wait for payment till you sell them." The man nodded vigorously. "And that arrangement includes me." He shrugged. "I receive a small share from all the merchants to pay for the guards and upkeep of the village corrals."

Abigail quailed at all she did not yet know or understand about the whole endeavor. "I . . . I am ever so grateful for your wise assistance."

"You already have friends in Nain, you know. The man you healed was the village headman before me." He gripped the ladder and started down, then halted to ask, "Do you carry the man Philip's gift of healing?"

Martha responded for them all. "We can lay hands upon those in need, and pray. Just as the disciple did. All else is up to God."

"And you will not charge?"

"How can we ask for money in return for what is not ours to claim?"

"The wizard will not like to hear you say that." Yelban's smile was the last they saw of him. His parting words came over the top of the ladder. "I warrant you will forge trust wherever you go."

Abigail gave herself to tasks she knew and understood. The stall and storeroom and living chamber all needed a thorough cleaning. She swept the floors with a thatch broom the previous tenants had either overlooked or deemed too paltry to take. Alban and Martha walked with Dorcas to the communal well and returned with two leather buckets brimming with water. They also brought rags and a makeshift mop—all borrowed from neighbors, along with the news that the entire market was talking of nothing save their arrival.

Alban added, "Some other stall holder wanted to take this place over, but Yelban would not permit it."

"He is both an honorable man and our ally," Martha announced stoutly.

Abigail asked Alban, "Shouldn't you be resting after all you've been doing today?"

"In truth, I feel as though Philip's prayers yesterday were meant as much for me as for the man upon the bed. I cannot remember feeling better than now," he assured her.

"It is not fitting that you be scrubbing floors like a servant," Martha muttered.

He chuckled. "You say that to one who began his military duty cleaning stables." He dipped a rag in the bucket, then paused and looked around at them. "Didn't our Lord himself wash and dry the disciples' road-soiled feet? I too want to have that servant attitude." He scrubbed another segment of the floor, then spoke the words Abigail had been half afraid she all too soon would be hearing. "I should be leaving shortly for Capernaum."

Abigail saw her daughter's lips draw down, and she quickly crouched beside the little girl to halt the protest before it was formed. She held Dorcas close and spoke to Alban. "Your own little son must be missing you. And your wife too. Isn't that so, Dorcas?"

Her daughter did not answer but managed a small nod.

Alban rinsed his rag, then switched his attention to wiping down the front wall. "I won't be leaving just yet, my friends. Leah would want me to make sure the weavers treat you fairly."

"We will be glad for every hour we have together, and then see you off with grateful hearts." Abigail gave her daughter another squeeze. "Won't we, dear one?"

Whatever Dorcas might have been preparing to say was cut short by a youngster who appeared so suddenly in the doorway that Martha gave a little cry of surprise.

The boy was perhaps ten or eleven and blade thin. He gasped out, "I am Yelban's son. My mother has been stricken. My father says, 'For the love of the one who guides your steps, please hurry.' "

As they quickly emerged from the empty shop, a caravan appeared on the northern horizon. "Phoenicians," the boy tossed over his shoulder as he ran ahead of them. "Bandits with camels. They will bargain for hours and spend coin like it was their own blood. This way."

He beckoned them quickly on through the square, now a hive of activity. Youngsters scampered out toward the approaching caravan, many with wares draped over their arms. Stall owners rushed about, rearranging and polishing their goods, calling to others with frantic impatience. The lad hurried his charges toward what appeared to be the largest stall. Abigail thought the sheltered front portico was as broad as her village house. Servants hurried to set the tables with fresh carafes and utensils, while two women had begun roasting an entire sheep over a stone fire pit in front. The boy motioned them through the tavern and into the rear alcove, where they found Yelban kneeling beside a pallet. "They have come, Father."

Yelban did not look up. "I am in your debt."

"There is no debt," Abigail responded, bending over the woman, lying white-faced and still as death. "We seek nothing save to serve our Lord." Alban and Martha nodded their encouragement, and said they would be praying back at the stall.

Abigail nodded as her two friends departed and settled Dorcas on the floor nearby. "Be a good girl and stay here while Mama speaks with our friend."

Dorcas's eyes were round and solemn. "You make her not sick?"

"Perhaps, with God's help." Abigail knelt beside Yelban. "What happened?"

"My wife is often seized by pains to her forehead and temples. One moment all is normal, the next, as you see her." Yelban dipped a cloth into a basin, squeezed out the moisture, then gently laid it on the woman's brow. His voice was scarcely above a whisper. "Everything hurts during times like this. Noise. Light. Movement. Sometimes the pain holds her for days."

The woman's expression showed a tightly concentrated stillness, as though unable to even draw a proper breath for fear of making the pain worse. Her brow was deeply furrowed, her lips compressed to a thin line, her eyes clenched shut. Abigail asked, "What is her name?"

"Jasmina."

"May I pray for her?"

"I would beseech you to do that and anything else that might help."

The son now ran into the room and stationed himself by his father's other side. He whispered urgently, "The Phoenicians are here."

Yelban clearly was reluctant to leave his wife. He looked his distress at Abigail. "As elder, I must speak for all the market. There are sheep to sell, and the corral—"

"You must go—please," Abigail said, lifting the cloth from his wife's forehead to dampen it again. "I will stay with her."

Yelban stroked his wife's cheek with one hand. "Be well, my dear one. I will return as soon as I can."

The clamor outside was fierce. In the darkened chamber, however, the stillness seemed complete. Abigail whispered, "Jasmina, can you hear me?"

The woman upon the pallet was as narrow as her husband. Even in the throes of her agony, she was a strikingly attractive woman, with refined features and lustrous dark hair. The only sound she could permit herself was a soft moan.

Abigail set the cloth aside. She laid one hand upon the woman's shoulder, the other upon her forehead. Her prayer was simple, a request for God to do his will in this room. The noise beyond the chamber receded further still. Abigail felt a small body snuggle up next to her. She started to tell her daughter to return to the corner, but there was a sense of rightness to the moment, a strong feeling of being enveloped by unseen angels, and she put an arm around the child.

Abigail did not know how long she remained, kneeling by the woman with Dorcas at her side, praying. Only that a moment finally came when she did not rise, but rather was drawn to her feet by the same power that she felt when watching Philip pray. Here, in this room, in this chamber, there was space for only one thing.

Abigail spoke in a voice that she hardly recognized. "In the name of our Lord Jesus Christ, be healed, Jasmina! Be healed, and rise up!"

CHAPTER TWENTY

The Megiddo Plains

JACOB STARTED AWAKE. He sat up and listened for whatever had drawn him from sleep. The caravan camp was utterly quiet, and it was dark, though he thought glimmers of dawn nudged the edges of the eastern hills. He rose from his pallet to look around the wagon, but all was still, the women evidently remaining asleep within its tapestry walls. His eyes swept the camp's perimeter. The guards on duty strolled calmly yet alert. Even so, something had disturbed him. Jacob was certain of that.

Their westward progress had proven much slower than hoped for. A camel had calved far earlier than any of the drovers expected, delivering twins. The calves were pale as a desert sunrise, with dark and liquid eyes. No one save Jacob had objected to remaining encamped for a night and a day so the camel had time to recover. The next morning they set off once more, with the calves lashed on the back of a camel plodding just ahead of their mother. Their plaintive cries and the mother's lowing response were a source of great humor up and down the line. They did not travel fast, then halted at midday for the caravan to deliver supplies to a Roman outpost. Which meant they had scarcely entered the Megiddo borderlands by nightfall.

Jacob now drank from the waterskin slung on the back of the wagon and studied the night. But his sense of unease grew stronger in spite of the quiet.

A low voice demanded, "You feel it too?"

Jacob turned to find the caravan master observing him. A sturdy man, his moustache curved about his cheeks and into his beard, giving him a fierce air, particularly now, when the only light came from a waning half circle of moon.

Jacob was about to say he had no idea what had left him so uneasy when it happened.

Far off in the distance the rumble of thunder.

The hairs on Jacob's neck stood on end.

The caravan master said, "How long do you give it?"

"Not before midday," Jacob said. "Too far to be certain it will strike us at all."

"Strange that a servant of two wealthy women has a nose for desert storms," the master said meaningfully.

"I am loyal to Jamal," Jacob replied quickly. "Jamal is your trusted ally. That is what you need to know."

"Well said." The master grinned. "What would you do, my knowledgeable servant lad?"

"We stand in the funnel where the Tiberias hills meet the opening to the Megiddo Plains," Jacob said slowly. "We must leave this region and seek safety in a town. Unless the Romans will grant us refuge."

"The closest garrisons are more than half a day in either direction. Both too small to take us all in. Even if they were willing. Which they would be, for a bribe large as my fee for this trek." The caravan master put two fingers to his lips and shrilled the alarm whistle. "Have your women ready to travel by the time the animals are up and packed, or we will leave you behind."

"We are ready now" came a voice from the wagon.

The master grinned again. "I would expect nothing less from Jamal's household."

As the caravan leader departed, Julia pulled the tapestry back and asked, "What is the matter, Jacob?"

"A *khamsin*, mistress. Windstorm. Several hours away still. Perhaps it will miss us. But we must find shelter in case it comes our way."

"We will hurry."

Jacob was busy hitching the first horse to the wagon when Julia climbed down. "What can I do?" she wondered.

"It is not fitting, mistress."

She waved a dismissive hand. "Everyone is too busy to notice. You need help. And you know I'm familiar with animals."

Though he did not welcome the reminder of their first awkward meeting, in truth Jacob appreciated the offer of assistance. "The horses need an extra feed in case we cannot rest them for a time. The sack of oats is on the ground next to where I tethered the donkeys."

Julia hurried away, her sandals slapping against the hard-packed earth. By the time Jacob returned with two buckets of water for the donkeys, she was fastening the first feed bag into place.

"Do you truly think the storm will pass by?" she asked directly.

He hesitated, then decided to offer her the truth. "No, mistress."

"Why not?"

"Because I can taste it," Jacob replied. "Can you feel the prickling of your skin, the way one's hair drifts off the neck, the way clothes rub harshly? It is the storm's approach that causes this." He pulled the first donkey over and tethered it to the back of the wagon. "The wind is straight out of the south. It will drive the storm right at us."

"But there is scarcely any wind at all."

"That is the myth that has fooled too many desert travelers. Even when the storm finally appears on the horizon, the wind still will appear too mild to be of worry. All the power is held in the storm's closed fist. When you finally do feel the wind, it is too late."

Julia checked the bridles and reins for each horse with a practiced hand. "But every caravan trader has survived storms."

Jacob did not wish to worry her unnecessarily. So he merely said, "That is correct, mistress."

"Have you?"

"Many times."

"Then why . . . ?" She must have seen the answer upon his features, for she said, "Bandits?"

Jacob nodded. "They have begun striking caravans from behind the curtains of sand. It is a very risky maneuver. They might miss us entirely. They might become overwhelmed by the storm themselves. But because caravans are becoming more well guarded, bandits have taken to such tactics out of necessity."

Julia spoke slowly now. "A bandit who is so desperate as to hide inside a sandstorm would truly be . . ."

Jacob refused to supply the word *savage*. But the stories of caravans that had been attacked in this manner gave him reason to quicken his steps.

With every creak of the carriage wheel, every snap of a drover's whip, every cry from a nervous beast, Jacob grew more certain of two things. First, the storm was headed straight for them. Second, the storm was massive.

Behind them little tendrils of reddish dust rose into the sky, twisting and turning like fragile dancers. Telltales, the old caravan drovers called them. The more telltales one saw, the greater the coming tempest.

By the time the sun crested the eastern hills, so many telltales rose into the southern sky Jacob could not count them.

Still the wind did not come. The air was breathless. Yet the oppressive sense of danger was everywhere. Jacob scratched at his robe and drew sparks. The horses snorted and pulled against each other, despite his best efforts to keep them working in tandem. The camels ahead of their wagon brayed with genuine fear and sought to bolt ahead. Drovers shouted and plied their quirts and hauled on leads. And all eyes watched the empty southern sky.

Every now and then, there came a rumble of thunder. To Jacob's ears it sounded like an angry beast slowly emerging from its cave.

Ahead of them, the plains seemed endless and utterly empty. There were no other caravans with whom they might join and increase their strength against their two still-hidden foes—the storm and the enemy it no doubt sheltered. Hard as they pushed the animals, the hills seemed to grow no closer. Julia drew the front drape aside and demanded, "The storm is coming our way, is it not?"

As if in response, the caravan master shrilled once again from up ahead, signaling a change in direction, urging his drovers to even more speed.

"I fear so, mistress," Jacob answered over his shoulder.

"Where is safety?" When Jacob hesitated, she added, "Please do not humor me with platitudes. I am my father's daughter. I must know the truth."

"The lines of hills you see to either side will focus the storm and heighten its strength. No village can survive here in the Meggido Plains." Jacob pointed ahead to where the caravan was veering off to the north. "The master is taking the track you see there."

Julia moved further out, peering across the empty reaches. "But I see no village."

"The village will be hidden behind the hills in the distance. Just like Tiberias. They will settle where there is protection for their fields and animals. Not just from such storms as this, but from bandits. And where there is a village, there must also be water."

"But what if there is no village?"

"If there is no village, mistress, why is there a road?"

Jacob heard Helena's voice from within. "Julia, come back inside the curtain. It is not fitting."

Julia started to retreat, then said softly, her voice low yet confident, "I am glad it is you guarding our safety, Jacob."

For the first time that day, he found a reason to smile. "*Hyah!*"

Jacob had no idea why the caravan master had chosen this road. The route they took was little more than a faint imprint across the plain. Perhaps the man had family who farmed there. Perhaps he had taken refuge there before. Or had heard from someone else that there was a protected alcove where the caravan could wait out the storm as well as find refuge from possible bandits. Jacob had no idea. The only thing he could have said for certain was that they were not going to make it in time.

Jacob pushed his animals very hard indeed. Though the horses labored to the limits of their strength, they could not keep up with the camels. Jacob stopped applying the whip. He could see from their lathered sides and the rolling whites of their eyes that the animals were giving him every bit of power they could. But the carriage was not made for speed, especially over such terrain. The wheels jounced and rattled and tossed them about. And with every passing minute, the distance between them and the rest of the caravan grew greater.

Finally Jacob could wait no longer. "Mistress, we must make a decision," he called softly.

Behind him, the drape was pushed aside. Julia said, "Tell us."

Jacob pointed to where the last of the caravan's animals were disappearing in the dust ahead. "We are falling behind. We must abandon the carriage. We have no saddles for the horses. Your mother and Zoe can ride the donkeys. I can ride the horse on the left bareback—he and I have come to understand one another. I am afraid you will need to ride behind me."

"No," responded Julia. "You must take Mother. She is not used to handling animals."

Jacob nodded his understanding. There was no need to explain further. "The second horse must carry our supplies."

"It sounds to me as though you have already made the decision for us, Jacob," Julia said quietly.

"No, mistress. The choice is this: Do we follow the caravan north, or not."

"What other choice do we have?" The tension in her voice was evident.

"Look at the hills over there. They are closer than whatever destination lies straight ahead. And see those dark spots along the base?"

There was a moment's silence as Julia and Helena studied the landscape where Jacob was pointing. But the jostling ride made any thorough inspection very difficult. Finally she asked, "Are those caves?"

"Perhaps. Or it could be simply sunlight and shadows. But I think caves. The wind hollows out many such depressions. They would be too small for the entire caravan. But we might find refuge."

"And you think we would be safer aiming for what we can see?"

"It is a risk, mistress. A very large one."

"But you think we should go there?"

"I do."

"Then we will do as you suggest."

Jacob hauled on the reins and called for the horses to halt. "We must hurry."

The three women swiftly followed his instructions, lashing together all their food and water—not enough, for most of their supplies were piled upon animals that were fast disappearing to the north. But Jacob had no time for such regrets. The air remained eerily still. Julia finally approached him and said, "Are you certain the storm will strike?"

"It comes." Jacob finished unharnessing the first horse and turned to the second.

"How can you be certain?"

"Look to the south. See how the cloud rises from the earth?"

"I see nothing but a hint of color. It is beautiful."

"So is the adder, and the cobra and the tiger." Jacob pointed to the donkeys. "Find blankets to cushion your ride, and quickly."

But there were no saddle blankets, only finely woven quilts intended to soften the carriage's interior. They were quickly folded, slung over the animals, and tied into place.

Just as Jacob was assisting the women upon the donkeys' backs, he heard it.

Helena asked, "What was that?"

Julia said, "It sounded as though the whole world moaned."

It happened again, louder this time, a low groaning that was more felt than heard. The donkey holding Julia shrilled a frantic protest. Jacob watched approvingly as Julia hauled back on the reins and forced the animal to submission. He pointed to the shawls wrapped around the women's hair. "Tie those as tight as you can across your faces, just below the eyes." He handed them two more he had taken from the wagon. "Tie these across your beasts' eyes. But not until the storm touches you. For doing so will slow us to a crawl. If you fall from your mount, whatever you do, hang on to the reins and let it lead you forward."

The two horses were fastened together with the donkeys, all in one line. It meant slower progress, but Jacob did not know how long before the wind struck, and once it did, he could not lose contact with the women. He first boosted a solemn Helena up on the animal's back, then took his position in front of her and firmly grasped hold of the reins. "We go!"

He felt Helena clinging firmly to the back of his tunic. He could hear her tight breathing and feared that in her fright she might lose her balance and fall. "Clasp your hands about my waist," he ordered. "Hang on tightly."

To his relief she did not hesitate to obey. He could feel her head buried against his shoulder. He wondered if in her fear and confusion she wept, but he heard no sound save for the low moaning of the coming wind.

The animals balked at first, lashed together in such a manner. But Julia and the servant woman followed his lead and applied the quirts, shouting and hauling upon the reins. Soon they were progressing as swiftly as Jacob might have hoped. Which was good, because behind them the storm grew ever louder. The sound was of some great beast in agony, a mournful note that rose and rose and rose, until it filled their entire world.

They were less than half a furlong from the rock face. Jacob now could see that his hopes were indeed realized. He counted three caves almost directly ahead, each deep enough for the rear walls to be lost to the shadows. He dug his heels into his mount, shouting at the frightened animals and using the whip with all his might.

And then the storm attacked.

One moment there was only the sound chasing them. Then the storm filled the air to nothingness.

The blasting sand came at them from every direction. Jacob tied his head scarf tighter and slipped from the horse's back. He tied cloths about the two horses' eyes, wound the reins around his wrist, and pulled.

His mind was so taken with fighting their way to safety that there was room for only one other thought. One regret. He and Jamal had used the women's presence as a cover for his journey to Joppa. A caravan including women made for a suitable ruse to hide contraband activity. Jamal and he had planned well. But what neither of them had taken into account was the danger from desert storms. Particularly a storm with the ferocity of the one that now surrounded them. If anything happened . . . Jacob could not even bear the thought. All he could do was pray and fight harder.

He had heard tales around the caravan fires. Of drovers who had lost contact with their caravans in the middle of the storm, and whose bones were found after the winds passed, the dust having eaten away the flesh. How some were within a few paces of safety, but were so blinded by the storm they simply gave up, lay down, and were no more. This storm was as fierce as any he had ever known—or heard of. It filled his senses. He could not think, not even question whether he continued in the right direction. There was nothing save the wind and his need to take one more step. Then another. For to stop walking was to die.

When his hand touched the rock, he would have wept if only he still had tears to shed.

CHAPTER TWENTY-ONE

The Megiddo Plains

JULIA SHIFTED IN an attempt to ease the discomfort of the rock against which she leaned. Tucked closely against her side was her mother, with Zoe next along the cave wall. Helena, though pale and weak from the recent experience, had fared rather well on the horse's back behind Jacob. Julia felt proud of her, knowing she had never mounted and ridden a horse before. Yet the woman had clung to Jacob through the terror-driven ride and managed to fall into his arms as they took shelter in the cave.

Jacob had waved the animals into the largest cavern. They went with little hesitation, anxious to be out of the storm.

Jacob then guided the women to the second cave. He led them as far into the back of the small enclosure as possible and settled them upon the rock floor. Once all three were safe, he had gone back to care for the animals and returned with bundles of provisions. It was too dark in the cave to prepare a meal. Not because of the time of day but simply because the storm hid all light from the afternoon sun. Jacob rummaged through the sacks and found water so each of them could have a drink. He even produced a few figs and some flatbread. Now the women huddled together, willing themselves to wait out the storm's fury. He had left them to their privacy, with the promise that he would be in the cave next over, where the animals sheltered, and would be within calling distance if they needed him.

From where she sat Julia could not see the storm. Nor did she wish to. The sound of the wind and the lashing sand was enough to make her quake with fear.

This time of waiting was also a time of quiet introspection. Julia found herself slipping easily into recollections. In the days before their hasty departure, her mother had continually refused all invitations to join Julia and Zoe and the followers. Julia had grieved silently over her mother's lack of faith. *What if the Lord returns and she is not ready?* She had prayed more fervently.

But even in her concern and grief, Julia's own faith grew. She prayed as she went about her activities, she sought counsel from Zoe, and she drank in every teaching, every word shared at the gatherings. *Oh, if only I had known Jesus when he was here. Had heard him speak. Seen him heal.*

And then one day recently, a gentle quiet had filled her soul. Julia heard again his words as they were retold by one or another of the group. She had seen him heal by the laying on of hands or the supplication of earnest prayers. He *was still* with them. His very presence filled the room each time they met together. Julia felt that presence within as well. When she knelt to pray. When she sought direction. And surely one day very soon she would lift her face to the clouds of the sky and see his glorious return. That thought held her confident and strong. And increased her desire to follow him.

If only her mother . . .

And her father?

Julia had grown up adoring her father. There was no one in her world that she had loved more. But the shocking truth she had learned from Zoe had brought such an enormous rift to that relationship. First, that her mother was not his legal wife. He had another family. Then, that Helena would not make a decision of which she feared Jamal would disapprove. And now, the latest news, that Jamal's wife in Damascus had become a believer.

That final news should have filled her heart with joy—and it did, in undeniable yet conflicting ways. It was a struggle she had never faced before, and now in their shelter, held captive by the raging storm, it brought her to tears. She knew such a battle of emotions contradicted her faith. One should not hold to love and anger warring within. Something was wrong. Something that with God's help she needed to make right. But how?

It seemed that prayer was the only answer. She would use the hours of their confinement to pray. To pray, and to shelter her mother.

Julia drew the shawl from around her shoulders and settled it over her mother's shivering body, keeping one corner of it to protect her own face from the sand and grit. She noted as she did so that Zoe's coarse woolen wrap was already in place over Helena. Between the two of them, surely she would be safe.

———

Julia could hear the roar beyond the mouth of the cave. She could feel the sand in the air. In her teeth. It stung her eyes and chafed at her cheeks. What must it be like out where it struck in its full fury?

She felt Helena shift her position. "Mother?"

Helena's head came up. She stretched out a hand to find Julia's in the darkness.

"Are you well?" Julia's voice was hushed. Her mother could not endure loud noise when one of her headaches was upon her. And Julia did not wish to awaken Zoe if she was able to sleep through the storm.

In reply Helena squeezed her hand. "We are safe. A miracle. I have even managed to sleep some. Another miracle."

"God be praised," Julia responded. There had been much to praise God for since she had come to faith, and the words were never more heartfelt than now.

She felt more than saw her mother's head lift. The phrase must have seemed strange. New to her. In the near darkness she studied Julia for a long moment and then said quietly, "You have changed, Julia."

The words held neither condemnation nor commendation. Only acknowledgment.

Julia nodded. She knew she had changed. But she also realized there was more to be done. "That is . . . that is what I would like to talk to you about."

Helena stirred on the quilted pad Jacob had retrieved from the donkeys. She half-turned from Julia. "You wish to convince me again. To come to your meetings. To try to change me."

Julia was quick to reply. "No, Mother. I wish to ask your forgiveness."

Julia could feel Helena's head turn toward her again and wished she could see her eyes. "Whatever have you done?"

"Just what you have said. Tried to change you. Argued with you. I am sorry, Mother. I had no right to coax and cajole. It is only God who can change a person's heart. It is his Spirit that will draw you to him. And it happens only when you desire it, Mother. God never forces himself on anyone. I was wrong to push—"

"Oh, my child," said Helena, reaching out to draw Julia into her arms. "I have been so overwrought. For so long. If I thought for one moment that this . . ."

Julia felt tears on her shawl, but she was unsure if they were from her own eyes or her mother's. It was so hard for her to hold her tongue in check. There was so much she wished to say—but she had said it all before. Many times.

"I need . . . I need your God. I have watched you and . . . and you have such joy. Such peace. Both you and Zoe. How I long for it. But, Julia, I cannot go to your meeting to find it. Your father would be very angry. He might disown both of us."

There it was again. Her father. The man whom at one time she had idolized. And now she saw as an opponent to all things eternal. Again she felt the anger rise within.

Then a new feeling flooded her very soul and gentle words were whispered to her heart. *Love. Forgive. As you forgive, you will be forgiven.*

Julia nestled close to her mother. That was her answer. The one she had been seeking through prayer. Of course. She must forgive. If she was ever to have peace in its fullness, she must forgive.

She slowly pushed back in hopes she might see her mother's face in the gloom. She lifted one hand to wipe the tears from Helena's cheek, but her hand encountered gritty sand.

"Mother," she began slowly. "You are correct. God has indeed changed me. I know it. I feel it. But there is one thing I have not let him do for me. Not until now. But he has just whispered to my heart the words that I needed to hear. Words of peace. Of forgiveness. He has forgiven me. Now I must forgive."

Helena seemed puzzled. "Who . . . ?"

"Father."

"Your father? What has he—"

"Not a thing. Nothing but care for me."

"Then . . . ? I do not understand."

"What he has done to *you*, Mother. I have felt angry that he has treated you with such injustice. Leaving you with no legal status. No security as a wife would enjoy. I have been so angry. And you don't even dare accept a faith because of his . . . his ownership. I . . . "

But Julia dared say no more lest she stir up the bitterness once again. She swallowed, said a brief prayer, and managed a smile, even though she knew it could not be seen.

"I cannot keep holding such feelings against my own father. Against anyone. Jesus teaches us that we are to love. To forgive."

Helena sat quite still. She finally reached for one of Julia's hands and clasped it in her own. "My dear," she said, her voice so soft that Julia needed to strain to be sure she heard aright. "You have just convinced me the faith you have found is what I need. What I have longed for. There is nothing further you could have said that would have convinced me. But this? This need to forgive. That is real, Julia. Genuine. I know it cannot come from within—except by the help of your God. Would you tell me how I might receive this ability to forgive from the God you have claimed as your own?"

Julia's arms tightened around her mother while her tears flowed unchecked. Never had she heard such beautiful words in all her young life. Outside the storm might still rage on, but inside, in the darkness and safety of the wind-lashed cave, peace flooded two hearts that reached out to their Lord.

CHAPTER TWENTY-TWO

The Megiddo Plains

ALBAN AND THE village elder both sensed the storm's approach at almost the exact moment. Yelban immediately shouted orders for the market's evacuation. Whether or not the tempest actually struck, there would be no trade until it passed.

Abigail had little in the way of wares yet. She had made arrangements with a few villagers for their weavings, but her shelves were less than a third full. She and Martha and Alban made swift work of stowing the articles and dismantling the shop, then went to help others who were shorthanded.

For safety's sake, Yelban ordered all the stalls dismantled and the corralled animals herded up the steep road to Nain and into the village pens. It was a hard trek, one made rougher by the required haste. Yet no one argued. Especially not with Alban constantly urging them to ever greater speed. All the villagers had survived such storms before. They could taste the friction on their tongues, feel the hair standing away from their bodies, as if the earth were quarreling with the sky.

The storm lasted two and a half days. Below them in the valley, the sand boiled and rushed, like a nightmare river. The Valley of Megiddo was filled from one end to the other, north to south, east to west. The sand was the color of old rust, and the noise was fierce. A howling dominated the world and did not stop, not to draw breath nor to let them sleep. Sand rattled against the doors, fistfuls of grit tossed upward like froth from a crashing wave. The dust settled everywhere. Abigail bathed Dorcas, and before the child was dressed again she would be covered with sand as fine as milled flour. It was in their food and in their water. It clogged their nostrils and filled their ears. They took to wearing their shawls wrapped around their faces even when indoors.

During the second afternoon, Yelban brought word that a young woman with a newborn had taken ill. He carefully led Abigail and Martha back through the howling wind and sand to the home, shawls wrapped tightly around their faces, and they spent all that day caring for the baby and praying over the mother. There was no sudden healing, but their presence seemed to ease the young woman's suffering and calmed her anxious husband. When they returned to Alban and Dorcas during the sullen dusk, the mother and child were both resting and seemed to be recovering.

Before dawn on the third morning, Abigail was awakened and could not find the reason. Then she realized the noise had stopped. She wanted to rise and see if indeed the storm was passed. But her limbs would not obey her. Dorcas stumbled over to her pallet, whimpering half-formed words, and snuggled down beside her. Abigail wrapped one arm around her daughter and both returned to slumber.

Abigail awoke to the heat of the sun's full light. She could not recall the last time she had slept so long. Even so, she heard nothing from the others. Abigail dressed and went onto the front porch. The entire village was silent. Not even the dogs were about. No rooster crowed. The lack of noise seemed deafening—eerie.

Slowly the village came to life, and they spent the day clearing away the sand. Every surface was swept, scrubbed, and left to dry, then scrubbed again. Helzebah and Alban worked upstairs, Martha and Abigail downstairs. They rarely spoke, for the dust had left every throat raw. They drank tea sweetened with honey and pomegranate, mug after mug. They walked back and forth to the nearest well so often they created a furrow in the sandy lane.

Dorcas played on the front porch with the little bird the drover had given to her. During the storm, Alban had fashioned a tether from a length of supple leather cord. He had shown Dorcas how to slip a noose about one of the bird's legs, then tie the other end around one of her fingers. Abigail had feared the bird would peck her child's hand during the process, but the bird had seemed to understand, or at least accept the situation. By the storm's end, it would hop onto Dorcas's finger and wait patiently for the child to fit the tether in place, then spend hours perched upon her shoulder, occasionally flitting about and making Dorcas laugh. All that long day, the bird filled the house with song.

The next morning they descended once more to the valley floor. Abigail had left Dorcas with the young mother, who appeared much improved that morning. It seemed to Abigail as though nearly the entire village walked down together. This was hardly a surprise, as their livelihood was dependent upon the market that lined the road junctures. The village owned five wagons, and all were used that day, piled high with canvas and wood and tools. The village had survived many such storms. They knew what to expect—before, during, and afterward

The Plains of Megiddo were a silent void. Nothing stirred—no wind, no birds, no animals. Even the buildings that marked where the roads joined were blanketed by sand, rendering them all the same shade of sunlit yellow.

The stone walls that had faced the storm's wrath were all heaped with sand as high as the roofs. Doors had to be forced open. The finest dust had sifted through the sealed portals and now coated every surface. The work done in the village above had to be repeated here, but there was no rush. Yelban predicted it would be at least a week before the next caravans arrived, perhaps longer.

They finished work on Abigail's stall long before many others had even made a good start. Alban and Martha went to help rebuild the corral and ready the stables. Abigail and Helzebah helped Yelban and his family with the tavern and the stoves. That night, the majority of the village camped there on the valley floor. The husband of the young mother returned to the village with a few others, promising to keep Dorcas with them overnight and report back the next day.

They ate a communal meal, filling Yelban's tavern and spilling out into the empty roads. They sang, they prayed, and then they sat and listened while first Alban and then Martha spoke of Jesus and his teachings.

Abigail's eyelids were growing heavy as Yelban stood and walked toward them. He cleared his throat, turned to Abigail, and said in a somewhat formal tone, "You have helped us at every turn. You healed my wife."

"It was God's doing," Abigail said quickly. "Not mine."

She might as well not have spoken, for Yelban continued in the same vein, speaking loud enough to be heard by the entire group. "You teach, and ask for nothing. You heal. You give of what you have. You are a friend to all."

Abigail stirred, uncomfortable, but Martha touched her arm. When she glanced over, Martha lifted one finger. Wait.

"The elders have spoken. We have decided. Your name will be

passed among the other villages and their elders. You will be spoken of as one to be trusted. All who weave will be told of you and your business here. The debts left by those who came before you are no more. You need only pay once you have sold the wares. You will be taught what is the proper price to pay the weavers. Any who seek to do you wrong will have offended every one of us."

Abigail felt her eyes fill with tears. Her throat felt tighter than at the height of the storm.

Alban clearly saw the struggle she was having. He rose and said, "On behalf of my sister in Christ, I thank you all. Soon I must return to my own family, who await me in Capernaum. I will depart with an easy heart, knowing that I leave Abigail surrounded by true friends, safe here in her new home."

They sang another song, prayed a final time, and then dispersed. Several of the villagers came up and offered Abigail a formal welcome, as though greeting her for the first time. Yelban's wife gave them blankets and bedding. Abigail walked out into the night, accompanied by Martha and Helzebah and Alban, surrounded by the soft hush of a desert night and the voices of people who welcomed her. She stared up at the wash of stars, and tried out the word that rang through her mind and heart.

Home.

CHAPTER TWENTY-THREE

The Megiddo Plains

JUST BEFORE THEIR third dawn in the caves, the storm began to ease. Jacob lifted his head from its rocky pillow to listen. In truth, he had not been asleep. His rest throughout the storm had come in starts and stops. He would drift away from the wind's howl for a few moments, then the discomfort of a dry throat or a sound from the animals or something else would draw him back to consciousness. His entire body ached. He was famished. Thirst was a constant enemy. But he was alive. And so were the women. And the beasts.

The women were in the cave to his right. Jacob shared his shelter with the animals. Neither cave had been deep enough to fully escape the storm. Fashioned by eons of wind, they were bowl-like depressions without the depth or the fissures that water could create. Jacob had searched the cliff face in both directions and found no better haven. They were at least sheltered from the worst of the wind. But the dust swirled about them in constant clouds. The animals complained constantly, until thirst rendered them unable to protest any longer.

They all were thirsty, all the time. There were five skins between them. Jacob rationed the water strictly, giving them one meager cupful twice each day. Even so, they had water for just one more day. He supposed the women wondered why he continued to share their scarce water with the beasts. The reason was simple. Without the beasts they would die out there in the desert. Jacob's greatest worry, never spoken aloud, was that the storm might last into a fourth day.

But by the time the first hints of light touched the eastern horizon, the wind had vanished. Jacob stood in the light as the women slowly emerged from their cave, their faces and clothes coated with dust. Julia's dark eyes were rimmed with red. She removed her shawl from about her face and shook out sand and dust. Even her lips were coated with the pale powder as of a death mask. She opened her mouth and tried to speak, but could only cough.

Zoe stared at the rising sun for a long moment, then dropped to her knees and clasped her hands. To Jacob's surprise Helena staggered over to kneel beside her. When Julia took her place at Helena's other side, Jacob crossed over and knelt also. If ever there had been a time for thanking God, it was now.

Afterward, they grinned ruefully at each other's sand-covered features, then lashed their meager belongings to one donkey and shared out all the remaining water. The animals pushed at Jacob, urgently wanting more. The women drank their portions slowly and did not complain. When Jacob tried to explain where he thought they should go, Julia waved his words away. "It must hurt you to talk," she rasped out.

He nodded. The woman's voice was rough and nearly unrecognizable.

She coughed and finished, "Lead us, and we will follow."

Jacob tried to guide Helena onto one of the horses. But she motioned him away. "Julia . . . will ride . . . horse."

"But, mistress—"

"I do not . . . have the strength," she finished in a barrage of coughing.

In truth, it made sense to pair the younger and stronger woman with the faster animal. If there was difficulty, she would have a better chance of controlling it. As Jacob helped Julia onto the horse's back, he said in a whisper, "Your mother is a true queen."

Julia's eyes shone with a joy visible even through all the grime. "My mother is now a follower of our risen Lord. The storm has turned out to be a blessing."

Jacob nodded and turned away, full of his own deep emotion at the news. He assisted Julia's mother onto one donkey, then Zoe on the other. Their few remaining supplies and the empty waterskins were fastened in front of each rider.

He had debated which route to take. Back to the main road, and on to the next well? Or further along the most recent track in hopes there was indeed a nearby village and that they would share their water? Jacob would not have minded a discussion. But since the decision was left to him, he chose to return to the Roman road. He knew that way, and he knew precisely where the next well stood.

At midmorning they passed what was left of Jamal's carriage. The wind had devoured the drapes and worn the carvings from the corner posts. The wheels had collapsed upon axles overloaded with sand. All the colorful tapestries were gone. As was every scrap of leather. The wagon's interior was almost buried beneath the sand.

Jacob walked over and burrowed down, using his hands as a scoop. Julia came to join him. She spoke, her voice still a raw whisper. "What do we seek?"

"Your chest. It would be good to have fresh clothing."

She dug alongside him. "And the two small bags. What I would not give for a bath."

"And I." But it was not a bath that most concerned him. "I have lost my bag of coins in the storm. We might—"

"Mother carried another. Father insisted she have plenty for the journey."

Jacob felt a band of tension ease from his chest. They would likely be charged top price for water. When his hands found the chest, together they hauled it from the sand and into the light. "Leave it closed for now. If you open it, everything will get covered with sand."

"It is very heavy."

"The horse has little else to carry. The skins are empty, and the small bags are light. We can lash this behind your saddle."

Together they carried the chest and tied it firmly into place. They set off again, and around midday they found the road. It was almost completely covered by the storm's sand. But the rocks that bordered it made a straight-line indentation, one that extended both westward and eastward, on to the horizons. They turned west. As they did, the women looked back, off toward Tiberias. Jacob waited for one or the other to speak. Behind them lay their familiar home and safety. And Jamal. But there was no well between them and Tiberias. The closest Roman garrison had been abandoned precisely for this reason. And Jacob knew they could not push the animals further than the nearest well. Not to mention bandits prowling the hills for just such stragglers . . .

In truth, going west offered no certain security. There was indeed a well, some three or four hours further. But the wind might have filled it, and if so, they would die with the animals. But the women did not question his decision, and he saw no reason to speak of his concerns.

Their progress was labored. Jacob dared not lead the animals faster than the pace they found natural. But the sun continued to crawl across the empty sky, and he knew they had to either reach the well by sunset or halt. And if they stopped for the night without water, he was not certain the animals would live through to morning.

The land was utterly empty. They saw no other living thing. No bird, nor even tracks. Jacob found no sign that their caravan had survived. The air was so still it was hard to believe the storm had ever happened. The cloudless sky stretched out to where it joined with the bare earth. The only sound was their labored breathing and the animals' shuffling steps.

By sunset Jacob was nearing despair. Zoe walked slowly beside Helena riding the donkey, the maidservant's arm around her beloved mistress. The animals had begun to falter. Julia slipped from the horse's back, though her footsteps were scarcely more stable than the horse's.

Then Jacob saw it. At least, he thought he saw it, though in his state he couldn't be sure. A faint rise on the horizon, a mere smudge that dimpled the otherwise flat landscape.

At that same moment, one of the donkeys brayed weakly. It was impossible that a beast might smell water at that distance. Even so, Jacob took it as a good sign.

The closer they came, the faster moved the animals. Jacob and Julia labored alongside them, drawn by a hope and a thirst that burned their bodies. Julia turned back to support her mother on the other side of the donkey.

When Jacob was close enough to see that it was indeed a well and the cover remained in place, he gave a hoarse cry of relief. He fell to his knees beside the rock perimeter, his hands trembling so hard he could not make them obey. Julia stilled his frantic fumbling by touching his arm. He glanced at her. She had lost the ability to speak, but her cracked lips formed the words *Tell me what to do*.

"Rope," he croaked. "Reins."

Together they untied the chest and dumped it down on the sand. He lashed one end of the rope to the wooden cover that enclosed the well's opening like a round door. Julia pulled on the horse's reins as Jacob slapped the animal's dusty rump. The horse was obviously so weary and thirsty its entire body trembled. Zoe took hold of the rope, and together they slid the cover aside.

This was a desert well, so deep that when Jacob dropped the leather bucket it fell for what seemed like eons.

When it finally landed with a splash, they all croaked a hoarse cry, animals and people alike.

The first bucket the four of them shared. Then they scraped the trough free of sand and poured in two more buckets. The horses and donkeys pushed at one another, drinking with impatient slurps. Julia and Zoe helped him haul up the ropes. Over and over and over. Jacob drank until his belly hurt, until he could not drink a single swallow more. He washed his face, then poured a bucket over his head and scrubbed at his arms and legs, then did it again. And a third time. He went for a walk to offer the ladies what privacy he could.

The last time he had come this way, there had been a dozen or so stalls. Poor structures offering the most meager of shelter and food. Of them, there was no sign. Not a stick of wood, nor a shred of cloth.

Jacob kept his position using the well and the setting sun as the only markers. He discovered a slight indentation and a small mound where he recalled the largest of the stalls had once stood. He began digging, and found confirmation in the form of a knee-high stone wall.

Julia walked over, rubbing her wet hair with her shawl. "What do you seek?"

"There was a stable here." He walked slowly along the line of buried stones, trying hard to remember the details. "The horses are in desperate need of fodder."

To his enormous relief, his recollections proved correct, for when they started digging they came upon a series of three wooden chests bolted to the stones, and in the second chest were oats. Together they carried double handfuls back to the well and dumped their precious cargo into the water trough. Once again the animals shouldered and jostled one another.

Helena said, "Maybe we can eat this too?"

"A tiny bit only, mistress. Else it will swell up your insides and cause great pain." He dribbled a few oats into her hand. "Chew long and hard, then chew again. This and no more."

They settled down beside the well, only sand for their bed and their pillow, and watched the stars come out. Jacob's stomach clenched with a stabbing desire for more food. Until then his thirst had been so great he had felt no hunger. But he could go a night without anything to eat. And so could the women, he was sure.

As the first stars came out, they joined hands for another shared prayer of thanks. Jacob bid the ladies good-night and lay watching the sea of stars.

They arrived in Ginae just before midday. They went to the inn at the center of town, where the women were directed upstairs, and water was heated for their bath. Jacob made do with a servant's wash at the stable's rear trough, sighing with pleasure as bucket after bucket sluiced away the dirt. He changed into robes loaned by the stable master and washed his clothes, then entered the inn to find every eye upon him. The innkeeper demanded, "Is it true what the woman says, you survived the storm?"

Jacob nodded. "We did."

The innkeeper set down a steaming bowl of stew and a platter of unleavened bread. "In a cave?"

"Two of them." Jacob spoke no more until he had finished his second bowl. The tavern became increasingly full with curious villagers. The three women returned downstairs, fresh-faced and clean, though their eyes still held the strain of their recent experience. Jacob supposed his own expression resembled theirs. When he could eat no more, he pushed the bowl away and related what had happened.

Julia and Helena sat across from him, watching him as they ate. Zoe had refused the invitation to join them at table, instead taking her place with the servants at the back of the room. Neither Helena nor Julia spoke until the bowls were finally taken away and tea was offered. Helena cradled her mug and said quietly, "Everything Jacob says is true. We are here because of his bravery and wisdom. And because of the Lord's care for us."

The innkeeper said, "We've had no word from either the south or the east."

"No caravan has passed this way?"

"Neither camel nor horse nor traveler until your good selves arrived."

Julia asked, "The storm struck here?"

"The hills offered us some shelter. But yes, we were hit. Most folk haven't ventured beyond their front door for days."

A voice from the crowd added, "It's a good thing the storm did not strike a week earlier. Else we'd have lost the fruit and olive crops."

The innkeeper picked up Jacob's empty bowl. "Some might call that a sign."

A woman's voice. "Or a miracle."

Julia said, "I have had that very word echoing through my mind since the moment we arrived in the cave."

Helena's eyes searched the faces in the crowd, then asked, "You are all followers of the Way?"

"Aye, mistress. We are. Some for a time. Others for only a few days."

"And I for three days only," Helena said quietly. "Has some event or miracle happened here?"

Jacob had often reflected upon that word, *miracle*. Alban's rescue of him, finding his sister, Linux's friendship, Abigail's healing, surviving the recent sandstorm. So many miracles. And yet another was added that very moment, when the innkeeper replied, "Aye, mistress, that it has. We were visited not so long ago by one who walked the earth with Jesus. A teacher, Philip by name. He spoke, and it seemed as though we heard not a man, but the voice of God. He baptized almost all the village." The innkeeper smiled at the recollection. "He came in the company of others from Jerusalem."

A voice from the crowd added, "And that woman from Sychar. Helzebah."

Helena's head swung around. "Helzebah of Sychar? Here?"

"Aye, that's the one. She traveled with two women from Jerusalem. Martha was one, she had spent much time with the Lord, and the other was—"

Jacob realized he had risen to his feet, as though pulled upward by an unseen hand. "Abigail?"

"You know her?"

"She is my sister!"

A rippling passed through the crowd, like the passage of a breeze over wheat. A woman said, "She taught us all day, and much of the night, and then again the next morning."

"Her face was filled with the same light as the man Philip's as she spoke of Jesus," said another.

Helena asked, "Where are they now?"

The innkeeper said, "They traveled north and east with the disciple and the Roman soldier."

"He was a Gaul," a man corrected, "and a soldier no longer."

Jacob breathed the one word. "Alban."

"You know of this man?"

"He is my guardian. Last time I saw him, he was most unwell."

"He was faring better, though still weak. He spoke little, but what he said . . ." The innkeeper shook his head. "After I was baptized, the Roman centurion embraced me and called me brother. I wept."

"And I," said another.

Jacob asked once more, "Can you tell us where they went?"

"That I can, for my cousin traveled with them as guard. Their destination was Nain. The woman called Abigail was to take over a market stall where all the roads come together."

"Was Helzebah with them?" asked Helena intently.

"Aye, mistress. She went to help them settle."

Helena said to Jacob, "Then I must travel to Nain."

Jacob nodded and tried to keep the concern from his voice. "I understand, mistress."

Julia said in a whisper, "This change of plan troubles you?"

Jacob nodded and answered in a low voice. "Jamal entrusted me with the care of you and your mother, but also with another urgent matter. I need to travel to Joppa. I am already delayed."

Helena must have overheard, because she looked about the small gathering. "Can any of you lead my daughter and maidservant and me safely to Nain?"

Several voices crowded together. The innkeeper lifted his voice to make himself heard. "We can and will, mistress."

"It is settled then," went on Helena. She looked at Julia, who nodded.

"You are free to follow your orders, Jacob."

"If you are well cared for and will excuse me, mistress, I will depart." He dipped a bow.

"What? You must leave now?" Julia questioned.

Jacob did his best to hide his weariness. "Jamal's errand holds a great deal of urgency. I should be off while the light and weather are with me. And I also need to find a messenger to carry back word to the master that you both, along with Zoe, are safe."

CHAPTER TWENTY-FOUR

The Megiddo Plains

THE CHANGE THAT Julia had seen in her mother over the few days since she had acknowledged Jesus as her Messiah was truly astonishing. Zoe also remarked on it. Julia no longer felt she had to serve as her mother's protector. Helena appeared quite able to make decisions on her own. Even their horrible ordeal of waiting out the storm, then traveling the seemingly endless journey across piled sand and trackless terrain, had not brought on another of Helena's headaches.

Now Helena had surprised her once again. Julia had not been able to believe her own hearing when her mother decided that the three of them would not travel on to Joppa as Jamal had planned but would divert to the small village of Nain to see a friend of years past. Surely Helzebah was only a name in Helena's faint memory from childhood. Though since her own conversion, Helena had several times asked Zoe to repeat Helzebah's story of meeting the Master during the time of his Judean ministry.

Julia was very aware that Jacob's presence and direction would be missed. For a moment she considered arguing that it would not be wise for them to travel on their own to a different destination. And if they did, how and when would they be able to return to Tiberias? Jamal had expected them to be safely delivered to Joppa under Jacob's diligent care.

As Jacob prepared for his journey, Julia felt the need for one last word with him. He was busy with a strong cord, tying one of his bundles of provisions onto the donkey's back.

"Does it concern you that we are not continuing on with you as planned?"

Jacob leaned back on his heels. "On the contrary, I think this is an answer to prayer."

"Won't my father feel we have not obeyed his orders?"

"There is no longer a caravan to guarantee your safety. No matter how hard I try, I will not be able to do this on my own."

"And what of yourself?"

"Had your mother not suggested this other destination, I would have remained here with you until we could connect with another caravan headed west. But after such a storm, all travel is disrupted. Perhaps it would take days, even weeks. Then I would be left with another dilemma. Do I send you back to Tiberias under someone else's care, or go with you and forsake my other assignment? Either way, I would not be able to serve Jamal as I should."

Julia nodded slowly as Jacob turned back to his task. There was more than just reassurance in his words. There was strength as well, and wisdom.

"Your mother has changed," Jacob said over his shoulder as he pulled a knot tight. "I have seen it in the brief time since she has joined with us as a follower. She is a stronger woman now. More able to face her world." He glanced quickly at Julia, clearly wondering if he should have made this rather personal observation.

But Julia quickly nodded her agreement. "I have seen the change as well."

Her response seemed to encourage him to continue. "This is an opportunity to meet with other believers before she returns to Tiberias. It may be what she needs to further strengthen her faith."

Julia felt immense relief at hearing some of her own thoughts given voice. "I feel the same."

As he gave a pull on the cord he said, "I wish . . . I would like to remain with . . . with . . . with the three of you and see you safely home, but I must be on the trail." He kept his face turned away from her gaze.

"I understand." Julia lowered her voice and dared to ask, "Do you have further warnings for the . . . for our fellow believers in Joppa?"

He gave a brief shake of his head. "I have been given one contact in Joppa. To see if . . . if they have further . . . news. Nothing more."

Julia nodded. She realized that she should not ask another question, nor delay him longer.

"Do you have enough coins?" he asked.

"More than enough for our simple needs." She hesitated. "And you?"

"I withdrew as needed from the chest. I am keeping an account—"

She waved his explanation aside. "I must thank you, both for your wisdom and your care. We would surely have perished had we tried to stay with the caravan."

"God is to be thanked."

Julia managed a quiet smile. She felt an unexpected warmth fill her. "I think there are times when God's servants need to hear words of gratitude as well."

He looked at her in a way that he had not before. Silently.

Longingly, as though taking to memory every feature of her face. Julia felt a flush creeping up her cheeks. "God go with you, Jacob. I will be awaiting your safe return."

"Thank you," he said just before he turned away. "I would appreciate your prayers."

Julia watched him go and wondered why she suddenly felt bereft. Alone . . .

Julia and Helena were preparing for bed in their shared rooftop room at the home of one of their new friends and fellow believers.

"Do you find it strange that I insisted upon this journey to Nain?" Helena asked as she combed through her hair with her fingers.

Julia turned from spreading out their pallets and arranging the coverings loaned to them.

"No. Not strange. You say you remember the name from childhood."

"Helzebah? Yes, vaguely."

"It is understandable that you would wish to see someone from your childhood, speak with her once more, Mother."

Helena removed her sandals and rubbed her weary feet. "Actually, I have two reasons to speak with her. She may have news of my family that I have not heard since my time in Tiberias. I . . . I have never learned what caused my mother's death." She paused and looked out the window for a moment. "And Zoe's story concerning her intrigues me. To think that a religious leader would forgive—"

"He was not a religious leader, Mother. He was—is—the Messiah."

"Yes, of course. I did not mean . . . Well, it is difficult for me to fully comprehend the fact that he has come. The one of whom we have long heard, the one for whom we have awaited. It seems like an impossibility, and now . . ."

"I know."

"I never thought I would live to be so blessed."

Julia smiled and moved over to embrace her mother. From her heart a fervent prayer of thanks floated upward. *Mother believes!*

When Julia stepped back, Helena removed her outer robe and tossed it aside. The embroidered garment that Jamal insisted she bring for the trip looked rather wrinkled and dulled by dust, but even with all that, still out of place in this quaint village of laborers. And now she—who was accustomed to sleeping on a raised bed in silks—prepared to stretch out on a floor mat for the night.

"I noticed you spoke with Jacob before he left."

Julia nodded.

"Did he seem distressed that I had decided not to go on to Joppa?"

"Oh no. In fact he was very understanding. He thought it wise that you take the opportunity to visit with Helzebah and the other believers before you return to Tiberias."

"Life is strange, is it not? Had we not come on this trip—which I dreaded with all my being—we would not have been caught in the storm that made us take refuge in a cave. And had we not been with Jacob, who knew of storms, we would have perished. And if we had not been forced to spend that frightening time together, I may not have been brought to recognize my need of your God. And now Helzebah . . ." Helena shook her head with a smile.

"Life is indeed strange. And wondrous."

Helena looked up at Julia. "My mind has settled much since I have come to faith. But there is one thing that causes an inner struggle."

Helena stared out the window, and Julia waited.

"Remember, you spoke of having difficulty forgiving your father?" Helena finally said. "I do not feel that I need to forgive him. But I . . ." She hesitated, as though the words were difficult to speak. Julia waited again.

"I do not know much about faith," Helena went on, now looking at Julia. "But I do know there are very strict religious laws about . . . about being a 'kept woman.' I remember someone from our village, an outcast. She was shunned. There was even talk of stoning her. I was a child, but it haunted me. It still does. I do not know what became of her. I think she was sent away—no doubt to beg."

Julia was silent. Listening carefully to her mother.

Julia noted the difference in her now. Instead of a woman who looked lost, confused, Helena sat tall and spoke with a strength in her voice. "I no longer will fear should your father decide to send me away. I would not welcome it, but neither will I despair. If that is what the Lord sees . . . as right, I will learn to bear it."

"Oh, Mother." Julia sat down on the mat and placed her arm around her mother's shoulders.

"You need not grieve," Helena said with confidence. "We . . . we both are in God's care. It is easy for me to trust him with my future. I will admit it is harder for me to trust you and your future to him. I cannot bear the thought of you being married to an infidel, should that be what he is. I pray and pray, but no answer comes. At least one I can hear."

Julia could not speak. The mother she had prayed for so earnestly was now praying for her. It touched her deeply.

Helena wiped away tears on a sleeve of her gown. "I still cling to faith that . . . that things will change. How or when I cannot see, but surely God will allow it to happen."

Julia tightened her arm around her mother, then stood and took her place on the second mat. She did not even want to think about the marriage that loomed in her future. It frightened and saddened her. She reached for the blanket and pulled it upward. Morning would come early. She was weary from their long day. She wanted sleep—but her mother's concerns for her whirled through her mind.

Helena was not finished. "I do not see the way to true happiness as being found in wealth. No matter how rich and prominent the family may be, sorrow can still fill the home. I do not think your father finds happiness in his riches. Instead they weigh heavily upon his mind. I now know there are things of more worth. Like forgiveness. Faith. If only your father could discover the *true* treasure . . . I pray for that to happen."

I, too, thought Julia, but she did not say the words as she lay down on her pallet.

The room was quiet. The night outside captured the calm after the storm. From some distance a sheep bleated. Julia felt herself drifting off to sleep when her mother spoke again.

"I have been watching our young man, Jacob. He seems to regard you highly."

Julia's heart started beating more quickly. "Why do you say that, Mother?"

"The way he looks at you. Particularly when you are not facing his way. He sees you for what you are. An attractive, strong, intelligent woman. I notice it in his eyes."

"Oh, Mother." In the darkness Julia put her hands on her warm cheeks.

"There are complications of course. You being the daughter of Jamal. But if your circumstances were different and your hand was not already spoken for . . . I quite like him."

Julia did not answer, and Helena said no more.

In spite of her exhaustion, Julia found it hard to calm her tumbling thoughts for sleep.

CHAPTER TWENTY-FIVE

The Megiddo Plains

THE WEEK FOLLOWING the storm was filled with feverish activity. A number of the stalls needed rebuilding from the ground up. Alban, Abigail, Zoe, and Martha pitched in with the others, winning even more friends. They worked late, often sleeping in the windowless rear chamber rather than making the steep climb up the road to Nain. When the Sabbath finally arrived, the entire village was in need of rest. The women joined with the community for a Sabbath service in the rather dilapidated synagogue. Later, after the evening meal, the followers of the Way began collecting together in front of Abigail's house, and it seemed very natural to gather in small groups to talk about Jesus, about what his life, death, and resurrection meant to each of them.

That night Abigail's sleep was fitful, and she finally left her pallet and slipped out the front door. She stood at the edge of the escarpment and watched the stars sprinkled across the sky, and felt anew the changes that now defined her life, like a leaf caught upon powerful winds.

Below her, the northern Megiddo Plains stretched out silver and empty. Unlike the Samaritan fields to the south, Megiddo held a desert dryness, with a hardscrabble surface that grew little save sand. While still in Jerusalem, Abigail had heard tales of the Samaritan wastelands and the loathed inhabitants who had lost their heritage and tainted their Hebrew faith. And yet this was now her home, and to her surprise she felt content.

The region's emptiness and strangeness were as had been described. But she knew God was with her. Abigail stared up at the sky, and did not pray aloud. Instead, she felt the Spirit's presence surrounding her. Her communion was deeper than words could accommodate.

Here in this silent emptiness, she had witnessed the impossible. Miracles of lives transformed, bodies healed. Her daughter was happy. Friends had remained at her side and helped her make new ones. She had found new ways to serve, had discovered a field needing harvest, just as the Lord had foretold. Villages filled with hungry hearts, yearning to know the Messiah.

As Abigail returned to her pallet, she resolved to begin a women's prayer and study group. They would meet to discuss the truths she had learned from Peter and others in Jerusalem. They would pray for each other and for the Nain community.

The next evening Abigail, Martha, and Helzebah closed the shop and prepared to climb the winding road home after another long day in the market.

Yelban's son pointed and called, "Riders coming this way!"

The women paused to shade their eyes against the setting sun, but this time it was not a caravan that approached.

Julia stood under an awning, sheltering more from the crowd than the sun.

They had arrived at Nain the previous evening, tired and dusty from a long day on the trail. To their surprised relief, they were heartily welcomed, not just by Helzebah, who quickly found accommodations for them, but by the entire community of believers who gathered to greet them.

It was a strange feeling to be among strangers who treated them as friends. So she watched and saw anew how the community of followers was indeed unlike others she had known. And Alban? Julia watched him in particular, for she wondered about his influence on Jacob. Surely this man held some of the secrets.

Their new friends gathered around Alban now, offering farewells before he left for Capernaum. Julia had heard how long it had been since he had seen his wife and young son, and she could see the anticipation in the man's face. She felt she understood at least some of his feelings. Hadn't she reacted in a similar fashion each time she had received news her father's caravan was coming home?

The group made a circle around Alban. They placed their hands on his head and shoulders and prayed for safety on his journey. They prayed for Leah, waiting at home for him with little Gabriel. They also prayed for Jacob, now wending his way toward Joppa.

But their prayers did not stop there. They prayed that as Alban lived from day to day, his testimony of the risen Lord would ring true, that others who would accompany Alban on his journey would bear strong witness wherever they went.

Alban and his small group heard blessing after blessing and words of encouragement and Scriptures to take with them as final good-byes were exchanged. It was an amazing scene and brought tears to Julia's eyes. Here they were, a group as diverse as one could possibly bring together. Jew, Samaritan, Roman, Greek—all united because of one who had come from God and returned to God only a few short years ago. Surely here was living proof that the eternal truths brought to life during Jesus' time on earth meant transformation was not only possible, it was real.

The man she had before known as her father's chief guard walked over to where she stood. Julia whispered, "Go with God."

Alban nodded and said, "When you next see Jacob, please tell him I am thinking of him daily—and also warn him to be careful." They both smiled. "I will pray for his safe return. And yours."

And at last the departing travelers were on the road, watched by many until they disappeared around the first bend. Julia was standing near Helena. She reached out and took her arm, moving in close to the side of her mother. Helena asked, "Why do I feel I have just said good-bye to a dear family member?"

"I suppose because he *is* family now. A closer kinship than we have ever known before."

Helena stared thoughtfully down the now-empty road. " 'Family,' " she repeated. "So many things I will be learning," she murmured.

"It seems like you rested well."

Helena responded with the hint of a smile. "I sat up with Helzebah and Martha. We talked far into the night."

"The moon was high, and you still had not come to bed. I thought to go looking for you—then I heard voices."

"Helzebah shared her story. Did you know she was married to five different men?"

"She was widowed five times?"

Helena shook her head. "She didn't say how each marriage ended. But after the five she merely lived with another man. That was when she met Jesus. She had gone to the well for water. The town women shunned her, so she went at a time of day when others would not be there. But he was there. Alone. This Jewish man who was not of their town. Who was not a Samaritan. At first she was frightened. She didn't know whether she should turn around and go home without the water. But she needed it, and he didn't seem to be paying any attention to her.

"He spoke to her—which astonished her. No Jew would speak to a Samaritan. Especially a woman. But his manner was kind as he asked for water.

"He told her that he was the Messiah, the promised one. Even more shocking, he seemed to know all about her, yet he did not shun her. He spoke to her with a respect she had not found from anyone—man or woman. I think that is what drew her most. Then he spoke of living water. Water that would satisfy her needs in the days and years to come. She found her heart longing for this living water. When she finally did leave him and hurry back home, she did not hide in shame. She called out to everyone she saw to come and hear him. She was convinced he was who he said he was. The Messiah."

Helena looked into Julia's face. "Think of it," she mused, "the Messiah—speaking to a woman. A woman living with a man to whom she was not married. Bringing her peace and forgiveness. Is not that amazing?"

Julia nodded, her eyes full. Helena too was weeping quietly, but behind the tears her eyes shone and a smile spread across her countenance, seeming to engulf her in a happiness Julia had never seen her mother express before.

"And he has forgiven me! This same Lord. This same master. My Messiah. He has forgiven me too."

"And me," Julia said softly. "And me."

"But I do still have questions." Helena gazed at the empty road once more. "We three discussed at length what I should do. They did not give me any advice or instructions, but we prayed. Martha said the Spirit would enlighten me. Would give me direction. Would give me strength and wisdom to make the right decision."

She looked calm, assured, as she went on, "And he will. I am confident of that. When I look back at how he led us through the windstorm and brought us to be here with Helzebah and Abigail and Martha, I see it all as his miracle. I have learned that I can trust Jesus with whatever lies ahead. Martha said that the decision may not be easy, but it will bring peace. And that is what I long for. What we all desire, I believe. Peace of mind and soul."

Julia reached out to embrace her mother.

Peace . . . Yes.

CHAPTER TWENTY-SIX

East of Jerusalem

FOR SAFETY'S SAKE, Jacob held where possible to the well-traveled Roman roads. By the second afternoon he had skirted the hills east of Jerusalem, and he spent the night in the same box canyon where he had slept after leaving Jamal's caravan. He knew donkeys possessed remarkably keen senses and were light sleepers. If they smelled or heard an intruder, Jacob would know of it.

He slept deeply, and the next morning after a quick breakfast he had reached the point where the foothills met the rocky coastal plains. This had become an increasingly lawless region. Only one main road descended westward from Jerusalem to the Judean plains. Zealots and bandits alike preyed upon unfortunate travelers. Roman soldiers patrolled the route, but they could not be everywhere. Jacob maintained his position just off the road, scouting carefully in every direction as he rode. Behind him, the way snaked up the Jerusalem hills, a yellow ribbon rising to greet the empty sky.

Where the road met the Judean plains, he made out the figure of a man walking ahead of him. He finally noticed the lone traveler carried a leather sack upon his shoulder and leaned upon a long staff. There was something about the man, perhaps his gait, that called to Jacob. He touched his heels to the donkey's sides and further closed the distance.

The sun was strong, and its rays glanced harshly off the scrub and rocks and on the traveler. Jacob grew increasingly certain now he knew the man. He called across the remaining distance, "The Lord's greetings to you!"

The man stopped and lifted a hand. "The peace of Jesus upon you, my friend."

A faint chill rose up Jacob's spine. "Philip?"

"Aye, 'tis I. And I know that voice."

"It is Jacob."

"Alban's charge." The disciple stepped off the path as Jacob rode up to him. "What are you doing, traveling alone in these hard days?"

"I serve the trader Jamal. He has sent me to Joppa. And yourself?"

"The Lord sent an angel." He spoke as easily as he might discuss the weather. Philip pointed ahead to where the road divided. The two main routes took aim for Caesarea to the north and Joppa straight west. But a smaller route, little more than a trail, broke off also. This one, Jacob knew, traveled straight south to the region known as Gaza. "I was ordered to travel the road to Gaza. Here I am. Why I have come, I cannot say. Do you think perhaps it was to meet you this morning?"

"Friend, I must warn you, the road to Gaza has been almost abandoned because of bandits. It would be far safer to head straight for Joppa, then turn south."

"Perhaps," Philip replied. "But the angel's instructions were clear enough. I go where the Lord leads me."

Jacob looked around with a small shiver. "Have you eaten?"

Philip patted the cloth bag slung over one shoulder. "The followers in Jerusalem were most generous. But I am short of water."

Jacob fumbled in his haste to unfasten his waterskin. When Philip had drunk his fill, Jacob asked, "If you have walked from Jerusalem, you must be most tired."

"I had a donkey, but he went lame."

"Then you must ride." Jacob shifted most of the second donkey's load to his own saddle. He arranged the remaining supplies and stretched the blanket across the animal's back, then helped Philip to mount. When they were once again upon the trail paralleling the Roman road, Jacob checked the hills behind them. He knew they faced grave peril, taking this way. And yet . . . He could not argue with the inner voice that bid him to accompany this man. Gone for the moment was all thought of Jamal's urgent mission. His thoughts were totally with Philip. "Did you say an angel?"

Philip moved forward so they were riding side by side. "I was deep asleep in your sister's main room. I heard a voice call to me, and I went out to the edge of the village overlooking the valley." Philip spoke with detached calm. "Have you heard your sister lives now in Nain, a village that oversees a great crossroads in the Megiddo Plains? Alban granted her a market stall there."

Jacob had immediate questions about the information, but all he could think to ask was, "May I ask what the angel told you?"

"I was bathed in a light as powerful as it was strong. I knew I was witnessing a miracle. I knelt in the sand. An angel said I was to travel the road from Jerusalem to Gaza. Nothing else. Nothing else was required."

Jacob hesitated. "If I had a chance to speak with God's messenger—"

"You would have a thousand questions. Yes, I do understand. If someone had spoken with me about such an event, I would have said the very same thing. But it was not like that."

"No?"

"When the angel appeared and spoke those simple words, I heard not just the command, but I felt the presence of God. There was no condemnation. There was no admonishment. Instead, there was . . ."

Jacob nodded his understanding. "You are a servant of God. You are doing his will. You are open to his command. He said go, and you obeyed."

Philip smiled. "When I spoke of this miracle in Jerusalem, I needed hours to make some of our group understand. You are indeed as clever, as well as devoted to our Lord, as your guardian claims."

With other of their leaders, Jacob might have felt a trace of awe. But Philip was unique among those who had followed in Jesus' footsteps. He was raised in a Hellenized family, as his name suggested. He had been appointed along with Stephen to take care of the widows and orphans in Jerusalem. He had served well, particularly those of Greek heritage. He had gone on to become a gifted evangelist. Philip carried himself with a sense of quiet transparency. Most content with silence, he listened far more than he spoke. And when he did speak, it was not about himself. The result was a sense of deep intimacy, not with the man himself but with the one whom Philip served.

"May I ask about my sister?"

"She is doing very well indeed," Philip told him. "Abigail's new home is situated upon a quiet lane leading from the village square toward the hillside. It is a protected place, and very peaceful. I shared quarters with Alban, who is feeling much better, by the way. From the porch you can look out over the crossroads far below, and the Megiddo Plains. Your sister and her daughter should be safe there. Abigail already is making friends and serving our Lord."

Jacob felt a pang of longing for his sister. It sounded like she was settled in a place that would be home. He was glad Alban seemed to have accepted that such a life was not for Jacob. At least not for the immediate time. He now walked a yellow plain beneath the glare of a wintry sun, the day as hot as the night had been frigid. He had slept without fire, wrapped in a single blanket, with only donkeys for company. And yet he had known then as he knew now that this was what he was to do until he was directed otherwise. "I am very happy for Abigail and Dorcas."

Philip glanced over at Jacob, and once more offered his quiet smile. "I am aware of the disagreement between you and your guardian. Alban told me about it, along with his sincere hope that there would be peace between you. I suggested to him that perhaps God's plan for you was as unique as the life you have known thus far."

"I do pray for God's guidance."

"I know this. And so does Alban."

The two looked at each other for a moment. Jacob clicked to the donkey and said, "To live confined to a market stall . . ."

"Is not your destiny."

Jacob's head jerked back so sharply the donkey faltered. "God has told you this?"

"No, my young friend. But I hear your heart's desire. And so must our Lord. And I also see how your sister flourishes in Nain. She needs safety. She needs a haven in which to raise her child and serve a community of followers. You, Jacob, must follow your own calling."

"Alban fears . . ."

"Of course he is concerned about your safety. But if this is how you are meant to best serve our Lord, then . . ." Philip smiled. "I shall pray for you both. Your safety, as well as Alban's peace in the matter."

"Thank you, Philip." Jacob felt a small quiver in his heart. "I hope and pray, if God does speak with me, I shall not grovel in shame over having taken the wrong course."

"I shall pray that when God speaks," Philip said, holding Jacob's gaze with his own, "you are open to listening first, then saying simply, 'Yes, Lord.' "

"You are right, and you—" Jacob stopped when Philip peered intently out to where the road curved south and disappeared around a rocky promontory. "What is it?"

"I thought I heard something."

Then Jacob heard it too. From ahead and around the bend of a small hill came the murmur of voices and the jangle of harness. Jacob reached out to restrain the older man but Philip was already eagerly pushing his mount forward. "Come, my young friend. Let us go and see the Lord's hand at work."

As soon as they rounded the hillock, Jacob saw stretched out along the trail a long line of armed men, some on horseback, accompanying the beautifully decorated chariot of an obviously wealthy official. Such an armed troop would have frightened off any bandit gang, no matter what riches the group might carry.

Somewhere in the distance, the Gaza road connected with the main Roman coastal route. There sprawled the unkempt fishing villages that made up the Gaza community. Jacob had journeyed upon the southern coastal road four times with Alban. Each caravan they guarded had met travelers coming from Egypt and the southern deserts. Alban had taught him to identify the strangers by symbols on face and body. Most desert tribesmen marked the rite of passage to adulthood by cutting the young men's cheeks. The knife slashes were filled with a mixture of pitch and lemon juice, so they healed cleanly but remained deeply scarred. The pattern of these scars declared to which tribe the men belonged. Understanding these tribal markings was vital, for some of the desert-bred men were easily slighted, leading to conflicts. Saluting them by their proper tribal name was an important means of gaining respect. And avoiding unnecessary clashes.

Now the men in the long line were resting their mounts and taking refreshment. Jacob was ready to advise Philip to take caution and restrain his donkey.

As they drew near the entourage Jacob told him, "These are Ethiopians."

Philip said, "I must go to them."

"I would counsel you not to do that." Jacob pointed to the caravan's center, at the chariot surrounded by a troop of personal bodyguards. It was a massive affair, three times the size of one intended for battle. The curved sides were covered with brilliant sheets of what could have been either bronze or beaten gold, shining in the afternoon light. Three men rode upon the chariot, a driver and a servant who held a sunshade above the third man. "That is no ordinary merchant. Either he is a king's messenger or someone . . ."

Jacob stopped because Philip was urging his donkey forward. Jacob swallowed hard and reluctantly followed.

Soon enough a guard caught sight of them and shouted toward the soldiers at the chariot. Three mounted guards wheeled about and raced toward them. Immediately Jacob did as Alban had instructed him in the past. He scrambled off the donkey's back and knelt upon the trail. He slipped the knife from his belt and laid it before him. Then he leaned down and pressed his forehead into the dust.

The Ethiopian warriors must have understood, for they kept their weapons sheathed. Jacob slowly lifted his head to see that the senior officer wore a chain of gold, thick as a snake, and held a miniature shield over his otherwise bare chest. As he opened his mouth, Jacob saw two of his front teeth had been knocked out, another declaration of tribal manhood. The warrior spoke in a tongue Jacob did not need to understand. "They want us to leave, Philip."

Philip too was off the other donkey's back, but he stood with his hands outstretched. "I greet you in the name of our Lord, Jesus Christ," he said in Greek.

The warrior stared at Philip from atop his horse.

"I wish to have words with your master. Please tell him that I come bearing the gift of eternal life."

The warrior gave no sign that he had understood. But he wheeled his horse about and rode to where the chariot had halted. He spoke to the official, who turned to stare back at them. Only then did Jacob realize what he was seeing. "The official holds a scroll," he said, his voice low.

The warrior saluted the official, then called to his men in the same guttural tongue. The rear guard motioned Jacob and Philip forward.

Jacob's heart hammered in his chest. Every person, even the camel drovers, was dressed in ornate robes. And was heavily armed. Whoever he was, this man held a great deal of influence in Ethiopia.

The three men in the chariot watched their approach in silence. The robe on the official was beaded with what appeared to be tiny gemstones, and every motion, every ripple of wind, created a flickering rainbow of colors. Soft featured and wide of girth, the man's skin was oiled, and as they approached, Jacob caught the fragrance of sandalwood.

The man's gaze was extremely intelligent. Cautious. Watchful. Jacob knew without the slightest doubt that this was a man who had long held the power of life and death.

Philip halted by the chariot, lifted his hands palms upward, and repeated his greeting in Aramaic.

The Ethiopian's accent was heavy but understandable. "Why are you here?"

"An angel of the Lord came to me in the night," Philip told him, bowing his head respectfully. "I was ordered to come south. When I saw your caravan, I was commanded to approach it and speak with you."

The Ethiopian stared at him a moment, then lifted the scroll, turning it so it faced toward Philip. "You can tell me what I hold?"

Jacob felt the hair on the back of his neck rise and his heartbeat quicken. He could see it was a scroll written in Greek. The text, known as the Septuagint, was a translation done by Judean scholars, and it had been completed a century and a half before Jesus was born. Jacob had studied those very scrolls in his youth, and he knew the text was usually referred to as the Seventy, representing the number of scholars who had labored on the translation. All students were required to memorize the prophets in Greek as a beginning to their studies. The Hebrew version of the Scriptures was used only during the formal reading of the Sabbath services.

Philip switched back to Greek and replied, "You hold the book of Isaiah, sire."

The official responded in the same tongue. "Tell me what it says."

Philip closed his eyes. His voice took on the songlike cadence of true devotion as he recited from memory, " 'He was like a sheep being led to be killed. He was quiet, as a lamb is quiet while its wool is being cut; he never opened his mouth. He was shamed and was treated unfairly. He died without children to continue his family. His life on earth has ended.' "

The official looked down at the scroll, smiled, and nodded

approval. "I am Yashkin, treasurer to Candace, empress of Ethiopia. And you . . . ?"

Philip bowed low. "I am Philip, servant of the Messiah."

"Do you understand of what the prophet speaks?"

"I do, sire."

"Will you tell me?"

"That is why I have come."

The official gestured and said, "Come up and sit with me."

Philip climbed up and joined the Ethiopian on the gilded bench. Together the two men spread the scroll across both their laps.

When the guards resumed their positions, the head guard called out loudly and the caravan resumed its trek. Jacob tethered the donkeys to the wagon behind the chariot, and took up a position between the two vehicles. He was offered a silver cup of water sweetened with pomegranate juice and honey. Otherwise he was ignored. He did not mind. He was close enough to hear Philip's words. Though the story was by now well known to him, still it held a powerful resonance. What he saw and heard was not merely a retelling of the Lord's coming, but rather the fulfillment of words written centuries before by their most revered prophet.

Philip had made himself ready, and the Lord had called him to service. Jacob watched the two men and heard far more than Philip's words. The breeze carried a second voice, one that spoke directly to his own heart. Of discipleship. Of making ready a life, so that it too might be used—even in ways he had not yet considered.

After a time, the caravan approached a grove of date palms. Yashkin cried out, "Look, here is water! Can I not be baptized?"

"If you so desire," Philip said. "If you truly believe . . ."

"I believe. I believe."

The official ordered the caravan to halt. The two men walked across the sandy expanse to the small oasis and the spring's edge, followed by Jacob and several of the guards. Yashkin stopped only long enough to remove his embellished outer robe and hand it to the servant who had not left his side. Philip grasped the man's hand and led him into the water. When they were waist deep, Philip declared in a voice that rang strong over the sunlight sparkling upon the water's surface, "I baptize you in the name of our Lord Jesus Christ. As the water washes your outer body, so may the Spirit cleanse the inner man. Rise up into the eternal life that has been prepared for you!"

The official came up out of the water, wiping both the spring's waters and his own tears from his face. "Amen," he said brokenly. "Amen."

The two men stepped from the water, Yashkin's voice and hands raised in praise to God. Jacob moved closer to learn Philip's wishes. Would they be continuing on with the Ethiopian?

But the disciple was no longer with them.

Jacob searched in every direction. He looked around at the guards, the servants. A ripple of astonishment coursed through the crowd. The guards hunted through the caravan. But Philip was not to be found. The only man not shocked by the disappearance was the official himself. He clambered back into the chariot, blind to all but the joy that overflowed his very being. He spoke a word, his voice still laden with emotion. The chief guard gave his call, and once more the caravan moved on in its southerly journey.

Jacob remained standing beside the road, the donkeys' reins in his grasp. The official's joyous song was still audible after the caravan disappeared into the golden dust.

It had all been so strange. And wonderful. And Philip . . . ? Jacob searched the area around the spring once more, then climbed onto his donkey's back and headed north, his own song filling the evening.

CHAPTER TWENTY-SEVEN

Caesarea

AFTER THE UNEXPECTED but rewarding meeting in the home of Cornelius, Linux spent the next five days at the garrison being ignored.

Each morning he presented himself before the commandant's aide. But Caesarea was the Roman capital of Judea, and the commandant was very sensitive to the political winds. These were uncertain times, and Linux no longer had allies among Judea's Roman leaders. The commandant risked disfavor by officially recognizing him. So Linux was made to wait.

He found solace among the community of believers. Linux was again invited to ride out to the home of Cornelius, centurion of the Italian Guard. After another time of prayer and discussion of Scriptures, Cornelius signaled for Linux to remain behind. Once the home had emptied of most other guests, Cornelius led him and Grattus, his escort from before, to the rooftop and motioned him to be seated on a lounge overlooking the sea. Without further preamble, the man declared, "What we do here is not illegal."

This centurion from the Italian Guard was a grizzled veteran with a commander's thousand-furlong stare. Linux guessed that this experienced soldier's eyes and ears could sweep any situation, no matter how chaotic, and assess its true nature within moments. Linux had felt that gaze come to rest upon him now and again during the evening and knew he was being measured. But he did not mind. In fact, the same sense of overwhelming peace he remembered from the Jerusalem compound filled him now. Let the man look and evaluate and make his conclusions as much as he wished.

Now the man gazed out over the moonlight grazing the sea's still waters and said to the night, "I am a loyal soldier of Rome. I serve my country, and my emperor. But I also serve my God. These times are full of questions and uncertainties. I prefer not to have my quest to know God lead my superiors to doubt my loyalty to Rome. Neither do I wish to bring danger to any of my friends or family. To any of the followers. So our meetings are held here in secret, restricted to those we know and trust."

The rooftop, like that of many Judean homes, was fashioned into an outdoor chamber, and it caught the night winds drifting off the cold Great Sea, but Linux did not mind. A pair of braziers burned brightly. His lounge was covered with an animal skin for further warmth. But in truth Linux was only vaguely aware of his surroundings and remained captivated by the time of prayer and teaching.

Cornelius said, "There are events in Rome which touch us even here. This new emperor, Gaius, is erecting a temple in honor of his own divinity. Other emperors have done as much, and it keeps the priestly sect happy. The crowds enjoy such spectacles. But Gaius seems actually to be convinced he is a god, and he now expects the people to burn sacrifices to him."

Grattus added, "This new emperor is also known by his childhood nickname, Caligula. It means 'Little Boots,' and was given to him when he went out to war as a child with his father, dressed in a small version of battle garb."

Linux shifted in his seat. "If you will forgive me, I would prefer not to discuss such things this night. I returned recently from Italy, and while there I heard every manner of rumor. No doubt some are true—perhaps all. But during both of my visits to your home, Cornelius, I have felt the Spirit's presence. I would ask for time to dwell in it for a moment longer."

"Well said." Cornelius nodded slowly. "But we seek to determine more clearly who you truly are, Linux Aurelius. What has brought you to us? What can you tell us of yourself and your life journey?"

So Linux began with his friendship with Alban, at that time a Roman soldier like himself, and of the unusual assignment to find the body of a dead Judean prophet. Of the escape of Alban and his bride on Linux's horse when Herod had issued orders for their deaths. He told them of his quest for Abigail's hand. Of Alban's intervention, and the resulting transformation of his life.

He talked long enough for his throat to dry out. Cornelius rose and served him tea by his own hand. Linux related his journey to Italy, the confession to his brother, his return, and his dismissal by the Jerusalem tribune. By the time he finished, the braziers had burned down to the last flickering embers, and even the night birds had gone silent.

They sat, three Roman officers wrapped in animal skins, listening to the sound of the waves upon the rocky shore.

Cornelius's hands were locked under his chin. "Your story is an inspiration to me, brother. Do you mind if I call you that?"

"I would consider it an honor."

"It is a common enough term among the righteous Judeans, which in Caesarea are few in number. We followers have taken to calling ourselves the same."

"We are bound together by our faith in the risen Lord," Grattus said. "And by the Spirit."

Cornelius asked, "Now that you have lost command of the Capernaum garrison, what will you do?"

Linux was quiet for a moment. "I do not have an answer for you, brother, save to say I am ready and willing to serve the Lord. Whenever and wherever."

"I like your words and the man behind them." The older soldier's grin flashed in the moonlight. "How would you like to serve under my command?"

Linux felt his heart leap. "Nothing would give me greater honor. But—"

"The tribune will think twice before attacking an officer in the Italian Guard." Grattus was smiling as well.

Cornelius studied Linux openly now. "The new consul has given me responsibility for all the garrisons in Samaria. I insist upon regular patrols. You can guess the result."

"You are taking losses."

"Between the brigands and the Zealots, my patrols are attacked almost daily. To maintain morale, I rotate them regularly. Six months on duty in the field, six months light duty in the Caesarea garrison. I have need of good officers. I can make a very convincing case to the commandant. And it might solve a political problem for him. What say you?"

Linux fought to hold his voice steady. "Your invitation would seem to be an answer to prayer, sire."

CHAPTER TWENTY-EIGHT

The Megiddo Plains

ABIGAIL'S DAYS HAD settled into a busy routine. There was much to do and much to be learned about overseeing a merchant's stall. Stocking it with goods, determining the price, finding those weavers with the best quality fabrics . . . and on and on.

Though they had come to visit Helzebah, even Helena and Julia were now working alongside her. And little Dorcas, who made a game of every chore and brightened the day for all who knew her, took delight in being the first to alert her mother when a caravan came in view.

But no one seemed busier than Zoe. Even though the roles of master and slave were less distinct among the believers, she truly had a servant's heart and could sense what should be done almost before the need appeared. Abigail marveled as she watched the elderly woman quietly take up any task before her.

Together with the followers in the village, the women shared a beautiful Sabbath. They met at the neglected synagogue. Their worship included a fervent prayer that the structure would be restored and again filled with worshipers.

In the days that followed, Martha proved to be an able merchant. She could lift her voice to carry from one end of the market to the other. Dorcas loved sitting among the stacks of fabrics and calling out to every passerby, showing them the fine weavings, loving the colors so much it shone in her face. They came into the stall because of her happiness, and they stayed to buy from Martha. The business was increasing quickly, Abigail noted as she looked around the well-stocked stall.

Abigail began going from house to house seeking out more sources for the weavings. Yelban had given his word for her, and that was enough for the villagers. As she visited the homes, she often stayed to speak with the women and tell them about the gospel of Jesus. Her natural warmth disarmed even the most skeptical of those who had been cheated by the ones whom Jamal had appointed earlier. At first Abigail wondered if it was proper for her to come to do business, then staying to speak of heaven. But she discovered it was all part of the rich tapestry of life. She was committed to be truthful in all things, to share from the heart, and return trust with trust. Always.

She soon had people stopping her in the lanes and upon the road. Seeking her out. Asking her to pray with them, telling of their concerns over an illness or heartache or husband or child. The weavings were now given to her with scarcely a word of negotiation on price. Trust was the bond that forged her place in the village. Trust and faith.

And both of these things brought her into conflict with Simon.

His was a very subtle discord, for he too attended the synagogue services. He joined the others at Abigail's home, prayed and listened. He had been baptized by Philip.

But on the other days of the week he still wore the robes scripted with secret writings. His hair was woven with ritual threads. He made amulets for those who sought favor from unseen forces. And he demanded coins for all he did.

Simon offered subtle hints, quietly spoken questions, about the power of this Jesus. He voiced misgivings about whether there truly was a need for the villagers to abandon the ways that made them Samaritans. He announced plans for leading a group up to Mount Gerizim in the spring, where they could seek guidance and forge new bonds with the old ways.

Abigail did not seek out knowledge concerning Simon's actions and attitudes. She did not need to. The villagers were confused and grew increasingly concerned, for they felt the tugs pulling them in conflicting directions. They asked her about what to do, how to respond. She answered as best she could. As did Martha. But neither of them felt fully satisfied with their efforts.

Abigail prayed and prayed about the situation. She prayed for Simon. She spoke of the problems with Martha and Helzebah, with Helena and Julia. And still she did not have clear direction.

The morning arrived when Helena and Julia, with their servant Zoe, would be returning to Tiberias. One of Jamal's caravans had been encamped nearby for a night and a day and another night. It was headed for Nabataea by way of Tiberias, and this was their opportunity to travel safely home.

Helzebah planned to leave at that same time, returning to her family. The women said their farewells to Martha and to Dorcas, and then Abigail walked with them to the caravan.

The caravan master assigned donkeys for the four women, then insisted one of his men serve as their personal guard. This was, after all, his master's family.

Helena embraced Abigail and said, "Your example is a beacon that will light my days."

"Helena, there is no need—"

"No, please. I do not wish to travel the road with these words unspoken." She took a long breath, then said, "I have learned as much from your example as your words. God has not made your life perfect. Yet in the midst of change and turmoil, you are living proof of his gift of peace. For this reminder, I am ever in your debt."

In the face of such praise, Abigail found her greatest doubts surfacing. "I am often beset by worry and fear," she admitted.

"Which is why how you live is such a great lesson. You are not removed from trouble. Yet God is there with you—through all of it. I need to learn that. To see that. I have walked with God for only a short time. I have much to learn."

Abigail wiped her eyes. "At night I still wake up and long for Jerusalem."

"The Jerusalem you knew is no more," Helzebah said from Abigail's other side. "You were there. You saw the changes."

"I saw," Abigail admitted. "And yet . . ."

Helzebah touched Abigail's arm. "Here you are safe. And they need you. Jerusalem will be a memory, a good one. Remain where you are, Abigail. Love your daughter. Serve your Lord."

Saying farewell to Helzebah was harder than Abigail had expected. "You have become a sister," she said as the two embraced.

The woman's features held traces of the life she had left behind. "I do not deserve such gifts."

"None is worthy," Abigail said. "All of us bear the burdens of things we should not have done. Should have done."

"Yes," said Helzebah. "Yes, that is so."

As Abigail turned and embraced Julia, the young woman said, "If Jacob should come back this way . . ."

"Yes?"

"Well . . ." She shook her head and stepped back.

Abigail looked a question at Helena, whose only response was to observe her daughter with some sorrow.

Zoe was the last to receive Abigail's farewell. The woman seemed to have drawn back into her role as servant rather than sister. She stood silently, hands folded in front of her, eyes studying her feet.

"Zoe, dear one, you have been such a blessing. I thank you for becoming a part of our little community and having eyes that see another's need. I shall so miss you."

Zoe's eyes reflected her surprise. Then for a moment she seemed to step out of her comfortable role, becoming more like the mother Abigail had lost and still missed with a child's longing. Zoe reached up and gently tucked back a stray lock of Abigail's hair, letting her hand run down the younger woman's cheek as she looked deeply into her eyes. "May God bring happiness back to those beautiful eyes, my daughter," she said, "and erase the pain I see. There is much of life still ahead for you. Embrace it in his name and for his sake."

She leaned forward and placed a kiss on one cheek, then the other.

Abigail waited while the women mounted their animals. The caravan master shrilled his cry, and the caravan started from the corrals. Abigail called, "Go with God."

Helena's eyes brimmed above her shawl. "When Jamal asks me what I think of his new stall holder, I will say that you are a gift from the Lord."

Abigail remained where she was, waving them off. Another farewell, another parting, another bit of her heart lost to time and distance. She waved until there was nothing in the east but a plume of dust.

CHAPTER
TWENTY-NINE

The Megiddo Plains

ABIGAIL WAS BUSY setting up her wares when Yelban's son appeared. He jerked his head, indicating he wished to speak with her alone. Once they were outside the stall, he said softly, "There is trouble. You must come."

"I should first see to my daughter."

"She is with your friends. This cannot wait. The future of our village is at stake."

Yelban's son was named Aboud, a common Samaritan name derived from Abel. He was lean-faced and tall for his fourteen years, with an intelligent eye and a ready smile. Only not this day. His features were drawn and tight with anger as he led Abigail down a side lane and behind a stack of barrels. When she started to ask their destination, he hissed once, a sharp sound. Abigail caught the danger and tensed as a stranger drifted into view. Even when the man was out of sight, she did not draw an easy breath.

Silently Aboud moved forward, beckoning her to follow. He

opened a small slit in the cloth wall of his father's tavern. Abigail could see yet remain hidden.

Nine men were Yelban's current customers, sprawled upon benches and the most comfortable seats. Two more men lounged by the tavern's entrance, their backs to Abigail. All eleven constantly scouted the front of the tavern with dark gazes. Through the wide opening Abigail saw another two men guarding their horses. Abigail drew the shawl up higher about her face and resisted the urge to flee. *Bandits*.

Though she remained hidden, she felt as if the bandits could sense her presence. Like wolves aware of prey, biding their time, ready to attack.

Yelban's voice could be heard through the tavern walls, sounding thick with the same apprehension that darkened his son's features. "What you demand from us is impossible."

"Nonsense." The spokesman looked tall even when seated. He wore a long beard, the end tarred and fitted with a silver spike. He popped an olive into his mouth, slurped loudly from his mug. "You serve excellent fare, my friend."

"You demand more than we make in profit."

"Then you shall simply have to raise your prices, is that not so?"

"The caravans will not stop here if—"

"Where else are they to go?" The bandit wore two curved blades on his belt, and long knives strapped to his back. Another curved bow lay across his lap. All his men were similarly armed. "Yours is the only market for miles. To the southeast there is nothing between here and Ginae, to the northwest the next place to halt is Nazareth, to the northeast, Tiberias, and southwest there is nothing at all!"

"The families here will wither and die. The villages—"

"The villages will endure. Is that not what Samaritan villages have done for centuries? Endure?" He threw back his head and laughed cruelly.

Three market watchmen stood stiffly in the sunlight beyond the awning. The bandits ignored them. Abigail could understand why. The bandits were professional fighting men, killers. The guards were simple villagers armed with staves and long knives.

Yelban glanced at his watchmen, then allowed his gaze to drift further. Beyond the market, out to where the lone hill rose in the far distance.

The bandit obviously knew what Yelban was thinking. "My friend, the only result of your running to the Romans is that the market would find itself a new headman."

Beside her, Aboud tensed and reached for the knife at his belt. Abigail gripped his arm with all her strength. Aboud turned to her, inspected her eyes above the shawl's edge, and reluctantly nodded. Abigail did not remove her hand until he released the knife's handle.

The bandit was saying, "The Romans will come, and they will demand payment for their protection. Perhaps not the silver that I ask. Perhaps only fodder for fifty horses, and meals for fifty men. And supplies for their fortress, for which they will give you script and never pay. Is that not why you have stopped doing business with them? They give you papers promising money, but never redeem it with silver?"

Yelban chewed on the edge of his moustache and did not respond. His focus remained upon the fortress atop the lone hill.

"So now you go to the Romans, after refusing to do business with them for months. I have been watching you, you see. I know. And the Romans will demand payment. And they will guard you. But for how long? A week? A month? And then they will leave. Because they are Romans, and you and I, my friend, are nothing to them. Nothing!"

The bandit rose slowly to his feet. His easygoing manner turned to a venomous snarl. "And when they leave, I will return. And you, my friend, will die. You and your wife and your son."

He gestured to his men. They rose as one, departing the tavern and walking toward where their horses waited. The men all wore the black of the Arabian tribes, with long cloaks flowing out behind them like the wings of spectral birds. The bandit leader mounted and reined his horse in beside the tavern entrance to shout, "I will return! I suggest that you be ready."

There were no other travelers that day. The villagers gathered in Yelban's tavern, and their discussions extended well into the afternoon. The sad conclusion was that their prospects were bleak. The bandits' demands were ruinous. The tribute they wanted would require them all to more than double their prices. There was every possibility the market would vanish into the sands, and their village along with it.

As the deliberations continued, Abigail felt eyes glancing at her. Even Martha looked her way now and then. Finally Martha rose and suggested they all pray for guidance.

Yelban chewed upon his moustache. "You are right."

The man seated next to him muttered, "Perhaps now is time for Simon to weave his amulets."

One of the other villagers snorted. "What good will that do us, save cost us more silver?"

Another called out, "He is a wizard!"

Voices rose in a sudden tempest, shouting for and against the wizard's involvement. Abigail waited and did not speak.

Yelban let them vent their frustration for a time, then raised his hand for silence. "All I can tell you is this. My wife was ill. Women prayed. The Lord heard. My wife is well."

"But they prayed over my child," another protested, "and the boy is still ill."

A woman said, "You remember they promised nothing but that

they would make the request to their God. They give to everyone from the heart, and they seek nothing."

"When they speak," another villager said with a nod, "I hear the truth."

"And my heart is filled with joy," someone else agreed. "When has the wizard offered anything save fear? When has he given without demanding more in return?"

Abigail waited until the only sound was the bleating of sheep from the nearby pen. When she began to speak her voice trembled. "I have never been comfortable standing before people. But the other night it came to me that I should start a women's group. We can meet together, and speak of the Scriptures, and pray. For our safety, and for our people."

The man who had suggested they speak with Simon waved her down. "We speak of crisis for our very livelihood and lives, and all she can say is to have the women pray?"

"Let her speak!"

"What good can come of this? Women sit in a circle, while outside the bandits bring torches and swords!"

Yelban walked over to stand directly in front of the protester. "I did not see you offer help when I stood alone this very day before the bandits."

The man muttered something, then went silent under Yelban's glare.

Yelban turned back to Abigail. "Speak to us."

"I have seen the power of God at work," she said, her voice sounding stronger in her ears. "In others, and in my life. I do not know what the answer is. I do not know so very many things. But I know that God is great, and that he waits for us to turn to him. Turn, and be steadfast in our turning. We must remain focused upon him, especially when times are hard and our way ahead is uncertain. Because at times like these, when our need is greatest, God offers us his wisdom, his miracles."

Martha's strong voice rang bell-like through the silence. "My sister speaks truth!"

When there were no more protests, Abigail said, "I would ask that those who hold to Jesus join with me now in prayer."

At that very moment, Abigail witnessed the Spirit's presence. Others would point to one thing or another and contend that it was the miracle coming from the prayers. But Abigail did not agree. For there were people who still wished to argue, and people whose fear was so great they did not even stand in the road alone. Even so, a silence descended that was far stronger than any absence of sound or any argument. Some in and about the tavern's enclosure rose as though lifted from their chairs, moved from their positions, and propelled outside. No protest, no sound save sandals slapping against the rough-plank flooring.

Those who remained numbered more than those who had left. But the numbers were far less important than the sense of silent accord. Here were the faithful. Here were those who shared with her the steadfast conviction in the midst of trials.

Abigail found herself filled with a calm power, one she knew was from far beyond her own self, a strength so great it vanquished her doubts and her hesitations. At least for this moment.

"Let us join hands and pray," Abigail said. "Our God waits to deliver us from this difficulty. As he has so often already. He is here with us now. He will remain with us forever."

"Travelers! Travelers coming!"

The village children bore the news as usual with shouts and

waves and wild dancing. The news of new arrivals always brought excitement to the market community.

Abigail lifted her head, expecting to find a caravan approaching, but she could see nothing. *Surely not the bandits!* She squinted against the noonday sun and tried to determine if the slight haze in the distance was travelers' dust or simply subtle shadows. She could identify nothing. But the young boys were still running about the market stalls calling out their news.

Would they be so mischievous as to . . . ? She turned her back on the uproar and began to count the woven baskets hanging from pegs on the wall.

Yelban's son, Aboud, now ran up. "Travelers are coming," he repeated, waving his arms.

"I do not see them," she disagreed, again squinting against the brightness.

"No. Not that way. Over there." He motioned with his hand.

It was not a caravan that approached, and fortunately not a mounted group of raiders with dark flowing capes, but a huddle of walkers, some with packs on their backs, some with walking canes. Even over the distance Abigail was sure they looked weary. She watched them for a moment, then turned to the young boy. "Your father will need your help. They will want refreshment."

Aboud nodded and ran off toward the family's tavern.

As Abigail watched the travelers' slow but steady approach, she had the strange sense of something familiar about the big man whose stride seemed to set the pace for the others. *Who might this be?*

As they drew closer she heard a roar of laughter, and her heart skipped within her chest. *The fisherman? Could it possibly be Peter?* Abigail strained to look more closely and knew without a doubt that it was he.

She almost ran out of the stall. She quickly realized it was John walking alongside him. *Peter and John! Why . . . ?*

They seemed as surprised to see her as she was to see them. "Abigail, dear one!" Peter's voice rang through the square. "I cannot believe my eyes. How are you, daughter?"

He laid strong hands on her shoulders, like a father welcoming his child.

Abigail felt tears burn behind her eyes. She had never anticipated seeing anyone from Jerusalem. Not here. In Samaria.

Peter stepped back to look into her face. "We had quite lost track of you. I wondered where you had gone. And dear Martha. Is she with you?"

"She is," Abigail managed to say. "And she will be as surprised to see you as I. Please join us for a meal. I will close the shop and take you up to the house. Martha is there caring for my Dorcas. Things are very quiet in the markets at this time."

Abigail swiftly counted the little group. Five. She would have no problem finding something to feed them. She greeted the others, then ran to close up her stall. She had scarcely begun putting away the goods when Aboud ran up.

"They are family?" he asked breathlessly.

"They seem like family. But kin, no. Their leader—the largest one—is Peter, a disciple of our Lord. And John. Another of the Lord's chosen twelve. I have as yet to meet the others, but I am sure that they are followers as well."

Aboud nodded. "And what brings them to Samaria?"

"They have yet to say."

"I will close up the shop for you. You go on home with your guests. Father will no doubt want to know if they would speak to a gathering this evening."

Abigail smiled. She would love to hear Peter speak once again. "I will make the request."

She left her stall in Aboud's capable hands and led the way up the hill to her simple abode. They laughed and talked all the way.

Peter wanted to know what was happening with Alban and Leah and Jacob, and Abigail was happy to give him the reports. She told him of the market stall and house that went with it, how much safer she felt than when in Jerusalem.

Peter grew solemn. For those of the Way, the persecution had not subsided. The man named Saul of Tarsus relentlessly pursued followers of the Messiah.

When they reached the house, Abigail led them inside to the main room serving as both kitchen and living quarters. She called upstairs to Martha and Dorcas, "Peter is here! And John, and others from Jerusalem."

From then on it was joyful chaos—everyone talking at once. Questions asked and answered—and others left unanswered for the present. Martha insisted on pouring more tea every time a cup emptied. Abigail used her small store of food to serve a light meal. The other members of Peter's group were introduced, and they exchanged stories of what the Lord had been doing while they were apart.

When things finally settled to a quieter mood, Abigail put forth the question that no doubt was Martha's also. "What has brought you here, may I ask?"

Peter's dark eyes took on the probing expression she had witnessed many times in the past.

"We have heard that even the Samaritans are becoming followers. Philip, the evangelist, has told stories of great responses here to the Good News. We came to discover if these converts truly are following the risen Lord. And if they are, to further instruct them in the Way."

Abigail smiled. "They are—it is true. They are coming to faith. Many of them." She wondered if she should add that there were also those who still sought out the sorcerer. But she said instead, "And they would welcome instruction. In fact, Yelban, the master of the markets below, asked if a meeting could be arranged for tonight so people might come and listen to you speak the words of our Lord."

Peter nodded, smiled, and turned to his traveling companions. "Our prayers are being answered before we even have settled in."

Later that night they gathered in the village square. Abigail could not believe how quickly news had traveled. People arrived even from nearby villages. She could see great interest upon their faces. Peter addressed the crowd, his voice as large as his person, and had no difficulty being heard. It was the message of the Messiah—the risen one. His mission, his death, and the resurrection that provided the way for all to have access to the Father. "Believe on him," Peter proclaimed in great power. "Believe on him and receive the gift of his Holy Spirit."

The next evening an even larger crowd gathered—and there among them Abigail saw the man she had come to fear. Simon, known for his work of omens and bewitchment, had joined the group. She could see his dark eyes following every move that Peter and John made. When the invitation was given to receive the Holy Spirit, many asked for the laying on of the disciples' hands and prayer. Abigail's heart sank as she watched the wizard pushing his way through the crowd toward Peter.

The group was beginning to disband for the night when Simon finally stood in front of Peter, money bag in his hand.

Abigail was praying with a woman, but she was close enough to hear the words.

"Impressive! Most impressive." The man's swagger was evident in his tone, and Abigail could hear the jingle of coins, no doubt making sure Peter saw the purse. "How much would it cost to obtain this gift you possess? I could use—"

"You think you can *buy* the gift of God?" Peter's tone was unmistakable, and his eyes blazed in the flickering torchlight that surrounded the square. "Put away your money. What that paltry sack holds could purchase nothing of eternal value! May your money perish with you—and perish you will if you do not repent of such wickedness. You have no part or understanding if you think that we—his followers—seek gold. He gives his gift freely, and his gift is of far greater worth than all the gold in the world. You had best turn away from this great sin while you still have time. Repent and pray that God in his mercy might see fit to forgive you."

The man fell to his knees, his hands reaching out to clutch at Peter's garments. "Please . . . please . . . pray for me. I don't want God's wrath to fall upon me. Please. Help me, please."

Abigail went to her pallet with many emotions washing over her—happiness for the wonderful visit from the Jerusalem leaders, for the familiar but always fresh message Peter had brought, a bit of sadness she was so far away from her memories of Jerusalem—bittersweet though they might be—and the uncomfortable scene with Peter and the sorcerer. Abigail set aside her fears of the man and prayed once again for him before closing her eyes.

CHAPTER THIRTY

Joppa

THE LONE FIGURE carefully made his way down the seaside lane, headed toward the home of a wealthy trader whose family was as ancient as the city, which was ancient indeed. Joppa was a walled city with a stone barricade curving like a quarter moon around the natural port. Along its length, seven watchtowers rose like pillars holding up the sky. The ancient port had long since outgrown its former boundaries, however. More people lived outside the city walls than within.

The trader's home where the man was headed stood on a hill less than five hundred paces from the main market street. Unlike that of most towns, Joppa's market did not occupy the town's center but ran alongside the ancient port. The harbor road curved to fit the shoreline, broad enough for portable stalls to sell fish and fresh produce. Even now, in the hour before sunrise, the smell of fish and offal was overpowering. The robed figure, hooded so his face could not be seen, shook his head briefly at the stench and hurried on.

From the opposite direction another man headed toward the

same house on the hill. The trader gave his surroundings little attention. He was accompanied by a guard and two sons scarcely old enough to be called men. The guard's torch cast a flickering gleam over the otherwise empty street. When the little group arrived at the massive portal of the house, the guard stepped forward and hammered upon the wooden doors. The merchant turned a cursory glance on his surroundings while they waited. Eventually a servant unlatched the hinge.

The trader expressed his displeasure at being made to wait. "I have an appointment with your master, Isaac," he growled, and the servant cringed as he bowed the man and his sons inside.

But before the doors could be shut, a wooden stave jammed through the opening and the one holding it called out, "I seek the trader Isaac."

The trader was a small man who walked slightly bent over. He was just inside the doors, and his hand moved swiftly to halt his guard before he could unsheathe his blade against the intruder. "Who dares disturb the dawn?" the trader demanded, motioning his guest and sons back.

"I am sent by a man we both know as a friend."

The man called Isaac hesitated, then motioned for the servant to open the portal wide. The guard quietly slithered the blade out as the torch revealed someone totally concealed by a dark cloak.

Isaac demanded, "Reveal yourself."

"I dare not, sire. There are enemies about." The voice was now lowered for only Isaac's ears.

Isaac peered at the figure and said, "Which is why I must see your face. Drop your cloak and name yourself!"

Instead, the unknown visitor stretched out one hand, opening his fist to reveal a letter sealed with red wax. "If you are indeed the man I seek, this is the only name I dare offer."

Isaac took a hesitant step forward. He accepted the letter and inspected the wax seal. "Let the man enter."

The guard protested, "Sire—"

"Be still." Isaac inspected the seal carefully but did not open the document. "This man and I must have words."

The robed figure stepped through the portal. "Alone," he said.

Jacob left the trader Isaac's establishment unseen. Not even Jamal's partner, this man Isaac, had been permitted to view his face. It was best so. What had not been seen could not be reported.

Isaac had made short work of his business with the merchant and sons, showing the grumbling man out himself while Jacob waited in another room.

Now Jacob traversed the main thoroughfare into the city center, halting before the synagogue gates. He saw he was early, so he slipped across the square to the street-side tavern beside the stables where his animals were berthed. As he ate, Jacob recalled the days when he had raced about Jerusalem's hidden alleys as a youngster, running with the other orphans to gain information for Alban. He reflected upon how far he had journeyed since then, arriving at a point where even his harshest memories now carried something of worth.

He left coins on the table and joined the stream of people moving toward the synagogue. Many elders and wealthy entered with beards still dripping from the ritual baths. Jacob joined the crowd of servants and village poor who lingered in the synagogue's dusty courtyard. He prayed the morning service, then settled upon the outer wall and waited while the congregants dispersed. Only then did he approach the elder locking the synagogue gates.

"I seek a man whose name I do not know."

The elder's beard, and what was left of the hair on his head, had yellowed like ancient parchment. He turned his head slowly and looked Jacob up and down. "How does this man look?"

"I cannot say."

"Does he live in Joppa?"

"Of that too I am uncertain."

"Then it should be impossible for any save Yahweh to help you, young man." Despite his negative response, the elder did not move. If anything, his ancient features had taken on somewhat of an eager cast.

"Then I apologize for disturbing your day." As he spoke, Jacob used one sandal to slowly draw something in the dust.

The elder responded by gripping Jacob's arm and whispering, "I have prayed hourly for your arrival. Come inside. There is not a moment to lose."

Jacob hurried back to the stables, lifting the cloak so it once again covered his head and most of his face. His heart beat rapidly against his ribs. The elder's news had filled him with a dread so strong not even the rising sun could dispel its chill.

The trader, Isaac, had turned out to be as good as his word. His eldest son stood just outside the stable doors. The young man tried to look brave, but the stranger's hidden face and his father's odd assignment clearly left him unnerved. "M-my father says, all . . . all is as you demanded."

"The goods?"

"Tied to your donkey."

"How many sacks?"

"Four."

Which meant as much frankincense as Jacob had transported the previous time. He stood in the alley leading from the central square to the harbor and pondered. But no answer came.

The young man mistook Jacob's silence for displeasure. "My father and I have done exactly as you instructed."

"Yes, I know. . . ." Jacob sighed. Not for the first time did he wish for Alban's wise counsel. But Alban might as well have been on the other side of the empire. Jacob cast a silent but frantic plea toward heaven . . . and waited. A pair of gulls screeched overhead. The young man before him nervously shifted on his feet. Otherwise, nothing.

"I have no choice," Jacob muttered.

"I'm sorry, I did not—" The young man blanched as Jacob stepped forward and gripped his arm. "I have done only as my father commanded!"

"And I mean you and your family no harm." Jacob drew the young man behind a scrawny desert pine that cast some shade upon the alley. "What is your name?"

"B-Benjamin."

Jacob could tell his shrouded face frightened the lad. He did not like what he was about to do, but he felt he had no choice. He drew back his hood. "Do you know Jamal?"

"My father's partner."

"The same. You know of the attacks upon Jamal's caravans?"

He jerked a tight nod. "I heard my father speak of them."

"I move in secret to try and keep this from happening again. But just now at the synagogue I have been given such frightful news . . ." Jacob halted at a scrape of footsteps. One of the stable hands emerged and turned the other direction from them. Jacob waited until the man vanished beyond the sunlit square. "This news carries the threat of death for many. I must return to Tiberias. I have no time for the slow and secret way of travel that I had planned."

The boy was perhaps sixteen years of age and very lean, yet his gaze already possessed a trader's shrewdness. "You mean my family no harm?"

"My only aim has been to protect your father's and Jamal's treasure. Now I must add a second goal. To save innocent lives."

The lad searched Jacob's face. "Tell me what you need."

CHAPTER THIRTY-ONE

The Samaritan Plains

JACOB LEFT JOPPA and halted at a small oasis three miles to the north, not far from the garrison. The ancient town had been difficult to subdue, and the Romans chose to largely leave it to its own devices.

The spring was shallow and less than ten paces wide but produced enough water to irrigate several farms and support a cluster of date palms. Jacob rested by the pond and let his two donkeys drink, merely another desert vagrant taking shelter. The day was warm. A faint wind blew from the south. Jacob could taste a hint of the sea in the air. Gulls wheeled and cried overhead.

He resisted the urge to rise and pace. Instead, he took a simple meal from the lone market stall fronting the oasis, a tattered affair run by a farmer's wife. The place was too small and too close to both Joppa and Apollonia to garner much trade. The only other customers were local farmworkers. The fare was meager, chickpeas ground with cumin and olive oil, flatbread, olives, dates, and cheese from the goats that bleated beyond the farm. Jacob did not mind.

He scarcely tasted anything at all. His mind searched frantically for some alternative, in case the trader's son did not arrive. But he could come up with nothing that had the slightest chance of succeeding. Jacob forced himself to eat, because if the lad did arrive, it might be his last chance to fill his belly.

The synagogue elder's news could not have been more calamitous. Word had come via the elder's own son, who studied in Jerusalem. Saul of Tarsus, the dreaded scourge of the followers, had gone before the Temple Council and requested letters of passage. The man had received word that the number of followers in Damascus was increasing daily. Saul intended to travel there, arrest them, and drag the whole lot back to Jerusalem in chains.

According to the elder, the Sanhedrin had previously assumed that once these followers were driven from Jerusalem, their numbers would diminish. It would then only be a matter of time before the remaining few were wiped out. To their consternation, the Council received reports from allies in various cities revealing that the opposite was happening. The church was *growing*. In Damascus, several synagogues had become overrun by followers of Jesus. The Sanhedrin was frantically searching for a way to formalize their persecution of the believers.

According to the elder's son, Saul had come before the Council with an idea. During the reign of Herod the Great, the Roman rulers granted the Temple's high priest and his Sanhedrin the right to extradite Judean criminals from other parts of the Roman empire. Saul proposed that they use this nearly forgotten law as a lever to arrest followers of Jesus from Damascus. Under Judean law they could be brought back to Jerusalem as common criminals. Once under the Council's power, the followers would be given a final chance to renounce their faith in Jesus. Those who refused would be killed. *Just as Stephen was* . . . Jacob thought with a pang, seeing his sister's face and feeling again her loss.

To Jacob's relief, he caught sight of the trader's son approaching on the road from Joppa. The lad rode one horse and led another by the reins. Jacob scooped up the last bite of his meal, left the payment, and hurried over to him. "Did you tell anyone?"

Benjamin was breathless with excitement. "I spoke exactly as you ordered, sir. I told my father that the stranger required our help—nothing more."

"You may tell him everything once I am gone."

"The promise that I would do so is the only reason he allowed me to come."

"Well done." Jacob leapt upon the back of his own donkey. "Lead on."

"Do you not wish to ride your new mount?"

"This will attract less attention. Quickly!"

They rode past Apollonia and the Roman fortress, then turned inland toward Capharsaba, Jacob on one of his donkeys and leading the other, the boy riding a horse and pulling the other by the reins. The road skirted the southern and eastern borders of the Plain of Sharon, following the northern rim of the steep Jerusalem hills. This Roman road was rarely used by devout Judeans, for it traversed Samaria.

When they entered the empty reaches, Jacob directed them off the road and into a stand of desert pine. He slipped from the donkey's back and stripped off his clothes. The trader's son dropped a bundle at his feet. "I brought all you requested. At least I hope I did."

Jacob heard the lad's unspoken questions. "I would share my assignment with you if I could. But lives depend upon my keeping this secret. At least for now."

Benjamin, to his credit, did not protest. He watched as Jacob dressed in the clothing he had brought and asked, "What shall I do with the donkeys?"

"They are yours."

"They are Jamal's," the boy corrected.

"He will be more than happy to grant you ownership for this assistance," Jacob replied. Then he added, "If I arrive in Tiberias."

"*When* you arrive," Benjamin corrected with a smile. "I do not know you, and yet I have every confidence in your success."

Jacob shifted the sacks of frankincense and lashed them tightly to the front of his saddle. "What can you tell me of this mount?"

"He is one of my father's finest. Strong, steady, and will go for days."

The stallion certainly seemed as described. He was tall at the shoulder and seemed immensely powerful, the muscles trembling with a sense of Jacob's urgency. Even so, the eye that observed Jacob transferring the sacks of frankincense and waterskins and food bags was calm, the hooves unmoving. "Thank your father for me, and tell him Jamal will gladly reimburse him for the horse."

"Of this I have no doubt. My father has partnered with Jamal for years."

Jacob swung into the saddle, took the reins in one hand, then accepted the stave that Benjamin held out to him. He unfurled the banner, grinned at the sight, and declared, "This is just as I had hoped."

"I thought as much."

"How did you obtain it?"

"My father owns the main stables in Apollonia. We service the fortress mounts and supply a number of their horses."

Jacob offered his hand. "Benjamin, I hope that one day you and I can become friends."

"As do I." The trader's son looked even younger when he

grinned. "You must lead a most exciting life," he said as he mounted the second horse, holding the donkeys' reins.

"There are times when I would be happy for a bit less excitement. And the worry that accompanies it." Jacob turned the horse toward the road. "For now, I am in your debt, Benjamin," he said over his shoulder. He urged his mount to a gallop.

The lad called after him, "For now, that will do."

Thankfully, the weather remained Jacob's friend.

His way was both straight and flat. In many places, it was well paved in the Roman manner, two layers of rounded stones laid upon a bed of milled sand. But this was not a vital route for even Judea's hated masters. The military relied upon the Caesarea harbor and largely ignored the port of Joppa. Patrols focused upon routes that fed Rome's coastal city. Which meant some portions of Jacob's more southerly route had not been repaired for many years. Jacob could not risk his mount going lame and settled into a steady loping gait. The horse was both strong and well rested, eager to fly. But now was not the time or place.

Jacob, with Benjamin's help, now looked the part of a Roman messenger, banner and all. The garrisons often hired a good horseman who was both trusted and willing to work for gold. These men wore cast-off Roman garb, most especially the leather vest that identified a Roman soldier on patrol. Attached to their back was a flexible stave, usually made of either water cane or willow. Lashed to this was the standard identifying them as a messenger. They carried neither money nor valuables, which meant they were usually left alone, at least by bandits.

Jacob's greatest ally was the road's utter emptiness. Three times he spied lone donkey herders trekking on one side of the road or the other. Jacob did not encounter his first caravan until late afternoon as he skirted the northern tip of the Judean hills. An endless parade of camels and donkeys and drovers and guards watched Jacob steer his mount off the road and pass to the caravan's right. He did not speak. Messengers seldom did. When he saluted the caravan master as he passed, the man eyed him with glittering black eyes and spat into the dust by his feet. Jacob's consolation was having his disguise prove so successful.

He stopped for the night in Sebaste, the ancient capital of Samaria, renamed by the Greeks. The town was little more than a crumbling relic, full of ruins and shadows of former grandeur. Jacob selected a stable Alban had used in the past. The stable master grumbled when he appeared, for Roman messengers often paid in stamped bits of paper known as chits. Merchants along the routes considered these chits next to worthless, for they were required to present them in either Jerusalem or Caesarea for payment. But the man stopped his grousing when Jacob dropped silver into his palm. He even sent his chief stable hand to the nearest tavern for food.

Jacob tended his mount by torchlight. The stable was rimmed by a crumbling waist-high wall. As he curried the horse, Jacob recalled how Alban had walked him to one corner of this very wall and brushed eons of dirt from the stone. Underneath lay the remnants of a mosaic. The colors had defied the years, a beautiful rendition of sheep grazing beneath a flowering tree.

Alban had often carried a small scroll, a part of the Scriptures, one that his friend Eli from his Jerusalem days had procured for him. That previous visit, Alban had read to Jacob from the book of Isaiah. The prophet's lament had reached across the ages and seared his heart. He still could almost hear the cries of the Israelites as they were led into captivity. *Turn from your sinful ways*, the prophet cried, and Jacob had shivered with remorse for mankind's darkness and sin.

When Jacob finished eating he rolled into a road-stained blanket. His entire body ached from the day of hard riding. His heart thumped a lonely beat. He cast his weary mind over all those who cared for him, now so far away. *Alban. Leah. Abigail.* The clan of believers he sought desperately to protect.

But the final image that flitted across his closed eyes, before sleep stole him away, was of a pair of dark, luminous eyes looking at him with a most astonishing mix of sorrow and joy, yearning and closed doors. He might even have sighed her name. *Julia.*

When danger struck, Jacob first had thought it was a puff of wind.

He was somewhere between Agrippina and Sennabris. Tiberias lay three hours north. The Jordan River ran through deep gullies somewhere to his right, and westward lay the Megiddo Plains with its great crossroads overlooked by the village of Nain. Jacob held a pace that felt as though it ground his bones. If the horse shared his discomfort, it did not show it. His mount maintained the same loping gait it had carried for the better part of two days.

Jacob drifted in a state that was neither fully awake nor asleep. He had heard Alban speak of this, when even experienced soldiers and guards grew so accustomed to their pace that they could fall asleep while still marching. Jacob did not fall asleep. But he was not alert either. And his drifting state almost cost him his life.

Something whistled past behind him, and Jacob reacted before he was fully aware of the threat.

In an instant he bent over the horse's neck, took a double-fisted grip on the reins, and yelled, "*Fly!*"

The horse jerked from an easy lope to a full gallop. The mane momentarily blinded Jacob. As he shook the strands away, a dark line sliced overhead, accompanied by that soft yet deadly *whoosh*.

"Hyah!"

He was being hunted by bowmen. Good ones, for though his horse dashed ahead, two arrows came within a handsbreadth of ending his life. One sliced across his back, leaving a searing track like flame as it passed. The other shot into the saddle just above his left thigh. The force was great enough to carry it through three layers of leather. The horse whinnied in pain and flew faster still.

Two more arrows struck sparks from rocks to his right, while another threw up dust from the road ahead. They dashed around a hill sheltering Jacob from further attack. At least for the moment.

Jacob heard the pounding of hooves behind him. His horse was strong, but it had been riding hard for two days. There was only so much more he could ask of it. Besides which, a dark stain began to spread from beneath the saddle. Jacob released one hand from the reins and ripped the arrow free of the saddle. The horse answered with another whinny, no doubt voicing its relief. Jacob swung his leg over the saddle, pulled himself low to the flying mane, and panted in time with his mount.

It was true that bandits seldom attacked a Roman messenger, but Zealots were another matter entirely. Now a well-organized fighting force, their assaults were increasingly bold. Messengers were considered fair game, both because they carried information from one Roman garrison to another and because they often rode horses as fine as Jacob's. The information was often useful when planning attacks, and the horses made for battle-worthy mounts. Jacob remembered he had once briefly thought he would join these renegades.

He knew he could not outrun the horsemen forever. The sun would set long before he reached the next town. He gripped the horse with both hands and thighs, panting out a prayer in time to the pounding hooves. *Miracle. A miracle, Lord.*

The response came so suddenly he cried aloud. For he rounded another hillock, and there before him lay not just a small oasis, but safety.

Jacob spurred his horse and leaped the outer shrub barrier, scattering a herd of sheep. He heard guards shout and saw men race for their weapons, and still he did not stop. Not until he was beneath the first line of date palms, and the caravan guards were holding swords and spears toward both him and the attackers behind him. He reined in his mount and swiveled in time to see the Zealots wheel and race off. Jacob sighed a quiet prayer of thanks as he climbed down from the saddle.

Only to discover that his legs no longer would support him.

He reached for the horse's mane, and the weary animal whickered softly, its lathered flanks trembling in exhaustion. Jacob patted the sweat-covered neck and slipped the bit from its mouth, then pushed the horse toward the trough. He fell to one knee and remained there, breathing hard.

A pair of foreign boots stomped over, and a voice he vaguely recognized demanded, "Who dares disturb the peace of this oasis?"

CHAPTER THIRTY-TWO

Approaching Tiberias

THE NOON STOP at the small village was more than welcome. It seemed they had been riding through sand and wind for days on end. Julia felt her legs would surely fail her as she stepped to solid ground. She watched her mother dismount, grateful for the guard who assisted her. Had both Helena and the guard not been followers of the Way, he would have been hesitant to help a woman of her position and wealth. Now he steadied her until he was sure she could stand on her own. Then he nodded toward the small tables scattered under the awning of the nearby food stall.

The meal was simple, but the tea was hot. Julia cradled her cup, hoping that its warmth would take some of the stiffness from her fingers. "This afternoon, God willing, we will arrive home."

Helena nodded but she did not speak. Julia could tell her mother was far away in her thoughts.

"Are you still troubled over your coming decision?" Julia asked softly.

Helena gave her daughter full attention and shook her head.

"No. No. I am sure that when the time is right, God will reveal his way for me."

"Then . . . ?"

"I was thinking of you, my dearest one. Of the marriage arrangement. We have been gone for some days. I wonder what awaits us at home."

Julia set her cup aside. Now the distress returned like a sudden downpour. How could she possibly leave her home and parents? Live in some strange household in some unknown country? With unbelievers? With a man she had never met?

She felt like her heart was being squeezed from her body. She reached for Helena's hand. She whispered in a trembling voice, "We must pray."

"I have been praying, my dear. Every day. Every hour, it seems."

"And we must reason with Father."

Helena shook her head and laid her other hand over Julia's. "Your father takes great pride in being a man of his word. He will not go back on a bargain. His very livelihood depends upon trust."

Julia pushed aside the plate. There was no way she would be able to swallow anything further now.

Helena reached inside her shawl and came up with a clean strip of cloth. "Wrap your food in this. You will need it later on the road."

Julia went through the motion without thought to what she was doing. She tucked the small package inside her own shawl.

"Martha told me a secret about prayer. The Lord himself said to his followers that when two or three agree in prayer, they may ask whatever they want to ask for, and the Father would hear and honor it. Two, Julia. *Just two*. You and I—the two of us—are enough. We can pray, and God will listen and act on our behalf."

"Three if we include Zoe." Julia's voice trembled. "How do we know it is not just something that is *our* will? Not his?"

"We will ask for his will to be done. If he has reason for this marriage to proceed as planned, he will show us. And we will feel his peace and blessing."

Helena waved to where Zoe sat talking with a distant relative. When the trusted servant joined them, Helena took her daughter's hands in both of her own. Her trembling prayer was simple but filled with heart and faith. She ended with words from her heart, "Thy will be done, Father. Thy will be done."

Julia's silent amen didn't fully allay her fears, but she knew it was the only path for her.

It was wonderful to ride into the courtyard and be home again. Julia hadn't been sure she would ever see the familiar house again. She could sense that Helena was equally thankful as they crawled down from the mounts. Two servants rushed from the house to welcome them, bowing and exclaiming over them in their familiar way. Julia looked at her work-hardened hands with a little smile, imagining the household's shock if they had seen her labors in Nain.

When Helena asked after Jamal, a servant responded, "The master is out at the encampment. Another caravan has just arrived from Damascus. Do you wish for me to send for him?"

"No," Helena said. "Leave him at his work. We will speak when he arrives home."

The servant kept his eyes downcast, but he must have known Helena well enough to respond, "The master may wish to be called. He has been very lonely with you away, mistress."

"Very well," said Helena. "You may send word that we have

safely returned—but explain that we understand he is busy and will await his return when he is free. In the meanwhile, we will have a warm bath and take tea and refreshment in the arbor."

The servant bowed again and backed away.

They settled together on the arbor bench, and Julia heard Helena sigh deeply. Overhead the birds chirped in the bower. The fountain danced, its little prisms of rainbows casting diamonds into the air. *It is still a place of peace*, Julia thought.

Zoe herself brought the tray. Helena invited her to join them, but the old servant had resumed her customary place within the household and respectfully declined. When Zoe departed, Helena poured tea from a copper urn.

"I had not thought I missed home. Now it seems good to be back. But it is also different. I think I can be happy here, now that I have found peace." She settled back and lifted her cup. "Strange, is it not? I had all this before—but I was so unhappy."

Julia dared to voice her thoughts. "I am still unsettled, Mother. I fear I will not be able to fully rest until I know what is to become of the marriage plans."

"But if he bids you—"

"I will obey, of course." Julia shifted and looked away. "I would not shame my father."

Helena nodded. "I was sure you would say that. And I respect you for it. But . . . but I must confess that I truly have peace about this as well. I cannot say why, but I feel the Lord will show his plan in this. Even to Jamal, though he might not recognize the Lord's hand."

Julia was glad to hear her mother speak with such confidence, but she still felt like her stomach was in a knot.

"And you?" she asked her mother. "Have you decided what you will do?"

Helena sighed deeply. Her eyes looked away into the distance—but again Julia could feel peace surrounding her mother.

"Yes . . . yes, I think I have. Tonight I plan to have a talk with your father."

They were just finishing their tea when they heard a commotion in the courtyard. From the volume of the voice it could be only one person.

"Where are they?" Jamal shouted. The next minute he was hurrying through the entrance to the small arbor, his face flushed, his eyes alert with anticipation.

"There you are, my dears," he called, his arms opened wide. "I was so worried. When news came of the storm . . ." But he didn't finish and instead embraced them both with one sweep of his arms. "You must tell me all about what happened."

Jamal sat in silence while the two described their journey, including Jacob's heroism during the storm. Alarm and relief creased his features as they spoke.

When Helena asked about his own news, Jamal's frown deepened. "There is both good news and bad, I am afraid. Business is doing well. Better than even I had hoped. But it demands my presence in Damascus. I will need to leave shortly. I feared you might not return before I had to be on the way. I would have been sorely troubled if I had not been able to see you before my departure. I need that young Jacob here to travel with me as well, so I've been waiting. He is to be . . . Well, I just hope he arrives safely and soon. I am concerned about him traveling alone."

"We have been daily praying for his safety," Helena said.

Jamal looked at her for a moment but simply said, "The bad news is, the marriage arrangement for Julia has been broken."

He was looking at Helena when he finished his statement. "I know, my dear—you are relieved. You never wanted this to happen. But truth be told, as much as we would desire it, we cannot keep our daughter forever."

Helena clasped her hands together and murmured, "How we have prayed for this miracle."

"It wasn't an act of any god, my dear," Jamal said. "It was the clan's doing. This groom-to-be was apparently a foolhardy young oaf. He was away on some hunting expedition with four other young men. They drank too much, and he ended up getting himself shot. An arrow straight to the heart. The family has sent their deepest regrets. They claim to have a distant relative, two years younger than Julia, and the clan is quite willing to apply the marriage contract to him."

Julia's heart plunged after the enormous exhilaration of her father's first announcement. She now felt a dread so strong it threatened to cut off her breath. But before she could form a protest, Jamal went on, "I told them that the original arrangement held no such provision. Since they could not honor the agreement, it was no longer valid. I did not say this to them, but if that was the kind of young man he was, I did not want his cousin for my daughter either. She deserves much better."

"So . . . ?" began Helena.

"This business of arranging a marriage is extremely time-consuming and costly. I am of a mind to let the girl make her own choice. She seems bright enough to know . . ."

Julia did not hear the rest. The emotions rising within were so intense that she moved from the room without even excusing herself. Her father and mother did not seem to notice. She heard her mother's voice agreeing that indeed Julia should be able to make her own decision in the matter.

When Julia reached the safety of her own room she laid her head against the cool stones of the wall and let sobs of relief shake her whole body. *Free*—she was free! She could scarcely believe it. God had answered. *Oh, thank you, Lord, thank you*, she breathed.

CHAPTER THIRTY-THREE

The Megiddo Plains

A FLASH OF raging wind blotted out the sky, so sudden they were caught unawares. Abigail, with Martha and Dorcas, were dining at Yelban's home when it struck. He stood in the doorway for a time, watching as the wind shrieked about. Down below on the plain the storm's force raged in full fury. Then, as suddenly as it had come, it was gone.

Yelban continued to watch the night. "The wizard would have claimed it is the old powers at work."

Martha said, "We are not to worry ourselves over the unseen. We trust in God, and rest in his peace."

"If I but had your strength of faith," Yelban murmured.

"We all have moments of doubt," Martha said. "At times we all feel the clutch of fear."

"That is why we need the company of fellow believers," Abigail suggested. "To help us see and remember."

"To pray with us," Martha added.

Yelban turned back to them. His head nodded slowly. "While

Peter and the group from Jerusalem were here, the bandits and their threat to our futures could not touch me. I prayed, and found myself able to set the worries aside. But now . . ."

Abigail glanced down at her sleeping child in her lap. Dorcas now stirred and whimpered, then settled once more into her mother's arms. Abigail stroked the little girl's face. "Sometimes I wonder how often we have been so shielded from troubles that we remain blind to the power of God at work around us."

Martha smiled her agreement. "Peter has departed. But the Lord's Spirit remains. We are ever in His care. As are you, Yelban."

He gave a brief nod, and the guests rose to depart. Yelban's wife followed them to the door. "I count the day you arrived here as a wonderful one, a great blessing."

More than the stars overhead, the words lit their way home. Abigail felt enough at peace to ask what had remained unspoken since they had arrived in Nain. "I have so appreciated your presence here with us, Martha. I am reluctant to even ask this, but how much longer will you be able to stay?"

In reply, Martha reached over and lifted Dorcas from Abigail's arms. She leaned in close to breathe deeply of the child's fresh scent. "How could I leave this child of God, so trusting, so full of life?"

Their footsteps were the only sound in the empty village lane. After a moment, Martha continued, "How could I go away from here, not certain that this one whom I have come to love more than my own life is safe and well and cared for? How could I deny myself the joy of listening to her prayers? How much I have learned from watching this one grow strong and trusting in the Lord our God. How could I leave all this behind?"

Abigail started to ask if Martha spoke of Dorcas or herself, but decided it did not matter.

In the morning the villagers descended to the crossroads to inspect any damage from the storm. They brought donkeys and one wagon loaded with tools and wood and cloth, for they had endured many such winter blows. Even so, there were bleak expressions all around as they drew near. The stalls were in tatters, the awnings shredded like sails. Many of the timbers were broken.

Yelban stood beside Abigail and said, "At least the corrals stood. The animals are still in place." She looked down at Dorcas beside her and wondered how long it had been since they had cleaned up after the sandstorm. But she took a deep breath and prepared herself for a long day ahead.

As Abigail walked through the jumble of torn canvas and broken timber, she found herself seeing not the storm's damage but rather, what the bandits might do. They were a far worse threat, and the harm they might inflict could be much more severe and long-lasting. Where would she and Dorcas go then? She had come to feel a part of this village. She truly had come to care for them and they for her. Was there no place she would feel safe?

She prayed silently as she worked alongside Martha. But not even the child's soft singing brought the usual solace to her soul. Over and over she told herself to be strong, to hold fast to the faith that she had urged Yelban to maintain. If only she could.

A familiar little voice broke into her thoughts. "Mama! Come see!"

"Not now, Dorcas. Mama is working—"

"Mama! It is Uncle Linux!" Her shadow danced across the front of their awning.

"Child, remember what Alban told us. Linux is in Caesarea. He can't—"

A shout rang from the northern edge of the market, "Riders approaching!"

Martha and Abigail exchanged glances, then together dropped their rags and brooms to join the other curious villagers.

In the distance five riders approached. It appeared they might indeed be coming from the distant Roman fortress. A yellow plume of dust rose behind them, a narrow ribbon tracing its way back toward the lone hill. The horsemen were little more than silhouettes against the empty sky, so far away Abigail could not yet hear the hoofbeats.

Martha squinted into the light and murmured, "Could it be?"

It seemed impossible that Linux might be arriving here at this outpost, far from distant Caesarea. Even so, Abigail could not still the sudden hope that sprang within her.

"Mama, Mama, lift me up!"

"You are growing too big, child." Even so, Abigail lifted the child onto her hip. Cheek to cheek, they watched the horses. "Why do you think it's Linux?"

"Because it is!"

Martha said, "They're too far for me to see."

"It *is* him! I *know*."

"Which one do you think—"

"That one. Right *there*. See?" Dorcas pointed to the rider who rode ahead of the others.

Perhaps it was the stance, the way he sat far taller than the others, or how his right shoulder was raised slightly, or the cock of his helmet. Something there in the silhouette caused her heart to grow wings.

"See! It is."

Abigail took a firmer grip upon the child and pressed through the crowd.

Martha called, "Where are you going?"

"To greet our friend!"

"Forgive me for arriving as I have." Linux was sitting on the tavern's rearmost bench in utter exhaustion. "We have been chasing bandits for days without rest."

His men were in no better shape. One of them remained with the horses, and another stood guard outside the tavern's tattered awning. The other soldiers sprawled at another table. None of the men were shaven. Linux wore an officer's uniform, but the brass was scarred and pitted, the leather worn by sweat and hard use. He did not wear the officer's crimson robe, which was normally fastened to the shoulders and hung down behind. His cheeks were hollowed, his eyes rimmed with exhaustion.

Linux coughed, a rasping sound. He nodded his thanks as Abigail poured more from the container of tea. "When we arrived at the Megiddo fort, we discovered the officer in charge and most of his men were gone, lost to that big storm. The fortress market was demolished, along with much of the village. Both of our wells had their tops blown off and are now filled with sand. We are on half rations while the remaining men dig out one well. There is almost no food. Not for beast nor man."

Yelban was seated across the table from the Roman officer, having found food for the travelers and making sure they had their fill. Abigail stood at the table's far end. Dorcas was beside Linux, her hand resting upon his arm. She had held the same position ever since he had first entered the tavern. "Uncle Linux. Are you tired?"

He looked down at the child and smiled for the second time since his arrival. The first time had been when he had seen Abigail and Dorcas hurrying toward him. The skin about his eyes creased like a man twice his age. "How is your bird, little one?"

"He hops and flies." She skipped in place to show him, her arms waving out at her sides.

"Does he? And does he sing for you?"

"Oh yes. I love to hear him."

"I am certain he is a great joy to you. And to your mother too?"

All eyes turned toward Abigail. She merely nodded to his question, but she could feel Yelban's eyes on her. She knew he was waiting for her to speak to the subject on everyone's mind. She also knew what needed to be said.

"We have food and we have water," she said clearly. "Both enough to spare."

Linux's head lifted, clearly recognizing the change in her tone and waiting for what would come next.

"We have other problems," Abigail said, looking straight at Linux. "Two of them, in fact. First, our market stopped trading with the Roman garrison because they did not pay."

"The garrison *stole* from you?"

Yelban spoke for the first time, and he also looked straight at Linux. "The garrison did not need to. You wrote out script. Pages and pages of notes promising payment. I have them still. A king's ransom in worthless script."

Linux grimaced. "I wish I could say I am surprised. But it is an old story. The garrison officer holds the power of a prince. What he does within the territory under his control is subject to no supervision but his own. More than likely this one received the silver for such costs and kept it for himself. If I were to find an officer willing to be honest with me, I would imagine his soldiers have not been paid either."

One of the legionnaires at the table said without raising his head, "Not in half a year."

Linux said, "We will make a search of the fortress. If I can find the garrison commander's hidden wealth, I will pay you myself. If the silver went with him, I will need to obtain funds from Caesarea. I do not have food to spare, and my horses are in worse shape than my men." His voice dropped, and he looked down at his hands. "You have no reason to trust me, of course."

Yelban turned and searched out the other elders, then said to Linux, "We will provide you with the supplies you need."

"And I will pay you," Linux said, looking straight into his host's face. "In coin. You have my word."

There was a soft rustling among the gathered villagers. Even Yelban visibly relaxed.

"There is another problem," Abigail said, nodding toward Yelban.

As the elder described the bandits' arrival and their threats, the Roman soldier by the front opening straightened and whistled softly. The soldier by the horses stepped into the tavern's shadows and listened also.

When Yelban was finished, Linux said, "Describe this bandit leader."

"Tall, though perhaps not quite so tall as you. Eyes like a desert adder, cold and dead. He wears two swords at his belt, and two more crossed at his back. And a bow of horn and ebony, curved like a serpent's back."

"His beard?"

"Long and waxed with the tip caught within a silver scabbard."

"I know this one," Linux said, nodding slowly. "He calls himself Kirtuk. It is the Nabataean word for death."

Yelban continued, "He vowed that if I sought the Romans'

help, he would wait until you departed. And then he would return. And—"

Dorcas cried out, "No. Don't go, uncle. Please."

Linux laid his hand on the child's head. "That is in the hands of our Lord, dearest one."

Yelban leaned back. "You are a follower?"

Abigail said, "He is. A dear and trusted friend as well."

Linux looked at her for a long moment, then returned his gaze to Yelban. "Here is what I propose. All but a handful of my men will come and set up camp here. We will patrol with the crossroads as our base. Those who remain at the fortress will dig out our well. But before I return here with my troops, I will search for the officer's unpaid silver."

He cast a quick glance at Abigail, then said to Yelban, "I have been assigned responsibility for this entire area. If you agree, I shall personally take charge of the soldiers on patrol about this crossroads. Unless you object."

"Object?" His hands lifted to each side. "Yours is the only offer of help we have heard since the bandits arrived." The relief and gratitude in the man's expression said more than his words.

"It is an answer to our most fervent prayer, Linux," Abigail said. "Please stay."

"Oh yes," Dorcas cried, clapping her hands. "Stay home."

Abigail watched as the Roman officer's gaze dropped to the child's face. Something in his smile caused a feeling she could not name to run through her entire frame.

CHAPTER THIRTY-FOUR

Tiberias

JULIA REMAINED AWAKE for hours that night, reflecting upon her father and the enormous change in her future. It truly seemed like another miracle. Finally she fell into a deep slumber. The sun was casting its rays through her window when she was awakened by tapping on her door. She pushed herself up, pulling her hair out of her face. "Yes?"

Her mother entered the room, smiling as she crossed to a small stool by Julia's bed. "It is early, I know," she began, "but I would like for us to talk some things over."

"Is Father still here?"

"No." Helena stroked her daughter's face. "No, Jamal spent the night at . . . at the inn."

Julia tried to absorb the meaning of the words. She had never known her father to stay at his inn. Then it came to her. "The two of you discussed . . . ?"

Helena nodded. "Long into the night."

"Has he asked that we leave?"

"No, not at all. I did offer to go. He said the house is ours. For as long as we want it."

"But . . . ?" Julia could not voice her real question, so she said, "What happened?"

"We can discuss all of that later," Helena said. Then more quickly, "For now we must prepare to travel."

"Travel?" They would once again take to the road? They had just returned, and she had a vivid memory of how arduous travel could be.

"Your father told us he is leaving for Damascus. I have asked that we be allowed to go there as well."

"To Damascus? What . . . ?"

Helena shook her head slowly. "I . . . I am not sure. I only feel that is what God has told me to do. I know no other—"

"Oh, Mother. You are not thinking of . . . of presenting yourself . . ."

"Truth is, I do not know what I am to do when we get there. I am sure, though, that I am to go. I would ask that you come also. God will make it plain step by step."

"But what . . . what did Father say?"

"He was shocked, of course." Helena smiled. "At first he said, 'What are you asking me? I send you on one trip, and now you think all you wish to do is travel about?' I reminded him that I had never asked him for anything before. He finally agreed. Though hesitantly, I think. I promised him that I would do nothing, say nothing, unless his—his other household invited me to do so. He will arrange for us to stay in his Damascus inn. Zoe again will travel with us."

By now Julia was fully awake. She wondered if her whirling thoughts would allow her to even think what she should do first. "How much time do we have?" she asked.

"I promised your father that we would not delay his departure. He would like to leave soon. He did not name the hour. But I want us ready and waiting when he announces he is prepared to take to the road."

Julia nodded and took a deep breath. Though another journey this soon had no appeal, she remembered her father's comment last evening—Jacob would also be going . . . if he arrived back in time.

She quickly began gathering the clothing she would need.

Jacob sat in the central courtyard of Jamal's home, hunched over the sacks of frankincense gathered together at his feet. The fountain sprayed musically into the morning, but he hardly noticed as he watched the caravan master pacing nervously back and forth. The man had not wanted to accompany Jacob, fearing Jamal's wrath. But Jacob had coaxed, and argued, and finally insisted. Now the caravan master's sandals slapped back and forth across the stones, and he pulled at his beard and moustache.

But Jacob took the caravan master's presence as a good sign.

Until yesterday, the last time he had seen this man had been in a dwindling cloud of dust as the man and his camels outpaced the trundling wagon. Behind them was rising a storm great enough to wipe them all off the earth.

Jacob now called over, "These dates are excellent." He held one up from the plate on the small table nearby.

The caravan master cast him a dark look. "I should never have trusted you."

"They are dipped in honey and wrapped in mint." Jacob pointed to another plate. "And this is fresh-roasted lamb adorned with onions."

"Do you not hear what I say? Jamal's fury is known from Damascus to Cairo. When he sees me he will—"

"He will do nothing. He will thank you."

"Thank me? I left his wife and daughter to die in the storm!" He dropped his voice for the last words, but his anxiety was most evident.

"You had two hundred camels and their goods under your supervision. Twice that number of donkeys. Eighty drovers." Jacob poured the man a cup of mint tea and held it out. "Here. Drink."

They had arrived at midmorning to learn that Jamal had been called to a meeting of local traders. At Jacob's insistence, a messenger had been sent. By now the household servants realized that the young former guard held a far greater role than previously known. He and the caravan master were led into the courtyard and fed from Jamal's table. Jacob had gathered his courage to ask about Julia, to learn only that both mother and daughter had arrived home safely.

The caravan master finally collapsed onto the bench beside Jacob. The hand that accepted the tea trembled, and he seemed to swallow with difficulty. "It is easy for you to be calm. He will not want to put out your eyes."

"Jamal's family is now safely at home. He will reward you with silver."

"You are a spinner of myths."

"Listen to me." Jacob waited until the caravan master faced him. "What I saw yesterday when I rounded that bend was not simply an oasis and a caravan. It was a sign from the Lord."

The caravan master watched him intently now.

Jacob said, "It was not merely Zealots who threatened me yesterday. I carry dire news of a peril facing all those who follow the risen Messiah."

"How can—" A noise at the front gates halted the man's query. His features again turned pale. "My children will starve without their father."

Jacob rose to his feet, gripped his companion's arm, and lifted him as well. "Have faith."

But the first man to come rushing through the outer portal was not Jamal. Instead, Alban hurried over, calling Jacob's name and sweeping him into an embrace. "Thank God," his guardian murmured. "Oh, thank you, Lord."

Jacob was somewhat embarrassed. Alban was not one for openly showing his emotions. Yet the deep affection was clear on his face as he released Jacob and took a step back. "Jacob, I must admit I was afraid I would never see you—"

"How dare you show your face in *my house?*" Jamal's voice thundered into the courtyard.

Jacob walked past Alban and inserted himself between Jamal and the terrified caravan master. "Sire, one moment."

Jamal's forefinger stabbed the air. "This man deserves the vilest of punishments!"

"The man deserves your thanks, sire. And a reward." Jacob was astounded that he dared interrupt his powerful employer. Even more, that he had suggested giving away some of Jamal's money.

"I will feed him his own tongue!"

"You will fill his hands with silver."

The courtyard had gone silent as death. Even the fountain's splashes seemed to fade into the background. Jamal focused on Jacob. "You, of all people, stand in this man's defense?"

"He has saved my life."

"He left you to die!" Jamal's face of stone turned on the caravan master cowering behind Jacob. "I will—"

Jacob gripped Jamal's forearm. "Sire, you must *listen.*"

Jamal's fury changed direction. From the corner of his eye, Jacob saw Alban move toward them, alarm on his features. But not even this could disturb Jacob's calm.

Jamal growled, "Unhand me!"

Instead, Jacob turned the man about and pointed at the sacks piled upon the courtyard's stones. "Do you see that, sire? They are here, *I* am here, because of *this man*."

"But—"

"Sire, only a few hours ago the Zealots attacked and almost captured me." Jacob stepped once more directly in front of Jamal. "This man saved me. He and his guards beat off my foes."

Alban stepped closer. "Zealots? How close to Tiberias—"

Jacob silenced his guardian with an upraised hand. His attention remained focused upon Jamal. "Sire, I am utterly certain that our Lord's hand was at work here."

Jamal snorted, but obviously his heart was no longer in it. He waved a dismissive hand. "All of you people with your religious nonsense."

"I serve a higher power, sire. And though the caravan master may not realize it, so did he. He was there at the right time for a *purpose*."

"What, to protect my wares?"

"Not directly, sire. Far more than costly spice is at risk here. This man may have helped save hundreds of lives." Again Jacob laid his hand on Jamal's arm. "Sire, reward this man and release him. To do otherwise would be a terrible travesty. He has saved you a fortune, he has saved my life—and now we must hurry."

Jamal looked down at Jacob's hand. Jacob released the man and took a step back. Jamal inspected him carefully, as though seeing Jacob for the first time. "Twice you have saved my family's fortune. I am thinking it is time to reward you, not him."

"If a choice must be made between him and me, sire, he is the one who deserves your silver. But this is not the time for that discussion."

Jamal shook his head and said, "You have the makings of a

leader, young man." The merchant turned to the caravan master. "Come here."

The man approached slowly. "Sire, the storm—"

"Enough. I will hear Jacob's report, and then I will decide on the future of our trade. For now . . ." Jamal unleashed the purse from his belt and dropped it into the caravan master's hands. "Return to your caravan. We will speak later."

The man gaped at the purse, then at Jacob, then Jamal. He bowed deeply and backed from the courtyard. When the outer door shut, Jamal turned back to Jacob. "Gather up the sacks and bring them to my strong room. You say we must make haste?"

"Every moment counts, sire. We hope and pray we are not already too late."

"Come then." Jamal hefted two of the sacks himself and turned away. "Alban, join us."

Jacob and Alban brought the rest of the frankincense and followed Jamal into his private quarters. Alban murmured, "You are no longer the lad I rescued from bandits. What have you done with our boy Jacob?"

Jacob grinned, then sobered as he heard a servant hurrying along the corridor. Jacob stood before the table, as he had previously in this same secluded room. Jamal sat with his back to the stone wall, flanked by torches. The long table before him was piled as usual with parchments and scrolls, bills of lading and reports from the merchant prince's far-flung empire. Beside Jacob were piled the sacks of frankincense, a king's ransom in the most valuable of spices. Jamal lifted his hand, palm out, as the servant's footsteps scraped along the flagstones. "Wait."

The old servant, the same one previously so dismissive of Jacob, stepped forward and bowed. "Forgive me, master."

"I ordered that no one should disturb us."

"Yes, master. But . . . that is . . ." The servant bent low again.

"The mistress has insisted on joining you. She has heard of your guests." He cast a nervous glance at the two men, plainly uncertain over the change in their situations. "Mistress Helena and Julia both know of . . . of Jacob's return. They *ordered* me to come, sire."

Jamal looked at Jacob, then back to his servant. "Then I suppose we had best allow them in."

Jacob's heart leaped at the sound of the light footsteps, and it leaped further when Julia came into view. Her face was flushed, and her brief glance at him held a light that warmed him to his bones.

Jamal gave the two women a terse nod. "So you have heard of my trusted man's return?"

Jacob noted Julia doing her best to hide a smile. Helena replied solemnly, "We did not hear it was Jacob, sire. Only that two riders covered by the road's dust raced into Tiberias and came straight here. We merely hoped it was the young man who had saved our lives." She gave the head servant a pointed look. "It distresses me to see he was not offered an opportunity to bathe."

"No one told me anything, mistress," the servant quickly defended.

She ignored it and asked, "Might we have permission to greet him, sire?"

Jamal waved them forward, watching without a hint of emotion.

Helena stepped forward, both hands outstretched. "It does my heart much good to know that you are safe, Jacob."

"And you, mistress."

"Julia and I have prayed daily for your safe return."

Julia nodded, and Jacob bowed toward the daughter, who remained at a modest distance behind her mother. "I trust your own journey was successful."

"Our thanks to you, yes, it was." Even speaking these words added a rosy glow to Julia's face.

Helena said, "I bring your sister's greetings. From Nain."

"I am so glad. How is Abigail?"

"Prospering. As is Dorcas."

"Her little daughter is a delight to all," Alban said from his place at Jacob's side.

Jamal motioned again. "This is all interesting, I'm sure. But Jacob claims to have news that cannot wait."

Jacob turned immediately back to his master. "Sire, I ask your permission to travel to Damascus."

To Jacob's astonishment, his words caused Jamal to pale, but he said merely, "I have already made plans, but—"

"I have received word that the most deadly foe of all followers of the Way is headed for that city."

Jacob felt rather than heard the two women's small gasps. "Saul of Tarsus," he confirmed. "He carries legal documents from the Temple Council, granting him the power to arrest any Judean who is a believer in Jesus."

They all began talking at once. The rock walls echoed so that no single voice could be heard. Jamal simply sat in his chair, his gaze flickering from one face to another.

Finally Helena managed to make herself heard. "He is *here*!"

"Of course! It *must* be him!" Julia said quickly.

Jacob raised his hands for calm, his face showing both shock and concern. "One at a time, please! Mistress, you say Saul is here? In Tiberias?"

"Tell them, Julia. Tell them what you saw."

Julia looked around the circle. "Yesterday evening I went to the caravanserai . . . to greet the camels." She paused to look at her father and added, "Though it was getting dark, a caravan arrived. I overheard its master say they were from Perea—you know, east of the Jordan. He said he had a guest with him, an important Pharisee from Jerusalem. This Temple priest had refused to travel through Samaria. That man is now looking for a caravan traveling on to Damascus."

Jamal gave a harrumph, then waved his daughter on. Julia said, "I also heard the caravan's master say after the priest and his guards—he called them *Temple guards*—had moved away that the priest had a seal from the Sanhedrin and important business in Damascus. He also said he was glad to see the last of the man."

Jacob's gut clenched. "It can only be the man the elder told me about in Joppa."

Julia turned back to her father and took a step toward him. "Will you . . . will he be traveling with *our* caravan?"

Jamal rubbed his beard. "If he learns we are going that way, I can do little else than allow it. The Sanhedrin carries a lot of power. To refuse would be costly indeed."

Jacob said, "You are going to Damascus?"

Jamal gave a single nod, then sat silent for a moment. "Yes, I was planning to leave today, and I also hoped you would return in time to join me. I do wonder, though . . ."

When Jamal did not finish his thought, Alban said, "I would not usually say the word *miracle* when speaking of Saul of Tarsus. But I know of nothing else that suits this moment."

The group stared at Alban, no doubt as perplexed as Jacob.

Alban said, "This man who strikes terror in the hearts of every follower who hears his name would be under the watchful eyes of your guards, and—"

"And what?" But Jamal's voice lacked its normal timbre, though no one dared respond. "What will you do?" His fist pounded the table. "If this is indeed Saul of Tarsus, and he learns a follower—or who knows how many others there might be?—is among the caravan's people, he will put you in chains. I too know of this man.

His name has spread throughout the region. I do not need to be a follower to fear his wrath."

Jacob said, "I could ride on ahead—"

"Do so, and you will never reach the city. The Damascus Road has become the bandits' main site for attack. Not to speak of the Zealots you just barely escaped." He tapped the fingers of one hand upon the table.

Helena said softly, "Jamal, sire . . ."

"I am thinking."

"Yes, and think of . . . think about your . . . your family in Damascus," Helena said with a catch in her voice. "They too are followers. What if Saul . . ."

Jamal might have nodded. Or it could have been a shudder through the massive frame.

"They must be warned—protected from this man," Julia urged.

"We have prayed for a sign," Helena told him.

Jamal said, "It is true, what you are saying? You would not wish harm to come upon my family?"

Helena walked around the long table and stood near Jamal's chair. "Sire, you said it yourself. They are your *family*. And even though I do not know them, they are my family as well. They—with me and Julia and many others—are now part of God's family. I want their safety, for their sake as well as yours."

This time, Jacob was certain a shudder wracked the merchant's body. "You are a good woman," he said hoarsely. "Better than I deserve."

Helena knelt beside his chair, and Jamal stared down at the top of her head. The two remained thus, with the chamber's only sounds the torches hissing. Helena lifted her head and said, "This is a sign, Jamal, greater than you or me or all of us together. Greater even than my fervent prayers concerning our daughter's betrothal."

Jacob felt a great fist clutch his chest. He could not breathe. *Julia? Betrothed?*

Helena said, "Sire, the fact that the Pharisee is here at this very time and travels to the same city is a *sign*."

Jamal nodded once. "I do not deny the truth of your words." His voice was a husky rumble.

Helena stood to her feet. "Sire, forgive my boldness, but it is the truth of *Jesus* that cannot be denied." She waited through a long moment, then said, "Will you pray with me?"

Jacob felt a surge rush through him, a force that came from somewhere beyond himself. He heard himself say, "Pray with *us*." Alban put a hand on his shoulder, nodding his agreement.

Jamal's voice sounded hollow. "I will think upon all you have said." He rose to his feet.

Jacob sought Julia's gaze, then turned back toward Jamal. He said, "And we shall pray for you to know what should be done, sire."

CHAPTER THIRTY-FIVE

The Damascus Road

JACOB'S PREVIOUS EXPERIENCE guarding caravans on many Roman-built roads had taught him an appreciation for their design and construction—mostly running straight as arrows, constructed by planners determined to tame nature's hills and borders. They were built for the armies that invaded, conquered, and then protected Roman boundaries. Besides expanding the empire's reach, the roads helped to promote trade as well as collect the taxes that trade produced. Broad enough to carry two chariots abreast, they were bordered by flat expanses where foot soldiers could march for days on end. The Damascus way fit the physical description, but these days the military strength was mostly a myth.

To the south, the Damascus Road connected with Jerusalem and Perea and on to Egypt and Alexandria. On the military maps Alban had shown him, Jacob had seen the lines running straight and true, dissecting lands and covering a lifetime of distances. These maps suggested an unstoppable force, so great it could subdue the wildest lands. And in many ways this was true. Didn't Rome boast of conquering the whole world? But Rome's grip upon the east had steadily weakened. The Damascus Road had become a single strip of Roman rule through a lawless and dangerous land.

It skirted the southern tip of the sea of Galilee. Tiberias was the first major trading community and point of safety within Judea's boundaries. It lay some fifteen miles north of the sea's southern border. All caravans entering or leaving Judea used Tiberias as a final resting point. Here in the shade of Herod's brooding castle was a last chance at safety.

Jamal did not say why he chose to make the journey to Damascus. But Jamal had arranged that room be made for himself and the women, and of course the caravan master quickly had obliged.

Jacob now stood at a distance and observed the household scurrying to prepare while Jamal continued to insist that there be no delay. Everything was accomplished in impossible haste—the guards gathered, the mounts selected, the clothes and provisions packed and loaded. Less than four hours after the first order had been given, the caravan set off.

Alban traveled with them as far as the village of Philoteria, a small village resting at the Galilee's southern tip. With Jamal's permission Alban intended to travel back to Capernaum to rejoin his family for a much needed time of rest and recuperation before resuming his duties as chief guard.

In safer times, the journey from Tiberias to Damascus might require six days. Jamal intended to make it in three—or four at the most. He was not concerned with how hard his caravan master might have to push the beasts or how the travelers might suffer. Jamal wanted them to arrive safely, outpacing any trackers and thus thwarting any plans to gather a force large enough to attack. It was a good plan, as Alban said several times.

But the plan's soundness did not keep Alban from worrying,

Jacob soon discovered. For once, however, it was neither the bandits nor the road that occupied Alban's mind.

"I do not like the presence of these Temple guards," he muttered. He and Jacob watched them ride some distance ahead. They had formed a circle around their leader and several other priests accompanying the group.

"Nor does Jamal. But there is nothing any of us can do about them." Jacob had been officially assigned as guard of the women, partly, he was sure, because Jamal had hidden the frankincense in with Helena's and Julia's personal belongings. Jacob and Alban rode on the east side of the road, far enough away not to eat the caravan's dust. Jamal rode just ahead of them alongside his daughter, who had insisted on her own mount. Helena had the comfort of a very small horse-drawn conveyance, with Zoe to see to her needs.

Since they had left Jamal's private room, Jacob had not had further occasion to speak with Julia. Even so, Jacob felt her presence up ahead of them. *But she is betrothed.* The thought brought another pang to his chest.

Alban squinted into the distance, studying the cluster of black-robed priests and their guards. "Tell me what the elder of Joppa said."

"I already told you everything I know."

"Tell me again."

In truth, Jacob did not mind the repetition. He liked the way his own thoughts were clarified by speaking with Alban. What was more, he relished how the two of them were together again. This time they rode and spoke as equals.

He decided Alban must have been thinking along the same lines, for when Jacob finished relating once more the details of his contact with the Joppa synagogue elder, Alban took a moment to look at him, then said, "Jacob, it was wrong of me to insist that you take over the stall in Samaria."

"No, Alban, you weren't wrong. Not at all."

"Are we to argue about this as well?" His guardian flashed a rare smile, and Jacob returned it, though somewhat ruefully.

"You weren't wrong," Jacob repeated, shaking his head. "If I had not resisted, prompting you to more fervent prayer for me, who knows whether you would have thought of this for Abigail."

"You speak the truth. Another instance of this new Jacob." He reached over and playfully cuffed the back of Jacob's head.

They rode in silence for a time before Jacob said, "There is more that came from our disagreement. I was forced to think. And pray. And ask questions about . . ."

"Questions about yourself and your direction and your future. Very difficult but most important."

"Much of what you said was true. *Is* true. I am selfish. I am strong willed. Sometimes I try to bend God's will to what I want, rather than bow to what he desires for me. I still yearn for adventure. I live for the open road. I want to see new places and experience new things. I wish . . ." He stopped, took a hard breath. And confessed, "I truly don't know what I *really* want. I only hope I have the strength to ask and listen for the Lord's voice, even when I am gripped by my own desires. *Especially* then." His eyes sought out the feminine form riding ahead, and he resolutely looked away.

Alban reached over and gripped his arm. "Jacob, we now are talking man to man. I must admit it is an experience new to me. I cannot say that young scamp with the dirt-streaked face will not be missed, though, the one who used to hide under my bed when he was in trouble."

"There are many times when I still feel like that little boy."

"We all have those times." Alban released his hold and sat straighter in the saddle. "Being an adult does not mean we have all the answers, nor will all our faults and weaknesses be resolved.

A man, first of all, knows himself and learns the need for honesty. Even when it is painful."

The village of Philoteria did not possess a true caravanserai. The lake at this end was shallow and held few fish. There was no natural port. Most of the produce the ramshackle market sold came from Tiberias.

The Damascus Road stretched out straight and solid in the day's final light. From Philoteria the road ran north by northeast, weaving through the southern Golan before entering a broad desert plain. As Jamal's guards stoked the central fire and prepared a meal for the merchant and his family, Alban drew their course with his dagger and spoke of his own experiences upon the road. Jamal had of course traveled the road many times. But the merchant was not discussing geography with his guard captain. He was discussing risks.

Alban told of the attack when he, a Roman centurion, had rescued the young Jacob from a band of Parthian marauders. He spoke with warmth and pride as he told of Jacob's childhood, being raised in a Roman garrison. Jacob had been surrounded by gruff soldiers who adopted the lad as their own. Alban then recounted the attack on a caravan that he and the Capernaum garrison had foiled, describing in some detail the tactics the bandits had used—riding a small troop in from one direction, driving the caravan toward the hills where a larger band waited to pounce. But Alban had made allies of the Judean shepherds, who led them across the Golan heights and revealed the caves where the bandits hid. Alban's troops had surprised them from above their hideout and had captured the bandits' chief.

Even though he had witnessed the event those many years

before, Jacob listened with a new appreciation for his guardian and friend.

As they started their meal, the sun's final rays touched the caravanserai. The tall Pharisee and the other priests had walked away from the rest and faced south and west toward Jerusalem. With the leather pouches, the phylacteries, bound to their foreheads and wrists, they covered their heads with striped shawls and began their prayer ritual. They swayed back and forth, and a low droning chant drifted over the distance.

Jamal used a chicken bone to point at the devout-looking group. "You do not join them?"

"No, sire. I do not," Alban said.

"But they are members of your clan, yes?"

Jacob knew the merchant was testing, probing. It was Jamal's way of searching out weakness, even among his closest allies. Alban knew this also, and replied without heat, "The Judeans within the Temple power structure, the Sanhedrin, view the followers as their enemies. Thus the persecution we have told you about."

"Are they correct?"

"No, sire. They are not."

"But these are not unintelligent people. The Sanhedrin are many things—power hungry, quarrelsome, vindictive, ready to take offense at any slight. But not dull, not uninformed."

Alban took his time responding. "Our Lord took them to task, sire."

"You speak of this Jesus."

"I do."

"The one who was raised from the dead."

"That is correct."

"You believe this? You accept this as fact?"

"My last duty as centurion was to investigate this very occurrence for Pontius Pilate."

"You knew the consul?"

"As well as any soldier who served under him."

"What was the man like?"

"A harsh man, burdened by his responsibilities. But fair in his dealings with me."

Jamal gnawed the last bits of meat from the bone and cast it aside. "And what did you discover?"

"That Jesus did indeed die upon the cross. And was buried." Alban's eyes burned more fiercely than the fire. "Three days later, he came out of the tomb. He appeared to his disciples and to many others besides. He taught them further, and he directed what they were to do. Forty days later, he rose into the heavens and rejoined the Father above."

Jamal studied his trusted guard captain for a time, then pointed to the swaying, praying men and said, "We should kill them."

Jacob tensed and heard Julia's gasp across the fire pit from them. Alban, however, showed no reaction whatsoever. He simply sat and watched the merchant.

Jamal went on, "This caravan rides with sixteen guards. All are trusted men of my household. We wait until the caravan enters the empty reaches beyond the Golan."

Alban said quietly, "That is why you wanted me to come, is it not? Because I have been a Roman warrior. Because I know the ways of war."

Jamal picked up the bone again and tossed it into the fire. "The desert has swallowed many men. Only the desert knows why or when or where."

"The Lord Jesus is a man of peace and mercy, sire. I cannot serve him and do such a deed."

Jamal's features turned hard as stone. He leaned forward, his face revealing a savage core. "And I in turn cannot worship a god who does not protect his own."

"You are not seeking God's protection, but the sword's," Alban replied calmly. "And Jesus is not *a* god. He is *the* God, the Messiah, the Chosen One."

Jamal's mouth moved, but no sound came out. Julia met Jacob's gaze over the fire, her eyes wide with surprise. Normally such a direct confrontation would have given rise to fury. Now the man seemed to gnaw upon Alban's words as he had the chicken bone.

Alban said, "If you wish to see our Lord at work, you must wait and watch—"

"That Pharisee threatens my wife and children," Jamal said hoarsely.

"Sire, the way of the sword does not bring peace."

"Your answer, then, is to *wait*." He almost spat out the word.

Julia spoke for the first time that night. "And pray, Father. Pray and believe with all our might."

Jamal turned to his daughter, the traditional shawl draped over her head, as was proper in public. "You," he said, his tone softening. "You surprise me most of all. You travel at your mother's prompting . . ."

When he did not finish, Julia said, "And seek God's will."

Jamal gave a single nod. "And you claim only peace."

"To carry peace, yes. But I think something more as well. I did not know exactly why we had come until this very moment, Father."

"I hear your words," Jamal said with a sigh, "and I understand nothing."

"We both came because Mother believed this journey was vital. She could not tell me more. Now I understand at least some of what God intends. We are here to testify that Jesus is *alive*. That he is waiting for you also to accept him into your life. To follow him."

Helena said from her place at Julia's side, "What joy it gives me to hear such words spoken among this group. In my lord's presence. And to have you listen."

Jamal inspected Helena across the fire, his bearded features cast in a ruddy glow, his expression unreadable.

Helena met his gaze with an unwavering calm. "And what greater joy if only you were to join with us in worshiping the Messiah."

After a time Alban asked, "Will you pray with us, sire?"

Jacob saw Jamal twist his face in an attempt at scorn, but the tremor in his voice gave lie to his gruffness. "I know not to whom you pray."

"Then I shall ask the Lord our God to reveal himself to you."

"As will I," Julia said.

Helena echoed the promise, tears brimming in her eyes, and Jacob added his own voice. "We all shall pray with you, and for you, sire."

Jamal dropped his gaze to the fire. "I shall think on this."

Alban said, "And I shall ask the Lord to show both his power and his mercy. That before you arrive at the gates of Damascus, you will understand the forces at the Savior's command. You will witness his ability to do astonishing things, and his love that binds us to him with cords that cannot be broken. We all will pray that you will see his mighty arm at work and hear his gentle call. That you will receive him, accept him, as *the* God, *your* God."

CHAPTER
THIRTY-SIX

The Megiddo Plains

THE MORNING AIR held a distinct chill as Abigail hurried with Martha down to the market stall. A caravan had been spotted, and every merchant scurried to ready his wares. Sales of late had been scant. Winter tempests took their toll even beyond the immediate damage to stalls and goods. Caravans were delayed, and now everyone was in need of their business.

"Did the boy know who these travelers are, where they are from?" asked Abigail.

"I didn't hear him say. But Yelban had sent him to alert us, and he seemed excited and hopeful."

Abigail too was hopeful that the caravan master and others in the group would be willing to barter fairly for the weavings in her shop. She needed coins to be able to buy the food and other items she and Dorcas required. Which reminded her of something else. "I am glad Dorcas does not need to spend the day down here with us. She is growing so quickly I cannot keep up with warm clothing for her."

Martha reached a hand to Abigail's arm. "It is a heavy burden you bear. Alone with a child to care for and protect. I am praying that your lot will change, and that a good—"

Abigail's gasp stopped Martha. "What are you saying?" Abigail felt her face grow warm. "Surely you are not asking God to . . . to supply a . . . a husband?" She could hardly form the words.

"And why should I not?" Martha retorted in her customary brusque manner. "You need someone to help you shoulder the load."

"Oh, Martha. Don't. Please."

"It has been five years since you lost Stephen. He would not want you to continue dwelling on the past. Dorcas needs more than a longer gown and warmer wrap. She needs a father. And you need a husband. Someone—"

"Please," interrupted Abigail, "please—do not speak any more on it. I cannot—"

"You must hear it, sister. You need to be thinking about it. You cannot go on for much longer alone."

"But . . . but first I . . . I need to learn how to love again." Her last words were little more than a whisper.

Martha made a sound that could have been interpreted in several ways. "Love again. My dear, you already do."

"What . . . what can you possibly mean?"

"I see it in your eyes every time you look at him, Abigail," Martha continued in a softer tone. "Every time you speak to him. Even hear his name. And he loves you in return. It is clear to any who care about either of you."

"Please, Martha. I beg you—no more."

"I will not speak further on this," Martha said. "But I will continue to pray. I know it is very hard for you to even think of this, but Stephen would have wanted nothing less. He loved you. He would not want you to be struggling along alone."

It was quiet for a time, and Abigail breathed a sigh of relief. But Martha had one more word. "He selected someone he knew he could trust. His friend. Your friend. And now Dorcas's friend. Why else would Stephen have asked him to take on the care of you if . . . ?"

Abigail was thankful to enter the stall and busy her hands with the tasks before her. But her heart still fluttered in her chest. It was unthinkable. How did one halt Martha from praying such impossible things?

The long hard ride on patrol had turned up nothing. Even so, Linux sensed bandits lurking in the hills' deep shadows. Why he was so certain he could not say. Beyond his range of vision, he suspected a cloud of evil was poised to spread over the region. Yet he and his soldiers had found not even so much as ashes of a cold fire pit.

They rode back in silence, a tribute to his men. After two hard days in the saddle, Linux heard no discontent. Not even as they arrived at their temporary camp beside the Megiddo market area and unsaddled and cared for their exhausted mounts.

The weather reflected his sour mood. The sky was slate grey and the air very still. Linux expected a hard freeze before dawn. Not the kind of night a tired soldier welcomed. His greeting from the elderly conscript who served his meal would likely be as cold as the night itself. He only hoped the food, no matter how simple, would be hot. A small bit of comfort.

When he pushed aside the tent's opening, he was astounded to see Martha sitting on the one stool, holding a cloth-wrapped bundle. She nodded at his look of surprise and held the parcel out to him. "I thought you might need something warm to thaw your bones."

The servant appeared, shuffling his feet and grasping his hands nervously in front of him. "I asked her to wait outside, sir, but she insisted. . . ."

Linux could not suppress a grin. Knowing Martha, if she was determined to do something, it would be done her way. "She is welcome at any time. And I am glad to see her."

Linux indicated the old man should remain, knowing Martha would be more at ease with a third person on hand. "Fasten the flaps back and stir up the fire to warm us. And bring a spoon." The man bowed and busied himself with his tasks.

Linux turned to his guest. "Welcome to my humble abode, good woman. And what is it you have blessed me with?"

"Lamb stew. It comes straight from the cooking pot."

"It sounds like a soldier's glimpse of heaven itself," he said as his servant moved a table away from the tent wall. "Will you share this welcome repast?"

"I have already supped," she explained, but she rose and moved toward the table with her bundle. "I would be happy for a cup of tea, though."

His servant prepared tea while Linux shifted a pile of maps and parchments to make room for Martha's gift. Despite his fatigue, Linux was glad for the unexpected company. It was an uncommon pleasure to have someone besides a soldier to talk to over his meal.

"I thought the Roman army did better by their men," Martha observed as she opened the parcel and set the bowl on the table.

"Maybe those appointed to Rome itself. We out here in the field take what we can find. Besides which, I don't spend much time here. As you well know." On impulse he asked Martha to pray, and found himself moved by her heartfelt words of thanksgiving.

He lifted a bite to his mouth and declared, "You have turned lamb into a delicacy fit for a Roman king." He ate in silence. When his bowl was empty, he watched Martha refill it and asked, "How are things at the market?"

"A little better today. Abigail . . . But she can tell you all that herself. Dorcas has been asking after you. The little one fears you have forgotten her."

"I certainly have not. I do think of her many times, be assured. But we have had some extremely long days in our search for those bandits. When we manage to return to our camp here after a patrol, it often is so late the market is already closed. And Dorcas would long be asleep."

"Even so, you should call at the stall. Many of the merchants don't climb the hill at night."

He looked at her. "Such a visit would be seen as . . . well . . . proper?"

"I will be there. No one would find any cause for gossip when a long-time friend visits us of an evening."

He nodded slowly and took another bite. "Is Dorcas now bedded for the night?"

"She was still singing to her bird when I left."

"And that was how long ago?"

"Not long. That man of yours would have taken the dish and sent me on my way. I was afraid it would all be gone by the time you arrived. I saw his nose twitching at the smell of it."

It was the first reason to laugh for some days. "I am very glad you saved it for me."

"I also wanted you to know that you are welcome to visit." Her eyes sought his over the rim of her mug.

His weariness and disappointment with the day were swept aside. Leaning forward on his elbows, he asked, "How is Abigail? Is her terrible loss less painful now? Sometimes she looks . . ."

Martha set aside her cup and leaned forward as well. "She is lonely, Linux. Dreadfully so. Only she is so busy worrying over her daughter and learning her new business that she does not allow herself the time to fully realize how she is feeling. But I too see it in her expression, in her eyes. Hear it in her voice." Martha rubbed a hand over her face. "It breaks my heart, and I have tried to talk to her, but she refuses to discuss it. I have told her I will continue to pray for her, even if she will not allow me to speak of her situation."

Linux rose to his feet and walked to the tent's opening. He stared at the night for a time, but in truth saw only the turmoil within his own heart. Finally he turned back to Martha, and said, "You know I love her."

Martha nodded. "I have seen it."

"For a long time."

Another nod.

"But I do not wish to cause her further pain, or make her uncomfortable."

"Sometimes a woman needs a change of circumstances to begin thinking in a new way." This normally direct woman chose her words carefully. "She is not ready yet. But she will come to it. One day—soon, I hope—she will realize that she does love you. But not yet. She still needs time."

A new resolve burned in his heart. "You are a bearer of light. Abigail has all the time she needs. I will still be here, waiting."

He stood and reached for his dust-covered robe. "Let's go see Dorcas," he said with a grin, and Martha smiled her agreement.

The next morning, Linux rode back to the fortress of Megiddo. His journey was lightened by recollections of the previous evening's joyful encounters—that initial talk with Martha, followed by a visit with his little friend. And her mother. Abigail had greeted him with kindness, but he had resisted the temptation to interpret her every word, every gesture, and gave his attention to a delighted Dorcas.

After a full and fruitful day, he and the band returned to the crossroads market in the fading light of late afternoon. Linux was not the least bit sorry to leave the old fortress behind. It stood isolated upon its lonely hilltop and brooded over the Samaritan plains. The Romans had taken it over for their own use without doing much to improve its condition. The rocks were black with dirt and age. From a distance, Linux thought it did not look like a fortress but like an angry stone vulture, ever ready to pounce.

Earlier that afternoon, Linux had finally located the garrison's missing funds. The commanding officer, the one now lost to the storm, had hidden the money in a compartment behind a loose stone in his private quarters. The coins filled four sacks. Before their departure from the fortress, Linux called the troops to order and paid their back wages. Their loyalty to Linux was sealed. The remaining silver he carried with him to present to Yelban. The funds would not be enough to satisfy the outstanding debts, but no doubt they would go a long way toward repairing the relationship between the garrison and the merchants.

Linux had split his Megiddo garrison into two groups. One he led himself, the other was directed by a crusty sergeant who hailed from distant Germania. Together he and Fabian planned their patrols so one band always remained near the Megiddo market to protect the shopkeepers.

Linux had been careful in selecting his own men, choosing those soldiers who were followers of the Way. They numbered seven. Added to these were another four with reputations for honesty and diligence. Most of the merchant families were followers of Jesus, and he sought harmony with them.

Linux arrived back at the crossroads just as the sun was setting.

Little Dorcas ran across the sand, calling his name. He let her help curry and feed the horses. All the while she sang a song she had just learned, one of King David's psalms. By the time the men were done with their chores, the men were grinning and joking with each other.

Dorcas led the way to Yelban's tavern, where Linux's sergeant waited with his own patrol. It had become their habit to take a meal together whenever both troops were at the Megiddo encampment. Linux and Fabian discussed any sign they had discovered, what reports or rumors had been passed on by villages they had visited, or where the next patrol might need to go. This day, however, Fabian met Linux outside the awning. He saluted the officer and reported, "A message has come from Caesarea, sire."

Yelban, attending the tavern's cooking fire, called over his shoulder, "Surely the news can wait until the man has eaten."

Martha appeared, wiping her hands on a cloth. "We have been roasting a sheep for half a day now."

"The aroma has had my men groaning with hunger," Fabian said.

"Bring your news inside," Martha insisted. "Sit, rest, pray, and eat. Then news."

The meal was as good as the fragrance promised. Most of the villagers drifted over. Some ate, others hovered around the edges. Dorcas stood by Linux's side and ate from his plate.

Abigail watched them both, a curious expression on her face. She did not disapprove, Linux was certain of that. Neither did she turn away. She seemed content to watch from her place by the awning's side wall, apart yet joined to the larger group.

As the tables were cleared, Fabian passed on the message from Caesarea. Cornelius, senior centurion of the Italian Brigade, had ordered the officer in charge of the Megiddo garrison back to Caesarea. There was to be a gathering of all the outlying forts' senior officers. Linux was ordered to scour the region as he came, looking for any indications of bandits.

Linux half expected a wail of protest from Dorcas. But the child continued to eat calmly from his plate, then settled down to play with her doll by his chair. Linux stroked the little girl's hair. "Will you miss me at least a little?"

"Oh yes. But you will come back," she said, nodding confidently.

The calm statement was enough to cause heads to turn his way. Linux said to the child, "There is no telling what I may face upon my return to Caesarea, child. Or where duty might call me."

Dorcas patted the sand-covered planks, smoothing the area around her doll. "You will come home. Here."

He risked a brief glance at Abigail. The woman did not meet his gaze.

Linux signaled to the corporal who had returned with him from the fortress. The man walked into the night, returning with Linux's saddlebags. He pulled out the sack of silver and handed it to Yelban. "It will not cover all those chits. But it is something."

"*Something?*" Yelban's fingers trembled as he untied the drawstring. He reached into the sack and hefted a handful of coins, lifting them high for all to see. "This is what we need. God is caring for us!"

Yelban raised his voice above the clamor that now filled his tavern. "We will dole this out in fair portions to all who are owed money by the Romans." He turned and said to Linux, "Someday, perhaps, I will find the words to thank you."

Warmed by the elder's response, Linux joined the others in their nightly prayers. This was the only time Abigail spoke since his appearance. Her prayer emerged so softly that Linux caught only a portion of what she said. But her voice sounded beautiful and stirred him as he listened.

Afterward they sat there, the Roman legionnaires and the villagers, in the peace that often came with such times. The sergeant was the first to break the silence. He leaned over his knees and said, his voice low, "I find myself growing curious about this God."

Linux could feel eyes turn his way. Clearly the villagers considered him the one to speak to the sergeant. Soldier to soldier. "What you are feeling, my friend, is the Lord's spirit at work within you."

The sergeant nodded at the sand by his feet and did not speak.

Linux gestured to the gathering. "Look about. Some of us are Roman legionnaires. We are gathered in the tent of a Judean merchant. In the heart of Samaria, surrounded by danger and strife. But we know peace. We are here because we care for each other. In a land that considers us their greatest enemy, worse even than the bandits, we are experiencing peace."

Linux gestured to Martha. "This good woman saw the Messiah die upon the Roman cross. She saw him laid to rest in a Judean tomb. And she saw him rise again to walk the earth and speak to them, sending them out with the Good News wherever they went."

Yelban spoke then. "Just as we have heard it here in Samaria. Challenging us to faith, to hope and love."

Linux said to the sergeant, "I ask, not as your commanding officer but as a friend, would you like to pray with us?"

CHAPTER THIRTY-SEVEN

The Damascus Road

JAMAL SAID NOTHING further about attacking Saul. The travelers rose two hours before dawn and were off long before the first light touched the eastern horizon. Alban embraced Jacob, prayed with his friends, old and new, and departed for Capernaum. It was too dark to identify any beyond the ones immediately around them, but Jacob had the impression Saul was watching everything.

By midmorning they had turned away from the Sea of Galilee. They trekked hard all day, stopping only once at a small well surrounded by a few flea-bitten stalls. The further they journeyed, the more remote the road. The guards constantly circled about the caravan, raising more dust than the camels. Outriders took their places at the front and back of the line.

They were not challenged and by sunset had arrived at the empty desolation of the borderlands. Trachonitis was the name given to this region by the Romans. Jacob surveyed this hardscrabble area that revealed little life. They passed a few destitute-looking shepherds and goatherds, and upon distant hills could see what might have been the ruins of ancient villages. *Or perhaps poorly constructed hideouts of bandits and Zealots*, Jacob thought.

They spent the night in a tightly drawn circle surrounded by ever-vigilant guards. None slept much or well.

Twice that next day they came upon the wreckage of other caravans. The first might have been a small band caught in a storm, possibly the one that had struck Jacob and the women. But the second pile of debris was a vivid warning to them all. The wind and the vultures had not yet managed to eliminate the remnants. Jacob rode up alongside Julia, trying to block her vision. But she had seen it already, he could tell. He thought he saw her lips moving, no doubt in a quiet prayer for families torn apart.

Saul of Tarsus proved a hardy traveler. Three times daily, he and his men separated themselves from the caravan to pray. That day the caravan did not stop for the noon rest, but Saul and his group still halted to cover their heads and turn toward Jerusalem. Afterward they raced to catch up with the rest of the caravan. Saul either rode one of the group's donkeys or walked in his turn.

As Jacob circled the caravan with the other guards, he took time to study this sworn enemy of all followers. Saul's tall form carried an intensity that made his physical attributes of secondary importance. Lean and strong, he bore the road's strain and toil with seeming disregard. Though known as a scholar and revered religious leader, he had the hands of a man who knew hard work. His eyes were his most compelling feature. Like those of a bird of prey, they were tightly focused, endlessly moving back and forth above a long and carefully tended beard.

On the third day since leaving Tiberias, they saw no others save a band of mounted Roman legionnaires who rode in tight formation but gave way to the much larger caravan. They exchanged a few words with the caravan master, who pointed back toward the remnants of the destroyed caravan. Jacob was close enough to note that their centurion showed no surprise at the news.

That night, Jamal paced around the caravan while the servants prepared their evening meal. He motioned for Jacob to accompany him. The other guards acknowledged the merchant with short bows, but not even the caravan master dared approach. Jacob could well understand—Jamal brooded with his entire being. He walked with body bent, a dark frown creasing his face. Jacob walked beside him, waiting for the man to give some reason for the invitation. But none was forthcoming.

When they returned to the campfire, the man addressed Julia. "Where is your mother? Is she not well?"

"She is well, Father. But she will not be joining us for the meal." Julia looked hesitant, then added, "Mother feels the need to fast and pray. She is . . . she is seeking God's will for the days ahead."

This only served to darken Jamal's scowl further, but he took his place on a small rug by the fire and accepted the meal laid out by a servant.

The three of them ate in silence. Several times Julia cast a quick glance Jacob's way. Clearly she sought reassurance that all was well. But Jacob had no answer save to wait and watch.

Finally Jamal set his plate aside and growled, "I grow restless, waiting for this God of yours to act."

Julia said softly from across the fire, "He is not just our God, Father, but the Lord of all."

Jamal studied his daughter, but did not rebuke her as he might have. "You are the brightest ray of sunlight to my day. You have been since the first time I heard you cry. You were a beautiful child, and you have grown into an even lovelier woman."

Julia clearly was taken aback by these comments. She blinked away tears that caught the firelight. "Thank you, Father," she whispered.

"The one reason I cannot reject this God is because I have seen the effect he has had on you and Helena."

Jacob hardly dared breathe at this extraordinary acknowledgment from a man he both feared and respected. And for him to be saying this in front of others was even more astounding. Jacob could hear Julia swallow before she managed to say, "There is no finer compliment you could ever offer me than this."

If Jamal noticed his daughter's emotion, he gave no sign. "You and Helena do not go to Damascus in order to make trouble for me with my other family. Neither of you is seeking a greater portion of my inheritance."

"No, Father. None of these things are important to us."

"Then why?"

"It is as Mother said. We seek peace and kinship with your family—but only if that is acceptable to them." Julia wiped her eyes. "We are fellow believers in the Messiah, and this fact draws us together into a family circle that does not require the normal earthly ties."

"This I do not understand."

"Mother has prayed and prayed again about this. Sometimes with Zoe and me, but mostly on her own." She took a deep breath. "She has an impression that God is calling her to reach out to . . . to your wife and family. She feels this is a small fulfillment of his command to love each other, even in seemingly impossible situations."

Jamal's gaze turned inward. "I did not mean to hurt anyone."

Julia nodded. "Both of us know that. But the truth is that you have, Father. You have hurt Mother very much." She hesitated, then added softly, "And me."

Jamal rubbed an impatient hand through his grey-streaked hair and across his face and down his beard. "I can't allow her to leave me. Neither can I send her away. . . . I can't."

"Mother has always loved you, Father, and has lived to serve you." Julia stared into the dying flames. "Her faith gives her strength to do whatever must be done."

Jacob rose and silently moved just beyond the campfire's reach. He felt he should not be part of this most personal and private conversation. But Jamal turned and said, "Come, sit with us again." When Jacob had done so, Jamal said, "What say you about this absent God of yours?"

But it was Julia who spoke into the silence. "He is neither absent nor silent, Father. He is ever with us, even when we are not conscious of it."

Jamal's gaze remained fixed upon Jacob. "Does this young woman speak for you?"

"As though the words were drawn from my own mouth," he said.

Jamal seemed to think on this for a long time. But when he spoke again his thoughts must have moved on, for he turned to Jacob and said, "You asked me to stay my wrath." Jamal thrust his arm out toward the northern sky. "But up ahead lay the hills of Damascus. Before nightfall tomorrow, we shall reach our destination. Tonight is the last chance we have to make these troublemakers disappear."

Jacob did not speak or move.

Jamal pounded the ground by his side. "Your God has done *nothing*. He is such a powerful God that he will allow this danger to spread from Jerusalem—attack the city of my birth, perhaps even my own flesh and blood?"

"My own sister was married to a disciple named Stephen," Jacob told him. "Five years ago he was stoned to death by a mob that was under the orders of the Temple Council. The man who travels with us, Saul of Tarsus, was among them."

Jamal sat as if turned to stone. He finally said, "I had not heard of this. Indeed, this makes it even more—"

"Please, let me finish, sire." Jacob took a hard breath. "Since we left Tiberias, I have prayed as I never have in my life. And the only clear answer I have received was today, upon the road. For the first time, I understood how difficult it is to remain steadfast in the threat of death, to serve our Lord while being attacked. I could almost hear the Lord ask me these questions. If I am to die a martyr's death, can I set aside my ambitions and my future and love him, serve him, to that last breath?"

The last log on the fire split and fell, releasing a shower of sparks. Otherwise the only sound was a tiny sob from Julia. The three of them remained there, gazing into the coals.

"I learned something more," Jacob said after a while. "I learned how hard it is to be left behind, as my sister was. How it may be even harder to continue on as she does. I am sure she has had moments when she wishes she had died with Stephen." He paused, then said, "All these things I had thought about before, but never with this clarity. I do not know what lies up ahead. For any of us. But I pray that if I am so called, I will be able to set aside everything else and serve my Lord as he calls me. Even if it means giving my own life. Even if I must . . ."

Jacob did not intend to look at Julia just then. But he was glad he did, for she stared at him with tears running down her face, giving him an unspoken message of such tenderness he could not breathe for a moment.

Jamal studied his daughter, then turned back to Jacob. "You are talking about the impossible."

Jacob shook his head. "I am sorry, sire. But it is impossible only if I rely on my strength alone, without God."

CHAPTER THIRTY-EIGHT

The Damascus Road

BUT WHEN DAWN broke and the caravan prepared to depart, Jacob found himself once more surrounded by doubts. It troubled him that the message he was to take to the followers in Damascus was being delayed as he shared the journey with the very man he was to have warned them about. What could he do to prevent a disaster?

He watched the Pharisee, Saul of Tarsus, draw his Temple guards over to one side. There were seven of them: Saul and a black-robed assistant priest and the five guards. They had not previously invited any other Judeans among the travelers to join with them in prayer, and they did not do so this time.

The Temple Pharisees were known as keepers of the tradition, staunch defenders of the Jewish law—and the minutiae with which they had surrounded it. Unlike the Sadducees, ardent foes on the Temple Council, the Pharisees traveled about Judea, lecturing in synagogues and searching out any perceived wrongdoing. Jacob watched Saul and the guards wind the phylacteries into place, then drape the prayer shawls over their heads and shoulders. By now most of the caravan had become accustomed to their droning chants and paid little mind. But Jacob found himself unable to turn away. He was Judean, as pure of blood as any of these. Yet they excluded him. And for what? Because he had found a Teacher who had come from God and drew him close to God.

And they would kill him for it.

Perhaps Jamal was right.

Jacob felt the sword at his belt almost hum with furious anticipation. He gripped the scabbard with one hand, as though to keep it still. The path Jacob had not taken called to him—the way of the sword and the warrior. The path of blood and destruction. It was a siren's lure of fierce actions and swift vengeance. Saul was an enemy. Jacob had the power to end this threat. All he needed to do was shout, and every one of Jamal's guards would leap to do his bidding.

Jacob heard the crunch of sandals over sand and knew by the light, swift tread that Julia approached. She stood beside him a moment, her gaze also toward the praying Pharisee, and said, "I know what you are thinking."

Jacob took a shuddering breath against the almost overpowering desire.

"You are a strong man," she went on, "and you hear the rationality in my father's perspective. And you fear for a family you have never met. You seek to protect other followers, people of a city you have never seen. I have observed my father's other guards, how they respect you. How they would respond to your word to strike." She paused, and he could have denied these things. But she then said, "Jacob, you have the right reasons, but you are drawn to a resolution that does not include our Lord."

He felt a shudder run through his body.

"Hear me, Jacob. I spoke with God last night, and he with me. I too was drawn by my father's arguments. I too felt the urge to unleash his guards, end this threat, leave their bodies in the wasteland." She stared into his eyes. "The Lord's Spirit confirmed to me that what you said last night was his voice speaking in you and through you. That your statements revealed a new man, one he is fashioning according to his plans for you."

Jacob felt something new and unfamiliar flow through him, a strengthening of purpose he knew came from outside his own will. That overwhelming desire for revenge—because of Stephen's death, the capture of Latif, the fear and turmoil that were scattering believers far from home and families—and now the opportunity to once and for all cut off the serpent's head and save more from persecution, all simply flowed out of him. Nothing remained but the ashes of that vindictiveness and rage.

As he turned to Julia all he felt was the now-familiar helplessness at his inability to do what he had been charged to do. Save his brethren. But it was no longer his lone battle. They were in God's hands.

He swallowed hard, then managed, "Thank you, Julia. I have heard the Spirit speak through your words."

Her only response was to smile. "Come. Mother is waiting. Let us pray together for God to further reveal his direction in all this."

By midday the mountains of Damascus were visible on the horizon. A faint haze drifted in the distance, a sign that the caravan was approaching the city. A world of rock and scrub and yellow earth stretched out on either side, and the air was utterly still. A faint charge surrounded them, like the power gathering before a lightning strike.

Jamal was a seasoned traveler, and he along with the caravan master and the guards continually swept the southern skies, seeking some sign of a coming storm. But the expanse behind them remained utterly empty, the sky a pale blue wash that seemed to mock their concerns.

Jacob circled the caravan twice, passing Saul and his companions with nothing more than a prayer in response to their dark looks. Julia rode a guard's stallion and remained by her father's side. Several times Julia's eyes met Jacob's as he passed, and he saw no concern. No tension. Only the same quiet confidence he had himself sensed the previous night.

Jacob gripped the pommel with both his hands and lowered his head. His prayer was simple, only acknowledging what was happening. *I am ready, Lord. Come, Holy Spirit. Come.*

He lifted his head and looked around once more. Perhaps other people sensed something too. He noticed Jamal muttering something to his daughter, and she leaned toward him to respond, her expression alight with anticipation. Jacob had a growing impression of the divine presence at hand. *Show me, Father, what I must do, how I might serve you. Here and now, and always.*

Then it happened.

The entire caravan suddenly stopped as if they had heard a shout of alarm from the caravan master.

A light appeared upon the road ahead. If the sun had descended from the heavens, it would have gone unnoticed in the intensity and power of this light.

Jacob saw the Pharisee, the enemy of the Way, fall prostrate upon the road. Jacob heard a voice, but could not make out the words. It did not matter. God's presence surrounded him, filled him. And then Jacob heard Saul of Tarsus cry out, "Who are you, Lord?"

Jacob slipped down from the horse and knelt upon the earth. He knew he was witnessing something beyond human understanding or experience, a miracle directed at another. Yet he somehow felt included. As though the moment was not merely intended for the man to whom God spoke.

The light faded, and Jacob slowly stood and walked forward. The Temple priest, the man who had sworn to destroy the followers of Jesus, remained face down on the road. Jacob reached down and gripped the man's arm. "It is concluded." He barely recognized his own voice.

Saul allowed himself to be lifted up. "I . . . I cannot see."

Jacob held his arm. "I will guide you," he said.

Saul's attendants were scattered about, looking stunned and uncertain. Yet none approached. The caravan master finally shrilled a signal. Gradually, almost reluctantly, the drovers once again called, the guards shouted, the animals responded, and the caravan moved forward.

Jacob held the Pharisee's arm and led him up the road. Neither of them said a word for a long time. Then Saul whispered, "The Lord Jesus spoke with me."

Jacob's eyes burned at the astounding opportunity of witnessing such a moment. "What did he say?" he finally said.

"He asked . . ." Saul's beard trembled. The man made no attempt to hide his emotions. "He asked why . . . why I persecute him. Him!"

Jacob felt something leap inside him. *This enemy of Jesus has heard his voice directly!*

Saul went on, his voice broken, "He . . . Jesus told me to get up and go into the city, and I will be told what I must do."

Jacob needed some time to shape the words, "I will help you."

CHAPTER THIRTY-NINE

Damascus

THEY ARRIVED AT the city just as the sun dropped below the earth's western rim. The legionnaires manning the city walls had seen the caravan descending from the southern hills, and the first gates were open to receive them. Jacob did not protest as Saul's Temple guards approached and cautiously took charge of the man. Since relating to Jacob what the Lord had said, Saul had not spoken again. Jacob had not minded the quiet. The power of what he had experienced lay like a mantle over the dusk. The entire caravan watched as the Pharisee, along with the other priest and the Temple guards, passed through the city gates and disappeared.

What now? lingered in every pair of eyes that watched Saul go. *What now?*

Jamal remained subdued, as did the entire caravan. Even the beasts seemed affected by the supernatural experience. Despite the long trek and the speed at which they'd traveled, no animal bellowed a complaint for water. There was no shouting by the drovers, no whips, not even orders from the caravan master himself. Instead, the long line of dusty beasts marched into the caravanserai and made camp in near silence.

Jamal's first instruction upon arrival was for three guards to escort Helena and Zoe to his inn and see to their accommodations. They were to have the best available, he told them. In an unusually subdued voice, Jamal said he would wait and present himself to his family in the morning. The day, Jamal said, had been already too full.

Julia had insisted on remaining behind to help see to her father's needs. By the time the animals had been settled and fed, it was fully dark. In the light of torches Jacob and the other guards erected tents for Jamal and his daughter. A meal was purchased from the finest of the stalls surrounding the caravan. As the attendants laid out the meal upon the carpets of Jamal's tent, the merchant gestured for Jacob to join them.

Jacob seated himself upon a cushion facing the tent's opening, as was befitting a guard. The three of them ate in silence.

Finally Jamal made use of the copper finger bowl to wash his hands and wipe his mouth. He spoke facing out into the night beyond the tent. "I detect no gloating from either of you."

Now that Jacob's belly was full and the Pharisee was somewhere inside the city walls, he felt like his mind had slowed to one step above slumber.

Julia replied for them both. "We are all humbled by the Lord's doings today, Father. Something we would never have contemplated."

Jamal grunted and dragged a damp towel across his face and down his beard. "Even so, I suspect your priests will be much pleased to count another rich man among your company."

Jacob countered, "Sire, forgive me. But you are mistaken on several counts."

Jamal started to bark. But Julia reached over and touched her father's arm. "Hear him out, Father, I beg you."

Jacob knew he should adopt a more subservient tone. But just then he was too weary to care. "First of all, the relationship you are invited to begin with Jesus is not done through priests. You do not any longer need to enter the Lord's presence through sacrifices at the Temple or through incense or offerings."

"What of those who just left our company? Would they agree with you?"

"Father," Julia softly urged. "Wait. Listen."

Jamal looked between the two. "You know what he is to say before he opens his mouth?"

"On this point, yes. I do."

Jacob went on, "Your passage into the holy presence has already been arranged. Jesus, the son of the living God, allowed himself to be the one and true sacrifice for all. You move into God's kingdom when you acknowledge him as Savior. Ask him into your life. Turn from your sin and selfishness, and determine to grow in your faith."

Jamal's words emerged very slowly. "What you have said creates more questions than answers. But I cannot refuse the truth of them. Not after what I witnessed upon Damascus Road. Not when my heart burns within my chest."

Jacob heard Julia's breath catch in her throat. She blinked fiercely, reached over, and took her father's hand.

Jamal stared at their two hands intertwined. "Jacob."

"Sire."

"Close the tent opening, please."

Jacob rose and did as he was ordered, signaling to the guard on station beyond the shadows that all was well. When he returned to his seat, the tent was illuminated by a trio of oil lamps.

Jamal reached beneath the cushion on which he sat and

withdrew two packets, both sealed by red wax. He settled one on the carpet between himself and Jacob. "Your reward."

"Sire." Jacob could not help but gape. The frankincense before him represented more wealth than he could have hoped ever to earn in a lifetime of guarding caravans. He knew he should say more. But just then he was too overwhelmed.

Jamal seemed to understand, for he nodded slowly. He turned to his daughter and placed the second packet on the carpet before her. "I offer you this as your dowry. Along with your permission to marry whomever you choose."

"Oh, Papa." She broke down and wept.

Jamal stroked his daughter's hand. "You have not called me that for a long time, daughter."

She required some time to say, "Thank you. Thank you, my papa."

Jamal nodded once more and turned back to Jacob. "Your abilities are wasted in guard duties. Here is what I propose. You shall make another trip or two for me, handling the frankincense. By that point, your role may be known and any chance of subterfuge lost."

Jacob fought to bring his swirling thoughts into focus. What the merchant was saying was important. Vital. "I agree, sire."

"Since my talk with Helena I have become aware of the fact that I will no longer be spending much of my time in Tiberias. I need a trustworthy man to run the business there for me. Of course much of what is now there will be moved back to Damascus, which will be my main location. But I will still need someone there. Someone I can trust who can speak for me. Jacob . . . ?"

Jacob's heart surged once more. "Sire, that is beyond—"

"So you agree?"

"Oh yes. That is . . ." Jacob looked across the carpeted expanse to where Julia still struggled to regain her composure.

Jamal also looked at his daughter. "You wish to wed this man?"

"We . . . we have not spoken of a union." Julia flushed, and she bit her lip.

Jacob felt his own face flame. "How could I speak of it when I had nothing to offer? And what of her betrothal to another?"

Jamal waved a hand. "The fellow got himself killed by a stray arrow."

Jacob felt the breath leave his body.

"And had you something to offer—would you speak?" asked Jamal.

"Sir, I feel so humble and—"

"Ask."

Jacob swallowed hard and leaned forward upon his knees, bowing deeply toward Jamal. He finally found enough air to form words. He settled the bag of frankincense back in front of Jamal as his bride-price and stammered, "Sire, I am asking for your permission to become betrothed to your daughter." He looked toward Julia. "If she will so honor me, sire."

"Well, Julia," Jamal prompted. "Would you wish to accept this young man's offer?"

Her voice caught but did not break. "With all my heart."

Jamal lifted his daughter's hand and kissed it softly. "You have my blessing." He reached for Jacob's hand and put them together in front of him.

Jacob found his own vision blurring. So many dreams, so many vistas opening before him . . .

Julia laid her other hand over that of Jacob's. She was openly crying.

"And now I have a request," said Jamal. "If I could have your full attention."

Julia laughed through her tears and exchanged glances with Jacob.

"It is not for me. For your mother. You have heard that I have given her the Tiberias home. I am asking that you live there with her. Care for her. I do not want to leave her alone there."

Julia looked at Jacob. "Jacob . . . ?"

"We both would be honored, sire," he said to Jamal.

Jamal's astounded gaze swept between them. "Well—it greatly relieves me to have this agreement." He turned to Julia. "I had worried about your mother. This is your gift to me. I will rest much easier knowing that you will be there with Helena. Her financial needs I will provide, but she needs someone there who truly loves her as she deserves to be loved."

Jamal lifted the bag of frankincense and tossed it back in Jacob's direction. "Now, take your reward, and may I suggest in the future you offer it more sensibly than what I just witnessed."

The laughter they shared only strengthened the bond already forming.

Jacob watched Julia turn serious and reach for her father's hand. "You have sought long and diligently for treasure, Father, and now I wish you to claim the greatest treasure of all. The priceless one. Worth far more than mere frankincense. And it is freely offered to all—rich, poor, young, old, Judean, Greek. . . ."

Jamal shifted on his cushions. His face too had taken on a serious look as he gazed at the carpet on which he sat.

Jacob moved slightly, thinking he should leave father and daughter to this moment.

"Stay," said Jamal without lifting his eyes.

He stayed.

Still Jamal did not raise his face. At length he sighed deeply and shook his head. "Everything has turned upside down for me. And now this . . . this Messiah you talk about will not leave me in peace."

"But that is exactly what he longs to give you," Julia assured him. "Eternal peace."

Jamal seemed not to even hear the words. "First my daughter, then Helena. Now has come the news of my wife and sons here in Damascus. . . ." He shifted and sighed, then again looked at Julia and Jacob.

"I could not understand it at all when I first heard it. Still cannot. But this I know. This great power I have witnessed today could come from nowhere else but a mighty being. The whole experience spoke to me. That everything you have been telling me is truth." He paused a long moment. "The—what should I call it?—tranquility I see on your faces is a treasure indeed. A treasure that far exceeds what you carry in that bag."

Julia leaned toward Jamal, clinging to his hand. "Will you pray for that peace we have found, Father?"

CHAPTER FORTY

Damascus

THE SUN OVER the eastern plains revealed a verdant landscape in spite of winter's cold. The merchant's tent remained silent, and there was yet no sign of Julia, so Jacob breakfasted alone. He made a quick circuit around the caravan's enclosure, surveying the beasts, speaking with the drovers, and assuring himself that all was in order. His heart continued to exult with a refrain of many voices. Julia was to be his betrothed, Jamal had offered him the kind of future in which he would thrive, and the merchant had prayed with them.

When he heard movement inside Jamal's tent, he placed himself by the opening, reported on the caravan, and asked permission to visit a synagogue for morning prayers. He felt a need to join with others in the familiar liturgy of thanksgiving. Jamal came to the door and responded that he would be traveling with his daughter to his Damascus home and would be gone for the day. Jacob bowed and departed, praying as he passed through the second set of gates that Julia and her mother would indeed be granted the reception for which they hoped and prayed.

Damascus could not have contrasted more sharply with Jerusalem, the only other great city Jacob had known. Jerusalem crowned a vast hilltop and possessed not a single straight avenue. Jacob knew people who had spent their entire lives within Jerusalem's walls, and yet still became lost when visiting a different section. Its lanes wound about, climbed hills and descended steep slopes. The inner city contained a second wall, far older than the first, weaving through the most ancient sectors and causing the city's lanes to do the same.

Damascus was perhaps as old as Jerusalem, yet it rested upon a vast flat. The Lebanon Hills rose to the north and west, forming a half-moon barrier that protected the city from most storms. These same hills also created two rivers that spilled in waterfalls down the neighboring cliffs, and poured like broad avenues—one through the city's heart and the other at its northern edge.

To the south stretched the vast deserts of Golan and Perea, wastelands extending all the way to Arabia. Yet to the east and north lay lush fields, rich farmlands fed by the same rivers that gave Damascus its life. The Romans had refashioned most of the city's main avenues so they ran straight and true, north to south and east to west. Jacob had no difficulty finding his way.

Nor was it hard to find fellow Judeans. Jacob had heard that as many as twenty thousand Judeans lived within the city's walls. He walked down the central avenue, a street called Straight, and immediately came upon a group of men carrying prayer shawls. He asked them for directions to the baths, which he suspected was their destination as well. Most observant Judeans would make a stop by the baths before morning prayers, as immersion was a component of spiritual cleanliness. For Jacob there was far more here than merely cleaning off the road's dust. He knew that the act of immersion was considered a symbol of change. Of elevating oneself from the earthly to the heavenly realms. Jacob wanted to mark all that had happened with such an act, and to complete the action with prayer.

Afterwards Jacob followed the men to the synagogue with a borrowed prayer shawl. He had heard them speaking as they dressed and knew the place of worship was dominated by followers of the Way. Apparently the news he had heard in Judea was true, that a large number of believers had found safety in Damascus.

The synagogue was a low structure set back from Straight Street within a waist-high wall. The building's interior had recently been lime washed. Yet no amount of light, nor even Jacob's joyful mood, could brighten the somber gathering.

He quickly realized that the voices around him were speaking of those residing just opposite the synagogue. They had just arrived with a caravan last night, he heard. The Pharisee's name muttered about him sounded like news of a plague. *Saul of Tarsus*. Dreaded hunter of the followers of Jesus. Here in Damascus.

Several hundred men filled the main chamber. Women's voices could be heard from beyond the cloth screens running down the eastern wall. The gathering quieted for the service, which followed the same pattern as in Judea: a song and then a Scripture reading from the Torah scrolls, followed by a prayer from the Psalms. Some men departed to begin their day, but most remained. Jacob stayed where he was, repeating silently the Psalms that resonated with the emotions filling his heart. *How precious, O God, is your constant love. You let us drink from the river of your goodness. You are the source of all life.*

Eventually the voices of concern and fear around him again intruded on his thoughts and prayers. He heard men whispering that perhaps they should take their families and flee. But where would they go? If Saul chased the followers all the way north to Damascus, what was to keep him from traveling on to Sidon, or Philadelphia, or even Babylon?

His mind rang with another passage from the Psalms, *God is present in the company of the righteous*, and he knew what he was being called to do.

Following formal prayers in a synagogue service, it was customary for the lectern to be opened to anyone who felt moved by the Spirit to come forward, so long as the elders leading the service approved. Many of the congregation now remained hidden beneath their prayer shawls, their eyes clenched shut and their beards trembling with the intensity of their prayers. Jacob slipped from his seat and moved forward. He bowed to the three elders seated before the dais and waited. The senior man inspected him, then nodded.

Jacob stepped up on the dais and stood behind the lectern, facing the congregation. He began, "I have never spoken in a synagogue before, but my name is Jacob, of the tribe of Benjamin. I live in Tiberias. I was orphaned by raiders on Damascus Road, rescued and raised by a Roman centurion. He is now a God-fearer and a follower of the Way. As am I."

A few heads had turned his way. Some who whispered worriedly with each other in the back glanced at him. But not many. This too was customary. Any could speak, but no one was required to listen. Jacob knew such a synagogue gathering would often silence a speaker like him through the shame of ignoring him. If the speaker raised his voice, those who chose not to hear would pray louder, or raise the volume of their conversation, or leave.

Jacob went on, "I am a senior guard in the service of Jamal, merchant of Tiberias and Damascus. It was with our caravan that Saul of Tarsus traveled here."

The silence was so sudden, the change so swift, the entire place might as well have been turned to stone. Every eye was fastened on him as Jacob continued, "The worst disaster of my entire life happened upon the Damascus Road when I lost my beloved parents. And now the finest moment has occurred upon the very same road. As the caravan approached Damascus, a light appeared from heaven. A light too bright for me to describe. It shone on Saul of Tarsus." A murmur of voices began again, and Jacob said loudly, "And Jesus appeared to him. I know this because Saul told me."

A voice cried over the growing din, "Can this be?"

"Shah! Let the man speak."

Jacob gripped the dais more tightly. "Saul was blinded by the appearance of the risen Lord."

"It is as I heard!" another voice called. "Saul and his group are residing in the priest's home just across the avenue. The Pharisee remains blind even now!"

The senior elder at the front confirmed, "The Pharisee will not eat nor drink. All night he has prayed. He prays still. He says he waits for God to tell him what to do."

Jacob lifted his voice. "One of the reasons I am here in Damascus was that I was sent by the elder of the Joppa synagogue to warn you of Saul's arrival. On my way here, I arrived in Tiberias to learn that Saul was demanding space within the next caravan departing for your city. Jamal the merchant had been preparing this caravan for days. So the man I was sent to warn you about came with me in the same caravan. God's hand was in all this. Of this I am certain."

"The Pharisee has sworn to drag the followers of Jesus back to Jerusalem in chains!" The shout was echoed by many others in the congregation, and the clamor of voices again filled the room.

Jacob raised his arms for silence, and the group settled down to listen once more. "That was before," Jacob told them. "I am certain of this. The man Saul has met Jesus. In person. He has heard the Lord speak to him. As the elder has reported, Saul is waiting to hear further from God."

There was another moment's tumult, and then a man called out, "What if this stranger is wrong?"

"No," Jacob said. He spoke softly, yet it was enough to silence the room. "When we left Tiberias, I was offered the chance to kill Saul and the Temple guards and hide them in the desert. I confess to you that for a time I was tempted. I could have protected those who have fled from his wrath, such as you here in Damascus. I had doubts and fears, just as you do now. But I prayed, and I felt God's hand holding me back from such a deed. I could not bring myself to act. I stand before you now, today, to proclaim that our Lord guided me. He spoke to me, and I truly believe he spoke to our enemy, Saul."

A man demanded, "What does the Lord say to you now?"

"Two words." Jacob had never felt more certain of anything in his life. "Fear not."

CHAPTER
FORTY-ONE

Damascus

JAMAL TURNED TO Julia as they walked together through the Damascus streets from the inn. "Would you please wait by the portal while I go in alone?"

She nodded. "Of course, Father."

"You do realize Florina may not wish to see you?"

Florina? It was a lovely name. Julia swallowed down the sorrow of hearing it for the first time. "That is her decision, Father. Mother and I both know she has the right to grant our request . . . or not. We will not insist."

"Your mother is a wonderful woman, Julia. I argued with her at first over her decision. I did not wish to lose her—and I also attempted to dissuade her from this visit. But—" He sighed deeply. "I know she will do only what she feels is best—for all concerned."

Jamal hesitated a moment, then went on, "I cannot hide the fact that I will miss her. Deeply. She has been my jewel for many years. But now I must respect her decision. As she said this morning when I came to the inn with my news, perhaps what God has before us will be an even better relationship. As fellow believers rather than . . ." He didn't finish, but then said, "I do not pretend that the road ahead will be easy. Pray for me, Julia."

She nodded and choked back a sob. His sorrow touched her deeply.

"Always remember, my dear, your mother may not have been my wife, at least in a legal sense, but you have always been—will always be—my daughter." He reached for her hand, gave it a gentle squeeze, and released it.

Julia felt she could not have been given a greater gift. She wiped her tears and followed her father toward the door ahead.

The outer portal opened into a vestibule where servants and messengers might wait. Julia took a seat on the side bench. It seemed a rather long time before a servant bowed in front of her. "You may follow me," he said.

Julia's heart pounded within her chest as he led her through a gilded hallway with marble floors. She wondered if the man who silently led the way could hear her heartbeat.

He pushed open a richly paneled door of polished wood and brass and motioned her forward. Her father was not there. A woman sat alone on a cushioned chair with gilded back and arms.

She was older than Helena by what Julia guessed might be at least ten years. She was not what Julia would have described as a particularly attractive woman, certainly not so in comparison to her own mother's striking appearance. Yet she possessed a dignity that to Julia held both judgment and an air of authority. Julia knew instinctively that she was not looking at a woman selected from some small Samaritan village. Her very bearing seemed to announce nobility.

The woman's face looked strained. Maybe even unwelcoming. Julia wished she had not come. She hesitated, but the woman motioned to indicate that she was to take a seat across the room.

"You are Julia?" Her voice was surprisingly soft.

Julia nodded, unable to form words.

"I understand that my husband is your father."

She found her voice then. "Yes, mistress."

Julia saw the dark eyes intently studying her, making her feel even more uncomfortable.

The woman observed, "I see little of Jamal in your features."

"Some say I resemble my mother," Julia responded, a catch in her voice.

"She must be an attractive woman." The words were not said with malice. It seemed a simple observation.

They sat in silence while the woman continued to study Julia. Then she sighed and lifted a small linen square, fine as silk, to her mouth. Julia wondered if it had been used previously to wipe tears.

"Tell me, Julia. Why did you come?"

"I . . . I and my mother have . . . become followers of the Way. We recently heard that you also are a believer. We have prayed about . . . about the . . . our circumstance since we have come to faith, and we wished . . ." What could she possibly say that would make any sense to this woman? "I am not really sure," she finally admitted. "We have been praying, and Mother thought she should come. The Lord—"

"Your mother," the woman repeated. "Your mother is *here*?"

"At the inn. Father's inn."

"So why did Jamal—your father—not bring her to me along with you?"

"My mother did not wish to intrude unless she knew you wished to see her."

Florina stirred and fluttered the linen in her hand, seemingly deep in thought. "And what if I do not?"

"She . . . we will leave. Return to Tiberias."

Florina fell silent. Her dark eyes registered troubled thought. At length she spoke again, her voice soft but strong.

"I already knew about her. For many years I have known. Not about you, though. No one had informed me that Jamal had another child. I should have suspected, of course. Tell me. Does Jamal have other secrets? Do you have brothers? Sisters?"

"No. I am the only one."

"A daughter," she said. "We—Jamal and I—do not have a girl. I suppose Jamal has spoiled you."

"A little, perhaps." Julia dropped her head to cover her smile.

But the woman also smiled. It seemed to please her that Julia had admitted it. "Tell me, Julia. Do you live in a beautiful home?"

Julia unconsciously circled the room with her gaze, then looked at the woman. "It is very lovely, very comfortable, but not as beautiful as this one," she said frankly. In truth she had never been in such an elaborate setting before. She could not tell what the woman might think about her response.

But Florina made no comment. "Jamal is waiting for my return," she said simply. "I promised him I would not be long."

Her weariness showed as she rose slowly to her feet. "We will talk again, Julia. I will send for you."

"Thank you, mistress."

She drew in a deep breath. "And when you come again, please, will you bring your mother."

Julia was in the act of rising, and she was so shocked she could hardly move.

"I do wish to see her. Yes. Though why, I would not be able to explain."

This decision had cost the woman, Julia could see that. She felt a deep compassion for Florina that she knew she would not be wise—or able—to express. "Thank you, mistress," she said with a brief dip of her head. "From both of us."

They were summoned the very next day. A horse-drawn conveyance waited at the inn's entrance. When she and Helena left the inn, Julia felt a shiver pass through her. It was only yesterday she had met this woman, and though she had not been spurned or disparaged, neither had she felt particularly welcomed. What would this day hold?

To her surprise, Helena seemed perfectly calm. She sounded pleased with the news that Florina was willing to meet her too. She and Julia had prayed together before retiring and again in the morning. Yes, God would give wisdom, Julia told herself as they were driven to the beautiful residence.

As they entered the large entryway into the courtyard, Julia could not but marvel again at its splendor. But her mother seemed not to notice.

They were admitted without delay and led into the small, elaborate sitting area where Florina had met Julia the day before. Julia could not help but wonder if this was the woman's own private space, like her mother's secluded arbor at home. Florina was seated in the gilded chair, much like a queen upon her throne.

This time she rose to meet them. Her eyes flitted over Julia and settled on Helena. Helena dipped her head in a respectful bow. Florina nodded. "Helena. Julia. Please sit with me."

A young servant girl pushed through the door bearing a tray of refreshments. All was silent while the maid poured the tea and distributed the cups. She passed a tray of food, mostly unfamiliar but enticing. Julia had no idea what she should try. She watched her mother select honey-dipped figs rolled in nut meal. Julia did the same.

Florina turned to Helena. "Your daughter tells me you have desired to see me."

Julia wondered if her mother would be as nervous as she had been the day before. But Helena surprised her. With a respectful yet confident manner she responded, "I was aware Jamal had another . . . had a wife and another family. For some time I have known and accepted it. But when I became a follower of the Messiah, it no longer seemed . . . well . . . seemed appropriate to overlook the situation. You are his wife. You and your family have a legal and moral right to his time and attention. I do not want to jeopardize your family—your home—in any way. I am sorry for any pain I may have caused you and your children."

It did not seem to be what Florina had expected. She took a long breath and looked at her plate. After a moment she raised her head. "Tell me, Helena, how old were you when my husband . . . acquired you?"

"I was nearing my fifteenth birthday."

"A fourteen-year-old?"

"Fourteen, yes."

"Not much more than a child. And I understand along with you came a small house, a market stand, and sundry other items in payment of a debt."

Julia looked quickly at her mother, but Helena did not shrink from the question. "That is correct. Jamal was most generous to my family. My mother would have been left utterly destitute and a pauper had he not acted as he did."

"So you see him as your benefactor?"

"I do. In many ways."

Florina seemed to consider this for some moments before

she spoke again. "Did you know he loved you? More than he loved me?"

"I am sorry if that is so. But no. I did not know."

"We have quarreled long and heatedly over you, Helena. Over your place in his life. His heart."

"That is very hard for me to hear. I am deeply sorry."

The woman sighed and set aside her cup. She stood and walked toward a large window looking out over a terraced garden. Her shoulders looked stiff but her steps were even, graceful.

It was a few moments until she spoke again, still facing the garden. "Actually, our past circumstances are not that dissimilar. I, too, was purchased—but as a bride. There was a large dowry that my father considered to be a great advantage. He was a nobleman who had fallen on hard times. Jamal offered wealth in exchange for standing. I was from Ephesus. My family was one of prominence. We worshiped the goddess Diana." She turned back to Helena. "Have you heard of her?"

Helena nodded.

"But Jamal would not abide observances of any gods in his house. He smashed my small statuette that I had brought with me from my home. I felt bereft and cried for days. I—well, I hated him for it."

She walked back to her chair. Helena was silent. Julia knew the story had not ended, yet she wondered why Florina was sharing all these sad details with them.

Julia also knew it was difficult for Florina to continue, but at length she spoke again. "You can imagine that our marriage has not been a happy one. I have obeyed. I have given every appearance of submission to him. But I have made no effort whatever to love my husband. Nor to make him happy."

Helena nodded slowly. "I understand."

Florina gazed a long time into their faces, as if to determine their judgment of her confession. Then went on. "We have two sons. They have been the only thing in my life that has brought any joy. It was my younger son who first became a follower. He led me to the group that meets here in Damascus. I was yearning for something beyond myself to give me peace. Purpose."

She stopped again and Julia watched as her countenance seemed to change. The tightness of her face softened, her eyes lost some of their shadow.

"And now that I know the true God, I have found what I was searching for. I no longer am in need of statuettes carved of wood or stone and plated with silver or gold. I am at peace. Or I was . . . until now." She gave a long sigh.

Helena half rose from her seat and Florina motioned her back down with a slight movement of her hand. "Jamal and I had a long talk last night." Once again she looked directly at Helena. "In fact, we talked for most of the night. He tells me that you have requested your relationship be terminated."

Helena nodded.

"Why?"

"It does not seem right to live without marriage when I know God has given specific directives about it."

"He would marry you. You must know that."

"But that would not be an answer that either you or I would favor."

"I understand why I would not favor it. But why not you?"

"Because . . . I would be claiming what rightly belongs to another—Jamal's time, his affection. It belongs to you and your family."

Florina again went back to the window. "I . . . I thought that surely Jamal must have been exaggerating when he spoke of you. No woman could be so . . . so honorable. So brave. How can you do this? Just step aside? You would have won, you know. He would leave me had you insisted."

"I could not live with that," Helena managed through trembling lips. "It would dishonor us all, especially Jamal."

When Florina turned around, her tears were flowing freely. She wiped them with the linen. "These may be the strangest words I have ever spoken. But I feel a kinship with you. I expected to feel threatened. Angry. Instead I feel like . . ."

"We are sisters in the Lord's family," said Helena softly, standing to face her.

"Yes. Yes, that is it of course. Odd, is it not? Yet . . . I have not been a believer for long, and I still have much to learn. But this I already know. One cannot hold bitterness and anger against another and also have the Lord's peace."

Julia had sat silently, listening to the strange exchange between two women who had shared the same man. She looked in awe at each of them.

"As I said," Florina went on, taking her seat once again, but she no longer looked like a queen. She looked like a lonely, needy woman. "Jamal and I had a long talk last night. He was not the only one in the wrong. I had to apologize. I have been a hard, angry woman. No wonder he did not wish to come home to me. But I promised him that with God's help I will change. I will seek to learn to love him. And I feel that with time—and God—we can fashion a relationship that will be pleasing to heaven. I . . . I thank you for making it possible for me to try."

And the next thing Julia knew her mother was kneeling beside Florina while the two women held one another and wept again.

And that was the way her father found them when he walked into the room. They didn't notice his coming. Nor his departure. For he left as quickly as he had appeared, tears in his own eyes. Julia started to follow him, but she could not see the way through the tears flooding down her cheeks.

CHAPTER FORTY-TWO

Caesarea

PUSHING HARD, A troop of mounted Roman soldiers could have made the journey to Caesarea in two days. Linux took five. They scoured the surrounding countryside on their way and spoke with village elders. They sent patrols out after shadows and whispers of sound, but found no threat. Linux suspected this was what the centurion Cornelius may have intended all along. Show aggressive force and reconnoiter hard. Hunt with a hawk's vigilance, and force the bandits to take their deadly business elsewhere.

They were up before each dawn, but none of Linux's band complained. Their destination was a city on the sea, a Roman place of safety, where food did not taste of sand and grit and desert heat, and the hot baths were the pride of the region. Every day their good humor strengthened, until by journey's end the legionnaires occasionally even broke into song.

But by the second day after arriving in Caesarea, Linux chafed under the forced idleness. Each morning he announced his presence to the acting garrison commandant. After that, the hours were his to do with as he pleased. Cornelius was out inspecting his forces. He had been accompanied by all the men Linux knew within the Italian brigade. Linux threw himself into the few tasks that came his way, and chafed at being so far away from Samaria.

Each night he found himself waking from a deep sleep, only to realize he had dreamed of a child's laughter. And of a woman's smile. He had promised Abigail's lost husband to protect her. Linux would honor that vow with his dying breath—whatever it meant. For Linux was certain the promise had not been made merely to Stephen, but also to the God they both served.

On the third afternoon a summons was delivered by Grattus, the young subaltern who had first invited Linux to the home of Cornelius. They rode out together at dusk toward the centurion's home. Grattus still bore the marks of his most recent road assignment. The dust might have been cleaned away, his hair oiled, his uniform fresh. But the strain of the past few weeks had aged him.

Linux asked, "You had a hard go of it?"

"We have been busy chasing ghosts. We lost four good men to arrows flung by the night. I accuse the night because we found no one."

Cornelius greeted them with his customary gruff courtesy, but the burdens were more evident upon his aging features. "Did Grattus tell you of our sorties?"

"Enough."

"The bandits and Zealots have one primary aim. They want to restrict us to our fortresses and our garrisons. There we are safe. But the roads they can then claim for themselves."

Linux hesitated, then said, "You must take the fight away from the roads."

The two officers stared at him. Linux understood their unspoken objections all too well. A Roman officer was trained to think in terms of dominance by force. And the roads formed their lifelines.

So long as they held the roads, they reasoned, Roman soldiers could be shifted into position, and massive attacks could be launched.

Linux continued, "The Megiddo crossroads have been under pressure to pay tribute to the bandits. Ever since my arrival, we have given chase. We do not attempt to engage. We want to tire them out, make it so uncomfortable for them that they leave the territory. And the only way to do that is by taking the fight to where they are most powerful, where they believe they have the upper hand. The hills. The caves. The hidden valleys. And the villages."

Both men looked aghast. "You patrol the Judean towns? How can you spare the men?"

"Two reasons. First, only half of my men remain in the Megiddo fortress, with orders that they must patrol daily. The other half are garrisoned at the crossroads."

"The Judeans make you welcome?"

"More than that. They consider us friends."

Several other of the brigade's officers had drifted over to listen. One said, "But the Judean villages give shelter and aid to the Zealots."

"Some do. And those we do not condemn. We do not have the strength to fight everyone. But we patrol their villages more often than the others, and we bring pressure on them in subtle ways. We search all produce and wagons. We inspect all their barns and outbuildings. Over and over and over."

Cornelius demanded, "And this scheme of yours is working?"

"We have not lost a man," Linux replied. "Only sleep."

An officer by the wall said, "If I garrisoned my men in a Judean town, they would slit our throats while we slept."

"Most villagers would not, but some connected with the Zealots might," Linux agreed.

"So how do you and your men remain safe?"

Cornelius understood Linux's hesitation, so he spoke out. "The Judean villagers to whom you refer are followers."

"Some. Perhaps most. But not all."

"You treat them with respect."

Linux nodded. "We treat the believers as brothers and sisters in Christ. And we pay all who provide us services. In coin."

"And your own men, what do they think of this?"

"Those who might resist this approach are assigned to the fortress. Of the others . . ." Linux smiled at the recollection of their last meal. "Some are coming to heed the Messiah's call."

"This is madness!" an officer protested. "The Judeans are our enemies!"

Cornelius shot Linux a warning glance, and Linux simply shrugged and did not comment further.

The officers ate a meal together. At least, they all ate in the same room. But there was a clear distance kept by those who scorned Judea and its citizens. Dark looks were cast Linux's way. Cornelius gave no sign that he noticed anything amiss. After the meal, he bade most of the officers farewell and ordered Linux to remain behind. He led his smaller band to the rear balcony, where his home's outer perimeter met the cliff and the sea. The torchlight revealed a face shadowed by worry and fatigue. "You are understanding the dilemma I face?"

"Yes, sire. I believe I do."

"For those of us who are coming to accept Jesus as the Messiah of all mankind, there is a growing desire for unity and peace," the man said. "This threatens to drive a wedge between us and the others, our fellow officers. Men I have trusted for years with my life. Men of Rome, good men."

"I do understand." The group as one stared out over the stone balustrade at the moonlit sea. Linux said, "It has been good being back in Caesarea. And difficult at the same time. Good, because it is familiar. This is a Roman city—orderly, safe, prosperous. But difficult, because it isolates me from the people."

"*Your* people?" Cornelius said.

"Not all. Not even most. Those who are not followers of the Way, those who do not know me, those who only see a Roman officer wearing the uniform of their hated conquerors, for them I am and will remain an enemy."

"And yet you are comfortable here in Judea."

Linux nodded slowly. "I did not recognize until I passed through Caesarea's gates just how much the Samaritan plains have become home."

"We have need of officers like you. Not here. Out there in the field." Cornelius turned to face him. "I would like you to return to Megiddo."

Linux resisted the sudden urge to shout his delight. "I hear and obey, sire."

"You will take with you men who share your sentiments about this land and the risen Messiah. You will carry silver to continue paying the stall holders for provisions. You will forge new alliances." Cornelius studied him intently. "What say you, Linux?"

Linux answered truthfully, "Your orders stir my soul and warm my heart, sire. They are an answer to prayer."

CHAPTER FORTY-THREE

Damascus

JACOB HAD RETURNED to the caravanserai to find instructions waiting from an absent Julia. The parchment had been folded and the edges sealed with wax. He was to go to a merchant on Straight Street, where she had already selected cloth for a new robe. The man had promised to have it ready that afternoon, and Jacob was further instructed to meet them before sunset at Jamal's Damascus home for the evening meal.

The merchant said to him when he arrived at the shop, "I did not attend morning prayers. But I heard you were there. Jacob, is it? Is it true what they are saying, that you traveled from Tiberias with the Pharisee known as Saul?"

"I did."

"And you spoke in the synagogue of meeting Jesus upon the Damascus Road?"

"I did not meet our Lord. Saul did."

The man responded with a shudder. "My family has lived in Damascus for over a hundred years. We Judeans take pride in our distance from the Temple priesthood. We chart our own course. We find our own way to God. When the disciples arrived speaking of the risen One, I and all my family heeded to this call. We have found great comfort, and more besides. We have grown closer, both to each other and to our God. We find such peace." He paused. "To think that Saul has come to destroy all this leaves me . . ."

"I understand," Jacob said. "But I think Saul may have been transformed by what happened. I know I was, and I did not meet Jesus face-to-face as he did. I saw a light. I heard a voice but could not make out the words. Saul saw and he heard what the voice said. And the light blinded him."

"There are those among the followers who think we should strike while his blindness lingers," the merchant said slowly. "That this is a gift from our Lord to rid us of this threat."

"I did not hear what Jesus said," Jacob repeated. "But I felt his presence. And there was no menace. Only peace."

"You led this Saul into Damascus?"

"He held onto my arm the entire way."

"Did he tell you what the Lord said?"

"Yes. That he should come to Damascus and wait. The Lord would tell him what must happen."

"And now he waits in solitude, and he fasts." The man stroked his beard. "He is blind and he is weakened. Like a lamb delivered to us, and now is waiting for the judgment he deserves."

Jacob shook his head. "I can only tell you what I saw and felt. And there was only peace in our Lord's presence. A feeling so powerful it defies description. I was left utterly shamed that I had once considered revenge."

Jamal's Damascus home was both grand and ancient. The original structure had been built in the desert manner, and the blank outer portal revealed little. A servant answered Jacob's knock and bowed him into the first courtyard, which was as far as most guests would ever come. Jacob was then led through a second portal, and entered a different realm. He was very glad Julia had arranged for his new robe.

The private area had been rebuilt in the Roman style, with an interior courtyard lined by pillars. The gardens were lush and contained three fountains, out of which splashed scented water. Birds sang to the sunset from flowering trees. The air was rich with the aromas of spices and roasting lamb.

They ate around a low table, seated upon divans. Five servants cared for their every need. Jamal sat at the head with Florina at his right. Their elder son, Gaius, sat at his left, with the younger, Titus, next to him. Across from them sat Helena, then Julia, and Jacob was seated nearby. Both Helena and Julia were dressed in gowns of silk equal in beauty to the one that Florina wore. In this unusual grouping, Jacob felt an underlying tension—but no resentment, unless it could be on the part of the two sons. They seemed to study the table guests with a mixture of curiosity and concern.

Gaius appeared to be a few years older than Julia. Titus seemed close to the same age. They watched Helena and Julia without masking their obvious interest. They avoided Jacob's gaze entirely.

Jacob marveled that these particular people could break bread together and discuss such things as weather, travel, news from the outlying cities, the next meetings to be held by the followers of the Way, and the strange and frightening news that Saul of Tarsus was actually in their city.

Jamal held the true mystery of the evening. Gone were his ebullient strength and his latent aggression. This evening, Jamal was even more silent than his two sons. He brooded, but without that smoldering hint of danger. Instead he studied each of the people around the circle. Jacob, Julia, his wife, his sons, Helena. Then Jacob again. Jacob thought the man seemed perplexed.

Jamal did not speak until the final plate was cleared away and the servants had departed. He looked around at them all once more and said, "If anything could convince me that this God of the Judeans does indeed exist, it would be this. How we are seated here today. But I could never have thought to ask for such an impossible thing, for I could not have imagined it happening."

The entire table seemed to breathe as one. The three women exchanged looks before Jamal's wife said, "Impossible for man. But in the company of God, joined to his wisdom and peace, all things are possible."

"Yes," Julia said. "Amen."

Jamal heaved a great sigh and looked at his daughter. "I prayed with you the other evening because you asked. Looking back at that, I feel as though I prayed as a merchant would. With my mind, but not with my heart. I wanted to negotiate. I was not completely truthful. But now I am coming to understand what happened to me . . .what is happening to me."

Florina obviously was fighting with her emotions and regained control. "How I have longed to hear you say such words. How I have prayed."

Titus said hoarsely, "As have I."

Gaius looked across the table at Jacob. Jacob understood the young man's expression very well. He had seen it any number of times when joining a new caravan, and all the other guards fingered their weapons and wondered if he was truly an ally. Or a foe waiting for the chance to strike.

Jacob lowered his head and prayed silently, not merely for himself, but for all of them. That God might find a way to continue this miracle, and strengthen his power and peace among the two households.

The elder son was still watching him. Gaius spoke for the first time. "You were praying?"

"I was."

"What did you ask?"

Florina admonished, "Gaius, that is between Jacob and his God."

"No, no, it is all right." Jacob took a breath. "I was praying that God would continue to work his miracles in this household. And make us friends." He hesitated, then added the final words of his prayer, "And heal the wounds I sense . . ." But he did not complete the thought.

Jamal leaned his head on his fist, a sound like a soft groan coming from his lips. Julia rose and walked over to seat herself on her father's divan. She took his hand. She did not whisper, but her voice was soft enough that the night almost captured what she said. "Part of coming to know Jesus is coming to know ourselves, Papa. Seeing all the things that we otherwise might wish to keep hidden. Even from our own minds."

Jamal lifted his face, creased in sorrows only he could know, to hers. He shook his head as if to clear it.

Julia said, "The closer we come to Jesus, the more we recognize his perfect love. And the more we see how far removed we are from this perfection. He calls to us with that love and forgiveness. He invites us to grow, to become more than we ever could be on our own."

Two of the servants reappeared bearing torches. Dotted around the garden were tall braziers, each fashioned like a flowering vine topped by a broad basin holding scented wood. The air became filled with the fragrant smoke, and light danced about them. Jacob was sure he was the only one who even noticed the servants.

Jamal asked quietly, "Will you teach me to pray for . . . for forgiveness?"

Julia said, "You need to ask this of Jesus himself."

"But . . ." Jamal's features tightened. "There is so much I have done wrong."

Jacob leaned forward and said, "You are no further from his forgiveness than the rest of us."

"That is true, Father." This time it was Gaius who spoke.

Florina straightened in her chair. "I have something to say." She stood and walked around the table to lay her hand on Julia's arm. "Julia, there is nothing I would desire more than to be able to . . . to share you as a daughter. Though I promise I will not attempt to come between you and your own mother." She turned to look at Helena. "She deserves you. And she needs you. But I would be so honored if, along with your father, we could welcome you to our home—your home—occasionally. You and Jacob. You are the daughter I have always longed to have. And if Helena will be so gracious as to allow this, I will be in her debt."

Helena already had stood beside Julia, and the three made a circle with their joined hands.

CHAPTER FORTY-FOUR

Damascus

JACOB WAS GLAD for his soft new robe, as it was made for the wintry chill. Over it, as with most of the men he passed, was a tan sleeveless cloak. The woolen belt was a rainbow of copper and red and ochre and royal blue.

He had insisted upon sleeping at the caravanserai for several reasons. First, because Jamal's attention remained upon his family at their home, and Jacob wanted the merchant to know his animals and his affairs were in safe hands. Also, because he felt that Julia needed the opportunity to be with her new family. God willing, Jacob had the rest of his life to come to know his beloved. And he had little role in this family saga.

Each morning he called on Helena and Zoe, who still resided at the inn. Then the day was his.

He took to attending all three prayer services at the synagogue on Straight Street. With each service, the number in attendance grew. By the third day after his arrival in Damascus, more than four hundred men were present. They spilled out the synagogue's front and side doors and filled the alleys to either side and the synagogue's forecourt. Even the Damascus Judeans who were not followers had little time for meddling Temple priests. They felt quite capable of charting their own course. Welcoming the persecuted followers from Jerusalem had come naturally.

Even those who did not acknowledge Jesus as the Messiah were incensed by Saul's presence in their city and what it portended. The idea of a Pharisee being sent by the Temple Council to arrest Judeans living peacefully in Damascus filled them with outrage.

From Jacob's place in the forecourt he could hear several groups muttering darkly. How they should cross the street and overwhelm the Temple guards and do away with this man. The clamor rose until those guards began to nervously talk between themselves, their weapons at the ready.

The message of peace Jacob had spoken from the synagogue dais was being overwhelmed by the rising fury. But just after the morning services ended, he noticed a curious encounter across the street. He was folding up his prayer shawl and stepping out the door when a man approached the two guards and bowed a formal greeting.

A voice near Jacob demanded, "Who is that?"

"Ananias. I would know him anywhere," said another.

"*Our* Ananias? What does he want with them?"

"I should know this? Go and ask."

"I will do that. . . . No, look, the guards are letting him enter!"

More eyes turned toward the now-opened portal. Someone said, "Ananias is a follower! What is he doing—?"

"Why should he have to face the dreaded one alone?"

Jacob could feel the crowd's growing sense of menace. He did the only thing he could think of to halt the likely violence before it began. He crossed the street and stepped through the front gate to face the guards. In a voice that would carry to all, he demanded, "Why did you let that one enter?"

The guards obviously did not want to respond. But in light of the crowd's growing ire, one said, "He *claimed* to have a message from God."

The other guard added, "This morning the Pharisee told us he had seen a vision as well. One named Ananias would come to see him."

Jacob nodded, turned, and held up his arms for quiet. He repeated what the guards had said. Then he waited.

A man said, "Are we going in or not?"

"Did God speak with you as well?"

"No, but . . ."

"God told Ananias to go. God told Saul to hear what the man came to say. If God is involved, what can we do?"

The bearded Judean reappeared in the doorway. Ananias was greeted with total silence until a man standing beside Jacob called over, "Did you see him?"

Ananias bowed once more to the guards and crossed the avenue. As he approached, Jacob felt a thrill course through his body. The glow on the face of Ananias looked like one he had seen before.

Ananias said, "The Lord Jesus came to me in a vision."

"When?"

"This very morning."

A sudden press of bodies forced Jacob up against the synagogue's wall. But he could still see and hear this man, Ananias.

Now the questions were coming from all sides.

"You are sure it was the Lord?"

"There is no question in my mind or heart. I did question it at first, because I too have heard of this man. But I obeyed—"

"And the Lord told you what exactly?"

"To come here. That Saul had seen my arrival in a vision and was waiting for me."

"And what happened?"

"I did as the Lord commanded. I laid my hands upon him. I prayed."

"For *him* you prayed? What did you say in your prayer, maybe that lightning should strike?"

"I prayed for his sight to return."

A sound like a groan erupted from the crowd.

"Why would you do such a thing?"

"Shah! Let him speak!"

The voice of Ananias was filled with the same awe that illuminated his features. "He says the scales fell from his eyes."

"So now he sees again! What does he do?"

"He eats. He drinks. He regains his strength."

"And what—"

"Look! There he is!"

The bearded figure of the Pharisee appeared in the doorway. One of the Temple guards spoke to him, clearly warning Saul of the crowd's mood. He gave no sign he even heard the man, though he obviously could see.

The man slowly crossed the road and entered through the synagogue's front gates while the crowd parted before him. Saul's features had an ethereal quality.

All who could forced themselves into the synagogue behind Saul. Others jostled for position by the open doors and windows. Together they watched as Saul stepped forward and paused before the elders. They bowed and backed away, granting him access to the dais. Saul stepped onto the platform and turned to the crowd.

In a voice that carried through the synagogue portals and out through the gates, Saul said, "I have been wrong in my thoughts and deeds. But God in his great mercy has given me light. Light through blindness. I now stand here to proclaim that Jesus *is* the Messiah, the risen Lord, the Son of God. He is come to save man from his sins. He is the gateway to heaven! Accept him as your Savior, and receive God's forgiving grace!"

After a stunned silence, a clamor of voices filled the air. Had this man just said what they thought they heard? The murderer, Saul of Tarsus, proclaiming *Jesus Christ* as the Messiah?

The questions once more turned to an uproar. Already people were choosing sides. Some whispered amen. Others muttered, "Blasphemy." And still others thought he was a liar.

Jacob thought it best to leave before the crowd erupted into a riot. He pushed his way through and headed for the door.

As Jacob finally made it to the outer portal a man beside him said to another, "Saul! After all we have suffered from this man, and now this! Do you believe him?"

His companion shook his head and shrugged. "Only time holds the answer," he said. "Only time will tell."

CHAPTER FORTY-FIVE

The Megiddo Crossroads
Early Spring

AFTER HOURS IN the sun's heat and the commotion of the busy market stall, Martha had sent Abigail home. She had hurried off to prepare a special meal. Linux had returned from another patrol through the nearby hills. And of course Dorcas had begged to see him again. When he had ridden into the crossroads market earlier that day, he had looked particularly weary. The thought of him returning to the crude quarters he called home and a cold meal served by a surly servant did not sound very pleasant, so Abigail and Martha had invited him to join the three of them at their evening table. He had smiled his thanks and returned the hug of his excited little friend. Abigail had then spent hours wishing she could be home making preparations instead of bartering with customers. Sensing that, Martha told her to go, promising to take care of the customers until closing time.

Abigail wanted the meal to be enjoyable but would not have the time to prepare as she would have wished. She had ordered a chicken from a neighbor. She set to work, plucking and cleaning, then seasoned it with herbs and began roasting it over the open fire. The savory meat, joined by root vegetables from Martha's little garden, looked as good as it smelled. Abigail set up their table on the front portico so they might enjoy the last rays of sun while they ate.

A meal seemed a small thing to offer the exhausted man, but Abigail hoped in this simple way to be able to provide a relaxing time for him. Dorcas was good at that, with her constant chatter and her easy laughter. Abigail had often thought she could see the fatigue drop from the man's shoulders as he and the child laughed and played happily together. It was very clear that Dorcas loved Linux—and that Linux returned the love in full measure.

With one last check of the chicken Abigail turned to welcome their guest. She noted the appreciative smile that lit his face as he stepped up onto the porch and Dorcas enthusiastically patted a seat at the table beside her, even though the meal was yet to be served.

As Abigail picked up serving dishes, Dorcas began bringing Linux up to date on all the household's activities. "Aunt Martha worked too hard at the stall today. But she drank her special tea to make her knees stop hurting, and now she is sleeping. Mama took her some broth and bread. But Mama thinks she will come to the table later. Today I fell down and bumped my arm. See? I only cried a little bit. That funny man Simon—he doesn't scare me anymore when he comes to the market."

Abigail set the platters on the table. Dorcas continued. "Did you know Mama had to take all the feathers off this chicken?" She wrinkled her nose and made a face. "And she took all the insides—"

"Dorcas. Please hush. We are going to eat now." Abigail took her seat and nodded to Linux, offering a smile she hoped would bring a sense of serenity to the meal. "Will you pray please before we eat?"

His prayer was brief and heartfelt, including his thankfulness for being able to partake of a meal with those he loved. And that, Abigail was sure, was what prompted Dorcas to ask a question as soon as she raised her head.

"Mama, do you love Uncle Linux?"

Abigail felt her cheeks burn. The question hung awkwardly in the air.

"Do you?"

"Your . . . your Uncle Linux is . . . is a very good friend—of many years," Abigail said, her heart pounding. She hoped her stammering rush of words would end the embarrassing scene. She tried to return her attention to the food on her plate.

"Do you love him?" persisted Dorcas.

Abigail heard, more than saw, Linux lay down his fork and place both elbows on the table as though waiting patiently for her response. If only she could jump up from the table and escape the difficult moment, but both pairs of eyes held her to her chair.

Thoughts scrambled through her mind, tripping over one another in their hurry to be discovered. More and more of late she had felt her heart opening up to a certain feeling—familiar but new. Was it love that made her feel safer, more complete in his presence? Could she deny this was love and be truthful? Even when she secretly wished he never had to head out on another patrol? Was it love that made her count the days until she saw him again? That breathed a deep-felt prayer of thanks to God each time he returned safely?

She stirred restlessly, not daring to even lift her eyes. She was sure Dorcas would continue to probe until she felt satisfied with the answer. But it was Linux who spoke softly.

"That is the question that I have ached to ask, my little Dorcas—but I have felt so constrained."

There was momentary silence as Dorcas pondered the meaning of his words.

Abigail forced herself to raise her eyes. Linux was looking at her with such tenderness that she found herself blinking away tears. Then a hand reached across the table toward her, and she found herself responding, placing her own in the grasp of the strong, travel-hardened hand of a Roman officer.

"Do you, Mama?" came the small voice.

Abigail swallowed, then nodded slowly, her eyes finally meeting those of Linux across the table. "Yes," she said in no more than a whisper. "Yes."

Dorcas seemed to take the admission as happy news, yet totally expected and in keeping with the way things should be. After all, who could not love her dear uncle Linux? She smiled and gave a nod, then turned her attention to her food.

But for Abigail and Linux the moment was the culmination of what seemed a lifetime of fears and dreams, heartache and happiness, now transformed by the one simple word. Abigail felt the warmth in the hand that held hers and saw the light that had come to his eyes. Could it be tears that made them glisten in the glow from the setting sun?

She took a deep breath and squeezed his hand.

A whole new world had just opened before them.

The hour was late and Abigail had already worked for many hours serving customers from two caravans that had crossed paths, requiring both provisions and wares. She had left her own shop in the care of Martha and Dorcas and gone to help Yelban serve the crowd of hungry guests. She was more than happy when both caravans moved on, leaving them with not only cleanup duties but more coins in their coffers.

She had mixed feelings about that day being so packed with activities. Glad because it kept her stomach from churning with nervousness, and sorrowful because her busy hands and hurried steps left her no time to savor the joy that already had replaced her intense loneliness.

Tomorrow she would be wed. Linux had been so patient. So endearing. It still seemed like a dream, but she had Dorcas to continually remind her of what was coming.

"Mama, only ten more days," she would say.

"Mama, only five more days."

"Mama, only two more days." On and on she went, ticking the time off on small fingers. The child's delight always brought a smile to Abigail's face. She would have a husband, and Dorcas would finally have the father she had so long desired. They would be family. That truth often brought tears to accompany the smiles.

And now Dorcas slept peacefully. Her happiness had not kept her awake. For Abigail, though, in spite of her weariness, sleep seemed far away.

She finally rose and crossed to the room's one small window to sweep aside the heavy woven covering. A placid moon looked down upon the sleeping village, causing dark shadows to gather in the hidden places. Nothing seemed to be stirring. The heat of the day had subsided, leaving the hint of fragrant garden herbs in the silent air. And on the hill to the west, the small dwelling Linux called home was just visible through the branches of a cypress tree. She wondered if he slept, or if he too was restless.

Suddenly Abigail knew she wanted to pray. Tomorrow would open the door to a whole new journey—but one she would not travel alone. From henceforth she would be the wife of a Roman officer. Once she would have scorned such a possibility. But Linux had changed all that. Linux, and the God he served. Her God. It was faith that securely bound them together. Perhaps the faith was even stronger than the love that they felt for each other. Abigail knew that even though the wedding tomorrow made her pulse race and her heart fill to overflowing, the future held many uncertainties. Even a Roman had no promise of immunity should the angry fingers of religious persecution reach again beyond the walls of Jerusalem.

Yet even with her awareness that their way was unsure, she knew she was in God's hands. They were in God's hands. He knew the future, and that their main desire was to serve and honor him. Abigail lifted her face to the wide breadth of sky that swept cloudless over the sleeping village.

"Thank you, Father," she breathed with deep humility and gratitude. "You have never left me to struggle alone but have always been with me. Have always placed loving and caring people at my side. Even in the darkest hours I have been blessed. Thank you."

But the short prayer, though sincere, was not enough. Abigail let the curtain fall back into place and crossed to the pallet where Dorcas lay sleeping. It seemed right that Dorcas would be included in this prayer. Abigail reached out and took the small hand in her own, studying her daughter's face in the faint light from the candle that still burned.

Dorcas did not stir but Abigail felt that the fingers curled a bit more tightly about her own.

"Father, my God and my salvation . . ." She paused. Where could she start? How could she hope to share the deep feelings of her heart?

She took a full breath and went on. "I . . . I never thought that the words *my husband* would ever pass my lips again. But . . . but you have provided another miracle, and I thank you. Both for the companion I have longed for and for the father for my little one. You know what she said to me when I tucked her in tonight, Lord—she said, 'After tomorrow I will never have to say *Uncle Linux* again. I will have a papa—like my friends,' and she clapped her hands with happiness. Thank you, Lord."

Another pause as Abigail tried to sort out her feelings. Tears fell through the fingers of the hand she lifted to her face. "And, God, I do not know how things work in your heaven. I only know that Stephen is there—with you. Can he see me, Lord? Does he know my happiness? It has been so long, but I am finally able to journey on. I know that this would bring him much joy. He would not wish to see me crippled by loneliness and fear. Yet I have been, Lord. Stephen thought my faith was strong, but I stumbled along far too often. Please, God, if you could just let him know that we are going to be okay again. He was such a wise, gentle husband in our short time together. He saw the goodness in Linux long before I did—and even asked him to take care of me. And now he will, Lord. Dorcas and me."

Abigail wiped her cheeks with a trembling hand. She had addressed feelings of the past—it was now time to think of the future. "And, God, please help me to be a good wife for Linux. He deserves happiness, Lord. May I be sensitive and loving—the kind of helpmate that I can be only with your presence in my life. May our journey together teach us much of faith. May we join our hearts and hands in service to you, and to your people. Show us the way, Lord. Teach us to follow where you lead. May our love for you, and for one another, continue to grow with each passing day. May we . . ."

Dorcas stirred. Abigail lifted her head to find the child's eyes wide open, studying her mother's face. Abigail raised a hand again to brush at her cheeks. She did not want to upset Dorcas with tears.

But it was a smile that greeted her. "Mama, is it morning?"

Abigail shook her head. "No, dear one. The night has hardly begun."

Dorcas squirmed and rolled over to her side. "Then I am going back to sleep. I want morning to come fast. I can hardly wait to have a real papa. Right, Mama?"

"Right," answered Abigail with a catch in her voice. "You are *so right*, my dear."

And suddenly everything seemed *so right*. So in proper order. Her churning stomach calmed, her anxious feelings left her. For the first time in many months—years—Abigail felt perfectly at peace. She reached out to brush the curls back from the face of the child whose eyes were already closing. Stephen's eyes. She blinked back tears, whether from sorrow or happiness, she did not know, nor would she seek the answer. It had been a long day. She needed her rest. She felt ready for sleep now. Dorcas was right. Morning would come much more quickly if she lost herself in slumber.

She smiled and leaned forward to kiss the cheek of the little girl who would soon have a *real papa*.

JANETTE OKE was born in Champion, Alberta, to a Canadian prairie farmer and his wife, and she grew up in a large family full of laughter and love. She is a graduate of Mountain View Bible College in Alberta, where she met her husband, Edward, and they were married in May of 1957. After pastoring churches in Indiana and Canada, the Okes spent some years in Calgary, where Edward served in several positions on college faculties while Janette continued her writing. She has written forty-eight novels for adults and another sixteen for children, and her book sales total nearly thirty million copies.

The Okes have three sons and one daughter, all married, and are enjoying their fifteen grandchildren. Edward and Janette are active in their local church and make their home near Didsbury, Alberta.

DAVIS BUNN has been a professional novelist for twenty years. His books have sold in excess of six million copies in sixteen languages, appearing on numerous national bestseller lists.

Davis is known for the diversity of his writing talent, from gentle gift books like *The Quilt* to high-powered thrillers like *The Great Divide*. He has also enjoyed great success in his collaborations with Janette Oke, with whom he has coauthored a series of ground-breaking historical novels.

In developing his work, Davis draws on a rich background of international experience. Raised in North Carolina, he completed his undergraduate studies at Wake Forest University. He then traveled to London to earn a master's degree in international economics and finance before embarking on a distinguished business career that took him to more than thirty countries in Europe, Africa, and the Middle East.

Davis has received numerous literary accolades, including three Christy Awards for excellence in fiction. He currently serves as Writer-in-Residence at Regent's Park College, Oxford University, and is a sought-after lecturer on the craft of writing.

Books by Janette Oke

Canadian West

When Calls the Heart • *When Comes the Spring*
When Breaks the Dawn • *When Hope Springs New*
Beyond the Gathering Storm
When Tomorrow Comes

Love Comes Softly

Love Comes Softly • *Love's Enduring Promise*
Love's Long Journey • *Love's Abiding Joy*
Love's Unending Legacy • *Love's Unfolding Dream*
Love Takes Wing • *Love Finds a Home*

A Prairie Legacy

The Tender Years • *A Searching Heart*
A Quiet Strength • *Like Gold Refined*

Seasons of the Heart

Once Upon a Summer • *The Winds of Autumn*
Winter Is Not Forever • *Spring's Gentle Promise*

Seasons of the Heart (4 in 1)

Women of the West

The Calling of Emily Evans • *Julia's Last Hope*
Roses for Mama • *A Woman Named Damaris*
They Called Her Mrs. Doc • *The Measure of a Heart*
A Bride for Donnigan • *Heart of the Wilderness*
Too Long a Stranger • *The Bluebird and the Sparrow*
A Gown of Spanish Lace • *Drums of Change*

www.janetteoke.com

Books by Janette Oke and Davis Bunn

Return to Harmony • *Another Homecoming*

Acts of Faith

The Centurion's Wife • *The Hidden Flame*
The Damascus Way

Song of Acadia

The Meeting Place • *The Sacred Shore*
The Birthright • *The Distant Beacon*
The Beloved Land

Books by Davis Bunn

Gold of Kings
The Black Madonna
All Through the Night
My Soul to Keep
The Great Divide
Winner Take All
Imposter
The Lazarus Trap
Elixir

Heirs of Acadia*

The Solitary Envoy • *The Innocent Libertine*
The Noble Fugitive • *The Night Angel*
Falconer's Quest

* *with Isabella Bunn*